HIGH PR
**UNICORN**

**"An intelligent, absorbing mo**... characters, a thoroughly satisfying plot, an attractive balance between humor and pathos and plenty of fascinating twists and turns; Bishop's finest work, and unequivocally recommended."
—*Kirkus Reviews*, starred review

"Richer and more complex fare than most novels with 'unicorn' in the title . . . Bishop maintains the balance between realism and fantasy almost unerringly." —*USA Today*

**"Fabulous** . . . Like me, you may have been assuming that fantasy writers had done all that could possibly be done with unicorns, and you may have been ready to swear off. Give 'em one more chance. You won't regret it; I promise."
—*The Denver Post*

**"One of the best writers in SF today**, Bishop's fiction is distinguished by his realistic, full-bodied characterizations . . . well worth the journey." —*Publishers Weekly*

**"Nobody is better than Bishop at mixing the grittily real and the utterly fantastic."**
—George Alec Effinger, author of *When Gravity Fails*

**"This is a breathtaking book."**
—Nancy Kress, author of *An Alien Light*

# UNICORN MOUNTAIN

*Michael Bishop*

BANTAM BOOKS
NEW YORK • TORONTO • LONDON • SYDNEY • AUCKLAND

*This edition contains the complete text of the original hardcover edition.*
NOT ONE WORD HAS BEEN OMITTED

UNICORN MOUNTAIN

*A Bantam Spectra Book / published by arrangement with William Morrow & Company, Inc. / Arbor House*

*PRINTING HISTORY*
*Arbor House edition published May 1988*



*Bantam edition / July 1989*


*Library of Congress Catalog Card Number: 88-913.*

*For information address: Arbor House, c/o William Morrow and Company, Inc., 105 Madison Avenue, New York, NY 10016.*

ISBN 0-553-27904-1

*Published simultaneously in the United States and Canada*

---

*Bantam Books are published by Bantam Books, a division of Bantam Doubleday Dell Publishing Group, Inc. Its trademark, consisting of the words "Bantam Books" and the portrayal of a rooster, is Registered in U.S. Patent and Trademark Office and in other countries. Marca Registrada. Bantam Books, 666 Fifth Avenue, New York, New York 10103.*

---

PRINTED IN THE UNITED STATES OF AMERICA

OPM 0 9 8 7 6 5 4 3 2 1

*For Jeri,*
*whose love sustains*

To anyone not instructed in comparative anatomy the unicorn is so credible a beast that it is difficult to understand why anyone should ever have doubted him. Compared with him the giraffe is highly improbable, the armadillo and the ant-eater are unbelievable, and the hippopotamus is a nightmare. The shortest excursion into palaeontology brings back a dozen animals that strain our power of belief far more than he does. What may be called the normality of the unicorn is just as evident when we set him beside the creatures of fancy. Compared with him the griffin is precisely what Sir Thomas Browne calls it, "a mixed and dubious animal."

—*The Lore of the Unicorn* by Odell Shepard

Who wants someone else to die? I mean, we don't want that to happen. But the Indians were right. When people die, they move on. The process doesn't necessarily have to be terrible. Get your tribe together, and you let the person die. And you help them to die, okay? *Give them the strength to die!*

—AIDS patient Arthur Felson, as quoted in
*Epidemic of Courage* by Lon G. Nungesser

# *Author's Note*

This novel deals in passing or in detail with several different topics—from AIDS to ranching to the Ute Indians to montane ecology to equine diseases to unicorn lore.

In December of 1985, I interviewed AIDS patient Jim Granger at the Cypress Street headquarters of AID Atlanta; I also talked to a support worker, Johnny Walsh. Both men gave me helpful information about gay culture, AIDS, and its harrowing impact on persons with AIDS, loved ones, and medical providers. I am grateful to them for their valuable contributions. Jim Granger died on June 8, 1986; he was not quite thirty-six years old.

I also owe a debt to these books: *Epidemic of Courage* by Lon G. Nungesser; *The Modern Cowboy* by John R. Erickson; *Cowgirls* by Teresa Jordan; *When Buffalo Free the Mountains* by Nancy Wood; *The Sun Dance Religion* by Joseph G. Jorgensen; *Above Timberline* by Dwight Smith; *Current Therapy in Equine Medicine*, a book loaned me by Pine Mountain veterinarians Noni Eakle and Dale Lott; and Odell Shepard's *The Lore of the Unicorn*. Astute readers will notice that I have ignored or contradicted huge swatches of this lore. I still recommend the book.

For dramatic purposes, I have taken small liberties with some of the material about Ute Indians. For instance, my depiction of Ignacio, Colorado, which really exists, is entirely a product of my researchers and my imagination. My Ute characters are fictional constructs and not meant to be constructed as either direct portraits or caricatures. The Anglo and Hispanic characters in my novel are also fictional constructs.

In August of 1987, I carried one pivotal chapter of my novel to the Sycamore Hill Writers' Conference in Raleigh, North Carolina. I would like to thank John Kessel, Mark Van Name, and all the other writers at this workshop for their suggestions and encouragement. Space limitations do not permit me to list everyone who attended Sycamore Hill, but Orson Scott Card deserves particular mention.

My editor, David Hartwell, knows how much I owe him. What is good in this novel is a reflection of his understanding of my real aims and purposes: what is clumsy or untrue in it is, as always, the result of my own writerly shortcomings.

Finally, I owe my wife, Jeri, more that I can easily say. She repeatedly assured me both that I would finish and that the result would be worthy of the effort. Others may dispute the accuracy of this latter assurance, but no one can argue that I failed to marry the right woman.

**Michael Bishop**
*Pine Mountain, Georgia*
*October 19-20, 1987*

# 1

Libby Quarrels was standing at the produce bin in the gigantic Safeway grocery store in Huerfano, Colorado, scrutinizing the bell peppers and hefting bag after cellophane bag of brown-edged celery stalks and runty carrots. You got lousy produce in winter, of course, and Libby didn't really expect to improve it by giving it some of her body heat, but she did hope to dig out the *best* stuff squirreled away in the frigid bin. For which reason she was eyeing and feeling up almost everything.

"My God, *shopping!* Annie Oakley Belle Starr Calamity Jane is actually standing here *squeezing vegetables*. If I hadn't seen it myself, I'd've never believed it."

The voice—the voice and the jolly sarcasm—identified its owner for Libby even before she looked up and saw Gary's grinning face reflected in the tilted mirror above the cabbages. He was wearing a sixty-dollar Resistol hat, a string tie with a turquoise hasp, and a fleece-lined denim jacket. In spite of the crow's-feet around his eyes, he looked about twenty again. But Libby knew too well that he was an aimless, silver-tongued, two-timing asshole, and the sight of his smiling self did nothing to wipe from her mind that hard-won knowledge.

Without turning around, she said, "Beat it, Gary."

"Dropped in to buy some Skoal. Got as much right in Safeway as anybody else, don't I?"

"To hell with Safeway. What're you doing in Huerfano?"

"You're a vision, Libby. Never seen you so pretty."

Libby was wearing jeans, a flannel shirt, a navy pea jacket that had once belonged to her father, a floppy-brimmed leather hat, two pairs of socks, long johns, and some well-scuffed boots that she'd picked up last year at a K-Mart in Pueblo.

If *I'm* pretty, Libby told herself, England's Queen Elizabeth is a surefire candidate for Miss Universe.

But Libby *felt* good—righteous, in control, and intelligently dressed for both the season and her mission into Huerfano from the Tipsy Q. Running into Gary wasn't her idea of the perfect shopping trip, but she could handle it. Just as, for almost fourteen years, she had met head on and handled his me-first boozing, buckle-bunny humping, and irresponsible rodeoing-around.

"I said, 'What're you doing in Huerfano?' One of the terms of our settlement was—"

"Hey, I'm not harassing you, Lib. I'm passing through. This is just a . . . you know, a serendipitous meeting."

"*Serendipitous* is your word, Gary. Mine's *maddening*. Have you been to see Covarrubias again?"

Covarrubias was a lawyer in Huerfano; he had an office over the bank, and Gary had pestered him endlessly about finding some way to reverse that item in their divorce decree—Gary always called it "that item," as if it were a simple nuisance—granting Libby full title to the ranch that he had bought with inherited money in 1969, the year of their marriage.

"I looked in on Julio. Just to say howdy. Nothing wrong with that, is there?"

"You're supposed to be at least three counties away. Unless you want to start paying alimony too."

Gary lifted his hands in a hey-wait-a-minute gesture, but Libby turned around and slapped his left one with a bag of carrots. He stepped back and began to rub the assaulted hand with a pained but completely phony look on his face. I'm just a little boy stealin' cookies, his off-center smirk told her. What'd you expect? It's the nature of the male animal.

He nodded at the bag. The blow had torn the cellophane, and a carrot was dangling from the split. "Whatcha cookin', Libby?"

"Chili."

"With carrots?"

"Yeah, I grate a few in."

"*Carrots?*"

"What's wrong with that?"

"You never used to put carrots in chili."

"I do now. For the vitamin A. I'm going to cook up enough to last Sam and me a couple of weeks."

"Lucky Sam. Lucky you."

"Snow keeps dumping on us. When you're trying to haul water, scatter hay, and keep a close eye on the puny ones, there's damn little time left to cook."

"I remember."

"That's *all* you do is remember. You didn't crack a fingernail to help with that stuff when the place was yours. I use the word *yours* loosely."

"Don't start, okay?"

"I mean, you never—" Libby stopped. As Gary had surmised, she had been about to start. And it did no good. It simply riled her up and drew the shades on any sign of intelligent life in her ex's baby blues. "All right. I won't. Do me a favor, though, and honor your part of our bargain—get your bronc-bruised tail out of Huerfano."

"Libby, you can't— " He reached for her arm.

She twisted away. "Mister," she said in a voice loud enough to shatter pond ice, "goose me again and I'll put a can of party nuts right in your own cheatin' assemblage."

Placatingly, Gary's hands went up again. Libby was pleased to note that several women with shopping carts were looking at him disapprovingly. A stock boy at the end of the produce aisle lifted his eyebrows—"Need any help?"—but she didn't and told him so by a grimace and a curt "No, thanks" and swung the bag of carrots into her own cart. (In any case, Gary would have taken the overeager stock boy apart.)

"Look," he said. "I need to talk to you."

"Yeah, well, there were times I needed to talk to you that I didn't get what I wanted, either." She put her foot on the cart's undercarriage, made it rear like a spirited horse, and wheeled the squeaking vehicle toward the checkouts.

"I'll buy you a beer."

She kept going. He tagged along like a chuck-wagon dog.

"I've got news, Libby. Family news. Do you remember Beaumont, my first cousin? My daddy's sister's oldest boy?"

"You and I aren't family anymore, Gary."

"You kind of liked him, Libby."

"Beaumont? You've got to be kidding."

"You recall Bo. He bucked hay for us one summer. Back in seventy-three, I think. He'd just graduated high school."

"For all I care, your cousin Bo can go screw himself."

"Well, Lib, it's nearly that perverted," Gary said cryptically, still dogging her wheeled basket. "*More* perverted, maybe."

Badly out of sorts, Libby stopped in a small fort of magazines and paperbacks near the checkouts. She snapped the tops of a dozen or so gaudy romances before uncaging a horror novel. Ah, good. She'd been looking for this one.

Reading it tonight might blunt the horror of this run-in with Gary—and briefly obliterate the drudgery of winter ranch work—by immersing her in a spooky story with no immediate connection to the farrago of her private life. If only she could twitch her nose—the way that actress on *Bewitched* used to do—and make Gary vanish. To remanifest (preferably without a space suit) on the far side of the Moon.

She wished she were back on the Tipsy Q, her chili made and her eyes on her novel. Meanwhile, the control on her electric blanket would occasionally click, keeping her toasty warm.

"Come on, Libby. Thirty minutes. For auld lang syne. Is that so damn much to ask?"

Was it? Libby looked speculatively at Gary. Then she held up the novel she'd pulled from the whirl rack.

"Buy me this book?"

"Sure. I like to buy you books. Gave you *Even Cowgirls Get the Blues* one Christmas, didn't I?"

"You gave this cowgirl the blues a dozen goddamn Christmases, Gary. Never mind birthdays, Easters, and Fourths of July."

"Libby, that's not— "

"The author didn't know cowflop about ranching. Four hundred pages of mystical flapdoodle and gratuitous feminism."

"I read it. I liked it. It was funny and it—"

"You read my copy before you ever gave it to me. Another Gary Quarrels two-time."

"Look, I said I'd buy that for you." He pointed at the horror novel around which her hands had angrily closed.

"Buy me these groceries too. Buy me these groceries and I'll let you talk to me. For thirty minutes."

Gary's baby blues flared sapphire. "Hey, I thought you got a kick out of your holy self-sufficiency. So why're you working me like a hooker lining up a mark in Vegas?"

"Take it or leave it. I figure you owe me about a *thousand* shopping carts full of groceries."

"You know what you can do with those carrots, don't you?" And Gary walked, striding from the fort of books and magazines toward the automatic entrance-and-exit doors. Good riddance, Libby hissed subvocally: Good goddamn riddance.

But when she entered the nearest checkout lane, Gary reappeared in the entrance door opposite the exit he had just used. He angled around the cashiers' stations, eased into her lane, and gripped the handle of her shopping cart.

"Forgot my smokeless," he said. "Might as well get these too, hadn't I?"

In Huerfano, an old coal-mining town in southeastern Colorado, three kinds of businesses outnumbered all the others combined: gas stations, liquor stores, and grimy little bars. Maybe that was because the coal had pretty much given out years ago, and anyone with any sense had moved to Santa Fe or Denver. The population was a quarter Slav, a quarter Italian, a quarter Chicano, and a quarter almost everything else imaginable: Anglo-Saxons, Scandinavians, Arabs, American Indians, etc.

Every Huerfanovian who owned a car or a truck needed the gas stations, and *everyone*—whether afoot or on wheels—eventually required a snootful. The pious frequented the liquor stores and took the stuff home. But more forthright or gregarious citizens ambled into the bars, paid their money, and sat in pine-paneled gloom—animated beer signs rippling on the walls—brooding over their Coors or their unabashedly watered whiskey.

Libby and her ex-husband were sitting in a booth in Tío Pepé's, trying to keep their elbows out of the overlapping mug rings on the scarred surface of the table. A wicker bowl filled with pretzels and another filled with corn chips sat between the Quarrelses like outsized counters in an arcane game. Libby ate nothing from either bowl; she didn't know how often the county sanitarian showed up to inspect the premises, and in January she'd gone a couple of rounds with a stomach bug that had made her deeply leery of food prepared anywhere but in her own kitchen.

"You're still calling yourself Quarrels," Gary said. "Thought you'd rush to change it back."

"Why? I was Libby Quarrels for fourteen years."

"Yeah, but from what you used to tell me, it wasn't a name you were all that proud of."

"It did a good job of summarizing our relationship, didn't it?"

"We don't *have* a relationship anymore. But you're hanging on to my name like it was a valuable heirloom or something."

"Maybe I'm trying to redeem it for your mother."

Pamela Fay McInnis Quarrels, Gary's mother, lived in a condo in Colorado Springs. Gary had just been to see her, taking a week off from the ranch work he was doing for a man with a spread not far from Dumas, Texas. Although Gary's mother had been glad to see her son, she'd been equally glad to bid him adieu again.

Miss Pamela relished the fact that Libby had won the Tipsy Q in the divorce settlement. Still, it was a better than even bet that had Gary's daddy—Don Reynolds Quarrels—been alive then, Libby would be frying hash browns in an I-25 truckstop instead of running cattle on the subalpine ranch purchased with some of Dear Old Dad's Otero Steel fortune. For the elder Quarrels had been a confirmed male chauvinist pig—he could have used *M.C.P.* after his surname the way that some men use *Esq.*—and Pamela Fay McInnis Quarrels had never been happier than during the twelve years since her husband's early but thoughtful demise.

"Mama doesn't care what folks think of the name Quarrels," Gary said. "You don't have to 'redeem' it for her."

"Then maybe I'm trying to redeem it for you. I'm sure as hell not hanging on to it because I think that one day you and me'll get back together."

"No?"

"No, sir. Em-damn-phatically not."

"Well, it's easier to say than a Polack name like Ruzeski. I guess *I* wouldn't want to go back to that one, either."

"Leave my family's name out of this."

"I will. I am. Just like you're doing."

"Look, the main reason I'm keeping yours—not that I didn't put up with enough shit from you to get to do whatever I want with it, including tattooing it on my rosy red rump—is convenience. Simple convenience. Feed-store clerks, equipment salesmen, other ranchers—everybody I count on knows me as Libby Quarrels. I'm not about to cross 'em all up by going back to Ruzeski."

"Sure. Who the hell's Ruzeski? they'd wonder It makes sense not to confuse 'em any more than you have to."

Libby, sipping her beer, looked into Gary's eyes. Already, he was on his second Coors, and already his eyes resembled those of a teddy bear's—hard, blue-black buttons with nothing but straw on mattress ticking behind them. The mockery that he was putting into his words, he deliberately held out of his eyes. And he had never seemed emptier or less attractive to Libby. But she had let him buy her groceries, and now she was bickering with him, sort of, over an utter triviality. She ought to be negotiating the asphalt hairpins between Huerfano and Snowy Falls, hauling her supplies back to Sam Coldpony and mulling ways to save her most vulnerable heifers from scours and pneumonia.

Two teenagers behind Gray were playing an old-fashioned bowling game. They kept sliding some sort of metal puck over the waxed and sawdust-sprinkled lane of the game box, trying to trip a bracket on its floor that would make all the wired pins fold back out of sight in unison. If the puck hit brackets to either the left or the right of this central trip, only three or four pins would fold back, and the bowler would have to go for a spare. Today, the kids playing were Chicanos, and jarring bursts of Spanish escaped them each time they slid their pucklike "bowling ball."

Why aren't they in school? Libby wondered. She took a last sip of beer, wiped her mouth, and began wriggling sideways. Gary bolted upright. "Hold on," he said. "It hasn't been any thirty minutes." He tapped his wristwatch.

"Seems like it."

"Sit, Libby. Sit. You made me a deal."

And a deal's a deal, Libby scolded herself. She ceased trying to wriggle clear of the booth and folded her hands in front of her, too distracted to imagine what Gary might have on his mind.

"You really don't remember my cousin Bo?" he asked. "Don R.'s sister's boy?"

"Yeah, I remember him. A little." So what? she wanted to add, boredom already creeping in.

"His parents—my aunt and uncle-in-law—they just found out that the guy's a swish."

"A swish?"

"You know, a pansy. A homo. A queer. A—"

"Okay, okay. I've got it."

"My own cousin. My own *first* cousin."

"Gary, it's not all that damn astonishing. Plenty of people in this country—it's a *big* country—swing that way. Even a girl like me, an innocent from Saguache County, has met a couple. It's not like tripping over a Bigfoot or anything."

"But this is Bo. Think about it. Who'd've ever guessed?"

Libby let go an exasperated sigh. (While married, she'd become a master of exasperated sighs.) "All right, if that's the case, how'd Bo's parents find out?"

"He has AIDS," Gary said. "Poor Beaumont's got AIDS. And he was always as smart as a Spanish quirt, too."

This news stunned Libby. She *did* remember Bo. The summer he'd come up from Pueblo to buck hay for them, he'd carried himself with endearing modesty. Not quite so tall—or so muscular—as Gary, he had nevertheless pulled his weight. Whenever the crew had begun to horse around at lunchtime or on breaks, Bo had cracked wise in a gently witty—rather than a smart-alecky—way that had doubled over even the nincompoopish Mitchelson twins from Pagosa Springs. Now Bo had AIDS, and AIDS was fatal.

God, it hurt to think of someone as healthy and full of spirit as the Gavin kid, Gary's cousin, falling victim to a . . . well, a *syndrome* that wasted its victims, depriving them of hope even as it turned them into latter-day lepers.

Libby said, "Bo could've been as smart as a nuclear physicist and still not've sidestepped that one."

"It's weird." Gary shook his head. His teddy bear's flinty

blue-black eyes finally struck a sentient spark. Plaintively, he said, "My own first cousin."

"He's living down in Georgia or Florida, isn't he?"

"Georgia. Atlanta."

"So when's he coming home, Gary?"

"That's what I've been working up to tell you. He's not. He's not coming home."

"Is he *that* sick? Almost gone?"

"What it is, Libby, is Aunt Josey and Uncle Nate don't *want* him to come home. They don't want nothin' to do with him."

"He's all alone then? He's got this horrible disease and his own mother and father won't let him come home to die?" Libby was appalled.

Purportedly, the Nathaniel Gavins had attended her and Gary's wedding in '69, but the Quarrelses—for various snobbish reasons of their own—had seldom socialized with the Gavins. Libby could not recall having talked to or seen them since. It wasn't very likely she would recognize them even if they were suddenly to pop up from the next booth in Tío Pepé's.

"Right. They've cut him off totally. I stopped to see them on the way up to Mama's, and they told me they don't ever want to see Bo again. 'Our son,' Aunt Josey said, 'isn't really a man. He's an in-between kind of monster. He *chose* to be that way to spite us for favoring Ned.' Swear to God, Libby. Aunt Josey's exact words, more or less."

"And they probably think his getting AIDS is God getting back at him for being . . . 'an in-between kind of monster'?"

"Right. Right again, Lib. I didn't try to argue with 'em. It wiped me out that they could even *think* such things about Bo."

Cheered by Gary's compassion for his cousin, an emotion he usually reserved for rodeo clowns and ranch dogs that ran afoul of porcupines, Libby reached across the table and put her hand on her ex's wrist. "Frankly, Gary, I'm amazed you're not on the bad guys' side. It really doesn't bother you that Bo's a— ?"

"Swish?"

"Gay, let's call him."

"Why should I care if he's queer? It's his life, I figure. It sure ain't any of my beeswax."

"Good for you."

"Except—"

Uh-oh, Libby thought. Except what?

The Chicanos at the bowling game began to scuffle. One claimed to have tripped the strike bracket, but the other held that he hadn't—that he had illegally folded all ten pins out of view by banging on the side of the box. In any case, he had thrown the puck out of turn.

"*¡Tu maricón!*" cried the accuser.

"You lying cocksucker!" shouted the accused.

The bartender, an average-sized man of thirty or so, came over to them carrying a polished oaken cane. He hit the alleged cheater across the buttocks and then used the crook of the cane to topple the accuser to the floor. "Behave yourselves or get out," he told them, And, muttering at each other rather than at the bartender, the boys apparently decided to behave.

To this brief set-to, Gary paid no attention.

"It's just that if Bo, my own first cousin, is a swish," he was telling Libby, "I can't help wondering if"—Libby saw, but found it hard to believe, that her ex's face was reddening from the roots of his hair to the cleft of his chin—". . . if maybe I've got those kinds of tendencies myself."

"My God, you're blushing!"

"Lib, please. Some folks think it's inherited. In the genes, like. And my daddy was Bo's mama's brother."

"You're seriously afraid *you* have homosexual tendencies?"

"Shhh. Remember how I used to run around on you? How I'd find me a couple of buckle bunnies at some two-bit rodeo in Wyoming or Idaho? How I'd take both of 'em to a motel and do my best to give 'em what-for? Or how I'd—"

"What is this, Gary? A confession or a brag fest?" Jesus, the man hadn't changed. He was still a pagan in a yoke-collared shirt, a lout to shame all louts.

"No. Neither. I'm just trying to ask you if you think I did those things—ran around like that, busting my balls—because I was . . . uh, secretly afraid I might be . . . well you know, like Bo's turned out to be."

"Back then, you never suspected a thing about Bo!"

"Of course I didn't. But I could've been worried on a . . .

you know, an *un*conscious level. Such tendencies get passed along. They're common to certain families."

"'If your father had no kids, chances are good that you won't, either.'"

"You think that's smart, but actually it's illogical. A guy who's mostly swish can still father a kid, just like a woman who's mostly lesbo can get knocked up and have a baby."

Are we really having this conversation? Libby asked herself. Is it possible?

Gary's blush, she noticed, had already faded. But if he truly had any *cojones*, he would realize that he had stopped blushing too soon. Not because he was talking openly about homosexuality, but because he was pontificating about it like the Chief Ignoramus in Charge of Obfuscation. He thinks he's an expert on the topic, yet he's afraid that because Cousin Bo has AIDS, all his heartbreaking infidelities were simply attempts to compensate for an inherited preference for guys.

With no warning even to herself, Libby began to laugh. She let her head wobble against the back of the booth, laughing and wiping her eyes and laughing some more.

The kids at the bowling game looked at her disgustedly, their expressions a lot like Gary's. One of them was cradling the metal puck as if thinking about throwing it at her.

Go ahead, Libby thought. I'm too damn numb to feel it.

On the drive from Huerfano to Snowy Falls, the heater in her GM pickup whirring as if a leaf had fallen into one of its vents, the slush-crimped fields on either side of the asphalt reminiscent of overfloured pie crusts, Libby realized that Gary had not taken her to Tío Pepé's just to spin a crackpot theory exculpating him of the responsibility for two-, three-, and even ten-timing her, but to apprise her of Cousin Bo's plight and to spur her to find a way to help him.

Or was that attributing too much ulteriority to Gary? Usually, he was as up front as a chorus girl's chest. If you couldn't read his motives in his eyes, you were probably waiting for some shyster to offer to sell you—cheap—the world-famous suspension bridge over the Royal Gorge.

But maybe Gary really had been looking out (in his roundabout, assume-no-true-responsibility way) for Bo, and he had come to her because he knew she wouldn't be able to get a decent night's sleep until she did something about the matter. But what, though? What *could* she do when she had livestock to care for, Sam Coldpony to nudge through the remainder of the winter, and creditors aplenty waiting for her to stumble into their snares?

Libby drove. The Twin Peaks were cone-shaped fortresses to her left, while Greenhorn floated to the north in a cloud bank crawling the downslope prairie like a phantom dreadnought.

A bitter winter's day, problems abounding.

Even a fleeting memory of the pale unicorns in the upland vale above her ranch house—beasts that had reappeared, shortly before or after Christmas, for the past three years—could not make her smile. After all, those half-fragile, half-indomitable creatures had problems of their own, and Sam Coldpony had already told Libby that some of them might be dying.

Slamming her foot down hard, Libby Quarrels made her protesting truck gobble up vaster hallucinatory stretches of highway. Up into the clouds and mountains, past bland-faced cattle, rusty windmills, solitary spires of sandstone, and the occasional melancholy ruin of a miner's adobe dwelling or a storekeeper's tumbledown dream. The color of her world showed monochrome, but its subsurface complexion was mottled.

For which reason Libby stopped thinking and simply drove, her mind as dimensionless and clear as a windshield.

## 2

Said the metal plaque on the dashboard of the taxicab she had caught at the Atlanta airport: ASPERIDON HOBEIKA.

In the rearview mirror, each time Hobeika glanced back to check the traffic flowing around them on I-85, his face had the swarthy, hatchetlike angularity of an Islamic Jihad terrorist. Lib could not help imagining him, AK-47 in hand, hijacking a TWA jumbo jet or browbeating a western hostage in a rubble-strewn hideout somewhere in Beirut.

Hundreds of cabbies in Atlanta and she got this Shiite fanatic who probably didn't even know Peachtree from Ponce de Leon. Hell, *she* didn't know Peachtree from Ponce de Leon—but, without either hassle or embarrassment, it was too late to stop him and flag down a cab driven by a Ron Howard clone.

"Have you ever been to"—checking the info that Gary's Aunt Josey had given her grudgingly over the telephone—"Chattahoochee CommuniGrafix before?"

"Sure. Joo got appointment?"

"An appointment?"

"Of course. Company very busy doing Fly-Fast ad campaign."

Libby was confused. In the rearview, Asperidon Hobeika's eyes drilled into her without even a twinkle. The logo on the flank of his dilapidated mid-1970s Chevy Impala had said FLY-FAST LIMOUSINE & TAXI SERVICE. Had Bo's CommuniGrafix Ltd. really undertaken to promote this tenth-rate transport company, whose logo might better read FLY-BLOWN than FLY-FAST?

"Joke."

"What?"

"A joke. I can't buy air for my tires, much less pay out like Pepsi for ads. Besides, I got already plenty of business."

"Good for you," Libby said. "You're Lebanese, aren't you?"

His eyebrows lifted: a response. Quickly, however, his eyes flicked back to the expressway, and his taxi switched lanes with a stomach-fluttering swerve. Another swerve. Another. Libby saw that they were going past Atlanta-Fulton County Stadium, where the Braves and the Falcons played. Meanwhile, pickups, sports cars, and vans were weaving in and out around Asperidon's madcap Impala as if piloted by so many dervishes on speed.

"How joo know that?" he asked her.

Libby kept a wary eye on the traffic. "Your name. We've got lots of Lebanese in Huerfano County—Hobeikas, Farises, Hasbanis. Maybe you've got relatives in Colorado."

Asperidon's terrorist façade fell away. He told Libby that he had always wanted to visit Colorado. Maybe he would go out there to live. Mountains. Fresh air. On the other hand, he *liked* the city, and the reason he had come to Atlanta—after fleeing Beirut with his wife and daughter in 1980—was simply to enjoy urban life as it ought to be enjoyed. Atlanta had a culture that appealed to him. Whenever they'd saved a little money, he could take the whole family to a café for pizza or to a movie for Stallone.

Libby tried to comprehend his enthusiasm for Atlanta but found herself, instead, bad-mouthing the traffic, the city's drivers, and the fact that the highway department had turned the expressway into a vast parody of desolation. Dear God, it looked like it had been bomb-cratered.

The cabbie grimaced. "Sickens me to hear out-of-towners—yes, Atlantans even—down-dumping the city for its crazy drivers and tore-up streets. Joo know why?"

"Why—?" Libby began. "Oh," she said. "Yeah, I guess I do."

"Joo bet joo do," Asperidon said.

In the rearview—Lib relievedly noted—his pupils at last dimly twinkled. But in them, too, were the cloudy psychic reflections of mortar shellings, sniper assaults, and car-bomb explosions.

He took the Cheshire Bridge Road exit—amid a confusion of ramps, overloops, and bifurcating lanes that would have addled a Department of Transportation sign maker—and somehow got her to the renovated house that was Chattahoochee CommuniGrafix Ltd.

A pale March sun shone down, but it was thirty degrees warmer than it had been that morning in Denver, and Libby gave Asperidon both her fare and an overgenerous five-dollar tip.

"Thanks," he said. "I will put it aside and start us to saving for vacation to Colorado."

Who in the world is that? wondered Carrie Plourde, standing at the solitary porthole in her den of fashion magazines, comic books, and birthday-suit albums.

Outside the offices of CCG, a fenderless cab was disembarking a woman who looked as if she had been beamed into town from the kind of peace-and-rock-music festival at which the hippies of the 1960s had made love, given birth, and raised their offspring, all of whom had inherited names like Zephyr Rose and Moon Puppy.

Floppy hat. Knapsack. Jeans. Boots. Maybe even a necklace adorned with a peace symbol or a zodiac sign—although the heavy coat she was wearing made it hard to tell.

Surely she's not coming in, Carrie thought. She must've had the cabbie let her out here by mistake. She probably wanted Bali Hi Imports. Only she must not realize how expensive everything in our neighbors' wicker-wacky place is.

But the taxi passenger walked toward CCG's porch, and the edge of the building eclipsed her from Carrie's sight. The bell in the foyer buzz-buzz-buzzed, and Jim Watling, directly across the hall, yelled, "Carrie, would you get that, please? I'm on hold to the executive vice-donkeybutt of Gainesville Chemtech and don't want to break my momentum."

So she put her paintbrush down, rearranged the sketches on her drafting table, and went down the hall to answer the door.

"I'm Elizabeth Quarrels," the woman standing on the porch told her. "I've come to take Bo Gavin home with me."

Abashed, Carrie thought, Who *is* this? The named Quarrels means nothing to me. Is she a wife that Bo attached himself to early on, to obtain the status of Regular Guy with his friends and family, or is she—possibly—a married sister with a different surname? It's clear she's a Coloradan, but a Coloradan from a mining camp or a prospector's cabin rather than from Denver or Aspen.

"Is Bo here?"

"No," Carried said. "No, he isn't."

"I called his apartment from the airport, thinking maybe he was too sick to come in to work. But he wasn't there."

"Well, Bo moved out of his apartment complex a couple of weeks ago, Miss Quarrels."

"Call me Libby. To where?"

You're acting like a housewife holding a vacuum-cleaner salesman at bay, Carrie scolded herself. Aloud, she said, "Come in. Come in. Forgive me for making you stand out here."

"He's living with—*staying* with— me," admitted Carrie, back in her office with her guest.

Libby had lowered her knapsack to the cluttered floor. Now she leaned against a pine bookcase, thumbing an old copy of *Vogue*.

Looking up, she said, "Why?"

"Things got a bit hairy in Savannah Glen. He could've sweated it out—he had the law behind him—but it was unpleasant having to face one hostile neighbor in particular. I took him to my place because I . . . I—" Carried stopped. Did she really want to tell this stranger, who on the way in had said that she wasn't even a blood relation of Bo's, that one stupid action of hers had estranged the elder Gavins from their son? "Well, because I *owed* him, Libby."

"Is that where he is now? Is he too sick to work?"

"No. Jim—Mr. Watling, our boss—has him come in until noon every day. That's when Bo's energy level's highest, and he's not usually fighting a fever. Afternoons, if he's feeling okay, he takes some work back to my humble *casa*—I'm renting a place over by Emory—and stays at it until he conks out. This afternoon, though, he had a doctor's appointment."

"He drove himself?"

Carrie said yes, and their conversation proceeded.

Even as the newcomer spoke, though, she seemed to be engaged in an inward quarrel. She had learned through a first cousin of Bo's about his illness and had flown all the way from Denver to fetch him home to . . . not Pueblo, but a two-pump mountain hamlet called Snowy Falls, nigh-on close enough to home to qualify. Now, though, Libby was finding out that Bo was neither jobless nor hospitalized nor lacking in local support, and she may have begun to wonder if it wouldn't be okay to abort her mission and return to Colorado via the next Frontier or Northern Pacific flight. The would-be Good Samaritan was rationalizing an early exit. To go home minus Bo would be to go home unencumbered.

I can't let her do that, Carrie realized. She's come here for him out of the goodness of her heart, and she's *almost* related to him. I'm not even close. In fact, I'm letting him stay with me for one simple reason: guilt. The guilt I feel for bringing about the breach with his parents . . . and the even worse guilt I'd feel if I didn't try to do something to atone.

Carrie remembered that back in January she had urged Bo to call his parents and to tell them that he was ill.

"What am I supposed to say, Carrie?" he'd asked her. "'I have some good news and some bad news. The good news is that I'm gay, the bad news is that I have AIDS'?"

"I don't know. You could try it."

"Or maybe this: 'The bad news is that I'm queer, the good news is that you won't have to sweat it too long'? That might mesh better with their feelings."

"But it probably doesn't. You need their support. Call them."

"Unh-uh. I'd be drummed out of the Gavins. They're militantly straight, and Ned has always been the apple of their rose-colored optical equipment. Why do you think I left Colorado?"

"Bo, you've got to—"

"Hey, Miz Plourde, I'm a grown-up. I don't gotta do anything I don't wanna. Except die."

That had ended the conversation, but later that evening Carrie had called information for Bo's parents' number in Pueblo and then rung them up to let them know that the older of their two sons was ailing. She had been careful not to say that he had AIDS, but had stressed that Bo was very sick, that he might need their help, and that they should telephone him as soon as possible.

Apparently, the Gavins had done that right after Carrie's call, and in their ensuing talk with Bo, he had informed them bitterly that he had a fatal disease called AIDS and he had not gotten it because he was a Haitian, an intravenous drug user, or a recent recipient of contaminated blood. The Gavins, as Bo had foreseen but as Carrie still found hard to credit, had hung up. Then, even though he had tried at least a dozen times to dial through to them again, they had pointedly declined to answer.

Hence Carrie's guilt. Hence her need to atone.

I'd like to be an angel of mercy, she thought, trying to adjust to Libby's sudden appearance, but I'm a nervous wreck. How many bottles of disinfectant have I bought since Bo moved in? And how many dates have I declined knowing that

I couldn't bring a would-be lover into my house with another fellow, body by Eichmann, roaming through it like Death's hollow-eyed herald?

"Look," Carrie blurted. "This arrangement isn't permanent. My landlord told me he'd let me rent his house as long as I didn't get married or have somebody else move in."

"No sweat," Libby said with humbling decisiveness. "I told you I was taking Bo back to Colorado with me."

Jim Watling appeared in the door. He had always seemed huge to Carrie, a bearded, ursine man who invariably wore a tie, even after he had cast off his coat and was eating his third mumbleburger from McDonald's for lunch.

"Bo's quitting?" Jim said. "I thought he was going to stay on until he couldn't hack it any longer."

*I* can't hack it any longer, Carrie thought. If you and Tanis want to carry him on the CommuniGrafix payroll, why don't you all give him a room in *your* house to die in?

Aloud, she said, "Jim, this is Elizabeth Quarrels, a relative of Bo's." My savior, she silently added, grateful that God—or a merciful facsimile—had answered her prayers.

For most of the remainder of that afternoon, Libby sat in Bo's office waiting for the end of the workday. Carrie had promised to take her home with her to meet Bo. She had even agreed to let her spend the night on the living-room sofa.

On her flight, Libby had drowsed in her seat, a pluglike blower needling cool air down on her face and the jet's wing jouncing just beyond her in the irreal altitudinal wispiness of 35,000 feet. Flight was a floating dream, and she had more or less dreamed her way from Denver to Atlanta.

Now, caught up on her Z's, she could do nothing but worry about confronting Bo. Maybe she had made a mistake coming. Certainly, she had invested a hell of a lot of money buying an airline ticket, even though the American Express charge for it wouldn't show up for another four weeks. And, certainly, she had presumed a great deal, supposing that Bo, uninformed of her visit, would rejoice to see her and leap at the chance to come live—and die—on the Tipsy Q, the ranch where he had bucked hay nearly thirteen years ago.

Libby had seen him only three or four times since, and on all those occasions he had been—outwardly, at least—just another bright, sure-to-go-far heterosexual lad. Tonight, though, she would be seeing him not only as a disease victim but also as a gay man—both for the first time.

Gay.

The word made her tremble. Now, in fact, all that Libby could think—considering her imminent rendezvous with Gary's cousin and her likely struggle to persuade him to come home with her—was that very little of what she knew about gayness would be of any use in making contact with him person-to-person. Maybe they'd hit it off at once. Or maybe one word with her would produce in him an aversion that, filtered through both his disease and his gayness, would keep them from connecting. If, of course, *she* wasn't the one who developed the aversion.

Carrie appeared in the door to Bo's office. "I called my house again. Still no answer. Maybe you should take a stroll, look in at Bali Hi Imports. I'm sure Bo'll be home by six thirty. We'll all have dinner together. Okay?"

"Okay. Who cooks?"

"The microwave, mostly. Reheated Chinese, reheated pizza, lots of Stouffer's Lean Cuisine." Carrie smiled and left.

Pretty neat lady, Libby reflected. Not the calculating career bitch TV says you're going to collide with in the Big City.

For the dozenth time, she looked around her ex-cousin-in-law's office. (Was there such a thing as a cousin-in-law? If not, she and Bo had no real family ties at all.)

Fascinating place. For Spartanburg's Emeritus Software, Inc., Bo had created a clever magazine ad featuring super-smart business people—the preliminary sketches were his; the laminated finished illos, Miss Plourde's—wearing hat-sized computer diskettes as if they were academic mortarboards. Each cap stood for a specialized Emeritus business program that would allow any company using it "to graduate at the head of its class."

Appreciatively, Libby smiled. Even Gary's folks had admitted that the Gavin boys—Beaumont and Theodore—were bright, and this work proved the fact . . . at least in Bo's case.

On the wall hung a huge framed poster from another ad campaign waged by Chattahoochee CommuniGrafix, this one for Piedmont Mills. It depicted a rugged emerald-green countryside—in Scotland, or New Zealand, or maybe the Falkland Islands—on which hundreds of sheep were grazing. Nothing unusual there. However, half a dozen of the woolly critters in the photograph were distinguished from the others by eye-grabbing plaid or checkered or striped fleeces unlike any ever found in nature. *For Out-of-the-Ordinary Quality*, read Bo's simple caption: PIEDMONT TEXTILES.

Another ad on the wall touted Heliodyne Industries, a Florida-based solar-power company. A big full-color photo montage showed a dozen American Indians in native dress dancing in the great room of a modern house whose circular roof was covered with reflective solar cells. Said the ad's caption, *We may not worship the sun, but no one makes better use of it than Heliodyne*. Among Bo's books—not coincidentally, Libby figured—was a copy of a scholarly work entitled *The Sun Dance Religion*.

Nice, thought Libby. Apparently, you can do this stuff like a late-night used-car pitchman or you can do it like an artist. Bo's been doing it—*trying* to do it—like an artist.

This insight predisposed Libby to like him, even in his adult incarnation as a gay and an AIDS victim. So did the fact that on his desk, half-hidden by envelops, folders, and technical manuals, rested a trio of photographs of the family.

Aunt Josey. Uncle Nate. Brother Ned. A gallery of judgmental blood relations who had excommunicated him from the circle of their love. And here *he* was—obviously, to them, an avatar of the Gay Antichrist—forgiving their holier-than-thou asses.

It was ironic. It was sad. It made Libby want to pick up each photo and ash-can it. But to hell with that. Lib shook her head, put her old navy pea jacket back on, and exited the CCG house.

Onward to Bali Hi Imports, the two-story bric-a-brac emporium just down the hill. She couldn't afford to buy anything, but maybe she could kill some time before Carrie Plourde finished up and took her home to see Bo. The only other establishments on this wide south-to-north street were the Roger Bacon Day School, above CCG, and a fried-chicken franchise and a gas station at the intersection below it. From the all-glass chicken castle wafted smells as vivid as any she had ever detected from a coop of wood and wire.

Libby entered Bali Hi. At once, a variety of pungent odors—incense, cinnamon, cloves, perfumed soap—strangled the scent of ripening poultry. Feathers rose up from ungainly glazed vases that were spotted like trout or striped like zebras. So did cattails, ersatz sunflowers, and an array of linen napkins folded to resemble either chrysanthemums or roses.

Glass. Porcelain. Teak. Handmade musical instruments. Cloth or plastic kites—long-tailed, spooky-faced, Day-Glo colorful.

So much junk that Libby almost regretted entering.

Upstairs, in an area partitioned with crating material and dyed burlap, she happened upon the bric-a-brac. West German figurines of fence-sitting children. Religious icons. Irish setters carved from redwood. And an entire paddock of mythological beasties made of either pewter or glass.

Among these items dwelled unicorns. Libby released her breath, not from surprise but from an anticipation fulfilled. She picked up one of the blown-glass animals. It was "beautiful." It was also phony. So were the pewter models, each one a romantic lie.

Elsewhere on the second floor, other customers were tiptoeing around, murmuring to one another, fondling merchandise. None was close enough to see her, though, and, knowing that, Libby scooped a dozen or more unicorns into the deep front pockets of her coat—an act that thrilled her.

Her heart raced, *kerr-chunking* like the engine in a rod-blown pickup. Someone was bound to hear. Even her grungy old peacoat wasn't thick enough to muffle this beating. She had to get out. She had to get out before, on her first day in Atlanta, she was caught crimson-fingered and booked for shoplifting. What would Bo think then? Carrie Plourde? Jim Watling?

Buy *some*thing, Libby told herself. If you don't buy something, you'll look even more suspicious than you think you do.

She left the area of burlapped partitions and wandered among the music boxes and stuffed animals at large on the second floor. She picked out a Hawaiian shirt at a rack near the music boxes, a dark blue garment with white and red poinsettia profiles splashed across it, and carried it downstairs to a cash register surrounded by cane bamboo. Would the shirt swallow Bo? How much weight had he lost? He hadn't been all that big in '73, and you always took a risk when you tried to buy for somebody you hadn't seen in a long time. What if he didn't like Hawaiian shirts?

"Will this be all?" said the woman at the cash register. She had a chain on her glasses; the stress that she gave the word *all* frightened Libby. Did her fancy-dan glasses give her X-ray vision, letting her see through the dense fabric of a peacoat?

"That's it," Libby answered, keeping her voice steady.

"Forty-nine dollars and ninety-two cents. Cash or charge?"

"Forty-nine dollars and—!" Libby began. Then she remembered and bit her tongue. "Charge," she said, pulling out her plastic. Who in the name of Sam Hill hauls around that much cash? The only person she could think of was Gary, back in his rodeoing days, and he'd never had it for long.

Testing her resolve, Libby had the shirt boxed and wrapped, a service for which she had to fork over two dollars, cash. Then she eased smilingly out of Bali Hi.

What was she going to do with the herd of stupid unicorns in her pockets? What had made her swipe them? Instead of going back to the CCG house, she went down to the gas station at the crossing and asked a burly man in greasy coveralls for a key to the women's rest room. He told her that its commode was broken; however, she could have the key to the men's, if she had no hangups about using it instead. She assured him that she didn't.

Inside, Libby flipped on the light, locked the door, and turned around to find herself staring at a machine that dispensed exotic condoms. It warehoused five different kinds of the same intimate product. Stuck to the surface of each dispenser chute was a color decal of a buxom young woman beckoning the occupant of the rest room to deposit the necessary pair of quarters.

Oh, boy, Libby thought. Adventure. Love. Excitement. All for fifty cents in a gas-house rest room

But from what Gary had told her about such machines, their best customers were teenage boys too anxiety-stricken to buy "rubbers" under the identifying glare of a drugstore flourescents. It was no surprise, then, that half the time the machines paid off and half the time they didn't. If you were sixteen or seventeen and still living at home, you didn't march around to the front of the station and raise a ruckus with the attendant about sacrificing a quarter or two to the ribbed-French-tickler slot of the men's rest room's prophylactic machine. No, you simply cursed your luck and skulked out into the night in search of a gas station with a more reliable dispenser.

Libby placed the package containing Bo's Hawaiian shirt across the mouth of a metal wastebasket and then began pulling glass and pewter unicorns from her coat pockets. She lined them up on the rear of the sink, on the upper edge of the urinal, on the chipped porcelain top of the commode, and, by standing with one foot on the toilet seat and a knee against the condom dispenser, even along the top of that machine. Beneath the rest room's naked 60-watt bulb, the unicorns either glinted or sparkled. Surveying them in their ranks, Libby congratulated herself on her decorating skills. This was exactly where they belonged.

She pulled a paper towel from another dispenser, found a pen in her shirt pocket, and wrote in block letters on the towel:

THESE AREN'T UNICORNS—THEY'RE COMMERCIAL STEREOTYPES. REDEEM THEM WITH OUR ATTENDANT FOR A FREE GALLON OF GAS OR A STRONG DOSE OF REALITY. ONE TO A CUSTOMER, PLEASE.

Carefully, she slid the top edge of this message into the upper frame of the mirror, pivoted, picked up her shirt box, turned out the light, shut the door, and carried the key back to the burly guy in overalls. He was as pleasant as before, and Libby hoped that when customers began bringing miniature unicorns forward for free gallons of gas—assuming that no one simply stole them all—he would refrain from giving them a dose of reality in a way requiring medical attention.

Striding back uphill to the CCG house, where Carrie Plourde was waiting for her in the parking lot, Libby knew that for the sake of a momentary anger she had committed two wrongs: the theft at Bali Hi and her pointless practical joke in the gas-station rest room. The latter could end up embarrassing a man who had been completely decent to her.

Immoral, immoral.

Libby wished she could blame her behavior on jet lag or

the change in climate, but, more than likely, it all went to her nervousness about meeting Bo Gavin again.

"Ready?" Carrie Plourde asked, gesturing her to the passenger side of her Chevrolet Cavalier.

"Sure," Libby replied.

Ready as I'll ever be, she thought, an unhappy queasiness afflicting her. As ready as I'll ever be. . . .

# 3

Carrie Plourde's rented house nestled on a tree-lined street not far from the shopping center called Emory Village. Like most of the houses on the right side of this street, it sat well back from, and below, the level of the curb—so that Libby was looking *down* on its roof until the Cavalier wheeled hard into its cracked drive and began dropping toward the garage, where another car—a foreign model—had laid claim to the stall. Carrie slammed them to a stop behind it, and the two women hurried up the back stairs to the fragrant warmth of the kitchen.

Inside, a lovely—but incongruous—smell.

Chili.

The kind that you make when you're snowbound or fear that you soon may be. Libby could not believe that she was encountering its fragrance in Atlanta.

"Bo!" Carrie shouted. "Bo, you here?" A ceramic Crockpot was plugged into an outlet near her stove.

Through the beaded moisture on the pot's glass lid, Libby could see the gorgeous meat-and-vegetable-laden bulk of the chili. Diced celery, onions, and green peppers. Osterized tomatoes. Bo probably hadn't grated in any carrots, but that was a private culinary touch Libby had seldom seen anyone else use.

"Here!" shouted a male voice from near the front of the house. "Bring any more work for me to do?"

"Not exactly," Carrie said, leading Libby into the dining nook and through it into a sitting area with tatami mats on the hardwood floor, Japanese woodcuts on the walls, and an array of rosewood or teak carvings—fisher folk, sunny Buddhas, willowy storks—standing on the mantel, a low plastic table, and two plastic end pieces, giving an Oriental accent to the otherwise high-tech décor. It all reminded Libby of Bali Hi Imports, where, she felt sure, Carrie had bought most of it. Probably on credit.

She saw Bo. He lay on the low-slung sofa with a Bloody Mary on the magazine table beside him while a portable tape player—"jam boxes," the kids called them—reeled out, faintly, a melody from the long-lost era of Big Bands. Libby recognized it at once. It was an old favorite of her dad's, "Relaxin' at the Touro" by Muggsy Spanier and the Ragtimers. A muted coronet solo—sassy, bluesy, laid back—gave way to a rhythmic tinkling piano that soft-pedaled into a clarinet turn. Hearing this ancient rag and simultaneously trying to size up a brand-new Beaumont Gavin made Libby stop in her tracks. Gary's cousin didn't look like Gary's cousin, and after the clarinet came a trombone, more coronet, and a final smattering of plaintive honky-tonk piano.

When the number ended, she was able to concentrate again. Bo, if that was really Bo, looked like a reclining shadow on which an artist—a cartoonist, actually—had drawn opium-bright eyes, a gash for a month, twin points for nostrils, and some thin, shaky lines for the pale hair falling in a swan's-neck curve across his brow. His skin was the color of a communion wafer, except where it seemed to be soiled by cancer lesions. He lay on the sofa looking at the two woman, and his attitude was one of amused tolerance for both the intrusion and their unabashed curiosity.

"I've brought a friend home with me," Carrie said. "A friend of *yours*, I mean."

Bo squinted at Libby. His cassette player swung into a tinny rendition—the box had lousy sound quality—of "Woodchopper's Ball" by the Woody Herman orchestra. The wood blocks percussing in this tune's background were an analogue of the headachy uncertainty rising in her. Possibly, this Bo Gavin was a *different* Bo Gavin, not the one who had lived in Colorado. His squint got squintier; he shielded his eyes with one hand, looking back and forth between Carrie and Libby as if trying to unite their separate images into a single Quintessential Female.

"Take off your hat," Carrie said.

He's not wearing a hat, thought Libby, giving Carrie Plourde an incredulous look. No, he wasn't. He was wearing a beige jersey, with a large rectangular pocket at its midriff and the words *Coca-Cola* emblazoned across its chest. His pants were pastel blue and pleated, his feet sockless, and his shoes, their laces dangling from his ankles like wet spaghetti, conspicuously designer-tagged. Libby had little doubt that his trousers, too, prominently bore a manufacturer's logo, probably on a hip pocket, but he was not lying in a way that allowed her to confirm this.

"Your hat," Carrie said again.

Whereupon Libby understood that she meant *her* hat, the floppy soft-leather pancake she had owned for sixteen years. My God, of course! Hurriedly, she drew it off, like a matador bowing to a crowd at a *corrida*. And felt herself blush, as Gary had crimsoned only three days ago in Tío Pepé's.

Bo continued to squint.

"Well," said Carrie, "don't you recognize her?"

He lowered his hand, scrunched his fanny backward on the sofa, and moved his feet carefully to the floor, all without taking his eyes from Libby. Libby could see that he *did* recognize her. But apparently he was having trouble believing that he wasn't simply hallucinating her presence in Carrie's house. He stood, not like a decrepit invalid but rather like someone who had just heard what he fears may be a burglar downstairs. Then, gingerly, he came to her, halted, touched her chin.

"Libby."

"Bingo. That's me." But she was thinking, This guy has AIDS and he's touching me. How can I be certain that his touch isn't—right now—fatally infecting me too?

Bo tilted his skull back and yodeled: "Libby Quarrels! Libby Quarrels! It's my dear sweet Lib-Lib-Libby Quarrels!"

What the hell. She embraced him. She kissed him on the cheek, the forehead, the nose, meanwhile patting his knifelike shoulder blades as if he had just completed the Boston

Marathon or hit an unreturnable serve at Wimbledon. He happily returned her kisses.

Carrie stood aside, laughing, while Bo's jam box began to play "Ain't Misbehavin'" by Fats Waller. *I* ain't misbehaving, Libby thought. I'm doing exactly what I should be doing. Exactly what Bo's parents wouldn't. Exactly what Gary is too irresponsible and cowardly to do, even if he at least had the gumption to point me to Georgia so I could do it myself.

Yes, sir, thought Libby, I'm a saint. I shoplift bric-a-brac only when I'm jet-lagged, and I uglify gas-station men's rooms with contraband unicorns only when they're too hot to handle and I can't figure where else to stash 'em. Yes, sir: Saint Libby the Good, Saint Libby the Beautiful, Saint Libby the Kleptomaniac Champion of Forsaken Cousins-in-Law with AIDS . . .

"God," Bo was saying. "God, Libby, you don't know how *great* it is to see you."

It *is* great to see her, Bo told himself, holding Libby at arm's length and studying her face as if it belonged to that of the *Pietà* of Michelangelo. Unlike the Virgin Mary mourning the dead Christ, Libby was smiling, but the melancholy suffusing her smile—the melancholy and her evident discomfort—made her look momentarily like a woman bereft.

But I'm not Jesus, Bo reflected, either dead or alive, and her showing up here is more like my resurrection than anything else. I was prepared to let Colorado, and all the people I knew there, simply die, but here's Libby Quarrels and suddenly it appears that my past is alive again. And if my past, then possibly the present , too and maybe even . . .

Bo yodeled Libby's name again.

Hat off, she looked almost as she had in the summer of '73, when he had gone up to the Tipsy Q to buck hay, working with Libby, his cousin Gary, and the other hired men to lay in enough fodder to get their stock through the winter snows, and she looked *exactly* as she had five years ago when he had stopped by the Tipsy Q to tell the Quarrelses that he was leaving Colorado to make his fortune.

On that visit, Libby had seemed standoffish and distracted, and only later had he figured out that she and Gary were going through some bad times. Her coolness to him—Bo realized that she had probably never felt as close to him as he had to her—had stemmed from a specific dissatisfaction with his philandering cousin and a consequent skepticism about every male of the species.

Bo had wanted to telephone her from Atlanta and say, "Look, I'm sorry Gary's such a world-class jerk, please don't color every guy in our family the same fast yellow, okay?"—but Libby would have thought that presumptuous and he could hardly have justified his buttinsky solicitude by pointing to their past relationship, which, were the truth told, had consisted of rare visits to the Tipsy Q to get away from Pueblo and his folks, using the fact that Gary was his cousin as an excuse and incidentally imposing on Libby because she happened to be married to big-talkin' Cowboy Quarrels.

Still, he had always liked her, and today it was a surprise—a heartening surprise—to find that *she* thought enough of him to seek him out at the height of this fucking plague, when he had tumbled into the slough of self-pity as well as that of despond.

"I've come to take you back to Colorado," she said. Her words strapped a power pack to his spirits.

Grinning, he lifted his glass. "How about a Bloody Mary?"

"I'd rather have a beer, if you have it," Libby said.

"You can fix me one," Carrie said. "There's no beer," she told Libby, "but if my live-in layabout hasn't already swilled it all, there's a bottle or two of Molson's Ale. Would that suit?"

"Sure." Libby gestured at Bo's shirt. "When'd you start doing walking advertisements for Coke?"

"Just last week. I bought me a complete wardrobe of name-brand clothes—stuff that, before Christmas, you couldn't have twisted my arm to try on, much less wear."

Libby puckered her mouth quizzically.

"You have to pay through the rectum for this crap"—Bo lifted his arms to better manifest the soft-drink logo—"and once you put it on, you're a shill for the people whose pockets you've lined for the privilege of shilling for them. The bastards should be paying *you*, you're a human billboard for their company's product—but no, they have it both damn ways."

"I've already heard this," Carrie said. "Pardon me while I get out of these heels." Then, clip-clopping sardonically toward the hall, she said over her shoulder, "He's jealous of the bastards for beating him to the ploy, that's all. Believe me, if *he'd* found a way to make our clients' clients foot their advertising bills for them, he'd be hyping himself as the Messiah of Southern Marketing. CCG and all our clients would be paying *him* bonus money. For the rest of the goddamn century."

"As is, they're only paying for these despicable clothes," Bo called after her, holding his shirt front away from his chest for evidence.

But Carrie was gone, and Libby looked bemused. He hooked her arm, led her toward the kitchen. "Let's get you that drink."

"If that's the way you feel," she asked, "why have you buckled under and started wearing their stuff?"

The question made him laugh. "Look at me. I'm not exactly Tom Selleck, am I? The soft-drink sultans of Hotlanta would most likely cringe to see me walking down the street in one of their licensed designs. Which is why I'm doing it. 'For only forty-six bucks, you too can cut a figure like the fatally sick sleazeball you see outfitted in our self-promoting jersey.' Or our whatchamacallit pants, or our whatchamacallit shoes." He opened the refrigerator. "My modest way of pissing on the commercialism that's kept me fed, clothed, and sheltered this past year."

"That sucks," Libby said.

Her words struck as forcefully as the icy air from the fridge. But he handed her a bottle of ale with as much savoir faire as he could muster and replied, "Why do you say that?"

"Because it's hypocritical. Either you stay out of the kind of work you're in, or you try to do it as honestly as possible."

"Which is exactly what I've been doing. I meant my 'pissing on commercialism' remark as . . . well, as self-deprecating irony."

"Oh. So you're saying that although *you* play fair, the other guys—the big guys—usually don't?"

Is that what he was saying? Essentially, it was. So he said, "Yeah. Of course."

"Right."

Bo fixed Carrie a Bloody Mary, and he and Libby returned to the living room. The chili would be ready as soon as Carrie was, and although he wasn't terribly hungry, Libby could probably eat. The portions they gave you on airlines were okay if you were dieting; otherwise, not.

Libby shed her peacoat, and they sat down beside each other on the sofa. Bo reached over, popped the tape in his cassette player, flipped it, closed the compartment again, and hit the PLAY button. After a brief run of white noise, Artie Shaw and his orchestra came on, shedding the vicarious nostalgia of "Moonglow"—dance music that had once had erotic import for his parents, as it may have had for Libby's and Carrie's too.

To Bo, though, it registered primarily as an auditory relaxant, not as a summoning of unforgettable experience. He had turned the player back on because, suddenly, he felt uneasy sitting next to Libby. Many of the people who had originally listened to Shaw's version of "Moonglow"—shuffling across a ballroom floor in sweaty transport or sitting half in each other's laps in a creaking glider as a cathedral radio filtered the melody through an open porch window—were dead, long dead, just as he would be dead within the next year or two. One day, Libby might remember *him* whenever she heard an orchestra play "Moonglow."

"Where'd you get the tape?" she asked.

"Christmas gift. From Ned."

"*This* Christmas?"

Bo nodded, sipped his Bloody Mary.

"Then Ned doesn't hold your . . . your gayness against you? Or does he even know about it?"

"He found out long before Mom and Dad did. I'm not sure that he knows I have AIDS. His gift came before *I* knew. Anyway, it's just like a tape that Ned made for our parents for Christmas. He and I don't write, or talk on the phone, or send birthday cards—but he never misses sending me something 'from Santa.' This year, a tape of Swing Era music. His own selections, I guess, and it's undoubtedly the nicest goody he's ever flung my way. Lotsa times, the music's kept me nerve-calming company."

"So maybe Ned'll support you in your illness."

"Not likely. He's satisfying the dictates of his Presbyterian conscience, that's all. Gifts at Christmas, but 'Repent, sinner!' silence the rest of the year."

Libby reached over and wobbled Bo's knee. Could she tell that it had all the size and resiliency of a walnut?

She said, "You *do* want to go back with me, don't you?"

"To die?"

"To do whatever you have to."

"Yeah," Bo said. He wiped his eyes, the moisture in which had welled up unbidden, and Libby seemed startled—taken aback—to find him soundlessly crying. "I've got to get out of here. This job. This city. This house. Not just to escape them, Lib, but to . . . well, to spit in Thomas Wolfe's eyes, I guess."

"To prove you *can* go home again? Good. I'm thankful. Because I don't have time to screw around waxing persuasive."

"Do with me what you will."

"We'll drive your car, Bo. I couldn't afford two more air fares."

"When? When will we leave?"

Carrie returned, wearing slippers and a silken-looking dressing gown patterned with cranes and butterflies. "Hey, hadn't you all better check with Bo's doctor?"

"Tomorrow," Libby told Bo. "As soon as we've gathered up all your stuff." To Carrie, she said, "Yeah, we had."

Bo told them that this afternoon's visit to Dr. Tedrow had gone really well. Bo was the perfect outpatient. His treatment to date had been low-dosage vinblastine chemotherapy, twice a month, with a couple of interesting sessions of acupuncture thrown in to satisfy his desire to touch all the bases, and the daily ingestion of so many fucking multivitamins that some times he felt like opening a curb-service pharmacy at the top of Carrie's drive. Right now, though, *he* was doing fine. Just fine.

"My hair hasn't even fallen out," Bo told the women. "It's dry and wispy, but I've still got it."

"One thing," Libby said, grabbing the sleeve of his jersey.

"What?"

"You've got to get rid of this. You don't wear an article of clothing just to thumb your nose at the hotshots licensing it."

"What? No antifashion statements? No anti*fascist* antifashion statements?"

"Look. You're running yourself down, not just the licensers—you're saying your own body's an argument against buying the shirt it's clad in. That's a sign of an unattractive self-hatred."

Dear Lord, Bo thought, a guy can't even wear a Kaka-Kola shirt without having his head shrunk. Five minutes after my cousin Lib drops in, she's psychoanalyzing me on the basis of my sartorial taste. Maybe this goofy lady's self-initiated rescue operation isn't going to work.

"I meant it ironically, Lib. I meant it to be funny."

"Well, Bo, it ain't."

"Don't tell me you're a fan of corporate America, the fat-cat titans of our exploitive free-enterprise system."

"I'm telling you that wearing that shirt—for the reasons you state—is a dumbass thing to do. Prideless and self-destructive."

Carrie Plourde took her drink from Bo and said, "Listen, it's time to eat. The chili's ready."

"Okay. Okay, then. I'll take the damn thing off." Carrie's house was cool, its furnace laboring to neutralize the omnipresent chill of the early March evening, but Bo stood up and in a single motion lifted the sailcloth jersey over his head. Then he flipped it to the hardwood floor and sat back down, hugging his naked chest and glowering at Libby. How's that grab you? he wondered, aware that he was nearly as gaunt as a malnutrition victim and that his liver-colored KS lesions stood out against his pale flesh like dirt clumps on a marble floor. Don't ever accuse me of self-hatred, or I may just organize a march of AIDS-afflicted nudists to prove what a wrongheaded oversimplifier you are.

"Am I the only one in this house who's hungry?"

"I am," Libby replied, looking up at Carrie.

"You mean I haven't ruined your appetite? The sight of noxious sores and protruding ribs doesn't offend your aesthetic sense?"

"It'd be thoughtful if you put *something* on, Bo."

"Want to pick it out? If you're going to scrub my Sanforized clothes in Freud, why not just be my wardrobe mistress too?"

"Okay. I will."

Carrie moved toward the dining room with her drink. "I'm going to set the table and bring the Crockpot in from the kitchen."

"I bought Bo a gift at that import place," Libby said, standing up, "but it's still in your car. Mind if I go get it?"

"Go ahead. It's unlocked."

Libby looked down at Bo hugging his own naked torso. "Stay like that, okay? I'll be right back."

What the hell? Bo thought, beginning to shiver. On Ned's tape, Dooley Wilson—the piano player Sam in the film *Casablanca*—was crooning "As Time Goes By." How long am I supposed to sit here? How long am I supposed to keep on breathing?

How about it, God? Am I doomed—as time goes by—to finish out my life with an opinionated cowgirl? With a gal who abhors honest cynicism?

Carrie looked across the table at Bo. He was a vision. The shirt that his cousin Libby had bought for him at Bali Hi Imports reminded her of an oil-rig fire blazing against a night sky in the tropics. It tented Bo, its short sleeves releasing his elbows and forearms as if they were guy poles.

The gift of this shirt had ended the argument between them, and Carrie was grateful. What if Bo and Libby had kept sniping at each other? Libby might've gotten fed up and left, and Bo might've dug in his heels and stayed—even with his rent at Savannah Glen paid through the month and Colorado wistfully beckoning.

"Good chili," Libby said. "Could use some carrots."

"Dump in a vitamin-A capsule." Bo pulled a bottle of vitamins from his pants pocket, emptied some capsules onto his palm, stirred them about with a finger, and chose one—which he then expertly cracked and whose contents he sprinkled onto his chili. He rolled a similar-looking capsule toward Libby. "Here."

Libby picked it up and noncommittally did the same. Weird.

But they'll be gone tomorrow, Carrie reminded herself. Annie Oakley and my live-in Poinsettia Fairy. I'll have my house back, and it's highly likely—inevitable, in fact—that Bo'll die out there without my ever seeing him again. Can I handle that? Well, sure. But I don't like it, and I'm not delighted with myself for relishing his departure. He was by far the best ad talent at CCG, and Jimbo Watling's going to miss the poor twinky.

More than I will.

"Mmmmm," Bo said. "I bet I'm the only PWA in the world"—PWA stood for Person With AIDS— "eating chili and wearing a Hawaiian shirt."

*Much* more than I will, thought Carrie. In the front room, Bo's jam box was playing the Benny Goodman orchestra's heartbreaking rendition of "Goodbye."

Bo was sleeping in Carrie's study, the room that she had given him after he abandoned his hostile apartment complex. Except that he wasn't sleeping. He was pitching and yawning like a T-33 in the hands of a rookie pilot.

At last, he sat up and peered through the gloom at the glowing dial of his clock radio: 2:27.

Aloud he said, "There's no law against driving at night." He dressed, pulling a rugger's sweater on over his new Hawaiian shirt, and walked through the house into the living room. Lib was asleep on the couch where, upon her arrival, he had been sipping a Bloody Mary and listening to Muggsy Spanier's Ragtimer's.

"Elizabeth. Cousin Quarrels."

"Nnnnn," Libby protested.

"Let's leave tonight. Now. My car's in good shape, and I can get packed in thirty minutes."

Libby's eyes widened. She shoved Bo's hand aside, swinging her legs free of the covers, kicked a blanket to the floor. She was wearing long johns rather than pajamas, but so what? Surely, she thought, muzzily trying to orient herself, Bo had seen a woman in long johns before.

"Cousin Quarrels," he said, "we're wasting time."

She regarded him with annoyed disbelief. "You need to talk to your doctor and settle things with your boss. Can't this wait?"

Bo shook his head. He clearly felt that waiting until morning would constitute a lethal variety of procrastination. "I've got unfinished business in Colorado. My mom and dad. My brother. As the bromide goes, I've been living a lie, but—God help me, Libby—I don't intend to *die* one."

Libby was struck by the importunate look on Bo's sallow face. "All right," she said. "Do what you have to."

Immediately, Bo dialed Dr. Tedrow's unlisted number,

passed Libby the receiver, and had her proffer his groggy physician an evaluation of the hospital in Huerfano and the competence of its staff. Dr. Tedrow, although obviously disturbed by this unexpected development, promised to forward Bo's treatment records to the Sangre de Cristo Medical Center. So long as Bo continued biweekly vinblastine chemotherapy there, he would probably do as well in Colorado as he had been doing in Atlanta.

After the telephone call, Bo said, "Why don't you get dressed? I'm going to wake up Carrie and round up some of my things."

Twenty minutes later, having loaded Bo's Mazda with suitcases and hang-ups, Libby and Bo hugged Carrie goodbye and backed out of her narrow drive on the first leg of their journey west.

Elm-peopled neighborhoods flowed around them. Traffic lights melted like acrylics on the windshield.

They made an initial stop at Chattahoochee CommuniGrafix, where Bo dashed in to pick up some of his art supplies and—as Lib could not help noticing—all the personal items on his desk.

Then they rode down to the intersection below Bali Hi Imports, where the only filling station open was the one in whose men's room Libby had earlier set out her display of miniature unicorns. She was relieved to see that a new attendant—a slender kid in spotless overalls—was on duty.

While this kid was filling the Mazda's tank, Libby told Bo that she had to use the rest room.

"Again? You went at Carrie's. You went at CCG. Are we going to stop at every gas station from Anniston to Amarillo?"

"It was the ale, okay? I won't be a minute." Libby left the car and asked the attendant for the key to the women's room. He told her—just as she had expected—that she could use the men's; the lady's was out of commission.

A moment later, she stepped into the claustrophobic rankness of the men's room. The unicorns were gone. So was the paper towel on which she had written her anarchic message. The condom dispensers, however, were still gaudily in place.

Impelled by curiosity, Libby put one boot on the commode

seat, pulled herself, and searched the top of one such vending machine for . . . well, for whatever was there. Her fingers groped about and finally collided with a small metal object. A figurine. A pewter facsimile of a unicorn. She closed her fist on it, pulled it down, and carefully dismounted the toilet.

A cute, and well-crafted, unicorn. A three-dimensional cartoon in an alloy of cheap tin and dull lead.

Libby pocketed it.

Speculatively, she studied the decal of a near-naked bimbo on one of the condom dispensers. What the hell, she thought. Why not? She rummaged a couple of quarters out of her jeans, fed them into the slot, and slammed the lever home.

Nothing happened.

Gary was right. These machines were designed to take you. And if you were a zit-afflicted teenage boy, you would probably mutter, "Oh, shit!" and stumble outside knowing both that you had been had and that recourse was out of the question.

But Libby was not a zit-afflicted teenage boy. She banged out of the rest room, headed through the arc-lit cold for the pumps, and put her hands on the shoulder of the kid airing Bo's tires.

"That machine in there ate my quarters."

He was a black dude the color of butter-pecan ice cream. His eyes betrayed both suspicion and confusion.

"My husband told me to buy a rubber, if you-all had a machine, and that's what I was trying to do."

The kid got the air-hose nozzle caught on the tire valve, and air began hissing evilly out. "Sometimes," he said, snapping the hose free, "guys lie to us about losing their money."

Bo got out of his Mazda and strolled around it to where she was arguing with the attendant.

"I put my quarters in a machine in there," Libby told him, "and got nothing back. I was trying to buy one of those French ticklers you've been promising to use, honey."

Bo looked at the nervous attendant. "You can't take money for an advertised item and then withhold that item."

"I'll give you your money back," the kid said.

"We want the tickler," Libby said. "That's the main reason, not counting gas, we came here."

The kid took Bo's credit card, led them into the heated

office, and did the requisite paperwork. Then, several quarters in hand, he escorted them into the men's rest room and levered two coins into the machine that had kept Lib's money. When it failed to pay off, he force-fed a second machine, which promptly supplied them with a foil-wrapped condom of doubloon-like antique gold. The kid extended this exotic doubloon to Bo.

"Give it to *her*," Bo said. "I've got venereal warts. You'd think that would be enough—but, no, Her Royal Highness has to have latex flagella."

"Here." The kid gave the doubloon to Lib, who slipped it into her coat pocket with the pewter unicorn. "Now," he said, studying her as if she were some sort of insatiable monster, "you guys get out of here before I call the police."

"What for?" Bo asked. "Making your damn machine pay up?"

Libby put her hand on his arm. "I know why," she said. "Let's beat it, honey."

A few minutes later, heading west on I-20, the two of them were laughing like . . . well, like pothead adolescents.

# 4

Sam Coldpony had been working on the Quarrelses' Tipsy Q since 1980. He kept house in an old prospector's cabin near timberline, at the uppermost limits of the Tipsy Q's range, and hiked down to the main adobe house and its nearby one-and-a-half-story barn every morning in the dark. In the winter, he often slept in this barn—to avoid having to screw around with snowshoes when drifts had meringued all the way up to his cabin's eaves and a man needed a flashlight to find his belly button.

For the past few days, though, Sam had been occupying Libby's house, sacking out in a quilted bag in the living room, while she pulled a Mother Teresa on a cousin of her ex-husband's who had had the bad luck to end up in Atlanta, Georgia, with this terrible new kind of VD that the media were calling a plague.

What bullshit. You had to be a fruitcake to get it, and even if it was a plague for fruitcakes, it was by no stretch of the male member the Second Coming of the Black Death for the population at large. It wasn't even comparable to the coming of the White Plague to the Great American West in the previous century, when Sam's own people, the Utes, and other plains and mountain Indian tribes had found themselves confronting those human-borne viruses—racial prejudice and Manifest Destiny—presaging their own enthrallment and likely extinction. So although Sam felt an ambiguous abstract sympathy for this Gavin fellow, he didn't understand Miss Libby's desertion of him during the depth of winter, and he wasn't looking forward to having a sick fruitcake on the place when their heifers began bawling to get light and the greedier beasts began eating all the lush spring wheat and fermenting it in their guts into powerful cases of bloat. Ranch work was demanding enough without going out in search of a sickie to triple or quadruple your troubles, and who wanted to hang around a plague carrier anyway, even if the plague he carried was only catching if posthole-digging other hombres—or being posthole-dug—was a sport you regularly, and more than likely indiscriminately, engaged in?

Maybe it's our *cows* that'll be in the most danger, Sam thought, spooning bacon grease into his egg yolk to keep it from oozing when he flipped the whole thing over.

A joe who'd posthole-dig another joe would sure as hell screw a heifer, wouldn't he? And the upshot of that'd be—before you could see your foreclosure notice flying—a whole damn herd with AIDS. You wouldn't be able to sell their calves or their milk, and you sure as hell wouldn't be able to sell the bulls who'd dicked around with 'em. Let's hope Miss Libby knows what she's doing, or we may be facing bankruptcy here on the Tipsy Q, and I'm not ready to run tuck-tail back to the reservation and hunker down again with all the BIA derelicts.

"Derelicts?" he could hear his ex-wife Dolores crying above his sizzling egg. "Who're you calling derelicts? The biggest hophead to trot down the trail at Ignacio was Samuel Taylor Coldpony, and I had the lousy damn luck to marry the sucker."

It was amazing how Dolores could still work her way into Sam's mind. After giving her a proper divorce in '72, he had abandoned the reservation, determined to make a life for himself free of the stifling paternalism of the Bureau of Indian Affairs. He no longer wanted handouts. No part of the government's per-capita payments for reservation mineral rights. No part of the oil and gas funds fed into individual money accounts—other Utes called them "I Am Money" accounts—in Albuquerque banks, administered by the BIA. And no part of any of the other windfall monies that, according to Sam's father, Clayton, had seduced their people away from the farming economy that had served them so well from the early 1930s until the mid-1950s.

Well, Dolores and Sam had been children of the handout era, and although she had always accused him of complacency and laziness, he had been molded to those traits by the same forces that had turned so many of his friends into free-wheeling, hell-raising warriors on the weekends and free-loading, ambitionless zombies so much of the rest of the time. Just like his buddy Benjamin Elk, Sam had blown his "eighteen money"—a BIA payout made on the birthday marking one's mythical attainment of adulthood—on a brand-new car. And, just like Benny Elk, he had wrecked it—totaled it—three days after first putting his skinny adolescent rump into the high-gloss upholstery of its driver's seat. Unlike Benny, he had come out of his wreck alive.

Six years later, in 1965, after much more skylarking and screwing around, Sam married Dolores Arriola, vowing to set himself straight: to find respectable work, to establish a household, to sire and raise responsible children, and to atone for the insanity of his and his wasted buddies' who-gives-a-fuck?/we've-got-it-made glory days by *staying* straight.

It hadn't worked. The Authentic Ute Crafts enterprise that Sam started in a failed gas station in Ignacio early in 1967—after working for eighteen months as a custodian at the Methodist Church in Durango—went down the tubes. It took almost two years of hard work and devout mismanagement to accomplish the wipeout, but by late '68 the feat was accomplished. All the money Sam had saved from his custodial work, and D'lo had set aside while wrestling a steam press in a Durango dry cleaners, had evaporated—like rain on a cracked stream bottom.

Half a world away, the Vietnam War was raging. Nearer to hand, troops of bedraggled hippies, including a coterie self-dubbed the Bizarros, were coming onto the reservation looking for Peace, the Great Rocky Mountain High, and Authentic Indian Wisdom.

And the Coldponys, instead of exploiting this influx to unload passels of Authentic Indian Artifacts—courtship pouches, magic eagle-feather wands, fringed powwow shawls—fell victim to the all-you-need-is-love communalism of the denim-clad young people. Sam found himself lifted, willy-nilly, to the pinnacle of 1960s coolth, for these bead-draped waifs regarded him as the Perfect Ascended Redman of Ignacio. They came into his and Dolores's shop, not to buy stuff but to listen to him harp about BIA fuckups and the resultant degradation of Ute society. They also pumped him for the real nitty-gritty about the Bear Dance, the Sun Dance, and the frequency of peyote rituals among both his own tribespeople and the Ute Mountain Utes over by Towaoc. Flattered, Sam solemnly spieled what he knew.

Worse, he even persuaded Dolores, who was at first skeptical of trading the shop's merchandise for pot, acid, and adulation, that these kids were the nation's best hope for a juster society and that the Coldponys should now despise the claims of getting and spending—not that they'd been growing wealthy—to support the wandering longhairs in their quest to realize this vision. Never mind that in Ignacio the snows always came by October and that most of these young altruists would set off for warmer climes well ahead of Halloween, leaving Sam and D'lo with a sadly depleted inventory and a mailbox full of bills.

By May of '68, the counterculture Bizarros were back, looking to trade brand-new controlled substances for the Coldponys' wares, including Sam's ethnographic gab fests about the mystical Southern Utes, but Dolores was big with child and logily disenchanted with the whole scene. On the third of May, she delivered.

Stoned to the gills on sweet Colombian grass, dogged by a

band of curious hippie hangers-on, Sam went out that very night to honor a venerable Ute custom—lately not much observed—of *running* to celebrate a baby's arrival. It was still cool in the evenings, but he stripped to the waist and, wearing only jeans and a grungy pair of Keds, set off at a trot to fulfill the custom. He ran south out of Ignacio along the Los Pinos River, near Highway 172 to La Boca. And as he jogged—in the days before jogging was a health craze among middle-class Americans—his long-haired friends paced him in their VW minibus, which, almost stereotypically, was spray-painted to suggest a bad LSD trip. They cheered Sam on. They passed him, alternately, lukewarm cans of Coors and hot, well-gummed joints "to make running easier." But the pain, because he had not exercised so rigorously in years, hobbled him anyway.

He eventually had to tell them to drive off and leave him: The last part of the run of a Ute brave honoring the birth of his baby was sacred matter, and he had to be alone—*all alone*—to do it right. Actually, he should have been alone from the beginning, but he was appealing to tradition *now* because he felt deathly ill and feared he was going to launch his cookies in front of all his spaced-out pale-faced admirers.

Obediently, out of respect for the sacredness of the birth run, they wheeled about and returned to Ignacio. Although it was only two more miles to La Boca, Sam tripped down the highway embankment, staggered across an open field, and fell into the river called Los Pinos. In its shallows, he had just enough sense to rotate himself sloshingly to his back, thus preventing his own drowning . . . if not the inevitable scolding that D'lo applied when a local rancher deposited him at the hospital the following evening, twenty-seven hours after his daughter's birth.

"Paisley," Sam Coldpony said aloud, wiping the last of the egg yolk off his plate with a limp piece of toast.

That was his and D'lo's daughter's name: Paisley.

Paisley Taylor Coldpony.

Chewing the last bites of his breakfast, slurping a final drop of scummy instant coffee, Sam remembered that Dolores hadn't wanted to call the kid that. She had already picked out a name, and she wrongly supposed that Sam was as delighted with it as she was. The name she liked was Alma—the Spanish for "soul"—but Sam had allowed the counterculture to coopt him, and because he had come to associate the fabrics dubbed paisley with the psychedelic head-trip paintings of his new friends, and with the mod art of Peter Max and Max's legions of imitators, he had the hospital personnel erase the name Alma from his daughter's birth certificate and replace it with the name Paisley. This act exhilarated him but outraged Dolores. From that point on—if things had not already been deteriorating, which they clearly had—the Coldponys' marriage began keening toward Dumpsville.

By the fall of the year, Authentic Ute Crafts was deep in debt, so deep that Sam could see no honest way out, and by Christmas the couple from whom they rented the converted gas station had already taken steps to evict them. The Coldponys returned to a reservation hamlet in the middle of blank open country, where they abided in a blank BIA-built house with Dolores's folks, and where D'lo's mother blankly took care of Paisley. Sam did whatever he wanted—which, mostly, was nothing—while D'lo got another job wrestling a steam press, this time in Pagosa Junction.

Richard Nixon was President, B-52s were bombing the blazes out of Hanoi, and none of Sam's hippie admirers ventured out into the badlands to find him and quiz him reverently about the Ute Way to Wisdom. Whereupon Sam began to hate them, and all that he supposed they stood for.

By 1972, in the same month that Nixon annihilated McGovern in the presidential election, Sam refused to contest the divorce suit that Dolores had brought against him, cinched up all his belongings in a bedroll, and thumbed his way off the reservation, up through Pagosa Springs and Wolf Creek Pass, until he had come to Del Norte, where, much to his own surprise, he managed to pass himself off as an able ranch hand and found three short-term jobs in quick succession with three different landowners along the slope connecting Del Norte and Alamosa. He learned everything he could about running cattle from these three jobs, primarily from the various experienced hands who were already working at each place. And in this way, deliberately denying himself the luxury of unbridled talk, he found not only his vocation but a quiet pride in the performance of it.

I'm one of the few guys around, he would inwardly brag, who can take both parts in a game of Cowboy and Indian.

And for the next seven years, until he drove up to the Tipsy Q in a buckboard pulled by a harnessed elk he had broken to the reins himself, Sam worked all over the Rocky Mountain states, on a dozen different ranches from New Mexico to Montana. Pridefully, he gave a full day's work for a full day's wage. Cowboys, he learned, weren't much like hippies—only occasionally would you run into a counterculture wrangler with a peace symbol for a tie hasp and long tangled locks flowing from his Stetson—and cowboys' attitudes, for the most part, were the polar reverse of their hippie brothers'.

Cowboys dressed conventionally, within the tradition of their calling; they preferred plug tobacco to Ye Olde Marijuana Roach; they thought *balling* a wimpishly pissant term for *screwing*; they relished Nixon's ongoing bombardment of Ho Chi Minh's gooky goons; and they knew in their guts that the only good place for the Stars and Stripes was at the summit of a flagpole or atop the casket of a soldier who had died fighting . . . even though lots of the dead grunt's quisling buddies had stitched Old Glory to their Levi's butts and hotfooted it off to either Canada or Safehaven U.

Sam carried his plate to the sink, nudged the faucet lever to the hot side. But it took a long time for the water to warm, and the dish detergent that he squirted into the basin refused to make suds.

What if Dolores could see him now, though? The one thing she would have never believed was that he had it in him to cast off his own Neanderthal notions of manhood so sweepingly that he could wash dishes every day without complaint. It wasn't a bunch of all-you-need-is-love hippies who had taught him, either. Or a braless feminist with a list of grievances in one hand and a tablet of nonnegotiable demands in the other. No, it had been his work, a life attuned to the uncompromising rhythms of animal life and the perpetual-motion carousel of the seasons. It would be wrong to say that cowhands had taught him the democracy of self-sufficiency, but it would be correct to state that his *becoming a cowhand*—him, Sam Coldpony, an Indian, a screwed-over Southern Ute—had turned the trick. What if D'lo could see him turning it?

"One-trick Coldpony." He could hear her taunting him.

"Think that washing the goddamn dishes makes you a man? By proving that you're manly enough not to be afraid of looking *un*manly by washing 'em? Well, you could sponge Ajax all over every fucking piece of china in Shanghai a million times a dish and still not go down in *my* book as a man, Mr. Coldshoulder. 'Cause the bottom line's that after our divorce, not only did you never once ask about Dear Old D'lo, you never once visited—or phoned, or wrote, or even asked anybody else to tell you about—your daughter Paisley. How could such a heartless sucker qualify in anybody's book, even his own, as a *man*?"

Sam put his plate in a drying rack, rinsed his silverware and cup, and began scrubbing the cast-iron skillet.

"Paisley," he said.

He hadn't seen her since she was four. In fact, he had skirted the Southern Ute Reservation a dozen or more times in his travels up and down the spine of the Rockies, moving from one ranch job to another, and he had skirted it deliberately. Why? Not because he had no feeling for his daughter. (He wired money—although *only* money—at Christmas and on her birthday, always from somewhere a long way from his current job.) Why, then? Because he believed that D'lo had long since poisoned the girl against him, and because he was afraid that to go back to Ignacio, or any other reservation town, would be to trap himself there forever.

Although you sacrificed a big chunk of your identity by turning your back on the place, you yielded even more by giving in to the despair and apathy common to so many of its inmates. *Inhabitants*, he meant. After all, you could leave any time you wished, you just forfeited any claim to BIA services and entitlements.

"Paisley."

She was nearly grown. In May, she would receive her "eighteen money." It might be time to go after her, Sam reflected. It might be time to see if she wants to make a life for herself on her own terms—not on the BIA's, or her white neighbors', or even our own diminished tribe's. Her own. Out in the real world. Where real things happen. Where you have to have grit, and stick-to-itivity, and self-knowledge, to face them. And where, by the Great Manitou, you always forge your own entitlements. . . .

Pulling on his fleece-lined deerskin coat, Sam thought about the cattle—the Tipsy Q's stock—standing in the cold awaiting his coming. There was no wheat in the pastures yet, no new grass, and the only way they could satisfy their hunger and continue to live was to eat what he brought them. He was essential to their well-being, he was their link to survival.

I was never that to Paisley, Sam told himself. Never.

He went outside. He tromped through the thin, brittle crust of snow on the ground to the barn. As he walked, stepping briskly, he composed his mind for the task of loading and unloading hay bales, and he thanked the Holy He-She for drilling a hole in the floor of heaven and for letting sift through it the primeval sawdust of the mountains. Where would he be if the Holy He-She had not done so? Where, for that matter, would anyone be?

Beyond the barn, a magpie cawed, and Sam Coldpony knew that he was the only person in the entire world who had heard it.

# 5

Libby's pickup, wearing studded snow tires, was already in the barn, gassed up and stingingly incandescent in the cold. Sam had driven Libby to Denver's Stapleton Airport in it, but he wouldn't have to wheel it up there to fetch her home because she and her fruity cousin were driving *his* car back from Atlanta. In another day or two, they'd come running up through Raton, Trinidad, and Huerfano to state Highway 69 and so into the Sangre de Cristo Range to Snowy Falls and the Tipsy Q.

Bless you, Holy He-She, for that small mercy.

For Sam hated driving in Denver; he hated, too, the deafening whine of jet engines at the airport.

So dark was it, here in the icy half-dawn, that he had to

turn on a safety light and hang it by its hook to a ceiling beam. The flatbed of the pickup rested under the rustic mezzanine into which, last summer, he and a pair of hired teenage boys had grappled Miss Libby's baled hay. All he would have to do this morning to load the truck was end-over-end the bales to the edge of this open loft and shove them into the bed. So he mounted a rickety ladder to the loft—amazed to find a huge cobweb winking among its rungs—and tightroped the edge with the instinctive balance that had led a cousin of his to become a steeplejack in Phoenix.

Sam's breath came smoking from his mouth and nostrils. He put his shoulder to the first bale, experiencing the contact—even through his heavy winter clothes—almost as if it were an ardent coupling with D'lo. His breath got thicker and more tattered. He pushed and pulled the reluctant hay as if he were trying to make it moan. He hugged it to the edge of the loft and evicted it from his arms into the pickup. *Krrr-thwunk!* Strands of loose hay rose and floated; the truck rocked as if an adult grizzly had leapt into it.

Sam continued hug-shoving the bales.

A dozen wrestling matches on the high ledge. A dozen victories over the fey, cold hay.

Tempt fate, Sam encouraged himself. In other words, jump from the loft rather than go down by the ladder. Undoubtedly a dumbass self-dare, because if he sprained an ankle or split a shin or broke a leg, he would be all alone up here, and even if he could goose Libby's hay-laden pickup into Huerfano to have a doctor check him out, the cattle would go hungry. He would have to try to find someone else to feed them until Libby got back. Who? You didn't just drive into town and find an A-1 ranch hand jockeying a stool in some bar, waiting for your finger snap.

Nevertheless, Sam jumped. He landed on an askew-resting bale, bounced to one side, and wound up wedged between two of the most buxom bales—frigid, musty ladies in grass skirts unsuitable for this altitude. He scrambled free, vaulted the gunwale, and climbed into the pickup's cab. The seat was so cold he could feel it burning the backs of his thighs through his jeans. But he bit his lip—Perfect Ascended Ute Cowboys are stoic, heroic, and heedless of frostbite—and, once the truck was in gear, tromped it out of the barn.

Sam drove down to the road fronting the Quarrels house—the high gate had a lopsided Q burned into its cap rail—then turned onto an auxiliary ranch road, unpaved, that led to the mountainside pastures still holding cattle. Frozen patches of snow dappled the ground, but nowhere nearby was there a solid blanket of whiteness. (When the days were fair, like yesterday, the sun often managed to melt the snow at all but the highest elevations.) Glancing up, Sam saw that the mountain called Abbot's Pate wore both a frosty toupee and a halo of pink-scoured cloud.

The truck's heater was on, rattling as usual. Sam relaxed just a bit, still not sure that this run was going to be uneventful.

No? he wondered. Why not?

Well, it had been a couple of weeks since he had visited the *inhupi'arat tubuts*—the haunted spot—where the single-horned, four-footed *ini'-putc'*—ghosts—sometimes appeared. Visited the spot, that is, and actually seen the creatures. Although they were clearly not white buffalo (the long-awaited apparition of which in the Sangre de Cristos and Las Platas would signal the end of the present order), they *were*—without the palest doubt—unnatural, or preternatural, animals.

What the culture at large called unicorns.

That was crazy, wasn't it? Unicorns didn't exist, not in the real world. Not in the hard-knock actuality of the Here-and-Now, where a man's business could go down the tubes, his marriage could break, and his last tie to his own child could fray and fall apart for no better reason than that he was afraid to take up the ravels and try to rebraid them.

On the other hand, Sam reflected, Miss Libby's seen them too. She knows about them, I know about them, and the two of us are the only people in all of the Holy He-She's creation blessed with such troubling knowledge. What are we supposed to do with it? And why has the Great Manitou bestowed it on an apostate Indian and a barren paleface squaw who's cast off her husband?

There was no good answer to this question—in any event, none that occurred to Sam Coldpony after several minutes of jumbled reflection—so he put it from his mind and wrestled the truck into the white-patched meadow where most of the

Tipsy Q's cattle had been sheltering at night. Seeing the familiar truck, many of them came sauntering toward him, chewing their cuds and bawling. Sam halted, got out, and began unloading hay bales at the animals' feet, unceremoniously rolling them off the back and telling the stupid beasts that *he* had never had such service in all his seven years of marriage. They didn't deserve it, and he hoped the next snowfall buried them under tons of "Colorado cotton," thus putting an end to his job. Nonsense talk to stay busy by.

After dumping the hay, he slid back into the GM's cab and began beeping its horn. This he did to let the cattle in other parts of the montane pasture know he had come. If they wanted a decent shot at today's delivery, they'd better haul their haunches in and shoulder aside the heifers already chowing down.

*Beep-beep-beep! Beep-beep. Beep-beep-beep!*

When about as many cattle as he expected had wandered near and started rump-brushing the truck, Sam turned on its engine. Several of the cows did hurried sidelong trots to avoid being bumped; soon they were languidly chewing again. Sam slewed away up the meadow—through a rising basin called Abbot's Saddle—toward the rocky margin of the mountain's "pate" and the troubling *ihupi'arat tubuts* where he had previously seen his one-horned ghosts, telling himself that if he saw them *today*, it would be a sign that the Holy He-She smiled on him. The upshot of the deity's goodwill would be that he and his daughter Paisley would meet again.

Meet and reconcile.

Seeing the unicorns would *guarantee* this happy reunion.

Let me see them today, he petitioned the kindly god Inu'sakats, so that she and I may embrace within the year.

Ten minutes later, Sam was prowling the edge of this haunted spot, cursing himself for tempting fate a second time this morning, once by jumping from the loft and now by daring to spy on a place visited by ghosts. Except, of course, they *weren't* ghosts. They might be fantasy creatures—animals from some washed-up hippie astrologer's personal bestiary—but they had appeared in Huerfano County in the too-too-solid flesh. For three years now, they had showed up in winter, around Christmas, only to migrate mysteriously out of the area by June.

Sam knew they were real because he had picked samples of their fine, milk-colored hair from the branches of Engelmann spruce and alpine fir. He had examined their forb-shot stools, and once he had even made a plaster-of-Paris cast of one of the creature's curious hoofprints. You couldn't do such things with animals that were . . . imaginary.

But so far this morning, no sign of the creatures. Sam stalked the edge of the stand of spruce that palisaded the haunted place, peering optimistically into its gloom. Here, snow lay everywhere, a foamy carpet fingering through the trees; it grew increasingly more plush as it neared the wide, rocky shoulders of Abbot's Pate, as if the Great Manitou had spilled a big pot of melted marshmallow over the mountain. Libby's cattle were two or three hundred yards away, at his back, but her pickup close enough that he could run to it if a bull elk charged or if the Abbot shrugged and an avalanche came down.

Where are they? Sam asked. Why don't they show themselves? At the same time, he realized that he was not much of a tracker, that the pickup had already alerted the saddle's animal population—pocket gophers, gray jays, martens—to his presence, and that it would have to be a deaf or an injured *ini'putc'* that allowed him to draw near enough to see it. Still, his unjustified optimism—the sense that today was a good day to run into his one-horned spirits again—persisted, and he kept walking up the narrowing cut beside the ragged evergreens.

Suddenly, Sam heard a series of high piping noises: whistles, squeaks, peeps. His heart fluttered, then settled again. It was only the colony of pikas—silver-furred little rodents—that lived in the boulder piles at the high end of Abbot's Saddle, now only twenty or thirty yards above him. Sometimes they were called rock rabbits or whistling hares.

Whenever they caught sight of a potential enemy or simply felt like singing, they set up a bizarre, high-pitched din that could unstring your nerves. They were making this eerie music now, several of them visible as silver-brown lumps on the lowest ledge of their pueblo of rocks, and Sam had to tell himself to give up any hope of sighting a unicorn. After all, the whistling hares were playing lookout for every critter in Abbot's Saddle, and Sam's one-horned hants were even more easily spooked than elk or mule deer.

Otherwise, how had they avoided detection in the Rockies for so long? At any rate, *he'd* never run across anyone who claimed to've seen them. And was that the sort of discovery you'd keep secret if you were lucky enough to stumble upon it?

Sure, Sam thought. Exactly the sort. To blab it around would be to ruin it. Even Miss Libby had agreed with him there. And so they'd said nothing about the unicorns to neighbors, to agents of the National Forest Service, or to her rodeo-mad ex-husband.

Damn those pikas, though. They were raising a shrill, unending clamor.

Curiously, Sam remained optimistic about finding the *ini'putc'* up here. He had put out hay for them a half dozen or so times on the edge of Abbot's Saddle, and always he had come back to find it eaten, with only a few thin scatterings of fodder to show that it had ever been there. Of course, mule deer or elk or bighorn sheep could have gotten to it, but Sam had seen the unicorns' tracks—eccentric prints like those of a horse *cum* mountain goat, as if a crazy rancher had crossbred those species for an upland environment exactly like this one.

Was there a word in Ute for Unicorn? Sam didn't think so. He had no memory of any Native American animal fable that featured the animal. Nevertheless, *unicorn* was the wrong tag to put on the guys he had seen up here. Another word, welling up unbidden from secret recesses of his mind, came to him even as he stepped into the stand of snow-laden spruce. When it did, Sam uttered it aloud:

*"Kar'tajan."*

And there one of them stood, its white body zebra-striped in a complex way by the sunlight ricocheting among the spruce boughs.

A kar'tajan. A living kar'tajan.

Sam wondered if the word had summoned the creature, or if the appearance of the animal had triggered his odd unforgetting of its name. Probably the former. The kar'tajan had manifested to him because he had "remembered" what to call it.

The beast was eyeing him warily. Its eye had a crimson tint, as if it were an albino specimen of its kind—but when it moved its head, the eye flashed violet and then icy blue. The creature was not much bigger than a small horse. When it flipped its tail and mane, it reminded Sam of a headstrong pony.

A cold pony, he thought. It's as well adapted to the mountains as I am, but we're both just a pair of misfits. Man and kar'tajan; Coldpony and cold pony.

Even so, looking at the miraculous beast made Sam's heart glow, and he stepped toward it with his gloved hand extended.

Then he froze, for there behind the kar'tajan, shadow-blanketed by the farthest trees, stood four or five more of the creatures. They were huddled together in a compact group. Sam finally numbered them by squinting and counting their horns. Owing to shadows and the silhouettes of thousands of branches, this was no easy task—but he did it by concentrating on the sapphirine highlights raying from their horns whenever they moved their heads.

Yeah, six kar'tajans in all, five behind the first, all peering at him as if he had an answer to their unvoiced question.

"You're hungry," Sam said. "And you expect me to go on feeding you, don't you?"

He looked back at the pickup. He had brought a bale of hay up here, thinking he *might* run into these animals. Now he had. But when he looked back at the kar'tajans, a moment of near-panic overtook him. The animals were gone.

"Damn!"

Sam crashed forward a step or two, wondering how they could have lightfooted it off without his even hearing them. And then he saw that the woods and the creatures' protective coloring had played an optical trick. They hadn't fled, they hadn't even moved—but the twigs, shadows, and snow in the evergreen stand had rendered them briefly invisible. They had merged with their habitat like equine chameleons. Sam saw them again only because the lead kar'tajan bobbed its horn, sending out a dark blue strobe that resensitized him to the presence of the entire group.

But if you didn't want me to, Sam thought, I couldn't see you at all. That right?

He was sure it was. These animals—previously unseen in

the Rockies, their reality disputed everywhere that sightings had supposedly occurred—had *chosen* to let him and Libby see them. A divorced lady rancher and a self-uprooted Ute.

But why would they do that? Because they were hungry? Because they were sick? Their species on the verge of extinction? Yeah, probably. For each and every one of those reasons, the kar'tajans had let Sam and Libby look upon them. And where the matter would end, since it undoubtedly *had* to end, neither he nor the boss lady yet had any inkling.

"Okay. Stay right there. I'll feed you."

Sam left the spruce stand, returned to the pickup, and drove it to edge of the grove. The pikas on the boulders above him began fluting and ten-penny-whistling like fiends.

"Shut your ratty traps," Sam said under his breath, off-loading the last bale of hay beside the opening in the spruce through which he had walked a moment ago.

Then he backed the truck down Abbot's Saddle about twenty-five yards, parked it, and tramped back up the snowy cut to the amelodic piping of the coneys. He wanted to see how close the kar'tajans would approach—how close they would let *him* come— when fodder was available. He felt sure his presence near the bale would do little to keep them from coming to eat it.

Thank you, Great Manitou. Thank you, kindly Inu'sakats. Bless you, sweet Jesus.

These were Sam's prayers as he walked, for now he knew that he and Paisley would be reunited this year. And what kind of guy, Ute or otherwise, would fail to thank the gods for bringing a dad and his daughter back together almost fourteen years after his . . . well, his desertion of her?

"Come on," Sam said aloud. "Come and get it." He walked up to the pika colony, climbed the lowest tier of boulders, and sat down so that he had a panorama of Abbot's Saddle—from the near upper end, through the long meadow where Miss Libby's cattle huddled, to the hazy stand of lodgepole pine far below.

Below those pines, Sam knew, lay the ranch house, the barn, the horse trap, and the road down the mountain past Snowy Falls, Farisita, and Carbonado into Huerfano. Up here, though, these places were mere dreams, and wilderness filled Sam's eyes the way that water backs up behind a beaver dam.

No pikas called. They had all gone to ground. But nitrogenous salt deposits on the boulders—like spills of sugar—left Sam no doubt that this was where the coneys lived year round. He was sitting next to such a smear. He smiled to see it. Whistling hares were such pragmatic converters of food and water into energy that sometimes they ate their own shit; they kept moisture in their bodies by pissing concentrated salt crystals. Sam scraped at the deposit with a fingernail, but it wouldn't budge. He wondered if the pikas, down in their burrows, were trying to nerve up to scold him for vandalizing their urinary graffiti.

At last, a kar'tajan emerged from the trees. This was the male that Sam had seen first. It minced to the cracked-open hay bale, lowered its head, and used its horn (in full daylight, ebony rather than sapphirine) to tear and spread out the hay. Only when it had finished this task, flattening the bale with its forefeet as well as rending it with its horn, did its fellows come through the trees to stand in shadow at the edge and patiently await their turns. Sam, who had never actually watched them eat before, was amazed at how daintily each of them fed.

Sam also observed the way that only one animal at a time came to the strewn hay. The other five hung back, hiding in the trees, while the eater took a modest mouthful or two, chewed it carefully, and then walked a half circle back into the grove so that the next animal could come forward and eat. Watching, he tried to evaluate the health of each of the six kar'tajans.

The most robust of the lot appeared to be the male, the unicorn stallion, that he had seen first. After it had fanned out the hay, the youngest—or, at least, the smallest—tottered forward. Sam noted again what he had first observed a couple of weeks ago, that this animal was in poor condition, maybe even diseased. It had a growth like a navy bean near one eye, hinting at canker eye, while its snowy hindquarters looked smudged and rumpled. Sam believed the colt had the kar'tajan equivalent of scabies.

None of the other animals—three adult females and a "long yearling" of fifteen or sixteen months—were as feeble as this animal, but they weren't all that damn perky either. The long yearling had matter in its eye and a glaze of snot across its nostrils, and one of the females seemed to be favoring a foreleg. All in all, a sad assemblage of "imaginary" fauna.

Well, even though the sky was clear today and most of the lower snowfields had melted back a time or two since early February, it had been a bad winter. Deer had come down out of the mountains to browse on suburban shrubbery in towns like Alamosa and Huerfano, and the state Fish and Game Commission had even gone so far as to arrange a few helicopter hay lifts for the beleaguered animals—although not without controversy and some publicly confessed second thoughts. If the deer, protected by law at this time of year, were having a hard time finding forage, how much harder it had to be for these incredible kar'tajans.

Further, Sam had no doubt that their discovery would also mean their death; the animals seemed to know this themselves—for they apparently never ventured into settled areas and so missed out on the controversial food drops.

The sick kar'tajan colt was wobbling forward to eat again. Sam thought, I'm surprised you've got the appetite. No sooner had he subvocalized this doubt than the creature crumpled to its front knees. A moment later, its hindquarters toppled too, and it lay there staring up the mountain through robin's-egg-blue eyes, up past the tier of the pika pueblo on which Sam was perched.

Then the dying animal cried out, a sound somewhere between a bleat and a whinny. My God, thought Sam. He could not remember ever having heard such a heartbreaking sound, and he leapt from the pika hotel to the inverted V of the snowfield.

Mind as blank as the sky, he crashed down the saddle, slipping and tumbling, toward the kar'tajan.

All its family—all but the stallion—bolted, flying away into the trees like clouds of livid plasma, vanishing with no more noise than the sun.

What will you do when you get there, Injun? Sam asked himself, but too late to ponder the question. He was there already, and the colt was eyeing him disdainfully. The male kar'tajan stepped out of the shadows to challenge his plans for the diseased—the *dying*—colt. When Sam reached to touch it, the stallion dipped its head, aiming its corkscrewed alicorn directly at his heart.

"Jesus!" Sam shouted. "I'm on your side!"

He twisted, but the alicorn caught the shoulder of his coat and ripped it with an echoing tearing noise. Sam fell. The stallion, which had swept past and then abruptly turned about, stood glaring at him with a scrap of deerskin on its horn. The animal lowered its nose to the snow and rubbed the horn across it to dislodge the coat tatter. Then it lifted its head and, with a kind of conniving desperation, studied Sam, who felt helplessly exposed.

The colt let out another pathetic cry, and Sam, rattled by its reverberations, saw that three hundred yards away, Miss Libby's cattle were gazing up the draw in bovine perplexity. What would the stupid mothers say if they could talk?

The pickup was still too far off to reach; the shotgun that he carried in it, useless. Besides, he didn't really want to shoot the kar'tajan, he just didn't want it to kill him for trying to help the colt. But he was down on his knees, and if the stallion charged again, taking aim with that beautiful ebony spike, he was almost certainly a goner.

So Sam began to talk. "Don't stick me," he pled. "I'm here to help, fella. Just to help." He continued to talk, his voice as soothing as he could make it, and the kar'tajan did not attack. It tilted its head, listening to him. Encouraged, Sam rose to his knees and walked on them toward the sick colt.

"I'm your buddy," he told it. To the adult alertly regarding him, he said, "Believe me, that's the truth."

The colt scythed its nose as he approached, swinging its horn like a murderous upright pendulum. Sam had to lean back to escape it. The stallion strode sedately up to Sam's shoulder and stood there as he tried to diagnose the colt's malady. Meanwhile, one of the females—the colt's mama?—reappeared among the trees like a ghost. Anxiously, she watched all three of them.

Wild-eyed, the colt began to flop. Sam knee-walked closer and put his gloved hand on the animal's side. It thrashed an abstract pattern into the snow. He leaned over it, trying to hold it still so that he could get a better read on its condition. The colt's head came up, swinging its alicorn.

Sam raised a hand to deflect this weapon, only to find that the horn had detached and that he was gripping it like a dagger. Blood oozed rapidly from the ugly wound on the colt's brow, discoloring its muzzle and staining the snow. Then its eyes rolled up, and the young kar'tajan itself fell back and died.

Why did you do that? Sam asked it, feeling the eyes of both its sire and its dam upon him. If you'd held on longer, I'd've shot a pike with my slingshot and sacrificed it to the God of Blood, who would have healed you. And we *both* would have lived. . . .

Sam had no great faith in the Ute God of Blood, but he did fear that the dead creature's parents might now turn their wrath—the fabled wrath of the unicorn—upon him, and he was ready to use the colt's alicorn, a dagger already a foot long, to defend himself against them. If he had to.

But although the female came out of the evergreens to nudge her child's corpse and lick its mite-infested ears, and to peer at Sam with mute bewilderment, no attack followed. The kar'tajan male circled both the kneeling man and the dead colt; then it leaned its body into the female's, moving her gently but firmly away.

In only a moment, in fact, Sam realized that the animals were leaving him, forsaking the scene of the young one's death, and that he had nothing to fear from them. He got to his feet to watch them go, but as soon as they had entered the spruce grove, the sunlight slashing in—and the sticklike shadows warring there—hid both of them from sight. He was alone at the top of Abbot's Saddle with the corpse of a creature that the world beyond the Tipsy Q had no real belief in.

In his hands, the obsidian-colored alicorn. A corkscrew with which to tap the world's kegged-up faith.

Bullshit, thought Sam. All I can do is hide it. All I can do is stash it away with my plaster cast of their footprints and with my idiot hopes of a reunion with Paisley.

Banging this heavy horn on his thigh, Sam Coldpony walked down the tilted meadow toward the pickup.

# 6

They spent the first night of their journey in a motel outside Conyers, Arkansas, where Libby told Bo to register them as Beaumont and Elizabeth Quarrels.

"Our surname's appropriate," he informed the clerk, "because we were just quarreling about whether to pull in here or to go on to someplace nice."

They ate at the motel restaurant, took turns showering, and hit the sheets—the room contained two double beds—while listening to Brother Ned's tape. They had not talked much while driving, mostly because Bo had shown little inclination to do so, and Libby finally fell asleep to Billie Holiday's painfully intimate vocal on "You're My Thrill": "How my pulse increases,/I just go to pieces/When I look at you."

They slept thirteen hours, dallied over breakfasts at a Waffle House, and headed west for Oklahoma, Bo at the wheel.

Once out of Arkansas, the sky turned an iffy, filament-shot azure. Libby intuited snow in this anemic blue; Bo had no opinion on the matter. They hit the outskirts of Oklahoma City about one o'clock; west of it, a vast emptiness, studded at intervals by the silhouettes of windmills or lopsided barns.

Yukon. El Reno. A forlorn federal reformatory (where a sign cautioned that hitchhikers could be escaped inmates). Bridgeport. Hydro. Weatherford. Clinton. Canute. And embedding all of these places, prairie prairie prairie.

Then Elk City emerged from the sagebrush waste, and Libby made Bo exit the interstate again. Leaving the I-40 bypass, they buzzed into town on venerable old Route 66.

"It's too early to stop, m'lady. If we reach Amarillo tonight, our final leg into Snowy Falls will be a cakewalk."

But Lib had seen a billboard advertising a motel with a heated pool, and when they drove past this motel, she cried, "Turn in, Bo, turn in! I didn't pack many clothes, but one thing I did pack was a bathing suit. I'm going for a swim."

"A swim! For chrissake, cousin, it's March!"

"The pool's heated. Come on."

Twenty minutes later, Bo and Libby entered the pseudotropical quadrangle sheltering the swimming pool. A steel-girded ceiling set with rectangular skylights arched over them, and tubbed ferns and flowers rested on the poolside carpet. Lib dove directly into the deep end.

Bo, wearing his jogging suit, sat down in a folding chair far enough away to escape being splashed.

Immediately, three young men emerged from the palm-tree-lined gallery at Bo's back.

All but one wore boxer-style bathing suits, and all had combed their hair back from their foreheads and ears in greasy ducktails. Cowhands, Bo decided. Or truckers. Or members of a no-acount country-and-western band. They began skylarking around the pool—for Libby's benefit.

Which meant, Bo knew, that they swung from Tarzan's side. Too bad. Particularly in the case of the young man in blue-and-white bikini briefs, apparently the rowdies' ringleader. Bo could only look and lust. This guy had a clean, broad face with a smile that was half cockiness, half impish little boy. His body was muscled as if he often engaged in light weight-training. The hairs downing his limbs and chest gleamed like incandescent filaments.

The trio behaved like kids, taking running starts and doing clumsy cannonball dives into the pool, their legs pedaling like those of cartoon characters who have just run off a cliff. The guy in the bikini briefs would mount and balance precariously on the aluminum crooks of the ladder at the deep end, then leap daringly outward. He and his buddies would land near enough to Lib to hit her with the fallout from their cannonball geysers, but far enough away to keep from crashing into her bodily.

Libby's head bobbed in the wash, and the whole courtyard echoed with the rowdie's cries of "Bombs away!" and "Banzai!"

Who *are* these dorks? Libby was thinking. And why doesn't Bo *do* something to make them behave? She was regarding him as if he were her husband, Gary's Elk City proxy, even though she had no call to do so. But rationality on one level didn't keep her from seeing Bo—on a less thoughtful level—as a 99-pound weakling who let beach bums kick sand in his face and hassle his girl.

Stop it, Libby thought. You're not Bo's girl. He doesn't give sheep bleep for girls—not romantically. And you're too long in the tooth to pass for a "girl," anyway.

She turned to avoid the fallout from another cannonball, then did a surface dive and a series of underwater flutter kicks along the pool's bottom. She spun to her back, still flutter-kicking. Two skies spanned her, one a chaos of bubbles and weirdly divided bodies, the other the courtyard's watery ceiling and skylights. But she was down, out of the rowdies' way, and although her limbs were still fighting the tides generated by their play, an easy serenity buoyed her.

Suddenly, directly above her, the leader of the trio appeared. His hair was floating, his eyes were open. He swam parallel to her in a way suggestive of lovemaking. Maybe four feet separated him from Libby, who feared that in rising to breathe again, she would bump into him. He, in turn, lowered one hand to his thigh, pinched the leg elastic of his suit, and deftly released his erect penis.

Oh, my crap! Libby thought. Another spoilsport egomaniac.

The guy was prodigious—bigger than Gary—and his cock cut the chlorine-tinted pool like a rudder. Although Libby wondered how he had managed to conceal it in that tiny suit, she mostly wondered why he thought that exposing himself—even if his dingus were as large as Moby Dick's—would impress or arouse her. What it rather did was convince her that no single lobe of his brain had as much bulk as his formidable cock.

She rolled to her stomach, the image of that libidinous alicorn burnt like a brand into her retinas. Then she twisted, kicked, and paddle-clawed her way toward the ladder.

A moment later, wrapped in a towel, she urged Bo to go back to their room with her. She'd had enough of the trio's boorishness for one day.

"Sit down a minute," Bo advised. "Maybe they'll knock off the rough-housing and skedaddle."

Libby sat down, and presently all three rowdies (the one in the bikini briefs decent again, diplomatically tucked away) climbed out of the pool and sauntered toward them.

As they passed, the chief rowdy halted, smiled at Libby, asked her if he and his friends could buy her a cold one. Nodding at Bo, she replied that her husband might not like that.

But the chief rowdy merely grinned. "We'll buy him one too," he said. "Just tryin' to be friendly."

Libby said, "Do it somewhere else, okay?"

"Yes, ma'am," said Mr. Bikini Britches, winningly, and he and his buddies retired to their table, where they sat knuckle-crushing their beer cans and laughing derisively about some damn fool who had hired on with their wildcatting crew last October. They were still too near for Libby's comfort, and she persuaded Bo—who had been as reluctant to come out here as he now was to leave—to take her back to their room.

"I know you're gay," Lib said, once they appeared to be settled in for the night. "How so? How did it happen?"

In the adjacent bed, Bo Gavin groaned.

"What's the matter? Is that entire topic out of bounds?"

"After two days on the road, m'lady, why bring it up now? Did my ogling of those hunks at the pool embarrass you?"

"I didn't know you were ogling them, Bo. I just thought maybe you might want to talk."

"Not really."

"Why are you so damned uptight?"

"Possibly, m'lady, it's having AIDS. On the other hand, maybe I'm sorry to have left Atlanta."

"My God, you were in such a rush to leave Atlanta you damn near rolled me onto the expressway on Carrie's couch!"

"Nevertheless."

"Nevertheless?"

"Listen, before I started trying to pass for straight again, I had a relationship in Atlanta—a monogamous gay relationship—that I thought would last forever. In every way but the legal one that the state acknowledges, this man and I were married. More truly devoted, and hence more married, if you want my opinion, then you and Cousin Gary ever were."

Libby propped herself up on an elbow. "What happened?"

"He died. Twenty-eight, and he fucking upped and died."

"AIDS?"

"It wasn't a fall from a horse."

"And you blame yourself?"

Bo barked a sardonic laugh. "Three months after we'd moved in together, we learned Keith had it. The tip-over diagnosis was PCP, *Pneumocystis carinii* pneumonia. But I didn't give it to him. That was more likely his legacy to me."

In the heated room, Libby experienced an unwinding chill but by dint of will refrained from shivering.

"In someone whose immune system is shot, m'lady, PCP's a mortal illness. So's cancer, of course, but Kaposi's sarcoma won't do you in quite as quick as *carinii* will."

"I'm sorry, Bo."

He was sitting on top of his bedspread, arms around his knees, and the purplish sarcoma lesions on his insteps and ankles seemed oddly innocent, more like childish boo-boos than the manifestations of a mortal illness.

"I'm sorry too," he finally said. "Two weeks after Keith's diagnosis, I left him. I cut and ran."

Libby surrendered to a second unwinding chill. She shivered. She kept shivering. She could not stop.

"And I went back into the closet. Last year, when the Watlings started CCG and hired me away from Software House, I began playing it straight. Emphasis on *playing*. I told myself I was playing it for keeps, too. That's how scared I was." He barked his sardonic laugh again. "Maybe there *is* some fucking justice in the universe, Cousin Quarrels. Maybe there is."

"You ran out on a person you'd made a pledge to?" The coldness she felt seemed bone-deep, blood-borne and chronic.

Bo, chin on knees, said nothing.

Thought Libby, I'm playing Saint Goody Two-shoes to a jerk who cut and ran—*his* words—on a loved one in the very straits he's now in. Amazing.

Libby slid her feet into a pair of bedroom mules and strode to the closet. Fretfully, she shrugged her peacoat on and yanked her floppy leather hat down on her head.

"Going out?" Bo asked.

This time, *she* did not reply. Instead, she plunged her hands into the pockets of her coat—incidentally making contact with the unicorn from Bali Hi Imports and the foil-wrapped condom from that nearby gas station—and crossed to the door. She wanted to storm out with no explanation at all, but either her conscience or her sense of decorum prevented her.

"I'll be back," she said. "I need a little air." With that, she exited, easing the door to rather than slamming it.

Libby paced the indoor-outdoor carpet near the motel's swimming pool. She was both relieved and annoyed that the hooligans who had ruined her swim were no longer around. The pool area was deserted, its only light coming from the blinking yellow bulbs festooning the eave of the gallery bar.

She halted and pulled from her pockets both the unicorn and the hermetically packaged French tickler. The pewter figurine made her wonder how Sam Coldpony was doing, while the fancy-dan coin put her helplessly in mind of the egotistical wildcatter with the enormous erection.

Kar'tajan, she thought, not immediately recognizing the word.

And then she understood that she had just mentally equated the hard-on of that guy in the pool with the horns of the mythological beasts haunting Abbot's Saddle.

Sex. Disease. Death. Kar'tajans.

That pretty well boxed the compass of her nascent relationship with Bo Gavin, who had just told her something genuinely dismaying about himself, and none of it yet made any sense to her. What had Gary—from whom she had supposed herself safely divorced—got her into, and why had she let him do it? Sometimes it seemed to Libby that her ex-husband had more to say about the way she conducted her life than she did, and more than a year and a half had passed since they had lived together.

"Crap," she muttered. "Horse hockey." She stuffed the pewter unicorn and the coinlike condom back into her pockets, then ambled morosely through the pool area to the car park. Outside, she found that light was sifting out of the sky: a myriad of tiny stars settling on window ledges, curbs, cars, marquees, and prairie.

Southward, I-40 glistened like a strip of clear tape. The sky swag-bellied down, diffusing its mute candlepower. A gauze of unraveling light gusted into the parking lot, flew on lace veils through the porte cochere, and delicately carpeted all the motel's stairway landings.

Beautiful, Libby decided.

But it could all turn ugly tomorrow. Driving through snow into the Texas Panhandle, and from there to Raton and Trinidad, would be dangerous. She and Bo might not be able to make it through. Raton Pass would test them—the steepness of its grade could nullify the exertions of an unhealthy automobile even on a fine day. But Libby was not really worried.

The light drifting down on skeins of feathery gauze had calmed and then exhilarated her. Briefly, she let it fall on her extended tongue. Out here in the cold, she was no longer cold.

Centered again, Libby walked back through the fake tropics of the courtyard to the room she was sharing with Bo and found him fast asleep on top of the covers.

The television set was on. Playing on some independent station out of Oklahoma City was an old episode of Mutual of Omaha's "Wild Kingdom," with Marlin Perkins. This episode had originated in the Nilgiri Forest in India, at a place called Mumadulai, and Libby sat down on the end of her bed to watch it. Perkins had died recently, but she had always found him an amiable, grandfatherly figure and listening to him discourse about the elephants of Mumadulai struck her as a fitting conclusion to an arduous day.

After the broadcast, Libby crawled into bed and descended into sleep.

The next morning, they got an early start.

In Oklahoma, snow quilted the prairie. In the Texas Panhandle, the northeastern desert of New Mexico, and the Sangre de Cristos in Colorado, it winked like sun-struck tinfoil on buttes, escarpments, ridges, peaks. In the same intimate way that the sea caresses ship hulls and the stanchions of offshore oil rigs, snow lapped against iced-over cattle troughs, the rickety legs of windmills. It was as if all the vast territory between Elk City and Snowy Falls had been illumined by an H-bomb blast at thirty thousand feet, and the land beneath it given the white-on-black irreality of a photographer's negative.

We're ghosts, thought Libby, trying to keep Bo's car's tires in the zigzagging herringbone ruts that other vehicles had already cut through the slush. We're nonexistent. . . .

# 7

Sam Coldpony was snowshoeing up Abbot's Saddle to see what had happened to the kar'tajan that had died there. He had hoped to check on it yesterday, but the evening before last, Miss Libby's ex-husband, Gary Quarrels, had appeared at her door, asking where she was and eelishly insinuating himself into the front room. Sam, trudging beside the spruces glittering like fairy-tale spears, remembered telling him, "You can't come in here, Mr. Quarrels."

"Why 'n hell not? Time was, I *owned* the damn place." (Liquor on his breath; fumes from a trillion distilleries.)

Sam gripped Gary's shoulders and pushed him gently backward. "Court order says you're not to come in. Says you're to leave your ex-wife be."

After knocking Sam's hands aside, Gary squinted at his former cowhand. "'V'you 'n' Libby got somepin goin', you horny goddamn Injun?"

"Go back to Dumas. Pueblo. Wherever you're living."

"Down by Dumas. Lately, though, been shackin' with a college cutie in the Springs. She saw me bronc ridin' las' summer over in Rocky Ford. S'perior ass, Sam. S'perior."

"Go back to the Springs, then."

"Can't. I'm smashed. You want me t' get smashed again on the way back down? It'd be on your conshunsh, Sam, 'n' *you'd* have t' live wid it." He jabbed a finger at Sam's chest.

Gary had ridden down from the Springs and up from Huerfano on a motorcycle—Sam saw it over Gary's shoulder amid the aspen stand in the front yard—an imposing black machine that looked as if it had been sired on an oversized electric eggbeater by a top-secret reconnaissance airplane wearing ebony camouflage. Sam had no idea what make or model the monster was, but it had a fuselage as thick as a torpedo's and a pair of "saddle bags"—built-in fiberglass carriers—large enough to hold a collapsible tent, three changes of winter clothes, and a pipe organ. A rifle scabbard, its rifle inside, was affixed on a slant near the wicked taurine handlebars. Even though the motorcycle's headlamp had the circumference of an antiaircraft searchlight, Sam couldn't imagine Gary—now stinko blind—roaring back down the mountain at this hour without flying off the road or dicing himself in an oncoming pickup's grille.

"I'll drive you to Huerfano, Mr. Quarrels. You got a buddy you can stay the night with, don't you?"

"Yeah. 'N' you won't hafta drive me t' Huerfano, neither. I'll jus' sack out on Libby's couch."

Sam didn't like the idea . Gary wasn't supposed to be here at all, and if he took a notion to go roaming through the house, Sam would have to intercept him. Even now, Gary was examining Libby's furnishings—the ratty overstuffed sofa, the periodical-heaped steamer-trunk coffee table, the stereo outfit and tape deck, the antique Bendix television set that Libby said she had bought at an auction in Pueblo back in '69—as if conniving how best to remove them during one of Sam's unavoidable absences.

"All right, Mr. Quarrels. But we go to bed in an hour, and you beat it first thing in the morning."

Gary tendered him a drunken salute. "You got it."

After washing his face and hands at the kitchen sink, and using a damp dish towel to dry them, he tugged off his boots, unbuttoned his coat, and collapsed on the sofa, pulling the coat over him for a blanket and covering his face with his hat—which looked to Sam like an inverted feed bag.

Satisfied that Gary was settled, he lay down on the living-room floor on his quilted bedroll. But having this guest, Miss Libby's ex, snoring noisily only four feet away made it hard to sleep.

Sam kept computing the odds that the guy was faking it, waiting for him to drop off so that he could tiptoe into the bedroom that Miss Libby used for a study and rifle her personal files. But at last Sam got his teeth clenched just right and drifted off.

When he awoke, he heard drawers sliding and cutlery clattering in the kitchen and went in to see what Gary was up to.

It was dark yet, as it was supposed to be, but Miss Libby's ex gave him a stubble-picketed smile and toasted him with a tiny can of tomato juice. Apparently, he had squeezed half a wizened lemon into the juice, for the wrung-out rind lay on the countertop like a speed brake for unicycling leprechauns, and whenever Gary put his lips to the can, he grimaced.

Sam had the unhappy suspicion that his unexpected visitory had been up awhile, but there was no law against rising early and nothing out of place anywhere outside the kitchen to cite against the bastard as evidence.

Gary was sober, cordial, solicitous. He insisted on preparing breakfast (banana pancakes rather than eggs), and after he and Sam had eaten, he insisted on helping wrestle hay bales out of the loft into the pickup.

He wanted to see the cattle again. He regretted that he was no longer involved with the Tipsy Q in any way, even though he had pretty much left its operation to Libby during their last few years together, and he was sorry that his fever for rodeoing had lost him his birthright. However, he *did* understand that Libby deserved the ranch, by virtue of her commitment to it, and he bore neither her nor Sam any grudge. Sam refrained from pointing out that the only legitimate grudge in this matter would have to run the other way; he didn't want to take Gary up to Abbot's Saddle, and he hoped that a tactful silence would induce the joker to leave.

The safety light hanging from a nearby beam kept flickering as if about to short out. Below them, the pickup was creaking beneath the weight of all its pitched-in bales.

"So she really did it, huh?" said Gary. His breath ballooned before him like a cold-loving, evanescent life form. "She actually flew out to Atlanta to fetch Bo home?"

Sam Coldpony said nothing; he had already admitted as much.

"How you gonna like havin' a sick swish live here, Sam?"

"He may not live here long."

"Long enough to germ up everything he touches, hey? But maybe you bona fide Injuns are immune to this AIDS shit."

Sam laughed a sharp, derisive laugh. "We haven't been immune to anything else you've brought us." Smallpox, he thought. The "joy" of alcohol. Good old Anglo greed.

Suddenly, there on the edge of the loft, Gary turned Sam toward him and gazed with unquestionable, if maudlin, sincerity into the Ute's eyes. He seemed to be trying to recover a dropped strand from the incoherent weave of their talk. "Isn't there anything *you* regret, Sam? Something you'd do over if you could?"

This was none of Gary Quarrel's business. A buttinsky, even a frightening, question. Sam glanced sidelong down. Over him stole the urge to whack the calf of Gary's leg with his own and to shove him off the ledge—all in one swift, fluid motion. He could hear Gary's scream, his skull ricocheting off the tailgate, his corpse going *whumpf!* in the scattered hay surrounding the pickup.

But he resisted the urge and tried to shake these images of unpremeditated murder from his head. Dwell on them too long and they would soon become the basis of an *intentional* assault—that was how close even a "good" person was to outright mayhem, how near the delicious irrationality of evil.

"Nothing, Sam? Nothing you regret? Leaving the reservation? Not seeing your kin?"

"I regret not driving you down to Huerfano last night." He had never spoken more than three sentences to Gary Quarrels about his life on the reservation, or his marriage, or his daughter. He had no desire to add to their total this morning.

Gary smiled ruefully. "Yeah, well, I regret the way I treated Lib. I regret tricking her into going after my own goddamn faggoty cousin when I didn't have the guts to do it myself."

"You can come and visit him while he's here."

Gary let go of the fleecy lapels of Sam's coat. He raised his eyebrows as if impressed with the Ute's no-nonsense way of dealing with half-baked regrets, of stemming the tides of bullshit. "Let's go feed the fucking cattle, Coldpony."

Okay, Sam thought. Maybe he'll scram when we're finished. He drove the pickup to the base of Abbot's Saddle, but parked it in a spot curtained by lodgepole pines from the boulder-strewn cut where the kar'tajan colt had died. And where, unless a predator had got to it either yesterday afternoon or last night, the corpse of that impossible animal still lay. He and Gary were four hundred or more yards down the saddle from that place, but the corkscrewed alicorn that had broken off in his hand, Sam recalled, was wedged crosswise in the pickup's glove compartment—less than an arm's length from discovery.

Sam beeped the horn to gather Miss Libby's cattle, meanwhile answering all Gary's nosy inquiries about the people in and around Snowy Falls and hoping that the guy's knee wouldn't accidentally jolt the glove-compartment door, which sometimes sprang open when the truck went washboarding over a cattle guard.

At last, however, the Herefords came, and Sam got Gary back to the house without revealing anything that had happened yesterday morning.

After which Gary insisted on taking him for a motorcycle ride to the post office in Snowy Falls and eight miles down the mountain in a hair-raising dash to Farisita, relishing Sam's fearful discomfort and intensifying it by leaning into every curve as if hoping to fly off the twisty highway into one of the slag heaps left over from coal-mining days.

Then, reluctantly, he carried Sam back to the Tipsy Q and told him goodbye.

"Been fun. Really enjoyed it. But it's going to snow tonight, and if I don't get out of here now, I won't get out at all."

"Then you *better* beat it," Sam said. The sky's mother-of-pearl opacity struck him, too, as a herald of snow, and he could imagine nothing worse than being snowbound with this pseudo-charming turkey, whom Miss Libby had ash-canned. Sam wouldn't even wish the joker on D'lo, and D'lo had made him think about revenge so many times over the past several years that showing her this graceful mercy *had* to earn him a few brownie points with Inu'sakats.

Once Gary was gone, he thought about returning to Abbot's Pate but puttered about the ranch house instead. He repaired a leak in the toilet tank, checked the valve on the propane cylinder outside the kitchen, loaded two burlap sacks of cottonseed cakes into the pickup, and rehung the off-center tool-crib door in the barn. When he had finished these undemanding chores, he clenched his teeth and drove down the mountain to Huerfano.

To the Huerfano County Public Library. A place he had seen on previous trips to the hardware and ranch-supply stores, but a place he had never visited.

The library was housed in a relatively nondescript bungalow of red brick right off Main Street—up from a defunct bowling alley and a flourishing funeral home; across from a convenience store and a stuccoed café. The café was shaped like a prairie schooner and acrylicked over with cartoonish cowboys and Indians.

Down from this café stood a ten-foot-tall statue of an Indian, the gift of an itinerant artist carver who had traveled about the United States offering his well-meant but bogus memorials to almost any community that would prominently display them. Sam, standing on the library's sidewalk, gazed at the carving with an odd mixture of disgust and perplexity. The statue seemed to represent a Plains Indian, a Cheyenne or a Sioux, even though in this part of the state it was the Shoshone Utes—the Muaches, the Capotes—who most deserved the memorial. On the other hand, the grandiose bulk of the carving failed to disguise—in fact, made conspicuous—the ineptitude of the memorialist's painstaking labor.

He's making memorials to himself, Sam thought. Putting statues to his own vanity everywhere people will accept them. And yet Sam had no doubt that the man saw himself, in all sincerity, as a self-sacrificing artist and humanitarian. Possibly, if you were white, you could buy into that sad fantasy. Most of the population of Huerfano had. . . .

Sam turned, went up the walk, and entered the library: a house whose interior walls had been removed, opening the floor to chairs, tables, shelves; a cosy, musty-smelling place insulated by towers of oak-stained bookcases and hundreds of lopsidedly put-up volumes, many of which—Sam figured, going by their looks—were acquired prior to 1960. Only the plastic-guarded best-sellers on the cart near the door appeared to belong to the 1980s, and who gave a good crap about them, anyway?

One of the library employees—a square-faced woman in a

bulky sweater and jeans—came up to Sam at the front desk. "Is there something we can help you with?"

"I'm looking for—" He stopped. What *was* he looking for? the last time he had been in a library was with Paisley, when she was three; he had taken her to Durango to check out dozens of picture books: *Where the Wild Things Are*, *Little Bear's Visit*, *The Cat in the Hat*, *The Velveteen Rabbit*. The titles flooded back unbidden, although it had been years since he'd even thought about visiting a library or reading to Paisley. Meanwhile, the librarian—a true pioneer type—was regarding him with patient curiosity, as if she suspected him of being stoned.

"You got anything . . . anything on kar'tajans?" he managed.

The woman blinked. "Cardigans? As in cardigan sweaters?"

"Yeah. I mean, *no!*"

"I'm sorry. I must've misheard you."

"Unicorns. Anything on unicorns?"

She showed him to the juveniles, where he found seven or eight picture books on the topic, none of them very enlightening. While he was examining them, however, she checked the card catalog and came to him a moment later carrying a volume called *The Lore of the Unicorn* by somebody named Odell Shepard.

"Do you want to read it here or check it out?"

When he admitted to not having a card, she helped him fill out the questionnaire to obtain one. Then she checked the book out to him, warned him that each overdue day would cost him a nickel, and thanked him for patronizing the library.

Whereupon Sam hightailed it back to the ranch, arriving in the front yard under a sky like bubbling oatmeal. An icy wind played harp music in the aspens, and the tool-crib door, which he thought he'd fixed, banged and banged. Bounty, Miss Libby's half-wild bird dog, who knew him, stood in this gale with a bent foreleg, barking at both the door and the rattletrap pickup.

Snow. Snow coming. Enough to make vanilla-flavored snow cream for every kid in the U.S.

In the kitchen, Sam sat at the table reading his book. It was hard going. Polysyllables. Latin names. Obscure history. But he discovered that *kar'tajan* was Sanskrit for "lord of the desert," a word closely related to the Greek word *cartazon*. He also learned that according to a Frenchman, Baron Cuvier, the originator of paleontology, "a cloven-hoofed ruminant with a single horn is impossible because its frontal bone would be divided and no horn could grow above the division." In other words, the unicorn could not exist, and the ebony alicorn—the natural dagger—that had yanked free in Sam's hand was a fantasy appendage, the product not of biological evolution but of somebody's overfervent imagination. The kicker, though, was that Sam had one in the glove compartment of Miss Libby's pickup.

Kar'tajans are real, he thought. They're *real!* He had known as much three years ago, but even after taking casts of their hoof prints and pulling tangles of their silky hair from tree limbs, he had not fully believed it. He had half convinced himself that the animals were bighorn sheep, mountain goats, pale deer, or possibly even wild albino burros, and that the single horns on their brows were tricks of the light, illusory shadows, or antlers seen from a cockeyed angle.

But now, with snow snapping over the Sangre de Cristos like immense sails, sometimes shredding into long vertical tatters and sometimes into blizzards of confetti, Sam Coldpony believed.

Cuvier had said that kar'tajans were impossible, but the baron had been a scientist and maybe the impossibility that he announced pertained only to the material sphere to which scientists usually confine their studies. But kar'tajans straddled our own material sphere and the ghostly one of the *ini'putc'*. Although they could give up pieces of themselves to this crass reality—feces, hair, horns, even their very lives—they obviously transcended it at some wacky metaphysical level and emerged into it from Elsewhere for immaterial purposes still cloudy to Sam.

Cloudy or no, he believed. And he believed even more intensely than he had before reading Cuvier's dogmatic declaration that the beasts wee impossible.

Lords of the desert, thought Sam, trudging the glacial spillway of Abbot's Saddle. He moved by snowshoeing—sidestepping—his way up the steep cut, and he squinted inside his polarized goggles to reduce the eye sting even further.

If *kar'tajan* is Sanskrit for "lord of the desert," then you'd have to assume that unicorns once roamed the wastes of the Indian subcontinent. Well, a snowfield like this is kind of a desert, too, and it wouldn't be off the wall to call our Tipsy Q kar'tajans "lords of the desert snows."

Very poetic, Samuel. Maybe you should've stayed in Ignacio and studied for the shamanhood. It's been years since us Southern Utes have had a *po'rat*—a medicine man—who wasn't imported from the fucking Navajos or Hopis.

But a new idea came to him as he tried to turn his head so that the pika pueblo below Abbot's Pate would reveal itself as a picture instead of a glare: Maybe the kar'tajans are "lords of the desert" in another way—in the sense that "desert" means *this world*, the one we live in. And they're "lords" of it—chiefs, kings, masters—because they suffer in it to lift up not only their own kind but those of us lucky enough to witness their suffering. If we think of our world as a kind of desert, then the kar'tajans breaking into it—from Elsewhere—are beings of great magic and power. They rule here because, in most of our sad run-ins with reality, they don't rule at all, they have no acknowledged place.

Hard thoughts, these. Sam could not tell if they amounted to mere nonsense, or if he—the Perfect Ascended Ute Cowboy—had hit upon a truth that could jump-start the mind even while lacking the prosaic power to melt snow or push up flowers. He felt that maybe he had.

Head turned, Sam was able to make out a shape on the inverted V below the pika colony. Coyote, he thought. A goddamn coyote. The runty animal was digging at a mound of snow, probably the very one entombing the kar'tajan colt. Sam knew the coyote had already seen him—the creature could have not have helped seeing him—but it kept furiously throwing powder between its hind legs, creating a small blizzard behind its scrawny butt and sodden tail. Sam heard himself laugh out loud at the sight.

His laughter carried. The coyote stopped digging, looked down the snowfield toward Sam, scrutinized him as if he were as alien to this pristine upland territory as a robot futilely got up in animal skins and furs. You can't fool me, the coyote's half-frightened, half-indignant stare said. You don't belong here. You're not part of our world, and nothing you do to try to make yourself a part of it is ever going to change that fact.

"I'm an *Indian*," Sam said aloud. "I've got as much damn right here as you do."

He kept snowshoeing. Grudgingly, the coyote tiptoed off the mound of snow into which it had been trying to tunnel and trotted into the spruce forest.

Sam reached the excavated mound of snow, busily patterned with coyote tracks, and knelt. He scrabbled at it with his mittened hands, hacked at it with the alicorn that he had carried along in the pocket of his deerskin coat, kicked at it like a man doing a bumpkin's parody of a Cossack dance.

"Wrong spot," Sam muttered.

But if it were, why had that damn coyote been digging at *this* mound rather than another? Coyotes had hotshot noses—virtually infallible noses. Fleet-footed and smart, they roamed just about any elevation, at any season of the year; he had once heard a well-traveled BIA agent tell of running into a coyote, an ordinary everyday sort of coyote, in a Costa Rican jungle. Coyotes were all over North America, and not because their noses played them tricks while they trotted around carrion-hunting, either.

Off came Sam's goggles. Everything in the landscape burned white, like clean porcelain. He reassured himself that the unicorn had died *right here*. No other place in the saddle was mounded in this telltale way, nor had any reason to be.

Sam pulled off his gloves, probed at the icy hole left by the coyote. His fingers closed on . . . a piece of hay. He held up. The wind whirled it out of his grasp. Well, that was proof, wasn't it? Proof that this spot was *the* spot, that he hadn't let the omnipresent whiteness disorient him.

Well, of course. Sam scooped handfuls of snow out of the mound and sifted them through his fingers. Soon, his palms were red and numb, and he realized that he was sifting—along with the sugary snow—the powered bones of the kar'tajan.

So much for corpse disposal, he mused, kneeling alone under Abbot's Pate, clenching and unclenching his zombie hands. The Elsewhere of the kar'tajans had reclaimed one of its own.

Surprising even himself, Sam tilted his head back and howled like a coyote at the grainy oatmeal sky.

# 8

We're ghosts, Libby kept thinking.

A dreamscape, Bo told himself again, half believing that they'd driven into a huge concentration camp of light. Addled light, like the kind he had seen as a kid looking east across the snowy prairie through the smoke belching from Pueblo's steel mills.

Dreamscape screamscape, he thought. A nightmare-scape, call it . . . except that it's daytime. Well, then, a daymare-scape.

"Is daymare a word?" he asked Libby.

"'Daymare'?"

"Yeah, daymare. Is it a word? A nightmare's a bad dream you have at night. But it's daytime, and we're having us the daytime equivalent, aren't we?"

"You'd know better than me if it's a word."

"How about daymare-scape? You like that? We can pretend we're rootin' Teuton cowpersons out here in the snowblind West, building up a whole new vocabulary by Germanic accretion."

Libby ignored him. It had taken them three hours to get from Elk City to Amarillo, and now—another five hours deep into their journey—they were on a narrow state highway in the upper eastern corner of New Mexico, heading for Raton and Raton Pass. They could see snow-blanketed desert, and distant snow-capped ridges, and snow in the vertical seams of nearby buttes, like cotton bursting from the boll. Occasionally, terrifying gusts of wind would broadside them, and Libby would have to wrestle the lightweight car to keep it from taking off and crashlanding on a section of some innocent rancher's barbed-wire fence.

Along the way, they'd seen vehicles abandoned in rest areas and ditches. A twelve-wheeler, like a pair of mating mastodons downed by a bazooka, was jackknifed across the median. Patrol cars slipped and slid past them with sirens wailing and spooky-blue flashers frenetically rotating.

Lib had kept the tachometer needle hovering between forty and forty-five, but even these modest speeds, given roadway conditions and the incompetence or timidity of some of the other drivers, had often bordered on the daredevilish. Fortunately, because Texas and New Mexico were states accustomed to bad weather, Libby and Bo had also seen snowplows at work and tow trucks helping those who had miscalculated either the slipperiness of the sheeted-over asphalt or the acuity of their own reflexes.

By six o'clock—five, Mountain Time—they reached Raton. After the desolation northwest of Dumas (outside of which Lib had tried to find the ranch belonging to Gary's boss), the roadside sprawl of Raton seemed a lantern-lit metropolis. Libby stopped for gas; the attendant told her that if they tried the pass tonight, they might end up back in Raton looking for a motel room.

"Is the pass closed?"

"No, ma'am. But traffic keeps backin' up, and the troopers up there'd rather you stop for the night than risk stalling out."

"My car will pull the grade," Bo told the attendant, who wore a hooded parka and trousers with cuffs ballooning atop his galoshes. In this garb, he was as anonymous as a scarecrow.

Libby said, "Don't you think we'll make it?"

"Where you going?"

"Snowy Falls. It's only another eighty miles."

"Sure you want to try it tonight?"

"Why wouldn't we?" Bo said. "You got a brother in the hostelry business or something?"

"Beat it, jackass," the man said, stepping back and waving them impatiently through. Libby hurried to obey. The attendant stalked off to the warmth of his office.

Meanwhile, twilight had begun to cross-hatch the sky above Raton and the cold to take on a damp al dente feel.

"You just insulted a guy who was trying to help us."

Libby knew why they seldom talked while driving: Bo's cynical negativity. Today, for instance, all their exchanges—

not many, really—had focused on the precariousness of travel conditions and the sinister beauty of the blowing snow.

"He'll survive," Bo said. But he knew that Libby was right and that he had questioned the man's motives because he had been riding all day with the relentless oppressiveness not only of the snow, but of Libby's unspoken censure. He was trapped with her disapproval, just as they were each trapped in his car.

Bo's Mazda did not pull the grade at Raton Pass. Not at once, anyway, for north of the city, they sat in a queue of cars, semis, and buses stretching toward the summit like a gaggle of impatient skiers waiting for repairs to a stalled lift.

The engines idling in this shady slant of I-25 were exhausting fragile plumes of vapor. Along with the gusting snow, these plumes had turned the steep corridor between New Mexico and Colorado into an alley of surreal wraiths and gritty noise.

Motors growled, tires lost and regained traction, horns blared, and more than one driver rolled down a window to shout curses at motorists nearer the summit.

Finally, nine spaces up the defile, a New Mexico state trooper showed up on foot beside the long train of halted traffic, stopping at each driver's window with a message. Lib cracked the window for him, catching the in-draft like a slap from an icy towel.

The trooper explained that only a few minutes ago a number of vehicles near the summit had collided in a messy chain reaction, tangling themselves across both lanes. If folks were patient, the untangling wouldn't take too long and everyone could cautiously proceed. If, however, folks tried to hurry things, troopers would cite the troublemakers and delay them further. Did Libby and Bo understand?

"Yes, sir," Libby replied, and the hawk-faced trooper, exhaling smoke, walked stiffly down to the next car.

Silently, Bo and Libby sat beneath the twilit wedge capping the pass. They kept their engine running for the same reason everyone else did—so the heater would work.

So near to Snowy Falls, Libby mused, but so damn far. And I'm taking a stranger home to live with me—a *sick* stranger. I knew him better, or thought I did, two nights ago in Carrie Plourde's house. Before his confession. Before he admitted his unattractive cowardice. But there's no turning back now. We're stuck here on the slope of Raton Pass, and we can't turn around. Once we hit the downside into Colorado, our lives will be changed forever, mine and his both. So this cold mountain pass is also a pass into a new way of facing life, of imagining reality.

"Looking for a way out?" Bo asked.

Startled, Libby said, "The trooper told us to be patient."

"I meant, Are you sorry you came after me?"

"I don't know. Are you sorry you let me collect you?"

"No. Grateful. Worried. A bit pissed at you for peeking at me sideways all day as if I were a war criminal."

"It's not for your—uh, orientation, Bo. It's for running out on someone who loved you—the same reason I often think of Good Old Gary as Genghis Quarrels."

"You *say* it's not for my 'uh, orientation.' But my running out on Keith lets you justify your secret homophobia under the guise of deploring my behavior toward my lover."

"I do deplore it."

"I know you do. But not just *that* behavior. All of it."

"Absolutely not. The way you treated Keith."

"You may believe that, but until I told you how I'd fucked him over, you had no excuse, given your Saint Joan Baez self-image, to see me as . . . well, as Genghis Gavin. Now, though, you do. You can uncloset your secret homophobia."

"What's all this 'secret homophobia' crap? I don't hate gays, I don't want to exile them all to Iceland."

"'Them'? One of *them* is sitting right next to you, m'lady; the least you can do is say, 'I don't want to deport *you*.' Which is what I mean by all the secret homophobia crap. Namely, that you're inwardly denying the very thing that my AIDS—a great chance for you to prove your broad-mindedness—undeniably proclaims about my life-style and values."

"You should have been a psychoanalyst. You're full of all the obligatory bullshit."

"You should see one. You're full of all the neurotic bullshit they're trained to purge."

"Why go to one? They cost. You're doing me for free."

Libby shuddered. Bo was getting to her.

Their disagreement, even with the heater whirring, had begun to milk-glaze the windows.

"May I ask you a personal question?"

"Where would I go to escape it?" Libby said resignedly.

"Have you ever gone to bed with another woman? And if not, can you *imagine* doing so?"

"No!" Her reply was emphatic. She couldn't imagine . . . what Bo said. She knew that some women might be able to—and *did*—but it had never seemed a viable option to her. Not, at least, on the rare occasions she had found herself speculating along such sordid, scarily fascinating lines.

"I believe you," Bo said.

"Why would I lie?"

"But the way you said no proves your repressed homophobia."

"Anyone who isn't bi or homo is a secret hater of both?"

"Not a hater of, m'lady, but a person who strongly disapproves and is fearful of them, yes. More often than not."

"You think I'm *afraid* of you? Because you're gay, not because you have AIDS?"

"You're afraid of what I am—because you disapprove of it and secretly fear *becoming* that which you don't approve."

"All this you understand because I think you acted like a creep when you ran out on your lover? Well, I can spout psychobabble, too, and I think you're attacking me to sidestep your own guilt—your *deserved* guilt. Which is pretty damn crappy."

Bo fell silent. Then he said, "Touché."

Nevertheless, Libby understood that Bo had not been too far off the mark and that she had counterattacked not only to shame him into retreat but to secure a little room to mull the worthiness of his accusations. Some of which, she knew, weren't just pretty damn crappy, but pretty damn insightful.

Homosexuality, no matter how hard she dissembled, offended her sense of aesthetics. The proper yin-yang symmetry that ought to prevail in the world was bludgeoned askew by the unnaturalness of male-male or female-female sexual congress. But then, the word *unnaturalness* told against her like a hostile witness. Bo had read her heart even as she had fought to hide that telltale palimpsest from him . . . and, in fact, from herself.

"May I ask *you* a personal question?"

"Go ahead. I owe you one."

"Have *you* ever gone to bed with—made love to—a woman?"

"Never. And never wanted to. Not one heterosexual experience in my entire life, Cousin Quarrels."

"Then I diagnose you as having a secret *hetero*phobia."

Bo smiled wanly. "Doesn't work that way. Our culture attaches no stigma to heterosexuality. But gay and lesbian behaviors are stink bombs at a big society bash. The party crashers who lob them are outlaws, criminal perverts. If anything, I secretly wish—or *used* to—that I were straight. I don't *fear* straights, I *envy* them, because I've been told over and over that my own preferences are vile. I spent most of the past year trying to pass for straight. That refutes your idea that I'm a secret heterophobe; it proves how thoroughly our culture indoctrinates us."

A tow truck from Raton, with chains on its outsized tires and an orange beacon flashing atop its cab, came rattling past them in the left-hand lane of the pass.

Libby ignored the truck. "You *dated* when you were at Southern Colorado, Bo."

"Not often. When I did, I dated for show. And I never asked the same young woman out more than twice."

"None of them came on to you? That's hard to believe. You're not unattractive."

"I *wasn't* unattractive, you mean. Now I look like an ad for a 'Save the Starving Ethiopians' fund-raiser."

"Bo—"

"Look, I had seven dates during college. Seven. And I chose those young ladies as carefully as most presidents—Richard Nixon aside—choose a candidate for a Supreme Court vacancy."

"Right. You went up to them and told them you'd ask them out if they didn't screw."

"Shy girls. Devout girls. To find them, I'd go to the Wesley Center or the B.S.U. or some Catholic gathering spot."

"Shy girls don't screw? Devout girls don't screw?"

"I was careful. Under optimum conditions, even out of wedlock, some of them undoubtedly do—but I used my second sense to scope out the doers and struck them from my list. Self-defense, Libby. Never did I unduly raise my partners' expectations; never did I treat them as anything other than absolute ladies."

"My ass," Libby said. There was something egotistical and self-congratulatory about Bo's phrasing, and she knew that she was reacting as much to this as to his explanation.

Above them in the frigid dusk, the tow truck's orange light was flashing behind a curve of the blasted-out wall of granite on the defile's left.

"Do you think I *liked* doing that?" Bo said. "I did it because I had parents, friends, a brother who'd've been hurt, or perplexed, to learn that my erotic impulses rode on homosexual frequencies. I mean *all* my impulses, Libby—every last one of them."

"Why?"

Bo stared at Libby. In the fogged-over bell of the Mazda, this monosyllabic question rang him like an iron clapper.

"Why. How did it happen that in this bigoted society all your erotic impulses 'ride on homosexual frequencies'?"

"The sixty-four-thousand-dollar question."

"You don't know?"

"Nobody knows. The people who say they do run up against other people, who say they do, whose theories directly contradict theirs, and vice versa."

Lib's knuckles sat on the steering wheel's curved horizon like whitecapped peaks. "Why do you *suppose* you're the way you are?"

"Don't know that either. My earliest semi-erotic memory goes back to when I was a kid of only two or three, and my dad had taken me swimming at a public pool in Pueblo. I played in the shallow end, waded in the wading pool, and puttered back and forth on the edge of the deep end where my dad was doing these show-offy handstand launches from the high dive. Nearly everybody was staring at him, and I was grinning from ear to ear to see the awed attention he was getting."

Libby remembered the show-off who had exposed himself to her in Elk City. A cretinous egotist. A jerk with no true self-respect. Had Bo's father, Nate, been a 1950s forerunner, only superficially more respectable, of that bikini-bottomed creep? Maybe.

"Your dad let you run free around the deep end?"

"No, ma'am. There was a young woman there—a friend of

Dad's from the steel mill, a receptionist or something—who was keeping an eye on me, just as she was keeping an eye on Dad."

"And you felt erotic stirrings seeing your father in a bathing suit on the high dive?"

Bo laughed. "Hardly. While everyone was watching him, I took this terrific urge to pee. I was a good kid—I didn't use the pool, the way some untrained kiddies might—I asked my dad's friend to take me to the changing room. She did, and while I was inside its dank cavern, I ambled past the shower and saw a grown man standing naked under one of the spigots, soaping his privates and inner thighs and turning around under the spray so that it could rinse the soap away.

"He could have been seventeen, or twenty-eight, or forty-five, but I knew in my kiddie's bones that he was *beautiful.* So I stood there on the margin of the shower room watching him, and when the guy caught sight of me, he didn't turn his back, or frown, or hint in any way that I was a naughty boy for looking at him. He smiled, winked at me, and very gracefully began to soap his chest. When I *kept* looking, he asked me my name, and I stood there dumbfounded, amazed by the gentleness of his voice, until I realized that maybe my staring was impolite—'Don't stare,' Mama always said—and so I hightailed it out of there in a state of pleasant confusion."

"You knew you were gay at the age of two?"

"Three, let's call it. I must've been three. At least. But I *didn't* understand what had just happened. I learned nothing about 'gayness' for several more years, and when I did, it was always in a context of outright disgust or ridicule."

"Now, though, you think that seeing that man in the bathhouse was . . . an erotic initiation?"

"Cousin Quarrels, *erotic* may be the wrong word. My feeling as I watched him showering was one of . . . comfortable awe, I guess. Something was *right* with the universe, and I sensed it at once. I knew that that specific sort of rightness would draw me toward it for as long as I lived."

Up the pass—the map in Bo's car said that it rose 7,834 feet above sea level—Lib saw the headlamps of two tow trucks burrowing tight yellow tunnels through the gloom, hauling a pair of crashed autos off the summit.

She glanced at Bo. His shoulders were hunched, and his face in profile resembled a wind-buffeted bird's.

She said, "I just can't believe a man's body was made to join another man's in the sexual act. It can't do so"— hesitating for a moment— "creatively."

"What the hell do you know about it?" Bo snapped.

Libby recoiled from his look of unabashed contempt.

"I asked you what the hell you know about it?"

"Are you gigging me because I've never had a child?"

"No. No, I'm not. But if creativity—*pro*creativity, I take it—is your measure of the lawfulness of the sexual act, you and Gary were as feloniously occupied as Keith and I. So don't give me that creative—*pro*creative—crap, okay?"

"Bo— "

"The body is amazing, m'lady. Remember what Mister Rogers used to sing on that kiddy program of his—'Your body's fancy / And so is mine'? He was right, and you don't know Crisco, Ms. Quarrels, about sexual creativity."

Touché yourself, Libby thought. But said nothing aloud. She'd prodded him to this outburst and probably deserved it.

Why were they still sitting here? The tow trucks were behind them now, grinding into the dark like Arctic war machines.

Over her yoke-collared shirt, Libby wore a woolen sweater vest with deep pockets. Her hands went into these pockets, withdrawing from one the pewter kar'tajan and from the other the foil-wrapped condom. She set them on the dash where both she and Bo could see them—strange totems, peculiar companions.

"Fantasy to the left," Bo said. "Reality to the right."

Libby tapped the condom. "You call this reality? This is a teenage boy's wet dream."

"Yeah, but it's capable of fulfillment, m'lady—especially if it's got a reservoir end. I discovered that with my first lover. Not that we bothered with 'protection.' The abiding reality of gay sex is that, procreatively speaking, it's risk-free."

"That's about the *only* way it's risk-free."

Bo conceded the point. Then, reaching to touch the unicorn, he said, "You'd have to believe in these to think that the act was an escape from pain. That's why I called *this*"— returning his finger to the condom—"reality. It's a symbol for sex, and sex is reality heightened: all your stakes raised, even your winnings on sufferance, your every loss potentially fatal. Which is why little girls go moony over horses and unicorns; they can fantasize control in an area where temporary mastery—to say nothing of control—is forever an illusion. Maybe a fatal one."

Philosophy, Libby thought. He's sitting here in Raton Pass, in a stopped automobile, drawing metaphysical distinctions between the symbolic significance of a French tickler and a tin unicorn.

Bo's crazy, she decided. His disease has pushed him over the edge, and I'm finding out about this frightening imbalance in his personality only eighty miles from Snowy Falls.

She shook her head. "Too deep for me, Bo."

He banged his fist on the dash, knocking both totems onto his car's rubber mats. "I'm talking sense!" he shouted. "I'm saying there's *no protection*—no goddamn protection! Let no one argue differently! Let no one hand you a two-bit unicorn when reality's so brutally expensive that only your life will pay for it!"

Libby feared that he was about to strike her. "Hey, Bo, calm down, okay?"

He was quivering as if galvanized by electricity.

"You're *not* making sense," Libby said, greatly daring. "You're making no sense about the real world, and not much in terms of your stupid unicorn/condom analogy. 'Protection' isn't—"

A metallic rapping on the window.

Libby and Bo flinched, and when Lib rolled the glass down, the trooper's face scowled in at them like a stern father's.

"'Preciate your patience," he said, vapor curling away from his lips, his growl contradicting his words. "Traffic's moving again. If you need any help in Colorado, pull over and hit your right turn signal. One of their guys'll mosey by to see what you need." He touched his hat brim and stalked around the hood of Bo's car to the shoulder.

The car ahead of them had already begun to move, and the pass, darkness folded over it like a tarpaulin, was slowly clearing.

"At last," Bo said. "At goddamn last."

* * *

"Why isn't your defroster working?"

"It'll do fine once we get moving. It's like that."

Bo turned out to be right. Although they conquered Raton Pass by unfogging the inside of the windshield with either their sleeves or crumpled luncheon napkins, once on the Colorado side, they found I-25 virtually free of ice or snow (although the land itself looked to have been slathered with shaving cream), and the defroster's efficiency improved as their speed increased.

Almost there, Libby thought. The title of an old Andy Williams song—a ditty about two traveling lovers nearing a hideaway where they could share "a paradise, a paradise so rare." It had come out during the British invasion led by the Beatles and the Stones, when it was unhip to admire ballads, but Libby, the original hippie, had liked it anyway. "Close your eyes," Andy had crooned: "Close your eyes / And we're almost there."

*Don't* close your eyes, Libby advised herself. We'll crash.

Ironic song to think of right now. Her ranch wasn't paradise, Bo wasn't her darling, and despite being less than eighty miles from home, she *felt* as if she were still a continent or more away. The snowy landscape made her wonder if she and Bo weren't unwitting passengers on a trip to Nowhere.

"Dit-dit-*dit*-dit, dit-dit-*dit*-dit." Bo eerily sing-sang these syllables.

"What?"

"*The Twilight Zone*. Its opening theme, just before Rod comes out to gooseflesh us over with that voice of his."

I'm thinking Andy Williams, Libby mused, and Bo's thinking Rod Serling. But that's what I was *beginning* to think myself—that we've just crossed over into "a dimension of sound, a dimension of light, a dimension of mind."

"Your point?" she asked, trying to shake the spooky grip of a twenty-year-old TV program's opening narration.

Bo put his hands on the dashboard and stared into the darkness slip-streaming past them. "We're going home, m'lady, you to your ranch and me to my Rocky Mountain roots—but I can't help feeling that we've both just entered an alternative reality. You know, a Phil Dickian world a couple of nudges beyond the twentieth century we've all come to know and love."

Libby laughed. Hearing Bo express her private fear aloud, in sentences she could parse and put back together, rendered her fear ridiculous, impotent.

"Go ahead and laugh," Bo said, and she couldn't tell if he was truly angry with her or simply playing his Rod Serling role to the hilt, frightening her with a make-believe that they understood to be illusory—even though they had tacitly agreed to *pretend* that it made up reality. Or *a* reality. "Because I'll turn your laughter into the sound of somebody gargling shattered glass."

"Dit-dit-*dit*-dit," Libby said, to disguise her nervousness.

Bo launched into a weird disquisition. He said that maybe they weren't *entering* an alternative reality at all; that possibly they had been *living in it* for the past three, four, or five years; and that Lib's coming to Atlanta had triggered his slow recognition of the fact that their post-1980 reality had suffered a major but subtle dissociation from the pre-1980 reality.

Only by venturing away from home and then returning to it with educated eyes could one see that this traumatic dissociation had occurred, and even then only if the prodigal—Bo enjoyed calling himself a "prodigal"—were somehow enmeshed in the evil machinery of the change but hip enough to look at all its ramifications with clinical detachment.

"I don't know what you're talking about," Libby said. But his words troubled her. They had application—or seemed to—to the arrival on the Tipsy Q of the unicorns that Sam Coldpony had been trying to study, with negligible success, ever since the winter of '82–'83. Had the creatures appeared in *this* reality, on *this* side of Bo's hypothetical historical fault line, because such a shift had really taken place? Were they proof of the reliability of Bo's otherwise kooky-sounding conjectures?

Trinidad, Colorado.

The city swept by them on either side of the raised interstate, jewels in the dark, lights on the western slope, a town as divided against itself as any other coal-mining/cattle-raising center. And then it was gone, and something Twilight Zonish crept out of the night again like a reality-traducing ogre.

Thirty-seven miles to Huerfano, Libby reminded herself. And another twenty-plus to Snowy Falls. Hang on.

"What I'm talking about is this," Bo said, still with his hands on the dash, as if to hold the whooshing darkness at bay. "Things went off the rails—a major reality disjuncture occurred—in 'eighty or 'eighty-one, when the first AIDS cases were diagnosed in California. I mean, this is like the Black Death, and that was a *medieval* plague. But as bad as that was, half the people who got it survived. While nearly everybody who develops AIDS takes a header into oblivion. Bye-bye forever. And that isn't supposed to happen in the twentieth century, that's supposed to be a . . . a Thing of the Past."

Libby relaxed a little. He was raving out of frustration, from the egotistical center of his disease, and that was understandable; she no longer had to make sense of his weird-o reality disjunction theory. Besides, it *didn't* make sense, at least not the way he was explaining it. The Spanish flu had killed twenty million people—including a few members of the Ruzeski and Kangas families—back in the second decade of the twentieth century. And even if half of *its* victims had lived, it wasn't an *ancient* plague; it had occurred only yesterday, so to speak. Bo couldn't logically argue that the twentieth century was a technological—uh, fairyland, germ-free and hence immune to any serious pathological assault.

But he was trying. "So it's already happened, m'lady. You and I are living in an alternative reality. We're privileged, or maybe cursed, to realize the fact, but nearly everybody else is ignorant of it—of the disjuncture that's shoved us into a continuum where a medieval obscenity like AIDS can still run amok."

"Bo, it's happened. You don't have to create another reality to account for it. That's the way *this* reality has always been."

"The rightness I sensed when I was there, that I kept on seeing even while being culturally conditioned to deny it—well, that's gone. Lost. Like Keith."

Libby wanted to say, But when was there ever a "rightness" in this century beyond your me-first notion of the rightness of male homosexuality? Was Nazism such a "rightness?" Or the A-bombings of Japan? The massacres in Cambodia? The famines in Africa?

But she bit her tongue. Bo, hunched beside her like a

wizened monkey, kept spieling his crackpot tale about how AIDS proved that a reality dissociation had sawed history into pre- and post-1980 continuums (the former benign and progressive; the latter sick and backward) and how the latter had captured them.

Sci-fi nonsense. Even so, Libby was aware that the unicorns on the Tipsy Q were a kind of askew corroboration of Bo's fantasy. The condom or the unicorn? What the hell did they mean?

For now, Libby Quarrels's only answer was to press harder on the gas pedal.

# 9

Blessedly, the house was empty. Her parents had died within a month of each other in the winter of Cowboy Ron's ascension to the high horse of the presidency. Alma, her daughter, was in Ignacio preparing for a debate with the kids from Cortez.

What is it they're debating? D'lo asked herself. Yeah, right—pesticides. For and against. Do we need 'em for healthy crops or do they screw up the environment so bad that it's knuckleheaded to keep using 'em?

D'lo stood at the only window in her front room staring out at—ah, her environment. She could see no crops, no bug-spray-poisoned streams. All she could see was acre upon acre of desolate Southern Ute Reservation, all of it snow-smothered and blank. Also the boxy prefab houses of her dead parents' closest neighbors, the Willows and the Cuthairs. Crazy damn funky sad. Families huddled inside them, dumb TV shows running, whiteness imprisoning parents and kids the way it always seemed to imprison everything.

For or against? D'lo wondered. Is Alma taking the "for" or the "against"? Or will she hippity-hop over and do the "against" right after the "for"? Does she have to—already the phrase rising in D'lo's mind was making her clamp down on a bitter chuckle—"speak with a forked tongue"?

Har-de-har-har. No. Not funny. Crazy damn funky sad.

D'lo glanced at the shotgun propped against her leg. She had carried it, loaded, to the window, keeping it out of view of anyone stupid enough to come tramping past her house in the aftermath of yesterday's eighteen hour blizzard. Now she closed the curtains and carried it with her to the only halfway decent chair in the room—a gut-sprung recliner that Sam had bought in Durango almost exactly twenty years ago. March the somethingth.

By the year Cowboy Ron took over, there'd been lots of cheap furniture—but after Papa Arriola's death, and again after Mama Rita's, D'lo and Alma had followed a Ute custom seldom observed nowadays: They'd given away as many of the old folks', and their own, belongings as they could spare. Papa's shaving mug, Mama shawls and beadwork, the TV, three quarters of the pots and pans. In fact, not counting Alma's books and clothes, they were down to the recliner, the refrigerator, the stove, and their beds.

And you could hardly expect a teenage woman—a senior in high school—to give up such things. Not, that is, if she was going to take part in debates called "Pesticides" or "The Place of Native Americans in Our Post-Rural High-Tech Society." Not when many of her classmates were either Anglos or Chicanos with an ill-disguised contempt for their Ute neighbors. And not when *some* of the fools Alma had to deal with were turncoat apples—Utes who were red on the outside but white to the core—who threw in with the bigots if she tried to assert her Indianness simply by wearing moccasins or a beadwork necklace.

And so Alma, who had her friends call her Payz while tolerating her mother's use of the old-fashioned Spanish name, wore semi-punk 1980s togs with various Ute accessories—buckskin vest, turquoise earrings, beaded leggings—and managed to be popular with nearly everyone.

But because her Anglo clothes weren't cheap, D'lo was earning enough to pay for them by sorting garments and running the steam press in the Arboles Dry Cleaners in Ignacio. In May, Alma would come into her "eighteen money," and already D'lo had set aside cash enough from ten years of this kind of fatiguing scut work to ensure that even if Alma blew this quick booty, she could still leave the reservation and go to college.

Pueblo. Colorado Springs. Fort Collins. Boulder. It was all taken care of.

No thanks to Sam Coldpony, who had mailed less than spectacular amounts of moola to them over the past decade. That clown had the loving-kindness and the dippy paternal instincts of a belly-bruised rattler.

D'lo leaned back in the recliner—at the juncture of the east and south walls—and placed the shotgun between her legs so that she could pull its trigger with her toe.

Glancing up, she saw high on the wall to her left the mounted buffalo head that Papa Arriola had inherited fifty years ago from Grandfather. It was sacred, this totem. And in the wake of Papa's death, neither she nor Alma had thought even once about giving it away. It belonged in the house. It meant that something of Papa was yet in this room with her, looking down one-eyed through its cataracts of dust on her preparations to rejoin him and Mama Rita in the spirit territories. Across the bare, cold room, between the window and the door, hung another sacred totem, a cross on which a foot-tall plastic Jesus was expiring. An awninged bulb above the effigy vividly spotlighted its wounds.

To D'lo, the buffalo head and the Christian savior represented two corners of a triangle that she was about to complete by flexing her toe. They offered equal measures of encouragement and comfort, and once her toe had done its job, Christ Jesus and Messiah Buffalo would escort her without delay to the land of the *ini'putc'*, where she would await with them the coming of the white buffalo that would stampede out of history the present balled-up topsy-turvy order. Where she'd no longer have to deal with the aggravations of this world or her private worry about how the cancer in her ovaries would demolish her cell by cell.

Three days ago at work in Ignacio, raising the lid to her steam press, D'lo had muttered, "I'm going to shoot myself."

Mr. Uhland, passing by, had heard her. "You're what?"

She repeated the statement.

"How?" (Not "Why?" but "How?" Typical Mr. Uhland.)

"I don't know. With a gun. A shotgun, maybe. I'll put it to my head and pull the trigger."

Her boss had once been a cop in Denver. "Listen, D'lo, women never blow their brains out. Take it from me."

"Women don't blow their brains out?"

"Naaah. They take pills, or slash their wrists, or put their heads in an oven—but they never blow their brains out. Offends their sense of tidiness, I guess."

*Their*. As if Dolores were not herself a woman. As if she were simply a kind of sexless man. Or maybe a specimen of a weird third gender not yet entered on the books.

Sitting in the recliner, D'lo thought, Hey now, fella. We have guts enough to blow our brains out. Retired city cop or not, you ought to realize that, Mr. Uhland. If you haven't seen it before, you were blind; you were just looking the wrong way when proof was offered. Someone should set you straight; somebody you know should prove to you that women sometimes blow their brains out.

Flexing her toe, Dolores Arriola proved it.

The next day, the front door stood open and the curtains were pulled to let in light. Paisley knelt in the corner with a bucket of soapy hot water and a scrub brush that she had borrowed from the Cuthairs. Cold air swept in behind her, but she was working hard enough at her self-assigned task to ignore it.

Larry Cuthair, a classmate, and his sister Melanie Doe hovered around the porch in their coats, now looking in, now wandering away a few steps. They were full of anger at their friend and confused about what they should do to aid her; Larry kept coming back to the door and weighing the risks of entering.

"Stay out there." Paisley said, sensing his presence behind her. "This is mine to do."

"The funeral's at two o'clock."

"I've got another hour or so, then."

Melanie Doe stepped up onto the narrow porch and spoke around her brother's shoulder. "Payz, you don't want to live here without your mother. Move in with us. We can be sisters."

"Thanks, girl, but you stink of hair spray or something."

Larry said, "She only puts on that styling-mousse gunk in the bathroom. After a while, you get used to it."

"Up yours," Melanie Doe said. "It doesn't 'stink' no damn more than this stinkin' place."

Hearing the Cuthair girl crunching off through the snow, Payz thought, It doesn't stink in here—too cold for it. And even if it did, even if it stank like bad meat in a summer dumpster outside Safeway, I'd *still* be doing this. I owe Mama that, it's the least she's got coming from me.

Larry would not go away. He shouted something unintelligible at his sister but quickly turned back to resume loitering around the open front door. He was an aimless loiterer. He didn't know what to do, he just wanted to help, and his hanging around angered Payz as much as if he were skulking there like a coyote waiting for its scrap after the cougar has fed.

"Go on home with your sister, you goddamn ghoul."

"I'm not a goddamn ghoul."

"A fool, then. A goddamn fool."

"I'm not a fool," he remonstrated. "*You're* the fool. There's plenty of people around here who'd do that, Payz. Plenty."

She kept scrubbing. When scrubbing didn't work, she picked up the putty knife that Larry's father had also loaned her and used its flat blade to scrape away the fleshy shrapnel either plastered to or embedded in the wall surfaces. Then she would wipe the blade on the edge of a five-pound coffee tin, banging the pieces of bone, scalp, hair, and brain into it as if dislodging dirty Kutzit or tacky glazing compound. After which she'd go back to the brush and practically amputate its bristles, pressing down on it to remove the telltale pinkness from the scraped areas.

"The cops shoulda done this!" Larry cried.

"They don't do grue," Paisley said. "Not when it's not their own."

"Let me help you."

"Why do you want to?"

Larry weighed appropriate responses. Even as far into her task as she had plunged, Payz could hear his mental gears turning.

"I don't mean just help you. I mean, let me *do* it."

"Go away."

"Please, Payz."

Tears welled in her eyes. "Why?" The bristles on her brush gouged visible tracks on the wallboard.

This isn't the way you should remember your mother."

"This isn't my mother."

"Her remains, Payz. Her remains."

"How am I supposed to remember her remains? Everything but her head's in a box in Ignacio."

"Let me do it. I *want* to do it."

Paisley continued to scrub and scrape.

"I'm going to come in and move your skinny butt. I'm going to take that brush away from you."

But Paisley sat up straight on her knees, showing Larry Cuthair the flannel-clad knobs of her spine. "One step more and I'll throw this pail at you."

"Okay, okay." A beat. "What if we did it together?"

"Why?"

"It'd be more fun, Payz. Quicker, I mean."

Right, Paisley thought. I'm having lots of fun—me and Tom Sawyer whitewashing Aunt Polly's fence.

"You don't want to live here. Even after scrubbing everything good. You just don't."

"Beat it, Larry." She realized that the more she talked to him the less chance of his following Melanie Doe home.

He kept trying to get her off her knees, away from the bloody recliner in which Dolores had disassembled her head, but she kept ignoring him.

Eventually, Melanie Doe crunched back through the snow, spoke inaudibly with Larry, and led him away. The wind scurrying across the land blew white powder into the house, and more coldness than even her energetic efforts to abolish the grue could hold at bay. She sat back on her heels to think.

Go to Mama's funeral. That's the first thing to do. Hold your head up and get through it.

Clean this damn chair as best you can and give it to somebody who needs one—if they're not so afraid of Mama's *ini'putc'* that they won't take it.

Graduate, she told herself. You have to get yourself graduated from high school.

Collect your eighteen money.

Then you go out looking for the man who named you

Paisley, the man whose last name is still your own. It's essential to find the old guy. To look him in the eye.

Those were her plans. The tears on her face felt like diamonds at absolute zero. She went back to scrubbing the floor and walls, erasing Mama's deed, exorcising it, willing her unthinking arm to move in spirals as purposeful as a hunting hawk's.

A while ago, Paisley had attended another funeral in Ignacio, that of the Southern Ute elder known to all his people as Yellow Wolf. But, of course, she had accompanied her mother to that melancholy event, riding side by side with Dolores Arriola in the backseat of the Cuthair family's '74 Ford Pinto wagon.

Now, standing by Mama D'lo's open grave, all her acquaintances and friends giving her plenty of room, Paisley remembered that the morticians had laid Yellow Wolf out in his Sunday suit with a bolo tie at his neck and a red stripe painted on his face as a greeting to the spirits who would receive him. There was no red stripe on Mama D'lo's face; she had deprived the tribal councilmen, not to mention the undertaker, of a face on which to daub the paint that would identify her to the spirits.

But, Paisley reflected, maybe Mama's facelessness in death will be all they need to know her. To most of the people of Ignacio, and to nearly everybody outside the reservation, Mama was faceless while she was living. Her blood is her paint, her devotion to me was the shawl that made her who she was.

Payz, recalling both Yellow Wolf's last rites and the burdened face of her mother in life, set her chin and stared at the lowering casket with mist-distorted vision.

This ceremony was occurring so soon after the suicide because the morticians could do nothing to "prepare" Mama D'lo for viewing, and Joey Cuthair, Larry's father, believed it important to get her sanctified before her flown spirit began wandering forever through the San Juan Mountains. Those mountains shone to the north of the cemetery like a rugged garden for the Ute gods.

Someone—Joey Cuthair? Larry?—touched Paisley's arm, but she shrugged aside the touch, absorbed in the burial.

Three different men had come to speak over the grave. First, a Baptist preacher from Ignacio, a man who had always shown goodwill to the Utes. Then, a caterpillar-browed priest in a cassock, who read the Twenty-third Psalm. And now, one of the tribal elders, DeWayne Sky, who held a burnished pipe in the air and spoke to each of four compass points—North, South, East, West—in guttural, machine-gun-fire Ute, the meaning of most of which Payz was largely, and contritely, ignorant.

Still, Elder Sky's utterances comforted her, especially when he spoke to the mountains, and when next someone touched her—it was the hangdog Larry—she did not flinch away.

"Come back to our house with us." He propelled her gently over the snowy ground toward the Cuthairs' station wagon.

"I still have cleaning to do. I don't want the next people to live in our house to find anything upsetting."

"It'll wait," Larry's father said.

But it wouldn't. Paisley imagined a new tenant's child playing in the corner, chancing upon a thumbnail-sized wedge of Mama D'lo's skull. It *wouldn't* wait.

"No," she said. "No."

At which point she saw in the back seat of the old station wagon a shawl-draped woman—an *ini'putc'* with no head.

Crying out, she fell to knees, aware that everyone leaving the graveyard must suppose her mad or epileptic. *Mama!* she wordlessly shouted, but when she looked again, the revenant was gone.

# 10

Bo's Mazda, Libby still driving, switchbacked the turns from Huerfano to Snowy Falls as neatly as a pony running a barrel race. And, despite the snow, they hummed into her front yard about nine that night with the brio of an experienced road-rally team.

A feeble dog stood beside the house, barking.

"Remember Bounty?" Lib said. "Used to help around here . . . before he got some age on him."

Now that they had arrived, Bo was frightened. Pueblo, where his parents lived, was better than sixty miles away, and you had to return to Huerfano to get there. Denver, where Ned lived, might as well have been Istanbul, an exotic promise of gold streets, condos, and brightly clad citizens. By contrast, the Tipsy Q was a humble, a nondescript, a damned *remote* spot to croak. And his coming up here to do so seemed, suddenly, a mistake.

"Where the hell is Sam?" Libby killed the engine and began to unbuckle.

Sam, Bo reminded himself. Sam Coldpony. Bo had managed not to think about Libby's lone hired hand for most of the past two days. But now he was about to *meet* the hombre who kept her two hundred Hereford and her thirty Beefmaster cattle fed and healthy, either with her help or by himself.

Usually, cowboys didn't much cotton to gays. And, Bo thought, Indians might have a similar aversion. He had no anthropological knowledge to back up this fear, but you seldom pictured a band of braves killing time between scouting parties and raids with bouts of recreational buggery.

The porch light began to burn.

"There he is," Libby said, getting out. "Come on, then."

Bo stepped into the stark Himalayan air, hugging himself as he walked toward the lean Indian on the porch.

Would Coldpony shake hands? No. He opened the door for them, then shut it behind them so that all the heat in the house would not escape.

Once inside, a handshake, which would have given Bo an insight into Coldpony's opinion of him, seemed superfluous. They settled for a few guarded glances. Then Coldpony said he had to go back to his own cabin and nodded a curt goodbye.

"Not tonight," Libby said. "It's too nasty."

She told Sam to bed down on the floor, where he'd been sleeping since driving her to Denver, then herded Bo into the bedroom/study connected to her own bedroom by a narrow bath.

An iron bedstand, painted with white enamel, held the mattress; a quilt featuring a sunny, stepping-'round-the-mountain pattern was the bedspread. A feather pillow lay atop the coverlet in a denim sham. The desk across from the bed was a big rolltop fortress that Lib had bought for Gary in Manitou Springs. On the wall, a pair of photographs—framed black-and-white enlargements—showed a windmill under a blurred winter sun, and a trio of 1960s street musicians, a straw boater at their feet for donations. Bo remembered these pictures from his hay-bucking work at the Tipsy Q in '73. Libby had shot them herself. Although Gary had disapproved of Libby's "hippies," she, by declaring the photos "a pair," had overruled his bigotry and hung them anyway.

"Still into photography?" Bo asked.

"No time," she said. "I've put all my equipment away."

They returned to the living room. Coldpony, now that his boss was home, seemed not to know what to do. He stood near the Buck stove, not warming himself but fiddling with the handle of a saucepan that he'd filled with water. Without that pan, Bo knew, the room would dry out like Death Valley, chapping lips, scorching lungs, desiccating mucous membranes. As a kid, he had always been both tickled and repulsed when his dad referred to Colorado as "the nose-picking capital of the world." Anyway, Coldpony tilted this pan to and fro, looking as incongruous as a cigar-store Indian in a video-game parlor.

"Sam," Libby said, "would you mind helping unload? My arms are shaking, and Bo doesn't need to go out there again."

Obediently, Coldpony bent himself to the task.

Bo sat down on the worn sofa and leaned over the steamer trunk on which Libby had been stacking magazines since the final year of the Carter administration: *National Geographic*, *Science 80*, *Western Horseman*, *The New Yorker*, *Cattleman's Quarterly*, *Redbook*. Despite afterimages of snow—calving kaleidoscope jewels—in his eyes, Bo thumbed the periodicals while Coldpony trudged in with hang-ups and bags. Lib pointed to this or that room. Coldpony stowed gear as directed, then returned to the car for more. On one occasion as he exited, a swirl of wind scattered the magazines.

Bo, stopping to pick them up, found a book amid the scatter.

*The Lore of the Unicorn* by Odell Shepard.

Bo laid it atop an open copy of *Western Horseman*. When Libby came back by, he tapped the hardcover. "You're one obsessed woman, m'lady. But I'd've never thought you'd go in for such . . . well, such unicorn-y nonsense."

She halted. "That's a library book."

Bo opened its front cover and found the pocket containing the due-date card. "That's true enough."

"But . . . but it's been a year or so since I last checked that out."

"Says here you've got twelve more days. The Atlanta libraries give you only two weeks and a renewal. But us illiterates out here in Clint Eastwood country don't read that much, do we?"

Libby ignored him. "Sam!" she shouted. "Sam, come here, will you?" She picked the volume up.

The Indian returned to her from the study, his ordinarily blank features betraying a hint of quizzicality.

Lib thrust the book at him. "What do you know about this?"

"I checked it out yesterday."

"Why?"

"What's going on?" Bo asked, puzzled by her anger. "Is there a law in Snowy Falls against letting the hired hands read?"

"Shut up." Immediately, she turned back to Coldpony. "What are you doing with this, Sam?"

"Trying to learn something."

"It doesn't belong here. You knew we'd be getting back soon. You should've checked it back in. Or taken it to your cabin."

"Why so uppity-tight about mere shelf space, m'lady?"

Glancing down at Bo, Libby seemed to recollect herself. "It's not that. It's just that . . . well, this is a very popular book in Huerfano, and we've had it out more than our share."

"But not since last year, you said."

"I've *never* had it out," Coldpony said. "I didn't have a card until yesterday."

Bo, rocking on the edge of the sofa, hugged himself. The front door was wide open—wind, snow, Bounty, hungry animals, just about *anything* could saunter in—and Libby was fretting over a book that Coldpony had left in a stack of magazines?

Weird. Bizarre. Dit-dit-*dit*-dit, dit-dit-*dit*-dit . . .

"Why *now*?" Libby was demanding. "Why did you decide *this* was a good time to get a library card?"

"How old are you, Mr. Coldpony?"

"My name is Sam," Coldpony said. "Forty-four."

"He's long overdue for a card," Bo noted. "But there's no fine for that, and his book isn't late. So why the furor?"

"I'm sorry," Sam told Libby. "I'll take it back tomorrow."

"Have you finished it?" Bo said. He felt lightheaded. Was it this cloud-cuckoo-land argument or a flaring of his AIDS?"

Libby put her hand on Sam's arm. "No," she said. "*I'm* sorry. Much ado about nothing. Bo's my houseguest, and if he finds out—well, he finds out. I just didn't want it to be so soon."

"Find out what?"

"I'll take it back tomorrow," Sam repeated.

"When you do—after our feed run—you can drive Bo down to the medical center to see about his outpatient routine."

Okay, Bo thought. Just as Dr. Tedrow wanted me to do. Then the peculiarity of Libby's anger with the Ute struck him again, and he urged her to aid Sam's education by giving him the toy unicorn that she'd brought all the way from Bali Hi Imports in Atlanta.

"Let him see it. It's small, but I'd lay money it's—what's the expression?—*anatomically correct.*"

"Bo—"

"Go on. Unless he betters himself through higher learning, he could end up tending a sewer ditch. For minimum wage."

"About what I make here." Sam said.

"And you know the motto of sewer-ditch guards, don't you? 'A waste is a terrible thing to mind.'"

The joke made Libby laugh. So she rummaged in the pockets of her sweater vest for the toy. And found, before the unicorn, the pornographic doubloon in its dazzling gold wrapper.

Sam Coldpony wore a look of almost comical befuddlement.

"Here, *you* take them," Libby said, dropping them in Bo's

lap. At last, she crossed the room to shut the front door. "I'm tired of hauling them around."

Bo held an item in each fist. They were cold, the foil almost as icy as the pewter. You travel fourteen-hundred-plus miles, he thought, and your reward's a rubber and a toy tin animal. Neither of them, given your illness and your adulthood, is of any value to you. A pair of tawdry Crackerjack prizes.

Find out what? he wondered. Find out *what*?

After stretching out on the floor, Sam struggled to make sense of his meeting with Bo Gavin. His boss's cousin—cousin-in-law—wasn't such a bad gringo, ignoring the fact that he looked awfully rundown. Was he really, as Gary Quarrels had declared, a "swish"? Probably. He had the plague, the wasting disease. In fact, that joke of his— "A waste is a terrible thing to mind" —was it the sick Anglo's way of saying something resentful about trying to keep his booby-trapped body alive?

In the meantime, Sam was troubled. Miss Libby had showered and gone to bed, and so had Gavin. They were both asleep, Sam was sure of it. So what other presence did he feel in the house? The ghost of the dead colt? The *ini'putc'* of an ancestor? Whatever it was, it stirred the winter air and made the pan on the stove hiss as if somebody were rubbing its rim with a dry finger.

"Sssssssaaaaam," it seemed to say.

The hair on Sam's nape lifted, rippled, lay flat. Something—*something*—had sneaked in during his treks to Gavin's car. Cuddled in his bedroll, Sam Coldpony clutched the unicorn book and muttered prayers. Meanwhile, this something sidled back and forth between the murmuring pan and the kitchen's upright cutlery block.

Outside, Bounty was barking as if a party of evil marauders had just driven into Libby's yard. It was nothing, Sam knew, but it *felt* like something. It truly felt like something—both inside and out. If only he could figure out what. Or who . . .

In the morning, nearly five hours after Libby and Sam had got up to load hay and feed the cattle, Bo rode down to Huerfano with Sam in the pickup. Sam was returning the unicorn volume to the library, while Bo was scheduled to meet a Dr. Nesheim at the Sangre de Cristo Medical Center.

Lib had made this appointment by calling her family doctor from the motel in Elk City. Her doctor had contacted Dr. Nesheim, an oncology specialist interested in AIDS and in victims of Kaposi's sarcoma. At present (Libby had informed Bo), the center had only one AIDS patient, a near-terminal case, and this Nesheim fellow was handling his treatment.

"A wonderful recommendation."

"The near-terminal business isn't Dr. Nesheim's fault, Bo."

"No?"

"The patient didn't seek professional help until he was almost a goner. He had this boxy trackside apartment in Huerfano, and he holed up in it like a hermit, living on disability payments—he's a Vietnam vet—and venturing out only when he had to buy something. Usually, a lady in a nearby apartment did his shopping. It was only when the landlord found him delirious in his bedroom that he finally got taken to the med center."

"I'm not the only AIDS case in the county?" Bo was amazed, and a little ashamed, to find that this fact disappointed him. As if the other patient, the ex-serviceman, had usurped his place as a unique individual in Remuda County.

"You will be when he dies," Libby had said.

Bo reddened. "Will it be that soon?"

"I don't know. Dr. Nesheim didn't confide in me."

"Why didn't the guy go to a doctor?"

"Like you, he didn't want anybody to know he was gay. Huerfano is clearly a worse place to have that found out than Atlanta."

Clearly, Bo thought. Sam dropped him off in front of the med center, a structure more nearly resembling a modern single-story school than a hospital. It nestled in the snowy lee of a ridge on Huerfano's northeast side, overlooking the economically depressed city and its jumble of houses and businesses. Entering the center, Bo was acutely conscious of the fact that he did not fit in here, that a gay man in this place was like . . . well, a unicorn on a subway platform.

Dr. Nesheim turned out to be a youngish, angry-seeming man with a no-nonsense air that failed to conceal the underlying strains of altruism that had apparently led him to medicine. Stereotypically, he wore a white lab coat, which, unstereotypically, made him look more like a cowhand in a duster than a physician. His shirt was pale pink. His tie, its knot yanked away from an open collar, was of skewbald suede, as if he'd surgically excised it from the hide of a painted pony.

A quick but thorough physical examination was Nesheim's first order of business. He seemed confident that copies of Bo's records would arrive from Dr. Tedrow within the week and that monitoring the progress of his disease on an outpatient basis would pose no major hardships. He approved the vinblastine therapy that Bo had been taking in Atlanta and stated his resolve to continue it.

Off the record, he talked about experimental treatments that he had been following, including the use of such drugs as ribavirin, mostly known as a children's nasal inhalant, and azidothymidine, or AZT, which actually seemed to inhibit the reproduction of the AIDS virus. Tests on this latter drug had started a year ago in twelve different medical centers nationwide, but already Nesheim had received encouraging feedback about AZT from a researcher—a former classmate—at one of these facilities. Bo swallowed this news as if it were a magic elixir, than fisted his hands and looked at the doctor with sudden wariness.

"Why are you telling me this?"

Nesheim cocked his head. "Why am I . . . ?"

"Why are you telling me about drugs that the government won't let you administer?"

"Oh. You mean, why aren't I keeping you completely in the dark about current research?"

"Look," Bo said. "Most doctors—my Dr. Tedrow included—won't talk about drugs that the Department of Health and Human Services hasn't approved for general use."

Nesheim leaned back in his chair and put his hands behind his head, so that his elbows jutted like wings. "And why not?"

The question startled Bo, but he dutifully ticked off reasons: "Testing isn't complete, harmful side effects aren't yet know, and patients may find their hopes falsely raised by word of treatments that they can't obtain. If they're desperate enough, it's possible they'll try to get them anyway. The fear is that they'll forsake orthodox medical approaches, scavenger-hunt drugs available only by breaking the law or heading for Mexico, and maybe wind up getting gouged by swindlers, no matter where they are."

"You've got it by heart." Nesheim smiled, leaned forward, and fiddled with the stethoscope lying on his desk blotter.

"But you've just hyped me on a miracle nose spray and something else—STP?—that sounds like a gasoline additive."

"AZT," Nesheim said. "Azidothymidine."

"Whatever. Anyway, these wonder drugs aren't available right now. Haven't you falsely raised my hopes, Doctor?"

"Did I tell you that these drugs constituted a cure?"

"No," Bo admitted.

"And what's your prognosis, as you presently understand it?"

Bo shifted uneasily. "Every full-blown AIDS case on record had ended—or most likely will end—in death ."

"Do you think you're an exception?"

"No."

"Then how have I *falsely* raised your hopes?"

Bo waited for Nesheim to continue.

"Actually, AZT may only benefit AIDS patients with pneumonia. But I told you about it because hope is one of the things we live on, Mr. Gavin. I can't keep you from dying of AIDS, but maybe I can help you stretch the time you have left."

"Ah. The Hippocratic equivalent of Hamburger Helper."

Nesheim surprised Bo by chuckling. "All I'm saying, Gavin, is that your knowing about these drugs, and knowing AIDS research is going on apace, translates—or *ought* to—into hope. And hope may be the only decent life-extending additive we presently have."

"What if I rob a drugstore for some of this kids' nose spray? What if I hitchhike to Mexico for a kilo of STP?"

"Because I raised your hopes about their likely impact on your symptoms?"

"Yeah."

"Are you one of those AIDS patients with a penchant for reading everything you can about your disease?"

Was he? He had to admit it. Ever since finding out that he'd developed AIDS, he'd gone to publications like *Scientific American*, *Discover*, *Science 85*, *The Atlantic Monthly*, *Time*, *Newsweek*, and the daily papers for everything they chose to run about it, and he was no longer shy about going to unlikely sources like supermarket tabloids, skin magazines, and Health Department pamphlets.

"Then, eventually, you'll *read* about these things. So why try to protect you from news I can't hide from you unless I put you in solitary confinement somewhere?"

"To preserve your aura of doctorly infallibility?"

"Yeah, there's that. It may be attractive to a few of my less secure colleagues, but I'm not on that kind of ego trip."

"And if I burglarize a pharmacy or buy some black-market dope from a scuzzy bagman?"

"Let me paraphrase Abel's brother Cain: I'm not my patients' keeper."

"Sounds responsibility-abdicating."

"I'm a medical provider, not a universal conscience."

And the finality with which Nesheim said so, implying not only his devotion to his calling but also his faith in the intelligence and moral strength of his patients, heartened Bo. The guy's okay, he thought, a straight shooter. The epithet coaxed a wan a smile to his lips.

"Libby told me you have an AIDS patient here," Bo said as they arrived together in the medical center's lobby.

Through the double-thick glass doors, he could see no sign of Libby's pickup in the muck-slathered parking lot.

Nesheim halted and grabbed Bo by the shoulders. "Yes, we do. And I meant to ask you if you'd like to see him."

"'See him'?"

"Visit him, I mean. He has no visitors. He was raised in a kind of orphanage and juvenile-rehabilitation center west of town, and when he came home wounded from Vietnam, there was no one here who remembered anything much about him. If it hadn't've been for his military disability payments, I'm pretty sure he'd've ended up homeless somewhere. Destitute and lost."

Lost. The word echoed between Bo's temples, ricocheting like a hard rubber pellet in a handball court.

"How's he paying his bills?"

Nesheim hesitated. "They're not completely covered, but our board of trustees think there're good reasons for extending . . . charity." He made this last word sound as bleak and brittle as a burnt saltine.

"What about his landlord? What about the neighbor lady who used to go shopping for him?"

The doctor's eyebrows went up. He was surprised that Bo knew so much about the man. "As soon as they understood what he had, they decamped." Nesheim gripped Bo's elbow as if it were the knob on a four-on-the-floor gearshift. "Please look in on him."

"Is he lucid?"

"Enough to appreciate he's got a visitor."

And although afraid that Sam would come during his absence, Bo let Nesheim lead him through a long tiled corridor and into another wing of the building. They passed at least three nurses' stations and a wall of operating-room doors before turning into a section of the intensive care unit that reminded Bo, oddly, of a locker room in an antiseptic and peculiarly equipped gymnasium. It seemed as if Nesheim's lone AID patient had been quarantined back here, and as this inevitable suspicion grew, Bo realized that he *had*—that although Nesheim was on the man's side, other med-center employees feared contagion, stigma, and death and undoubtedly wished that he were shuffling off his mortal coil in, say, Denver.

Outside the dying man's room, Bo asked, "What's his name?"

"Alfred Tuck. He goes by Alfie."

Inside the room, Bo immediately registered a corpse, cranked to a two-thirds sitting position in its bed, and a tangle of tubes like a prosthetic exoskeleton of soda straws. A nurse sat on a nearby stool perusing a copy of *Reader's Digest*, but when Nesheim nodded a gentle dismissal, she smiled self-deprecatingly and left. Tuck's hollow eyes were fixed upon a TV set on which a game-show host was inciting the studio audience to near hysteria.

"Introduce yourself," Nesheim urged. "Tell him you have AIDS. Tell him you have the same kind he does."

Bo didn't move. That's the way I'm going to look, he thought, just like that vegetating quasi-cadaver. He hadn't seen Keith Jory in the final stages of his AIDS—*Pneumocystis carinii* pneumonia—but only because he hadn't stuck around long enough to watch Keith deteriorate.

Well, Alfie Tuck, even with a case of the far less virulent

Kaposi's sarcoma, had deteriorated nicely. He'd become a peat-bog mummy. If Bo were thin, Tuck was etiolated. His lesions made him seem a perfect candidate for a George Romero horror film.

"Tell him," Nesheim said. "You're up and walking, it can only do him good."

Up and walking, Bo reflected—hope on the hoof. And he went to Tuck's bedside, introduced himself, and, after Nesheim dragged over the nurse's stool for him, talked to him for perhaps twenty minutes about staying the course and visualizing victory.

And listening to him, too.

He listened to the dying man—whom he had just been coaching to greater heights of stubbornness and endurance—talk about stealing milk bottles off doorsteps as an eight-year-old, boosting office equipment from a Pueblo loan company as a teenager, masterminding the fragging of a smartass second looey while a grunt in 'Nam, and paying for all his sins, both carnal and otherwise, by catching a piece of land-mine shrapnel near Hue and then coming down with this fucking gay plague in his hometown of Huerfano. A litany of petty misdemeanors, major crimes, and unremitting persecutions that broke Bo's heart.

At length, Bo looked up, disconcerted to find that Nesheim had left them alone. He put a hand on Tuck's thin upper arm, and the guy's eyes rolled up in his head as if he had just tasted a bracing spoonful of ambrosia.

"No one else has visited you?" Bo asked incredulously.

Alfie Tuck reached across his own fallen chest to grip, feebly, the back of Bo's hand. "Father Zinzalow. But I told that goddamn daddy bastard to amscray."

"Why?"

"Because I hate those bastards."

"You're not religious?"

"I was *raised* a fucking Catholic." He let go of Bo's hand and pulled from his gown a tiny gold crucifix; its chain also supported several dog tags. "See this? I keep it with me always."

"But, Alfie, you threw the priest out. Why?"

Tuck clenched the crucifix. "Always." He was squeezing it hard enough to gouge its shape into his palm.

Hope, Bo told himself. That's his ever-present hope, while I'm hope on the hoof—even though I'm just about to hoof right back to Snowy Falls.

As if on cue, Dr. Nesheim reentered Tuck's room. "A man by the name of Coldpony's waiting for you," he told Bo.

What can I do? Bo wondered. "I'll come back," he said. But that wasn't enough. He had to *give* Tuck something, a talisman.

In his coat pocket, Bo found—it seemed to crop up as often as the corpse in Hitchcock's *The Trouble with Harry*—the tin unicorn that Libby had shoplifted from Bali Hi Imports.

"Here," he said, pressing the figurine into Alfie Tuck's other hand. "A promise. I'll be back to redeem it."

"Thanks," Dr. Nesheim said when they were in the hall. And Bo walked along beside him, realizing that he'd never get out of this antiseptic maze without the doctor's guidance—just as he would need his help negotiating the labyrinth of the illness that would one day lead him into a cul-de-sac like Alfie Tuck's.

Sam Coldpony sat in the lobby thinking over the events of the past few hours. His heart was pounding so hard that it might be a good thing that the Sangre de Cristo emergency room was only a few steps away. Someone around here *had* to know CPR.

That night, he had scarcely slept. Once, when he got up to add more wood to the stove, the flames leapt as if he had just splashed kerosene on them, throwing his own shadow against the wall in such a two-dimensional caricature of his body that it had resembled not him but a headless figure in a tattered poncho. This shadow—maybe he'd been dreaming—contorted on the wall with no regard to his own movements, an independent thing.

As it did so, the pot behind him hissed, "Sssssaaaaam."

"Who are you?" he whispered. "What do you want?"

But when he turned around to seize the pot's handle, it stopped calling his name, and the shadow—he had glanced fearfully over his shoulder at it—resolved itself into an eerie projection of his own sinewy form. The headless poltergeist that had flickered there a moment ago was gone.

*Ini'putc'*, thought Sam, clutching the arms of his chair in the medical-center lobby.

So he had been awake when Miss Libby awoke. He prepared them each a soft-boiled egg and a cup of instant coffee, and they sat across from each other in the kitchen, eating. Miss Libby sensed his upset but attributed it to her scolding him in front of their guest about that damned unicorn book. She apologized again, asked if he'd seen any of the creatures lately.

"All six. But—"

"But what, Sam?"

"One of them died."

She asked for, and he gave her, all the details, including the chilling part about the disintegration of the dead colt's body, and she thought that over as if it did not unduly surprise her. After all, the first winter that the unicorns came—kar'tajans was the word they were both using now, prompted to it, he guessed, by their study of Shepard's book—well, Miss Libby had taken her camera up to Abbot's Saddle and tried to take pictures. Tried, Sam recalled, because none of them had turned out. Bad film, she said, and tried again a week later with a fresh roll, but *those* shots had developed with airy smudges where the animals should have been, an experience that put period to her ambitions to become a wildlife photographer of mythological beasties.

"Out of our gourds," Miss Libby said between sips. "Don't you think we're out of our gourds, Sam?"

"Yes."

"That's why I didn't want to let on about them in front of Bo. He's got enough to worry about. Why make him worry that the folks who've set out to care for him are raving wackos?"

"What you mean 'we,' white lady?"

"If he finds out, he finds out," she said. "But, my God, won't that complicate things for him?"

Sam had no idea.

"Show me where the kar'tajan colt died, okay?"

They loaded the truck with hay—having Miss Libby along made it a helluva lot easier—and growled up to Abbot's Saddle to feed the cattle. No kar'tajans showed. And when they examined the spot near the pika colony where the colt had fallen, died, and, so far as either of them could tell, biodegraded back through the ecotone separating the Tipsy Q from the Elsewhere in which its species had originated, they found nothing to prove Sam's story.

Of course, there was the alicorn, that corkscrewed ebony dagger that he'd put back in the truck's glove box—but, after last night, Sam hadn't wanted to show it to her. She would want it—despite his own belief that it was just what he needed, a reservoir of powerful spirit medicine, to protect him from the *ini'putc'* in Miss Libby's house. And now that he knew it was Dolores's ghost, he *had* to have that protection.

"D'lo," Sam murmured.

Four feet away, a woman sitting with her kid on a circular sofa island faced away from him, thinking him a raving wacko.

Of course I am, Sam thought. Every now and again, Miss Libby and I see imaginary animals that won't picture-take and that melt away like snow when they die. Of course I'm a raving wacko. And why not? Now there's a *human* ghost after me, the *ini'putc'* of the woman who bore my child, the woman I deserted.

He knew this because after returning *The Lore of the Unicorn* to the Huerfano Public Library, he had visited Tío Pepé's to make a phone call to the home of D'lo's parents outside Ignacio. With a handful of quarters from the bartender—even long before noon, the bar had customers—Sam rang up information, was told that there was no longer a listing for Dolores Arriola, asked for the number of DeWayne Sky instead, wrote it down, and placed his call.

Posing as a BIA agent, Sam lied that, if only the Bureau could find her, Ms. Arriola had a mineral-rights check coming.

"Goddamn it, Sam, you don't fool me," DeWayne Sky said. "You sound just like you always did."

"DeWayne, where's D'lo?"

"Dead. Buried. Done it two nights back. I chanted her into the arms of Inu'sakats—for all the fuck you care."

Suicide, Sam knew instantly. My woman's killed herself.

A moment later, he said, "What about Paisley?"

"Alma's fine," DeWayne Sky said. "She means to finish school. Don't you come down here—not until it's fucking June."

"DeWayne, I—"

"You do, I'll shoot your ass off. I'll tell everybody to keep a rifle loaded for you."

Sky rang off. Sam picked up his remaining quarters, ordered a beer, and watched two Chicano dropouts "bowling."

Now he was in the hospital, waiting for Bo Gavin to come back from somewhere deep in the bowels of the building and listening to his heart beat—the reports of an ax striking worthless rock in an exhausted mine. It had been over a decade since he had felt this hemmed in and besieged, and on that occasion he had cut and run. What now? Sam asked himself. What now?

My God, Bo thought when he saw Sam Coldpony rise to greet him. The Indian—a *redskin*, for God's sake—was as pale as a palomino. Bleached out around the mouth and eyes. Was he one of those people who went white-knuckled simply entering a hospital?

Even though they had met a few minutes earlier, Bo introduced Dr. Nesheim to Sam, and the two men shook hands.

"Look," Nesheim said, turning back to Bo, "let me warn you that the altitude's liable to get to you here. Don't assume every time you have some chest tightness, or a little dizziness, or a queasy stomach, that your AIDS is pistoning along again. That's possible, I don't say it isn't, but remember it may be nothing but the thin air. You'll adjust."

"I was born in Pueblo, Dr. Nesheim."

"Right, but you've been away. Call me if you need me. I'm almost always here."

A moment late, Bo and Sam were riding in the cold pickup.

In profile in the opalescent day, Sam's face appeared even more haggard and pale. Is it the altitude? Bo asked himself. Or have I already managed to infect the guy? He suspected that Sam resented his presence, feared his disease, despised the behavior that had occasioned it. They rode into the Sangre de Cristos—Greenhorn's sugary peak to the right, Abbot's Pate's bewigged summit straight ahead—without saying another ten words.

A mile from the Tipsy Q, the pickup's tires clattered over a cattle guard; the door to the glove compartment fell open. Bo was looking down at a shiny black spike, about a foot long, itricately grooved in spirals about its entire length. He took it and turned it in his hands.

"What's this?"

"Letter opener," Sam said quickly.

"Is it yours?"

"Yes."

"For Federal Express packets? Jumbo book mailers?"

Sam gave him a jaundiced sidelong squint.

"Where'd you get it?"

"Lillian Vernon's. Mail-order catalog."

A lie? The truth? An impatient sarcastic riposte? "What's it made of?"

"Obsidian."

"Obsidian's glassy and black, Sam—this is dull and black."

"Coral, maybe."

"Coral?"

"How should I know what it's made of?" Sam snapped. "I ordered it a long time ago."

Bo continued to turn it in his hands, marveling at the delicacy of the spiral edges. "Natural object? Man-made?"

"Natural," Sam said, clearly irritated.

"From what?"

"It's a narwhal tusk." Sam hit the brakes, halting them in the middle of the road. "A *baby* narwhal's. Adults' are a lot longer than this, but they're all corkscrewed and they make classy damn letter openers."

"I thought you said you didn't know what it was made of."

"I just remembered. Put it back."

"Back in the glove compartment?"

Sam just stared. Push him no further, Bo warned himself, this thing's valuable to him. So he returned the "letter opener" to the glove box and lifted its door. He banged the door with his fist to get the latch to hold. As soon as it caught, Sam eased the truck back into gear and depressed the gas pedal.

My hands're tingling, Bo realized. Sam's corkscrewed "letter opener" has set my palms to tingling.

Or maybe it's just the altitude, he thought. The altitude and my chauffeur's spooky demeanor.

When they reached the house, Bo sat for a moment on the shotgun side, convinced that weird business was afoot. Or ahoof. Once upon a time, European mountebanks had passed off narwhal tusks as unicorn horns. And that book of Sam's, and the figurine that Bo had given Alfie Tuck, all these things suggested . . .

Find out what? Bo asked himself again. *Find out what*?

# 11

That evening, Sam grabbed his bedroll and snowshoed up through the aspens behind Lib's house to the cabin where he had been living since first hiring on at the Tipsy Q. Bo told Libby, who had spent most of the day doing paperwork, that Sam's cabin struck him as an inconvenient place for her only cowhand to bunk.

"He likes it up there."

She explained that the cabin had been on this property for more than fifty years. A prospector by the name of Naismith had built it in the late 1920s; and each ranch owner since Naismith's failure to find gold in this part of the Sangre de Cristos had made various improvements to it—a new roof, a sounder floor, a more efficient stove. Until Sam's arrival, however, it had been a spring, summer, and fall retreat for hunters and hikers, not a billet for the hired help, probably because even in good weather it was a twenty-minute trek from house and barn. Of course, Libby conceded, the fact that it lacked indoor plumbing also told against it.

"What does it have instead?"

"The usual—an off-site comfort station."

Bo pictured the sort of lopsided kiosk that cartoonist always assign to hillbillies. "And Sam *likes* it? Lowering his bare butt to an unplaned plank when it's ten below?"

"I don't know about that," Libby said. "But when he found out he could have the cabin rent-free, I guess it beat taking a room at Mrs. Thrower's in Snowny Falls."

Bo, fully dressed, was sitting half under the quilt on his bed, while Libby sat huddled at the rolltop desk bulking just beyond the foot of the iron bedstead. That, it seemed, was where she did her paperwork, and if she did it days, while he was around, well, there went his privacy. Moreover, he could not regard the rolltop, even on a contingency basis, as "his." It was hers, all hers. And, he supposed, she might often be perched at it, working away, as he lay abed struggling to nap off yet another enervating fever.

But after his visit with Alfie Tuck and the leavetaking of the taciturn Sam, Bo was glad enough to have Libby nearby. Meanwhile, frames of Coldpony snowshoeing away—toward his cabin— flickered in his head as if on a relentless videotape loop.

"Tonight, Sam might've been happier boarding in Snowy Falls."

Libby glanced over. "Why do you say that? He's bunked in the cabin in far worse weather than this."

"Did you see his face?"

"When?"

"Just as he left. A whipped dog could've looked more downcast only if somebody had booted it off a bridge."

"That's Sam's wary look. He's shy around newcomers."

Right, Bo thought. So shy he sounded like General Patton, telling me what to do with his precious "letter opener." Bo also recalled that he had seen Sam pause at the pickup to retrieve this object before circling Lib's house on his way to the cabin.

"This wasn't 'wary,' m'lady, This was *worried.*"

"About what?"

"I don't think he likes me. I think he must believe I'm highly infectious—the Gay Plague's answer to Typhoid Mary."

Libby smiled. "If he thought that, he wouldn't even be here."

"He *isn't* here. How do you know he didn't just snowshoe off a couple hundred yards, then light out for Indian territory?"

"Believe me, he didn't."

"'Cause he's got it so cushy here, eh? Three squares a day, so long as you consider a chicken-bouillon cube a square. A chance to rise before five to throw hay at bawling bovines. And an 'off-site comfort station' in the Remuda County Alps."

"Oh, yeah," Libby said, laughing. "Yeah."

"What do you pay your indentured Ute, anyway? Last night, he made a veiled allusion to 'minimum wage.'"

"I try to give him about five hundred a month."

"*Try?*" Bo barked. "Unless my head for figures has gone blooey, that doesn't even *approach* minimum wage. If Sam's week were only forty hours, he should be taking home—taking *cabinwards*— close to *six hundred*. And yet the poor exploited native's on call *around the clock*—like an old-timey *horse-and-buggy doctor*."

"Will you stop talking in italics, please?"

"For pity's sake, Cousin Quarrels, that's *terrible*."

It *was* terrible, Bo thought. The man had overseen every aspect of the Tipsy Q's operations during her absence, and his work week was probably closer to eighty hours than forty. What a taskmaster Libby Quarrels was, what an avaricious robber baroness.

But when he gave her a chance to talk, she explained that the Tipsy Q was only marginally a profit-making enterprise. In fact, if she were to depend solely on her income from the sale of cattle, the ranch would go under. Therefore, every year from January to early April, she tried to cover at least three months' worth of Sam's salary preparing tax forms—at a hundred dollars a shot—for neighboring ranchers and whoever else came to her.

In addition, Libby had two Beefmaster bulls—animals one half Brahman, one quarter shorthorn, one quarter Hereford—that she had bought from their original breeder near Falfurrias, Texas, in the only year that Gary had made more money rodeoing than he had spent doing it. She put these formidable critters to stud often enough to bring in another three or four grand every year. Sometimes, she even trapped muskrats to sell their pelts. Even so, the costs of supplemental feeds, vaccines, fencing, working chutes, and standby roundup equipment—along with utilities, fuel for vehicles, food, clothing, and such occasional austere indulgences as a burrito at the Prairie Schooner Café—could sabotage her always iffy profit margin faster than you could say Ronnie Reagan.

"Is that the line you use to keep Sam's salary down?"

"It's *true*. Add in a rent-free cabin, the meals he takes here, and the clothes I sometimes buy him—it ain't trash, Bo."

"Maybe not." But Bo kept thinking about butt-freezing arctic midnights . . . and Sam's rustic privy.

"Of course not! Besides, he really digs working here. If he didn't why would he stay?"

Libby told Bo the story of Sam's arrival: "He showed up in our front yard seated on a buckboard—actually, a sort of makeshift trap with a polyethylene cab supported by what looked like umbrella rods. Sam was under this thermoplastic awning, holding the reins, but neither the trap nor Sam was the first thing your eye went to. The first thing your eye went to was the dray animal pulling his silly-looking contraption. It wasn't a horse, or a mule, or a ox. It was an *elk*. A well-fed but somehow gangle-shanked bull elk that responded to the tug of Sam's reins as if the silly thing had been born in harness."

"Then Sam's not a Ute, m'lady, he's a Lapplander."

"No kidding—he showed up here driving an honest-to-God elk."

"So many of your wapiti are notorious prevaricators."

Said Libby, "You think *I'm* prevaricating?"

"No, ma'am. Never."

Semimollified, she said, "He'd found the creature while it was a calf. It came wandering through a pasture on the ranch where he was working. Nobody knew what had happened either to it or to its mother. Maybe she'd broken a leg, or fallen to coyotes, or gotten shot out of season—it was early summer. Anyway, her calf was traversing this natural park high on the ranch. 'Sort of striding and sort of wobbling,' Sam told me. He dally-roped Ouray—that was what he finally named it—from horseback and led him downhill to the corral behind his boss's house."

"Maybe Ouray was stoned."

"Possibly. The rest of the story's pretty straightforward—Sam nursed the calf, fed it, petted it, worked with it. And so on and so on. Pretty soon it would follow him around as if *he* were its mother. When he put a bridle with a custom-made bit on Ouray, Ouray accepted it. Several months on, word got out that a crazy Indian on Sam's boss's place was illegally harboring a wild animal, a game animal, and Sam caught wind of a plan by agents of the the Fish and Game Commission to remove the elk from his custody and return it to the wild. So Sam absconded. He absconded into the Douglas fir on the upland border of the ranch, and he did it riding Ouray, going, I guess you'd say, elkback."

"How did they end up *here*?"

"Well, they laid low for a long time. Sam, riding Ouray, would sneak back down occasionally. Near La Garita, at a friend's place, a garage mechanic's, he built his plastic carriage and fitted Ouray with a floppy-brimmed straw hat that helped—a little—to disguise the fact that Ouray was an elk instead of a drayhorse. Then Sam set off on a tour that brought them, eventually, down past Alamosa and over La Veta Pass into Huerfano."

"Without getting tagged by the highway patrol?"

"Sam says they jogged along early in the morning or late in the afternoon. Most drivers probably thought he was a rancher of some antitechnological religious persuasion. Lots of folks stared. The sheriff in Costilla County slowed down and ran parallel to them for about an eighth of a mile in his Bronco—otherwise, nobody bugged or hassled them at all."

"Sam Coldpony in 'The Case of the Amish Indian.'"

"Something like that, yeah."

"But how did he and his pet elk end up on the Tipsy Q?"

"At Mrs. Thrower's in Snowy Falls, he found out we were looking for help, and that same afternoon he came trip-trapping up in his motorless plastic carriage, Ouray sashaying just as pretty as any Thoroughbred strider. So we hired the guy. Gary was suspicious, but who else were we going to get? Besides, I figured that anyone who could harness an elk had to be a whiz at working with animals, and animals is what a ranch is all about."

"Animals 'R' Us," Bo said. "What happened to Ouray?"

"We told Sam about Naismith's Cabin and insisted that—if he were serious about keeping Ouray—he keep him up there. We also told Sam not to expect to employ elk power to drive his polyethylene trap around Remuda County. We weren't going to turn him in for 'domesticating' a game animal, but we also weren't going to flout Colorado law by letting him pretend that Ouray had the same status as a *mechanical* all-terrain vehicle."

"So the elk's still up there?"

"Sam let him go the same day he settled in at Naismith's, and Ouray disappeared into the timber. He's been back a time or two, Sam says, but you won't see him lollygagging around the cabin like a teenager who can't find a job. Ouray's back out there somewhere, elking it up."

After telling this story, Libby put away her jumbled tax forms and slid the desk's rolltop into the lock position. Bo, she could tell, was hacked that she was working in "his" room, but she'd left the desk in it deliberately. She could simply leave if he demanded privacy, and if she were with him on a daily basis, finding her at his bedside when his condition began to worsen could hardly shock or frighten him.

And this was Bo Gavin's first full day as her guest. Sam had gone, Gary was no longer around, and she, like it or not, was this perverse quasi-stranger's nursemaid-in-training.

"Good night."

"Wait a minute," Bo said.

At the door to the room, Libby pivoted to face him. He looked like a teenager camping atop her bed, his temples almost naked but the hair above his brows brushed high and stiffened with styling mousse or wax. Like a clean-cut rock musician whose clean-cutness is a code for a cryptic sort of hip debauchery. Studying him, Lib felt the flesh on her forearms *crawl*. Eerie. It was almost as if, snakelike, she were going to shed her skin.

No, no, she thought. That's bigotry. That's fear. And Bo has values as good—or as defensible, anyway—as your own.

Aloud she said, "Yeah?"

"What were you and Sam afraid I'd find out?"

"Pardon?" The word popped out, a flustered stall.

"Come on. Last night, you told Sam, 'If he finds out, he finds out.' You said you just didn't want it to be 'this soon.'"

"I don't."

"But if I'm gong to find out eventually, why fret the 'day and hour'? You're playing God, and Nesheim, my new doc, disapproves of impersonating the Deity."

Okay, Lib thought, feeling strange. I probably should've told you on the trip back from Hotlanta. "There are unicorns on the Tipsy Q, Bo. Genuine, honest-to-God unicorns."

He stared at her, his chin on his knees, his legs concealed by a monument pedestal of quilting. He appeared to be waiting for her to spring a punch line.

At last he said, "Would you repeat that, please?"

Libby obliged him.

"Dit-dit-*dit*-dit, dit-dit-*dit*-dit," he said.

This mockery of *The Twilight Zone's* theme echoing in her head, she shut Bo's door, crossed to the stove, and stood there beside it warming her backside, perplexedly amused.

Let him make of that whatever he wants. It's the truth, and if he doesn't believe me, or Sam, or the evidence of his own senses—should he ever acquire any—well, he'll die thinking the universe is just as tawdry and predictable a joke as he's undoubtedly convinced it is right now.

Naismith's Cabin was an icebox.

A two-story log structure (actually, the second "story" was an interior sleeping deck), the cabin perched among spruce, not far from a stream, on the flank of Ptarmigan Mountain, behind and above the Tipsy Q ranch house. Sam reentered the place, after an absence of four days, to find snow dusting the lintels and windowsills; the cracks between its floor planks, brimming with gritty white powder, were breathtaking lines of coke for Old Man Winter.

Brrrrr, Sam thought.

He went to work making a fire in the stove. Then he scooped a mound of in-sifted snow off the worn army blanket on his bed on the sleeping deck. His every breath, despite the fire crackling in the stove, plumed and shredded. After a while, the wet wood began to spit and hiss—or was he only now beginning to hear it?—and he crashed back down the narrow stairs to look at the stove and check out his food boxes.

Some kind of animal, probably a pine marten, had assaulted one food box, in which there was seldom much but snacks—beef jerky, potato chips, fried pork skins—but the wide flat rock that Sam had used to keep the lid down had thwarted its efforts.

Thank you, Inu'sakats, Sam thought. Thank you, Jesus.

He set the rock aside, took out the bag of pork skins, tore it open, and returned to the stove to eat them, his teeth chattering so relentlessly that it was almost redundant to chew.

"Sssssaaaaam!" a voice said. (The stove's?)

Although he had just been upstairs, he heard movement up there, a clattering and a burbling that had nothing to do with the watery noises of the stove. Not a pine marten, Sam told himself. Not a squirrel or a porcupine. Something else. Warily, he observed the staircase, the hair in the small of his back tingling perceptibly, even through three layers of clothing.

His kerosene lantern, near the front door, projected spastic shadows—they seemed to be afflicted with Saint Vitus' dance—up and down the mud-chinked walls.

But the thing coming down the stairs, banging first into the rail and the fishing-gear locker opposite it, was no shadow. Not like the impalpable thing from last night.

*This* thing was made of earth, half-frozen earth, cut and shaped into human from as if from iced-up but thawing organic matter. The chemise wrapping its body, the prayer shawl on its shoulders, told Sam that it was female. The fact that it navigated without benefit of head suggested strongly that it was D'lo.

His dead ex-wife, whom DeWayne Sky had hinted to be a suicide, was stalking him in his own cabin, a hunting knife—*his* hunting knife—held across her belly as if she were the slasher in one of those gross-out horror flicks for jaded teenyboppers.

"Stop," Sam told her. "Stop right there."

But the things—his dead ex-wife—had reached the bottom of the stairs, and now, like a revengeful *ini'putc'* from a ghost story told by a mischievous grandparent, D'lo was coming for him. ("I'm coming for youuuuu, Sam.") Step by dragging hitch-along step, she approached.

A thing recently exhumed from a hole six feet deep in Rocky Mountain tundra. A thing galvanized by misanthropy. A gray thing so anomalously thawing that chunks of herself—vegetable flesh—were calving and knobbling the floor behind her like minute islands of grue. Although a comic-book nightmare, she was yet real enough to be upsetting.

Sam shouted, "D'lo! Damn you, D'lo! Stop!"

She would never listen. Faceless, only her chin and a cracked wedge of skull floating above her neck, D'lo qualified (it came to Sam) as a genuine airhead. But her will lay elsewhere, and he had better do something, he knew, to deflect or evade her juggernautish zombie wrath.

He picked up the rock that had covered his food box, brought it to his chest, gruntingly heaved it. It struck D'lo in the breastbone, knocking her down. Painstakingly, D'lo's dead self struggled from beneath the rock, from knees to feet, and resumed stalking the man who had once known her living flesh as well as any other person ever could.

To Sam's amazement—since he felt fear rather than desire—he had an erection. He was conscious of it because it seemed such a strange response to imminent dismemberment. If D'lo were actually going to wield his hunting knife against him, a hard-on, no matter haw splendid, wouldn't be much to parry with. Worse, she'd have a little extra body surface to target and dice if she kept coming in her unswerving, idiot-minded way.

But then, so cued, Sam remembered the alicorn in the pocket of his parka. He withdrew it, gripped it by the large end, and hurled it with a forceful backhand flip at the dead woman's heart.

A flying dagger to her source of power.

Inu'sakats forgive me, Sam thought. And the Great Manitou. And Jesus, too. I never wanted to rekill my wife. Always, I hoped to go back. Maybe I never acted on that hope, but always I felt that I would. One day . . .

When next he looked, Sam saw the alicorn quivering point first in the mud sealing a wall chink across from the stove.

D'lo, or the thing that had been D'lo, was gone, an evaporated breath. Even the marshy globs of herself that had fallen to the floor had vanished. The horn of the dead kar'tajan had magicked them away, had re-exiled his zombie wife and all her nauseatingly detachable parts to the spirit world of the Holy He-She.

Did this even happen? Sam wondered. He was limp again, and the cold perfusing Naismith's Cabin seemed not that of a bleak Colorado March but that of a stony winter grave.

# 12

It disturbed Bo that Lib was having such a hard time making the Tipsy Q go. Doing other people's taxes. Pimping, so to speak, for her Beefmaster bulls. Trapping muskrats. And skimping in a dozen different ways, from Sam Coldpony's wage to the catch-as-catch-can repair of fences, riding gear, windmill parts.

Independent cattle barons, or baronesses, weren't supposed to sweat such things. But Lib was less a baroness than a full-time caretaker, with a crucial stake in her operation's success, and he, Beaumont Gavin, AIDS patient, was going to be a financial, as well as an emotional, drain on her resources. So he agonized anew over the wisdom of imposing upon her charity.

His medical insurance—acquired, thank God, long before his immune deficiency—would cover his treatment with Dr. Nesheim. He also had a life insurance policy, with his parents as primary benficiaries, that would offset burial expenses. Everything else about his affairs—from the funds in his Atlanta savings account to the disposition of his earthly goods after his death—seemed too complex for linear thought.

Although Bo had been a canny ad talent, he had never had much of a head for . . . *business.* Not business per se, anyway. Making money had never flummoxed him, but doing stuff with it, making it grow once he had it, had never been his strong suit. He had no real-estate holdings, no fancy portfolio.

All of this Bo explained to Libby in a series of conversations over the next few days.

"Don't worry about it," she told him.

"What else have I got to worry about?"

The height obtained by Libby's eyebrows said, Plenty, but her mouth stayed mute.

"Look, I'm going to pay for your airline ticket. I'm going to chip in groceries and utility money. I'm going to change my will so it doesn't all go to my parents, who've black-sheeped me from our tight-assed clan."

"Black-sheeped?"

"It's like blackballing, only not so much fun. Especially if you're a honky with a sexually transmitted disease."

"When will you go see them?"

"I don't know."

"Call them, then. There's the phone."

"They'll just hang up. I'm their trans-oriented foundling, the consequence of a swish—I mean, *switch*—that took place in Mama's maternity ward three decades ago."

"Bo—"

"Just think of the poor gay parents who wound up with Papa Nate and Mama Josey's infant Robert Mitchum."

"*Bo!*"

"So I'm not calling." It was something he *would* do, later. He would have to. "Besides, it's long-distance."

"The money doesn't— "

"But I'll put in something toward the phone bill, too."

"Hush, Bo. If not your folks, then call your brother. Tell *him* you're here. He'll relay word—they must all think you're still in Georgia."

"Libby— "

"I'm not going to call them for you," Libby said.

"Who the hell *asked* you to?"

Libby shrugged, pulled on her jacket, and went outside to help Sam (who lately had been even more hollow-eyed and distant than on that bizarre trip back from the med center) go *prowling*—Lib's term for riding pasture and studying early spring range conditions, a job that involved setting salt licks, checking the waterholes and windmills, and sizing up the health of the herd.

Bo thought, I can't even help them do *that*, even though I ride as well as she does.

And he couldn't. They had talked about it, and Lib had decided that, as good as he felt now, she would be crazy to jeopardize his well-being by taking him on a spine-jolting horseback tour. Hadn't he wanted privacy? Well, this afternoon he could have some.

Never mind that Bo now had more privacy than he knew what to do with. Ranch work kept Libby outside for hours on end, and although she had those fuming tax forms to pore over when she came home, she had begun doing them, evenings, on the steamer trunk in the living room—a concession to his unhappiness at having her hunched over the rolltop in "his" room.

Shivering in his shirt sleeves, Bo followed Lib onto the porch, then watched as she strode across the muddy yard toward the barn. Only a few dingy fleeces of snow remained in the aspen-tree shade, inert as wool, and even gimpy old Bounty was capering through them at his mistress's heels.

"Don't let an imaginary kar'tajan gore your horses!"

Libby halted and turned around. She flapped Bounty in the head with her hat to keep him from pawing her coat.

Then she favored Bo with such an unreadable stare that he got lost in it, like a toddler in an orchard of legs on the walkway around a public pool.

"What did you say?"

Her question made him flinch. "I said, Don't let a fictitious unicorn gore your lovely horses."

"Actually, Bo, you said 'kar'tajan.'"

"I meant 'unicorn,' though. I was being snide. Snotty, if you prefer. *Snite*, if you'd like a Carrollian portmanteau word."

"I don't give a hoot about *snite*. It's the word *kar'tajan* that turned me around."

A tremor of uneasiness eeled through Bo. The word was familiar to him, but he had never spoken it aloud before. Where had it come from, and why was he so sure that it was an acceptable synonym for *unicorn*? He thought of the figurine he had given Alfred Tuck, and of the "letter opener" that Sam had packed to Naismith's Cabin, and of Libby's bravura assertion that on the Tipsy Q a herd of bona fide kar'tajans—unicorns—sometimes roamed.

Nonsense, all of it. Childish claptrap. The mind cheese from which two-bit fantasies were malodorously molded.

Libby said, "Have you ever read *The Lore of the Unicorn?*"

"Sam's bedtime book? No, but I'm a big Beatrix Potter fan."

"You're a huge pain in the gluteus."

"For not having read a book about a nonexistent animal?"

"Look. *Kar'tajan* means 'lord of the desert.' In Sanskrit. Do you know any Sanskrit?"

"I was a member of the Sanskrit Club at my high school, but all we ever did was gutter-argot translations of the *Kama Sutra*."

Libby's look transmogrified him into mere offal. Dear God, Bo thought, why I am so hostile to her silly unicorn fetish?

"I thought maybe you'd read it," she said. "Often, we remember more about old books we've read than at first seems likely."

"That's true," Bo said. Clearly, she was trying to winkle out an engima cloistered in her subconscious.

"Go back inside. You'll catch your death."

"Too late." He prayed his smile did not look smart-assed.

"Yeah. I guess it is." She put her floppy hat back on, did an about-face in the viscous mud, and headed for the barn.

"Careful, m'lady." He himself was careful to say nothing else about one-horned equines, whether kar'tajans or unicorns.

Inside again, Bo stood beside the Buck stove, mulling the debt that he owed his . . . his cousin-in-law.

And without writing his parents or brother out of his will, he was resolved to do whatever he could—in his remaining time—to help support her ranching operations. He would stay alert for ways to exploit his talents on Lib's behalf. For, as Dr. Nesheim would surely agree, he wasn't dead yet.

One evening, Libby, Sam, and Bo were seated around her kitchen table eating chili, the very recipe that Bo had prepared at Carrie Plourde's house—except that tonight, going by her instructions, Bo had grated in two carrots.

Almost no talk.

Sam, Libby noted, had been especially close-mouthed since Bo's arrival, and it was good to see that he could part his lips to take food, if not to state an opinion. Maybe he was sick of chili and simply being polite. On the other hand, Sam seemed inward even by his moody standards—aloof and preoccupied.

Bo, by contrast, was in good spirits. His jam box rested on

the counter, turned down low. The tune coming from it was Muggsy Spanier's "Relaxin' at the Touro." Under an unbuttoned cardigan sweater, he was wearing the gaudy Hawaiian shirt that willy-nilly recalled for Lib her shoplifting escapade in Atlanta. She wished he had chosen something else, but how could she say anything to him?

Bo had been preparing their dinner for the past several nights, everything from baked trout (Sam had put several rainbow filets in her freezer last fall) to barbecued possum and venison chili. Although she'd had a few involuntary qualms about a PWA doing her cooking, she had set them aside.

Lots of people lived virtually in the pockets of AIDS victims, with no exchange of the disease virus, and if she was going to shelter Bo, she couldn't ceaselessly worry about catching it from him. So I won't, she determined. As for Sam, he appeared to be fretting *something*, but not that Bo's presence in her kitchen might one day destroy his immune system.

Between bites of chili, Bo rapped his fingers on the table in time to "Relaxin' at the Touro." And when that number segued into "Woodchopper's Ball," he began to do a kind of rhythmic bounce in his chair. Nothing obnoxious, just a swaying of the shoulders, a gentle jiggling of the elbows.

Sam emerged long enough from his brown study of Bo's chili to give him a droll, poker-faced look—and then all three of them heard an explosive racket in the front yard. Libby put a hand to her breast, Bo stopped bouncing, and the roaring outside rendered the music of Woody Herman's orchestra's only so much static.

Paranoia framed Libby's first thought: *Vigilantes!* She had a sudden pseudo-prescient feeling that a crowd of gay bashers from Huerfano was going to break down her door, drag her cousin-in-law outside, and lynch him.

"Cryin' out loud," she heard herself say. "What's that?"

Sam swallowed a bite of chili. "Gary," he said.

"Gary? *My* Gary? My *ex*-Gary, I mean?"

"'Fraid so, honey."

"How do you know?"

Sam said something about a motorcycle and something else about Gary's having spent a night with him during Lib's trip to Atlanta. Then the roaring died, Fats Waller's "Ain't Misbehavin'" started tinkling from the box, and all three of them sat petrified waiting for the inevitable knock on the door.

Please, not now, Libby prayed. Not *now* . . . The knock came. It reminded Libby of the Big Bad Wolf pounding on a little pig's door. Would he reduce it to flinders?

"Bastard."

Bo, she noticed, seemed more amused than anything else. Well, why not? Gary and he were first cousins. And a first cousin, even a bigoted one, wouldn't croak his own kin simply for having adopted an unconventional sexual orientation, would he? Besides, *Gary* was the reason that Bo was sitting at her table.

With Bo and Sam behind her, Lib opened the door. On the porch, she saw Gary Quarrels, well bundled in a fleece-lined coat. Out in the yard, near the aspen grove between the house and the unpaved stretch of Highway 69 linking Snowy Falls and Westcliffe, stood the biggest, blackest, ugliest motorcycle she had ever seen. And seated on it, haloed by the twilight, was a pretty young woman with big brown, skeptical eyes.

Grinning—he almost always attacked with that grin—Gary nodded at the woman. "Melissa," he said, by way of introduction. "Hi, Libby." He peeked around her. "Bo in there?"

"Hello, Melissa," Libby said, blocking Gary's way. "I'm Libby, Libby Quarrels."

"Yeah, I'm here," Bo said, and Libby could not hold Gary out. He sidestepped her, walked into the house, and halted a yard or so from his cousin, recollecting at the last moment that he might not want to shake hands with, much less embrace, the prodigal.

Whereupon Libby decided to shut him inside and go talk to the obviously perplexed woman on his ugly motorcycle. No use heating up the outdoors. Besides, Gary had never brought one of his buckle bunnies home before. Although they were long divorced, this still seemed an audacious violation of . . . something.

"Wouldn't you like to come in, Melissa?"

"What did you say your last name was?"

"Quarrels."

"That's Gary's last name."

"Well, it's mine too, I'm afraid."

Melissa's eyes held a game intelligence, not just skepticism. "And I get the distinct feeling you aren't his sister."

Libby was happy enough to confirm this suspicion.

"A pox on the bow-legged jerk!" Melissa said, looking around as if to orient herself. "He rode me up here to meet his—his *ex*!"

Sam Coldpony walked onto the porch, nodded at the two women, and began buttoning his coat. Gary's arrival had hastened his departure for Naismith's Cabin.

"Why did he *say* he was bringing you up here, Melissa?"

"To see a ranch he'd once owned. I knew he'd been married, but he never told me his ex was homesteading the place. Hey, I didn't even want to come."

"Gary's an impetuous fool."

"Gary's a walking monument to his own ego." Like a gymnast on the pommel horse, Melissa leapt forward on the motorcycle. Then she turned its ignition key. (It had an ignition, Libby marveled, not a kick starter.) So much noise *varoomed* from the daunting machine that the branches of nearby aspens began waving as if a gust of wind had blasted through them.

"Tell the sucker goodbye for me!"

Libby had to step back as Gary's buckle bunny—a sensible girl, really—wrestled the cycle around, spun through the muck, and, with her butt lifted like a jockey's, let the monster spit gravel for ten yards before skidding up onto the unpaved highway. Then, wild to be wreckage forever, she gunned Gary's pride-and-joy back down the windy, indifferent mountain.

Summoned by this hubbub, Gary came rushing outside too late to stop her. "Hey!" he yelled. "Hey!"

Bo appeared on the porch beside Sam, and Gary turned to Libby with a look of such highly distilled amazement that she wished that she could bottle it. In formaldehyde.

"She stole my motorcycle!" Gary wailed. "She fuckin' *stole* my four-thousand-dollar baby!"

"It's the company you keep," Libby said. Privately, of course, she had to admire Melissa's daring.

Gary raised his arms. "What do you think of that bitch? What do you think of her?"

"S'perior ass," Sam said. "S'perior."

* * *

Bo couldn't figure out why Gary had come, or why he had brought Melissa with him, or why her theft of his "baby" hadn't led him to call the police.

"Never mind that," he said. "She'll get it back to me. This was just to teach me a lesson."

"Another course in Remedial Decency, huh?"

"Very funny, Lib." Gary stalked about the living room, ducked into the kitchen, served himself a bowl of chili, and returned to the living room, carrying it in one hand and spooning chili into his mouth with the other.

Once or twice, he sauntered to the hall and glanced at the bedrooms, as if to decide what sleeping arrangements prevailed. Sam had long since left.

"Good damn chili, babe. 'S good as I remember."

"You'd better thank Bo. He made it."

Gary paused with a spoonful nearly to his lips.

Wondering if I've contaminated it, aren't you? Bo thought, but stood by the wood stove, arms crossed, saying nothing.

Gary was putting him to the scrutiny of a naturalist, trying to find an appropriate genus and species for him. They were cousins, they were strangers, but Gary could not get a handle on a suitable taxonomic category in which to stuff him, and this was important to the cowboy. At last, he permitted himself to take another healthy mouthful of the chili.

"You fixed this, huh?"

Bo nodded.

"Well, you would, wouldn't you? I mean, that's something you'd just naturally do, isn't it?"

Libby and Bo exchanged glances.

Still eating, Gary explained that spring was coming and that he was headed back to the ranch near Dumas where he had been working, off and on, the past two years. There were a couple of thousand cattle there, and the annual spring roundup would give him a chance to hone his roping skills. The pay wasn't bad, either, considering that his boss had a dozen other hands to cross with greenbacks, at least at roundup time.

His smartass girlfriend had his motorcycle, but if Bo or Libby would give him a ride into Huerfano in the morning, he could catch a Continental Trailways to Dumas and have someone at the ranch skip into town to pick him up. It was possible that Melissa was heading that way herself, since they had set out with that in mind as their ultimate destination, and maybe *she'd* be the one to meet him at the bus station, not only to get him back out to the Prentice Ranch but to apologize for abandoning him.

"More apology than I ever got."

Gary ignored the sarcasm. He pointed the chili-smeared tip of his spoon at Libby. "Is *this* the way you're going to do it?"

"Is what the way we're going to do what?"

"I mean, is Cousin Bo going to live here alone with you while he's . . . while he's sick?"

"Yes."

Gary ducked Bo's gaze. "But, Lib, it doesn't *look* right."

"Would you repeat that incredible statement?" Libby waved her hand. "No, forget it. The Philanderer King of Remuda County wants his ex-missus to appear as upright as Caesar's wife? I'm sure that makes perfect sense—in *some* universe."

"I'm not kidding. Folks are going to see Cousin Bo living here with you. They're going to assume . . . what people assume."

"You've been playing house with Melissa the Motorcycle Moll and you're afraid of what people are going to assume about *me*?"

"People around here don't know what I'm up to, but you're their neighbor. They know all about you. Haven't you ever heard of, you know, 'community standards'? Standards here aren't what they are in the Springs. Never will be, either."

To encounter Gary again, Bo reflected, was to be reminded anew of Lib's saintliness in staying with him for thirteen years.

Bo stepped away from the stove. "Gary, you're manufacturing a needless worry."

"Easy for you to say." He gestured again with his spoon. "You can swagger around like a stud, eating up all the gossip about how you've moved in on her, looking like Don Juan."

"Gobble-gobble," Libby said.

"What?"

"Gobble-gobble. A turkey gobble. Thought maybe it'd help get me on the same fouled-up frequency you're on."

Bo said, "Listen, Gary, I'm going to let everybody around here know that I'm gay and that I'm dying of AIDS."

Maybe that's a bit strong, Bo thought, that word *dying*. For, except for his thinness and his far-from-ghastly facial lesions, he looked almost healthy again. His death was several months, maybe a year or more, away. But, of course, you calmed the excitable with whatever worked.

Sadly, this stratagem *didn't* work. "You can't do that," Gary stammered. "That'd be even worse."

"Why?" Libby asked him.

Bo clenched his teeth, expecting a spiel about the prejudice of small communities against both gays and persons with AIDS, but Gary said, "Because he's my goddamn cousin!"

"Accident of birth," Bo said.

An expression of amazed distaste appeared on Libby Quarrels's face. "Not that again."

Not *what* again? Bo wondered.

"Yeah. That again. Why not? The folks around Snowy Falls know Bo's my cousin. If they find out he's a flaming fruitcake, they'll begin to think I'm"—Gary made a mocking, limp-wristed gesture so wildly out of character that Bo had to admire it—"one more prissy cupcake, too."

"Guilt by association?"

"By relatedness, Lib. These things are hereditary. They get passed down. Believe me, there are *genes* for swishiness."

"That's so stupid. That's so backasswards stupid I can hardly believe even *you* said it."

"Bo can't go around here telling people he's a faggot!"

"I'll try to find another word," Bo said.

Libby said, "First, Gary, you're assuming your old neighbors aren't a whit smarter than you, that they'd be moronic enough to think you're gay because you have a gay cousin."

"Well, they—"

"And, second, Bo says nobody knows—not exactly, at least—why some people are sexually attracted to other people of the same sex. It's still pretty much a mystery, hon; it isn't necessarily programmed into the Quarrels family DNA."

"People are funny," Gary countered. "They'll believe all kinds of things that aren't true."

No argument there, Bo thought. And they'll deny all kinds of things that are. Take, for example, my parents.

Gary set his chili bowl on top of the stove. Hands fisted at his sides, he turned to Bo. "If you go around *announcing* your faggotry, I won't be able to visit up here again—I'd be too damned ashamed to show my face."

"Then why not show everybody your pale posterior on your way south, Gary? Who'll notice the difference?"

The next thing Bo knew, he was coming down for a landing on his scrawny backside in front of Lib's steamer trunk, scattering tax forms as he groped for a handhold on consciousness and hearing Lib curse Gary for knocking him ten ways to Tegucigalpa: "You ball-less brute! You . . . you lily-livered klutz!"

Bo realized that he was on his back. He had no control of his limbs. A face—a male face, a distraught male face—floated above his own, peering down with pathetic remorse, going in and out of focus like an image on a TV set with no outdoor antenna.

Hands—male hands, desperate male hands—gripped his shoulders, pulling him up and then lowering him again, over and over, as if the physical manipulation of his flaccid upper body would bring Gary's tormented face into permanent, or at least protracted, high resolution.

"Forgive me, Bo. Forgive me. I've never hit a family member before. Swear to God. . . ."

A shiner the size and color of an eggplant wedge decorated Bo's left eye. Libby left him a pair of mirrored sunglasses to wear to conceal the bruise, and Gary, who had spent the night on the couch, told him half a dozen ways to reduce the swelling and leach out the unsightly purple, meanwhile beseeching forgiveness and promising no future repetitions of the assault, no matter the provocation. It was quite likely, he said, that neither Bo nor Libby would ever see him again anyway. He was an intrusion in their lives. He was a fuckup who had dishonored the Quarrels name, and his true place was on the Prentice Ranch or in some rodeo arena, bulldogging heifers and spurring the buck out of bridle-shy horses.

"You're forgiven," Bo said, squinting at Highway 69 through his mirror-shades. He was taking Gary to the Trailways bus station in Huerfano, while Libby and Sam went out on horseback to check the "heavy springers"—pregnant heifers close to calving.

The bus to Amarillo would be through Huerfano at noon. Bo left Gary sitting on a cigarette-burned bench in the narrow Continental Trailways station and drove to the hospital to see Dr. Nesheim and Alfie Tuck.

The doctor was writing something in longhand across the bottom of a medical chart.

"I'm glad you're here," Nesheim said, looking up distractedly. "Alfie Tuck's death is imminent."

"How imminent?"

"This afternoon, possibly. Maybe this evening. The odds are about nine to one against his being here tomorrow. Can you stay?"

Bo hesitated a moment before saying yes.

"Are those fun-house goggles absolutely necessary?"

Bo answered by gripping them by the frames and carefully taking them off, revealing the purple crescent under his eye.

"That's probably not as alarming as the sunglasses, Bo. If you wear them, Alfie may see a metallic locust looming over him, a huge silver insect. He's out of it, more or less."

"Okay, they're gone." Bo folded Lib's mirrorshades and stashed them in an inside pocket of his corduroy sport coat.

"Let's go." Nesheim, discomfited, gave a self-effacing shrug. "I should never've left him. After a while, though, it all begins to grind you down."

Alfie Tuck was on patrol. He and his platoon mates were hiking the ridge of a rice-paddy dike, at twilight, with mortars going off and the cries of villagers echoing from the torched hooches blazing like bonfires behind them.

The platoon had air cover, Alfie noted, but it was a weird-ass variety of air cover, and although he knew he ought to be grateful for it, he wondered if a dirigible—a balloon like the Goodyear blimp, for Christ's sake—was the best aeronautical prophylaxis against an ambush by the Cong.

"Stay directly under it!" their know-it-all second looey was shouting. "Or if Charlie don't get you, I bloody will!"

But Alfie doubted that this dirigible—the U.S.S. *Hector*, a navy blimp of all things—would do anything but make them more conspicuous than they already were. Its sausage-shaped bulk glowed pink against the ultraviolet sky. Beneath it, he and the other grunts were skinny silhouettes given definition, even prominence, by the monstrous shadow of its vast hovering shape.

The blimp was supposed to protect them, but Alfie's gut burned with the fear that it would betray their mission—the rooting out of Charlie—and leave them all broken and dying on the rice-paddy ridge. Indeed, its gaudy crimson reflection in the rice pools to either side was cut into discontinuous halves.

Alfie began griping to the fellow in front of him, Rudolfo, who told him it was the goddamn *blimp* that was likely to draw VC fire. It was amazing that it hadn't already caught a few rounds and sprung about a zillion leaks.

"Shut your fuckin' mouths!" their shavetail cried. "If you wanna get out of this alive, keep 'em fuckin' shut!"

That's something, Alfie thought, our second looey shouting at the top of his lungs for us to keep our mouths shut. . . .

And then—the inevitable. Incoming from the north turned the rice paddies into dance floors for a hundred phosphorescent geysers, and the U.S.S. *Hector* exploded. Alfie and his platoon mates were belly-down on the dike, trying to dig their ways back to Texarkana or Tenafly, while the ribbed sheath of the navy airship was folding in upon itself, collapsing dreamily, blazing at its seams in a way that lit up half the Indochinese peninsula.

Burning, the burst skin of the blimp began to fall, coming down like an ignited shroud as big as a football field, bidding fair to settle upon and incinerate them. Their tough-guy second looey was screaming, "No! No! No-o-o-o!" And Alfie, struggling to get to his feet so that he could hurl himself into the mosquito-peopled rice paddy, was screaming too.

"Everybody else gets helicopter gunships!" Rudolfo was crying, rolling over and over as the *Hector* wafted inexorably down. "*We* get a slow-as-a-mole's-ass, sitting-damn-duck blimp!"

Alfie couldn't argue with his friend, or fathom the rationale for such unorthodox "air cover," or comprehend the full idiocy of the brass at headquarters. But he could scream, and he screamed to protest what was happening and to make himself impervious to the screams of his equally doomed platoon mates.

"*Rubbers!*" Alfie Tuck suddenly cried. "*Ru-u-u-uh-berrrz!*"

Bo took the emaciated man's wrists and leaned over him. "I'm here, Alfie. It's okay. It's okay."

Alfie opened his eyes. They flitted here and there with the aimless alacrity of minnows.

"I'm here," Bo said. "Right here."

Beneath the exoskeleton of plastic tubes sustaining him, Alfie brought his clenched hands up to his chest. "That daddy bastard told me . . . I wouldn't be dying now . . . if only I'd've bought me . . . some lousy rubbers."

"Who?" Bo asked. "Who?"

"The priest. That lousy priest. Told me . . . I shoulda used . . . condoms." He smiled wanly. "*Rubbers*, Bo."

"Your priest told you that?"

"He had . . . no right. They're . . . forbidden. Against the law of God."

Bo looked at Nesheim, who was seated on a stool about six feet from Alfie's bed. The doctor shrugged perplexedly.

A priest has told Alfie that he wouldn't be an AIDS victim if only he'd had the good sense to protect himself, thought Bo, and now Alfie's outraged at the man for suggesting the use of a product regarded by all Roman Catholic authorities as a ploy of Satan's, a sin against life.

"So I told . . . the daddy bastard . . . to amscray."

"Has the priest been back to see him?" Bo asked Nesheim.

"No. Other than staff, you're the only visitor he's had these past several days."

"I . . . want some . . . now," Alfie said in a gruff whisper.

"Some what? Visitors?"

Alfie whispered, "Rubbers, Bo. Rubbers."

It turned out that Alfie Tuck, knowing that he was not long for the Sangre de Cristo Medical Center, wanted Bo to create a festive backdrop for his leavetaking. He wanted Bo and Nesheim to festoon his death chamber with balloons—actually, inflated condoms—and to tie them by colored thread or shoelaces to the ceiling so that they hung down around his bed like charms.

He wanted to go out in dignity, sure, but he also wanted there to be something gala about his going. A few prophylactic balloons, he told Bo, would do the trick better than anything. It was too late to use the damn things for what they'd been made for, but not too late to draft them into play as decorations for the obligatory celebration of extreme unction. And if they would call the priest that he had once told to amscray, this priest would surely perform the sacramental rite necessary to his salvation.

"Fine by me," Nesheim said.

He told Bo that the hospital sometimes received free samples of condoms from medical-supply houses. In twenty minutes, using some of these samples, they had Alfie's room, or a small area around his bed, looking like a target-practice booth at a county fair, and Bo had to admit that their efforts, involving both some lung work and some knot tying, had made the scene appear more life-affirming and cheerful than . . . well, morbid and grotesque.

Soon, the priest whom Alfie had once made amscray arrived—a young man, younger than Bo, who came into the room to administer extreme unction. He entered almost as if he were being drummed to his own hanging, but if he understood that the "balloons" bobbing around the bed were inflated condoms—among them, the fancy French tickler that Libby had bought in Atlanta—he gave no sign, merely pushed a couple of the tiny translucent dirigibles aside and set to work rescuing Alfie Tuck's soul.

Finished, he excused himself and departed.

Bo sat down by the bed again, and Alfie haltingly recounted the occasion of his first homosexual experience. A fight with another teenage boy—at a keg party on a remote part of that boy's father's ranch—had evolved into a wrestling match that had in turn evolved into a brutal variety of love play.

"I never wanted . . . to be a woman. . . . Only dumbfucks say a queer like me . . . musta wanted to be . . . a woman."

"Easy."

"Gimme . . . gimme a cigarette."

Bo glanced toward Nesheim for approval. The doctor shrugged and nodded at the bedstand, where a pack of Camels lay. Bo tapped out a cigarette, place it on Alfie's bottom lip, lit it.

Alfie sucked its tip into flame. Smoke began swirling around, giving him the aura of George Raft in an old gangster flick. He sighed, as if he had just become a naturalized citizen of Heaven.

"Listen," he said, drawing Bo closer.

"Yeah, Alfie?"

A bronchial whisper: "Hear that? Somebody's comin'."

Bo could hear nothing but Alfie's uneven breathing.

The dying man squeezed his wrist. "Never mind. It's somethin' else I . . . I got to tell you."

"What, Alfie?"

"Just somethin' you already know. You gotta be . . . a helluva tough guy . . . to take a big one . . . up the old wazoo."

Alfie's bottom lip dropped and his eyeballs froze. Bo took the cigarette from his mouth and gently closed his eyes.

"Shit," Bo said. "Shit."

Nesheim, who had just found a hypodermic syringe, began using it to burst Alfie's balloons.

What Alfie had heard while talking to Bo was the sound of hoof taps in the corridor, and when Bo took the cigarette from Alfie's lips, he saw a pale unicorn enter the room. The animal circled the bed, slipping past Bo and the doctor as if they were not even there. It then approached the buoyant condoms and popped them one by one with the tip of its ebony horn.

Firecrackers going off. Bombs bursting in air.

Then, its task accomplished, the kar'tajan snorted, backed away from Alfie's bed, and went *tap-tap-tapping* into the corridor like a lord. Gratified, the corpse watched it retreat.

Opening the dead man's clenched left hand, Bo found within it Libby's shoplifted unicorn.

# 13

Gary and I never had kids, Libby thought, kneeling in the hay beside Sam Coldpony, trying to help a pregnant heifer get light. So this is one of the things I do to make up for that lack. This is the way—running the Tipsy Q, caring for animals—I try to be—well, *creative*.

Bo stood behind them, periodically inquiring, "What can I do? Is there anything I can get you?"—but Libby wished that he would simply go back into the house and leave them alone.

On the other hand, being present for this delivery was probably Bo's way of balancing the death of Alfred Tuck, which had upset him so much that he'd returned from the funeral with his shiner riding high on his grief-blotched cheek, a purple tumor. Well, hooray for him. Maybe he couldn't go prowling, but he could stand by watching them deploy the calf-pulling chains. Libby hoped that a successful labor would sweep away his fidgety melancholy.

Except that things weren't going well. The heifer was grunting or bawling with every contraction, and the smell of the antiseptic lubricant in which Libby had bathed her arms—as well as the chains and the come-alongs—was hot in her nostrils, an agonizing blast of fumes. Moreover, the flood lamps that she and Sam had set up in this dank crib were focusing so much magnesium-white glare on the hay that she could imagine it catching fire and igniting the entire barn. Impossible, but the idea still troubled her.

"Is the bugger facing head out?" Sam asked.

"God help us if it isn't." The sleeve of the heifer's vagina was strangling her arm.

"Want me to see if *I* can grab a foot?"

"She's tight back here, Sam. Every contraction mashes my

hand against her pelvic bone. You hand's even bigger." Libby groped about some more. "Ah. Ah. There's the head."

She had been fishing for the hock of the calf's leg, trying to fit the loop at one end of the chain around it and wondering why it seemed to her that the calf's head kept moving from side to side in the arm-cuffing birth canal. How could that be? There was hardly room to wiggle her pinkie, much less for the calf to shove its head first to the left and then to right. Freaky. She visualized the head budding in one place, spontaneously shrinking, then budding again in a spot just across from the "original" head. She couldn't find a foot at all, only a elusive, ever-sifting noggin.

"What can I do?" Bo asked for the twelfth time. "Tell me what I can do." (Or was it the thirteenth?)

Shut up, Libby thought, but she was too intent on locating the calf's hock to tell him that.

At last, she found a foot and attached her chain. After more groping, she found the other foot, managed to ease the other end of the chain around it, and withdrew her arm into the air, stunned not only by the omnipresent cold but also by the fact that the calf's feet seemed oddly far apart. Usually you found a foot on one side of the calf's head and the second on the other, only a little space separating them. But, in this case, the narrow birth canal had become—eighteen inches above Lib's elbow—a veritable Lincoln Tunnel, with the calf's forefeet in its outer lanes.

Sam connected a set of fence stretchers to a post not far from the heifer and started taking up slack in the pulling chains around the unborn's hocks. He did so from a crouch, applying pressure at a downward angle. The chains began to winch the calf as smoothly as possible into the hay, already beslimed and blood-tipped, under Bossy's massive hips.

Aching with weariness (it was near midnight) and shivering (it was still March), Lib stood up to watch. There was not much that she could do now but pray that the calf didn't die in the birth canal. If it did, they would have to call in the vet to do a Caesarian, dismember the calf, and remove it piece by bloody piece—or accept the loss of another valuable specimen of livestock, a monetary set back that Lib didn't want to think about. If too many of her heifers failed to get light, she'd do better going into tax accounting full-time.

Fortunately—for the moment—the come-alongs were working, and the calf, greasy with lubricants and steaming as if it had emerged from an oven, plopped out into the hay.

"My God," Bo said. "Holy Jesus."

Libby didn't blame him. The animal on the ground was what the Good Book would call an abomination. It had two blind heads, evil nubbins for horns, and forelegs so short that, if the creature were unlucky enough to live, it would totter about the Tipsy Q with its rear end a good two feet higher than its deformed heads.

Libby glanced at Sam. His usually imperturbable face betrayed shock, possibly revulsion. The panting heifer that had given birth to this monster lay exhausted, flanks heaving, nostrils contracting and dilating. Bo touched Libby's arm as if for reassurance, while Sam, rising, gaped at the calf from a mental territory that Lib had no clue how to map or explore. Then he approached the abomination—this outrageous word kept flashing on and off for her, like a beer sign in Tío Pepé's—to scrutinize it.

Sam scrutinized it from head to tail, from crippled forelegs to stolid hindquarters. When he turned back to Libby and Bo to give his report, he told them, "It's a bull calf and a heifer calf both, folks. It's got it a pizzle and it's got it a pocketbook. I don't know what the hell to call it, exactly."

"A hermaphrodite," Bo said. "A natural hermaphrodite."

Sam looked at Bo as if he had uttered an imprecation in a dead language.

Why has this happened? Libby wondered. She remembered that on the last lap of their trip home from Georgia, Bo had said something about a "reality disjuncture." Was this abomination's birth—its disquieting presence here on the floor of her barn—evidence that he hadn't been talking simple rot? (Dit-dit-*dit*-dit, dit-dit-*dit*-dit.) It seemed possible. It almost seemed likely.

Thought Libby, We've been captured by an alternative reality, a post-1980 continuum in which miracles (kar'tajans) and abominations (this calf) may both occur.

"It's dying," Sam said. "Hell, it's dead."

"What are we going to do with it?" Bo said.

"Bury it," Libby said emphatically "Just bury it."

"You could make some money with this. You could— "

"Bo, don't. Okay? Just don't."

"Then think of science. You owe the world a chance to see this thing."

"Why?" Sam asked.

"Because it's rare. People might learn something from it."

A new uneasiness settled on Lib's old one, like one transparent lamination atop another. First, the two-headed calf. Second, Bo's insistence that she *do* something with it. Charge admissions. Give it to a museum. Something. Anything. It led her to hate him a little—in the same way that she hated the deformation of nature embodied by this grotesque . . . *thing*.

Libby put her hands to her temples and stared down at the calf as if through a makeshift slide viewer. Why? she wondered.

And why am I equating this indisputable deformation of nature with my doomed cousin Bo? Didn't the way he cared for Alfie Tuck compensate—at least a bit—for his betrayal of his lover? Can't he see that trotting out this abomination—either for profit or for science—would be sort of like trumpeting his shittiness in Atlanta instead of his kindness of Alfie here in Huerfano?

Libby began to shake. Her brain was a compost of smoldering convolutions. Everything was so goddamned confused.

Putting an arm around her, Sam said, "You okay, honey?"

"Abominations can't live," she said. "The world rejects them. Hermaphrodites can't live. Nature weeds them out." She pointed at the dead calf. "Drag it outside somewhere and bury it."

Abruptly, Bo came between her and the grotesquerie that she had mid-wifed into brief existence. "Fuck you, m'lady!" He flicked her on the cheek with his finger. "You're a bigoted cowgirl puritan!" Impudently, he repeated the finger flick. Harder.

Sam grabbed Bo's jacket and shoved him over the corpse of the two-headed calf. Stunned by the unexpectedness of both Bo's verbal attack and Sam's physical response to it, Libby held Sam away from her ridiculously sprawled houseguest.

"Why are you angry with *me*?" she cried. "What have I done?"

It made no sense to her. After long and painful labor, one

of her heifers had delivered a stillborn monstrosity, and her command to bury the thing—rather than to exploit or dissect it—had led to this hair-trigger outburst.

What was wrong with Bo? Sure, he was under a death sentence himself, but he didn't have to act like a revolutionary confronting the piggish elite. Wasn't she a victim here too? Her heifer's hideous miscarriage hurt all of them.

Bo crab-walked away from the monster, levered himself upright against the manger wall. "I'm no fucking bovine—but maybe it'd be a helluva lot easier for everybody if I were."

He rearranged his jacket, brushed of his jeans, sidled out of the stall, and limped through the dark to the house.

Shit, Libby thought. Triple shit and a dead hermaphrodite to boot. I couldn't' feel much worse than this. I'd have to be in the last stages of AIDS to feel worse than I do right now. I'd have to be dying without benefit of human sympathy or painkillers, and Gary would have to be sitting at my bedside watching. . . .

"Get the mama up, Sam," she said. "Get her on her feet. Then go bury this . . . thing."

Sam stared at the . . . abomination. Gazing down upon it, with no other person in the cramped birthing crib, disconcerted him. It seemed to him that, in some malign way, Dolores had engineered this disaster. She'd committed suicide on his account, and although he had not been bothered by her ghost—her headless *ini'putc'*—for several nights now, he suspected that she was trying to repay him for leaving her and "Alma" and for never again seeking face-to-face contact with either of them.

Now, of course, D'lo had no face to contact. No eyes to peer into, no lips to speak, no ears to hear his stupid explanation and apologies. But she was still determined to effect contact, and Sam believed this two-headed monster was all her doing. Indeed, its second head was probably a grisly surrogate—blind, deaf, and dumb—for the one blown from her body in a suicide that must have been spectacularly gory.

Using chains and Miss Libby's pickup, Sam dragged the calf out of the barn and into the horse trap behind it. He began digging a grave in the rocky earth. He stopped long enough to go back inside and get the worn-out heifer to her feet by covering her nostrils with his hands and cutting off her wind, then returned, sweaty and empty of thought, to finish digging the grave. It took two hours, the ground was so hard, and when he finally rolled the monstrosity into its shallow resting place, the eyelids on the smaller and more deformed of its two heads rolled up like window shades—he could see this by the equinoctial moon—to reveal a pair of intelligent brown eyes so much like D'lo's that he was staggered.

"I'm sorry," he said. "I'm goddamn fucking sorry."

He shoveled dirt back into the grave, mounded it, tramped it down, and dragged several good-sized rocks into place on top of the site to discourage coyotes and pine martens from trying to disinter the corpse. It would have been easier with a little help, but he managed, proud of himself both for managing and for refusing to let his fear run him off the task. He'd have only a few hours to sleep tonight—what was left of it—but, assuming that D'lo stayed buried with this goddamn calf, he ought to sleep good and hard. He was so weary that stars had begun to pinwheel and his feet to shuffle beneath him like a toy robot's.

But you've still got to trek up to Naismith's Cabin, Sam told himself. You've still got a ways to go.

Hadn't Miss Libby stopped to think how pooped he'd be when he finished digging this grave, that offering him her couch to sleep on would've been nice? Well, no, she hadn't. That stillborn calf, along with Bo's bitchy behavior, had kept her from it.

Sam returned the pickup to the barn, put up his tools, turned off the floods, buttoned his coat, and stalked outside again.

Fifty yards away, on the other side of the horse trap, stood an elk silhouetted in a gap between Ptarmigan Mountain and the inky stand of Douglas firs southeast of the ranch house. It's antlers occupied this pale gap like a rocking chair balanced atop its head, swaying minutely each time the beast tilted its muzzle to scent the wind. It should have shed them in February, this five-foot rack of concentrated mineral matter, but it hadn't. Damn puzzling.

"Ouray!" Sam cried. It had been forever since he had seen the elk. His heart lifted. He walked across the horse trap, climbed the fence, and lowered himself tenderly onto Ouray's back.

Astride the animal, Sam felt several stories tall and charged with power. The wind slicing across the upland pasture could not sabotage this feeling, nor could the sharp reality of the wapiti's bones or the musky shagginess of its coat.

Ouray, he thought. Ouray, you've returned. He felt like a war chief. Squeezing the elk's flanks, he prodded it into a trot.

Soon, however, Ouray was running, climbing, flashing up narrow draws and between tangled pines, and Sam was staying aboard by a combination of effort and instinct that astonished him. Ouray and he had melted into each other, a pair of galloping symbionts. No longer was he fretting about D'lo's *ini'putc'*, or his boss lady's lack of regard for him, or his once dire need for sleep.

"Inu'sakats," he shouted, gulping the cold spring air, "deliver us from evil!"

When Lib entered the house, it surprised her to find Bo sitting on her lumpy sofa watching television, for he claimed to hate the offerings of the commercial networks. Also, her Bendix—which she had nabbed at an auction seventeen years ago for the grand sum of eight bucks—could pick up only a single station out of Pueblo, and that station only on clear nights. Even when Little Ben received it, the images cavorting in the box's oblong window seemed to be dancing in a salt-and-pepper storm. And the sound was bad. You could turn it up, but that amplified the roar, while the picture remained unrealievedly grainy.

Tonight, though, the sound was good. Libby, going from living room to kitchen to scrub and disinfect her hands, noticed that she didn't have to strain to hear the audio. But it *was* a clear night, and the Bendix had always been unpredictable. Once, without an outside antenna, it had received a station from Colorado Springs long enough for Gary and her to watch nine tenths of an old James Dean flick, *East of Eden*. Whereupon Ben had gone blooey, video and audio both, and she still had no idea how things had turned out for the tormented Dean.

Bo said nothing as she went by. He was pissed because she had refused to spread word of the birth of a two-headed calf all around Remuda County—hell, all around the state. He was pissed because she had called the hermaphrodite an abomination.

Christ, was he sensitive! He should be wired to receive beetle belches originating in other solar systems.

Her hands and forearms scrubbed nearly raw, Libby returned to the living room. Now, Bo was sitting cross-legged on the floor in front of the Bendix, ratcheting the channel knob. She sat down on the sofa so that she could see the amazingly sharp pictures coming into focus one after another as Bo ran through the channels. Briefly, she wondered if he and Sam had done something—put up a new rotary antenna, replaced the Bendix's guts, bought a satellite dish, installed cable—to attain such range and clarity. But no, none of those things had occurred.

"What's going on?" Libby said. "How are you managing that?"

Bo stopped clicking the channel knob. He scooted back so that she could see even better. "I don't know. Little Ben's incredibly keen tonight. He's picking up stations I've never seen before—movies, public-affairs programs, series episodes that are totally . . . hell, m'lady, I don't know. Look!" He waved at the oblong screen. "I mean, give a gander at this one. It's as if a team of mad scientists has commandeered the airwaves and refitted Benny Boy to pick up the results."

The hairs on Libby's nape erected. The program on this channel was being broadcast in color. That was no surprise. The surprise was that her Bendix, a black-and-white anachronism, had translated the color signals into an apprehendable color picture. A blue sky, a brown building, green grass, a brindle dog.

A computer-colored version of an old *Our Gang* comedy featuring, prominently, Alfalfa and Buckwheat.

Eyebrows raised, Bo glanced at her over his shoulder. She bit her lip and shook her head. The 1980s were a video decade, but how could you take part in the revolution without a color set, a decent VCR, and, ideally, even a cable hookup? Well, you just uncrated your old Bendix, plugged it in, and flipped it on.

"Bo, what did you *do*?"

"Nothing. Swear to God, cousin, *nothing*. When I came in,

I was too wrought up to sleep—so I turned on your set, whumped it with my fist, and, bingo, we've got a color connection to a dozen different surrealistic channels. Dream channels, call them. You can't get them in Atlanta, Ted Turner or no Ted Turner."

Alfalfa's angular face floated around pinkly, Buckwheat's shone like a ripe eggplant. The coloring process used on the film had to have been amateurishly hit-or-miss.

"Change it," Libby said.

Bo scooted forward and did so, keeping a grip on the knob.

In view, a program called *Erotic Practices of the Renowned and Powerful.* Segment one originated from the bedroom of Secretary of State John F. Kennedy and his current paramour, an actress named Grace Rinehart. Segment two emanated from the Moscow home of the late Soviet leader Yuri Andropov.

Shockingly, the segment devoted to Kennedy starred John Kennedy himself, now approaching seventy—silver hair, age-spotted hands, pendulous jowls. He had survived Oswald's assassination attempt in 1963, and his allusions to President Mondale, plus the incredible anomaly of his survival, hinted strongly that this program had its home studios in a parallel reality.

So did the fact that the woman next to JFK—reputedly both a director and an oscar-winning actress in her early forties—was no more familiar to Libby or Bo than a charwoman in Liverpool would have been. But Grace Rinehart did most of the talking, and what she talked about, as Kennedy gazed on with looks alternating irony with an inappropriate uxoriousness, was methods by which a clever bed partner could rouse an elderly swain to "breathtaking heights of youthful passion."

"Want to go back to Buckwheat and Alfalfa?"

"What happened to Jacqueline?" Libby said. "If Oswald didn't kill him, did Jackie divorce him? Did she still marry Onassis?"

In the old days, Libby had admired JFK fiercely. In fact, she had always believed that, had he lived, he would have extricated the United States from its evil role in Vietnam. Somehow. Never mind that during his presidency he had deepened U.S. involvement and that today it was everywhere reported that he had been a discreet but incorrigible philanderer.

But Bo could not say what had happened to Kennedy's marriage to Jacqueline. He was about to change channels again.

"Don't."

So Bo stayed his hand, and after commercials for a nonaddictive recreational drug called Sky High, a Tanzanian marital aid, and a limited run of signed Andy Warhol silkscreen prints, the Andropov segment aired—with the deceased Andropov himself showing off a collection of arcane devices that Libby couldn't believe any Soviet citizen, in any true Marxist continuum, would have had the temerity to assemble. It was fascinating, this peek into Andropov's closet; it was also fantastic, hard to credit, and discomfiting. Some of the devices, declared the translator, had come into play only when Yuri disported himself with former KBG underlings.

"Underlings?" Lib said. "Go back to the *Our Gang* comedy."

"Wait a sec. You got your titillation from the Kennedy piece. Now it's my turn."

So Libby watched with Bo. Really, she should be helping Sam, but if he left, what guarantee did she have that her set would still be working in this unbelievable way upon her return? None. And Sam could cope. He'd understand if she stayed inside watching this eye-opening episode of *Erotic Practices of the Renowned and Powerful.* Wouldn't he?

When the program ended, Libby made a change-the-channel gesture at Bo. He obeyed.

A taped stage production of Shakespeare's *The Moor of Venice* from the American National Theater in Kansas City, Missouri, with Dorothy Stratton as Desdemona, Laurence Harvey as Iago, and Paul Robeson as Othello.

*Click.*

A talk show hosted by Tennessee Williams—Libby had never seen him in that capacity before—on which a film actor, a pianist, and a sought-after stage actor, whose career Libby had never followed, discussed the incidence of AIDS among the celebrity communities in Hollywood, Las Vegas, and New York. All three men admitted having AIDS, and Williams, gesturing with his cigarette holder, praised them for speaking so openly.

"Tennessee Williams is dead," Libby said. "He died in 1982."

"He hasn't got anything on Kennedy. Or Dorothy Stratton, or Laurence Harvey, or Paul Robeson."

"We're dreaming. Tennessee Williams never hosted a talk show, and those three guys would never go on the air to tell the world they've been lying about themselves all these years."

"Protecting themselves," Bo contradicted her.

"Yeah. Not very well. They're dead men too, aren't they? Or are they simply in the process of dying?"

Bo made no reply, but they watched the talk show to its end, by which time it was three thirty in the morning.

*Click*.

MTV—or a station bizarrely like MTV—had Swing Era videos, all produced in either *film noir* chiaroscuro or an eerie sepia tone that pulsed with the rhythms of the music. The stars of the only segments they watched were Glenn Miller, Muggsy Spanier, and Duke Ellington and his orchestra. It was hard to get Bo to move beyond this channel, for these unlikely videos fascinated him. But, after Ellington conducted "East St. Louis Toodle-oo," Libby said, "Change it!" so forcefully that he finally twisted the dial.

A televised cattle auction originating live, and on video tape, from Fort Worth. With a direct line and a little cash, Libby told herself, I could bid for some of those beauties.

*Click*.

A documentary about Pope John Paul I going into the slums of São Paulo and Rio de Janeiro to distribute both free condoms and pamphlets in Portuguese on how to use them.

*Click*.

A rerun of a lost episode of *Star Trek*, with Steve McQueen in the role of an alien who has stowed away on the *Enterprise*.

*Click*.

An animated remake of Arthur Miller's *The Misfits*, as rendered by the artists at two major comic-book companies. The characters had computer generated voices, but they moved with uncanny grace and fluidity.

*Click*.

Everett Dirksen, once a Republican senator, reciting excerpts from the prose of Jack Kerouac. *On the Road*, apparently.

*Click*.

*Wild Kingdom* with Marlin Perkins. Here, in a manner that made Libby's nape tingle, Perkins's narration accompanied film footage of a kar'tajan roundup on the edge of the Great Indian Desert, near Jodhpur, in the province of Rajasthan. Perkins and his cohorts—some of them Indian wildlife officials—employed helicopters both to sight and to herd the kar'tajans (the only word Perkins used for them), and each time they swept down over the panicked beasts, dust from the rotor was spectacularly billowing, a sharpshooter from the wildlife department would lean out and fire a tranquilizer dart into one of the fleeing animals.

Wow, Libby thought, I'm *not* crazy. Neither is Sam. They're real. Even Marlin Perkins believes in them.

"See?" she said. "*See?*"

"See what, Cousin Quarrels?"

"They're real. That's all. They're real."

"If Kennedy didn't die in Dallas. And if Muggsy Spanier's on MTV. And if the Pope's in Brazil passing out prophylactics."

Libby stared at Bo. His shiner, in the miraculous light shed by the Bendix, was throbbing purply.

"Then, and *only* then, may either of us believe that kar'tajans are real, m'lady."

Bo was right, of course. Little Ben was performing not only above and beyond the call of duty, but so far above and beyond its technological capacity—at least in the universe that Libby had to regard as real—that she'd be an idiot to credit *anything* issuing from the damned box.

"These lovely kar'tajans," Marlin Perkins was saying from the damned box, "have undergone an unprecedented population depletion here in western India. Some have even wandered into villages on the desert's edge. They seem to be looking for people to take care of them, and many of the Hindus of Rajasthan feel that to turn them away would be a crime against the gods.

"But Indian wildlife experts have noted that the kar'tajans' dwindling numbers may be the result of an epidemic of a disease very much like equine infectious anemia, better know to Westerners as swamp fever. So they have cautioned people against exposing their own livestock, of whatever kind, to the sick creatures.

"How infectious this Indian swamp fever may be, and what other types of animals it may endanger, are questions that this exciting roundup had been organized to answer. And we at *Wild Kingdom* have devoted ourselves to recording the event and to helping our Indian friends preserve as many of these beautiful one-horned 'horses' as it may still be possible to save."

"Swamp fever?" Bo said. "Among unicorns? On the edge of the Great Indian Desert?"

"Forget the name, Bo. It occurs all over." Lib recalled that during one strangely hot summer, several years ago, horseflies had congregated in swarms in their barn, and she and Gary had wound up losing two good mounts to—yes, swamp fever, a.k.a. equine infectious anemia. It was a viral disease that had made both horses sweat, go wobbly in their legs, and shed body fat as rapidly as if they were taking an aerobics class.

"The worst thing about it," Libby went on, "is that there's no treatment for it. Sometimes, the infection goes away. More often, your horse just up and dies."

And now, in Little Ben's eye, three men in safari jackets and multipocketed khaki shorts were examining a tranquilized unicorn—kar'tajan—and Perkins was saying, "On this weakened animal, our friend Dr. Prakash Chakravarty of the University of Hyderabad had found, near the pale nostrils, several lesions hinting at advanced infection by the swamp-fever virus. Such cases offer our dedicated wildlife workers but few options."

In closeup, Chakravarty looked at Perkins (who received a quick intercut closeup of his own) and resignedly shook his head.

"In the case of this animal, the good doctor says that we must either destroy it or risk having it spread its affliction to other members of its species. Often, in the Wild Kingdom, man is forced to be cruel in order to be kind."

Libby took in this platitude—one among many—as if it were a steam-exploded popcorn kernel in a bowl of popped kernels. She was scarcely aware that, finally, Little Ben's picture was beginning to suffer occasional interference—askew phosphor-dot fault lines—and that the audio was fuzzing out. Perkins had begun to sound as if he were gargling salt water. Well, so what? Libby was having a revelation that overshadowed the significance of a nature program syndicated from an alternative reality, a revelation that made most of its scripted narration sound like jejune babble.

"The kar'tajans on the Tipsy Q," she said. "That's got to be what's wrong with them."

The purple knot beneath Bo's eye trembled as if about to hatch something. "Swamp fever?"

"Equine infectious anemia. That's what's wrong with them, Bo, that's why they've been dying."

Libby ignored the bemused, skeptical look he gave her. Never mind—not now, anyway—that the infection was usually a summer disease. No matter—at least for now—that it had no reliable treatment. And to hell with the fact that none of her neighbors—so far as she knew—had any notion that mythological beasts from another reality were roaming her high mountains pastures.

"You know, m'lady," Bo said, "your otherwordly swamp fever has all the earmarks of a kar'tajan kind of AIDS."

Ouray carried Sam up to Naismith's Cabin. But the elk did not stop there. It went surefootedly up a tortuous trail above the cabin to the mine that Naismith and his partner had hewn out of the wooded flank of Ptarmigan Mountain.

The mine's collapsing entrance, its rotted timbers drooping or standing knock-kneed, loomed in the cold like a door to the spirit realm. Although Sam had never before wanted to explore Naismith's Mine, a figure—the *ini'putc'* of his birdshot-beheaded D'lo—stood outside it, beckoning him and blazing with blue electricity.

Ouray, meanwhile, pointed his antlers as if to receive through the spurs of his out-of-season rack a broadcast from the Holy He-She programming these uncanny events.

As the elk climbed, Sam fought to stay aboard. Never ceasing to beckon, D'lo retreated deeper into the mine—so that the shaft was kindled a kinetic silver-blue and her semaphoring arm suggested an eel manufacturing its electric messages in an undersea grotto. Once on the ledge fronting this shaft, Ouray snorted, as if to say, Get down, Coldpony, and go inside.

So Sam dismounted, and the elk nudged him between the shoulder blades. Dolores's *ini'putc'* was no longer clearly visible, but the silver-blue glow that had called him—the ghost fire crepitating along the lineaments of her headless form—continued to flicker from the mine's recesses. Thirty or thirty-five feet in, the Ute estimated. Nevertheless, he felt compelled to abandon Ouray on the high stone ledge and enter that disturbing darkness.

What if I die up here? Sam thought. What if D'lo is plotting a belated revenge? I'll never see Paisley again.

Sam stumbled on the hand-cart tracks that Naismith and those in his employ had laid down in the tunnel. But he caught himself and kept going. Once, he turned to see that the great elk had assumed the posture of a sentry. Starlit antlers tracking him, the elk grew steadily harder to see, as if poised beyond a filmy veil or a warped pane of glass. Meanwhile, ahead of him, his ex-wife's *ignis fatuus* continued to draw him after.

As on the first night that D'lo had appeared to him, Sam found that he had a hard-on, a stiffness already painful. What was wrong with him? A man wasn't supposed to become aroused—not that Sam felt any *true* erotic ardor—when at bodily risk. Not unless he was a weirdo. Well, for a Muache Ute, Sam silently mused, you've always been pretty damn weird.

His erection pressed against the cold metal of his zipper like a divining rod, pursuing D'lo's spiritual aura toward a destination still uncertain. And what of the magic horn of the kar'tajan colt that had died near Abbot's Pate? Well, that talisman was in Sam's cabin, utterly inaccessible. He rued the fact.

Merciful Inu'sakats, how cold it was! The ceiling of the shaft dropped lower and lower as Sam crept deeper inward. The walls, too, seemed to narrow, like perspective lines converging on the point at which all perspective disappears.

D'lo's blazing *ini'putc'* vanished. Utter darkness eclipsed the mine shaft. Sam's hard-on remained, divining rod and pointer. He unzipped his jeans, not only to free it from constricting denim but to let it function more effectively as guide.

Outside, far behind him, Ouray bugled a long note. The elk's steadfastness prodded Sam onward.

The drooping ceiling and the in-closing shaft walls forced Sam into a crouch (though he wasn't yet performing autofellatio), and suddenly, almost as if the Holy He-She had spoken a commanding "Let there be light!" into the darkness, an immense vista of plains of dusty hovels exploded from the cul-de-sac at the rear of the mine, disclosing a panorama of ocher dust and quivering heat mirages that could not possibly exist inside the mountain's stony ribs.

"Have mercy, Inu'sakats," Sam mumbled.

This vista—a ceaseless barrage of pitiless desert light—unmanned the Ute. Gaping at it, he returned his flaccid member to the protection of his undershorts.

Seamlessly, but not inconspicuously, this impossible territory graded into Naismith's mine, rising up from below—all fissured redness—to clasp the floor and walls of the shaft, which in the transition area seemed to be lined with fun-house mirrors. On all sides but right in front of him, Sam could see himself amorphously reflected, even downward beneath the soles of his boots. Three or four more steps and he would fall into this sudden desert, maybe to his death.

On the lip of this opening, Sam felt that he had tunneled from one side of the world to another. He watched a cloud of dust lift on the far horizon and come billowing toward him as if raised by the feet of a thousand infantrymen.

In this neighboring dimension, it was naked midday. Squinting against its unexpected stinging light, he heard the sound of rotors *whup-whup*-whupping over the desert and at last managed to make out two dragonflylike machines shepherding the approaching dust cloud on either flank.

In the middle distance, to the right of the helicopters, Sam spied a squalid little village of mud and wattle huts. Some of its people had come out to see what was going on. Against the blowing dust, they shielded their eyes with their arms—skinny turbaned men in breechclouts, women in filthy saris, a bemused white cow chained to a rock. The helicopters careened over them, dipping and tilting to keep the approaching dust cloud contained.

Sam heard a low vibrato of hoofbeats. Soon, he was able to see through the forward veils of dust that the beasts were kar'tajans. The helicopters were herding them. As he watched, a group of eight or nine kar'tajans broke off from the main herd, which had begun to turn to Sam's left under the high cliff face from which he—from the beasts' point of view—was spectating. This splinter group darted into the rocks at the base of the cliff and picked its way up the slope toward him.

In Sam's view, they seemed to be trying not only to escape the pesky helicopters but to find relief from the oppressive heat and desert lifelessness of their barren world. Until only a few years ago, he figured, they had probably done okay here—in fact, they may have prospered. But now—well, the poor critters looked as if they could use a rain, a big rain. Why they were being hounded be men in helicopters, Sam had no idea.

Below, he could hear these kar'tajans struggling for purchase on the rocky track leading up to his blind. He stepped back. The lead animal was a stallion, like the one he'd seen below Abbot's Pate during Libby's absence. First, its alicorned and bearded head appeared, then its sinewy white throat and pale chest, and then its powerful ghostly legs. Another stallion crowded through behind the first, and a motley harem of six females, one with a yearling colt, squeezed through the natural chute right after the males. Sam took yet another step back.

That's why it's so hard to run them down on the Tipsy Q, he told himself. They probably retreat to the reality they came from, only to wander back when pickings seem really slim down there and they want to add to their colony in Colorado.

Breathing heavily, the kar'tajans filed by Sam, who had braced himself against the mirror wall, the chambers of his heart beating like so many timpani. Unless his ability to recognize individual animals had deserted him, these were kar'tajans that had never been on the Tipsy Q before. The lead stallion strode past the Ute with the gait of a medieval lord. It cast an indifferent eye on him, as if he were an ore cart or an abandoned pick.

The other kar'tajans passed in the same stately way. However, one female was breathing raggedly and the others had mauve sores on their flanks and chests. The yearling colt appeared in the best condition. It stamped its forefoot in the cramped defile. Sam's nostrils twinged with the uncommon stench of sun-baked kar'tajan flesh, a smell like dust-laden Oriental rugs.

Ouray bugled again. The elk's trumpet call echoed through the shaft and out over the meadow below Ptarmigan Mountain, summoning the kar'tajans and promising spring. Sam could imagine Ouray and these equine immigrants herding together.

Then he was alone in the mine, the artificial ecotone between Here and There, teetering on the threshold of the kar'tajans' bleak reality. Their world was a body length away. Sam inched forward, gripping the frictionless wall with the palms of his hands, begging Inu'sakats not to let his boot soles slip from under him.

About fifty feet below, in the lane of rocks through which the kar'tajans had climbed, Sam saw a man in shorts, safari shirt, and pith helmet—an elderly man with a trim mustache. He hailed Sam in a friendly way and asked if he had seen many members of the larger herd wandering nearby. The animals were being checked for equine infectious anemia, and it wouldn't do to let any of them get away without an examination.

"No!" Sam emphatically cried. The word echoed in the mine and out across the desert. The elderly man thanked him, turned, and disappeared back down the natural aisle, as much a ghost in Sam's imagination as his ex-wife's *ini'putc'*.

Baffled, Sam hurried back through the mine to its opening. Ouray was gone.

Down the mountain, D'lo's electric, headless ghost sat astride the great wapiti. They cantered along behind the untethered string of kar'tajans, all of them flickering with Saint Elmo's fire. When they disappeared into the trees, taking every vestige of light with them, Sam hiked back down to his cabin in a mood somewhere between joy and funk. Crazy, he thought. I'm probably crazy.

Little Ben's picture went out entirely. Electrons ricocheted across the screen in indecipherable insect swarms. The sound was a relentless shower spray.

What a night, Bo thought. Had he dreamt it? The back of his neck felt as if someone had laid a hot mustard plaster against it. Nausea pooled in his stomach as if from an acid drip.

"Come on to bed," Libby ordered. She raised him from the floor and escorted him into the bedroom. Then she was gone, and in the darkness Bo lay gazing up at a pair of framed photographs—one of a windmill under a haggard sun and one of a trio of sixties street musicians playing their hearts out for handouts.

# 14

After a while, the trio of street musicians in the second photo began to favor Bo's parents and his brother Ned.

Mama sat in the middle wearing jeans and sandals and playing a fiddle. (A street musician's violin was always a fiddle.) Dad, in bib overalls and low-topped boots, sat to Mama's left strumming a guitar. To Mama's right, Ned clutched a banjo, his goateed chin tilted upward so that he and Dad could harmonize on the lyrics of a song forever unhearable.

At the base of the three-stepped tier on which they sat, a hat for contributions. Only a single anonymous bill had been folded into this straw boater.

Why is Ned singing with them? Bo wondered. Why aren't I in the picture too? Neddy's nearly six years younger than I am, but he's there on the street helping them hustle money, and I'm totally out of the picture.

Hey, I'm a Gavin too. I love our parents as much as Ned does, even if they think AIDS is God's hickory stick for "sins" and have acted like insensitive shits ever since finding out I had it.

Even if Ned, who finagled himself a snooty-hooty job in Denver right out of college, has done more to support them these past four years than I have. Hell, only recently did I begin getting my feet under me. A novice is a novice, and an ad man's almost always at the mercy of his firm's client list. . . .

Light poured through the bedroom's rear window, telling Bo that he had slept at least an hour or two—for Libby had sent him to bed near dawn, after a night of impossible TV watching. Viewing so rare that Bo had a hunch they would seldom enjoy its like again, if ever. It had mystified, stimulated, and upset him, and he was sure that it—not Sam's impromptu shove in the barn—had triggered his headache and nausea.

AIDS was funny that way. It responded to the traumas that you yourself regarded as traumas. Sam's shove he had deserved, but the Bendix's alternative programming—after the birth of a two-headed calf—had assaulted Libby and him with no concrete provocation. (Was the calf's birth that provocation? If so, Bo had had nothing to do with it.) And it was traumatic to learn that the world you lived in, even with all its flaws and disappointments, had no more, and no less, reality than a TV *Movie of the Week*.

Bo blinked. The people in Lib's photo weren't his family; they were three folk-singing students from the sixties counterculture. Where had Mama Josey, Papa Nate, and Brother Neddy gone?

He folded back the covers. His head felt as if it were capped by an unshed rack of antlers. (Great God, how did a male elk or a mule-deer buck stagger around under such weight?) Bo, hunched on the edge of the bed trying to adjust to the sunlight, rubbed his temples. He needed more sleep, but more important, he needed to find his photos of his family.

A moment later, he was rummaging in a suitcase in the bottom of the room's only closet. He found the triptych of hinged pictures, all of them filmed with dust, and shammied the glass in each frame with his pajama sleeve. Then he set them on Lib's rolltop, studied each of them minutely, and felt his way back to bed.

Phone home, Bo thought, hearing himself parody the pitiable cry of the alien in the movie *E.T.*: Beaumont, phone home.

In his midmorning dream, Bo *visualized*. He recognized, while dreaming, that the images sprocketing through his mind were not just tension-releasing dream images but the manifestations of a subconscious effort to heal himself.

Pretty good, Bo dreamt. If you can do this in your sleep, you may end up among the first AIDS patients to triumph completely over the merciless tyrant.

For in Bo's purposeful dream imagery, Alfie Tuck was entering the booby-trapped maze of his bloodstream to hunt down and kill the Kaposi Cong that had turned it into their private warren. Alfie was crawling through these tunnels with a flamethrower pack. Each time he encountered a commie cancer cell, he drenched it with fire, illuminating the translucent walls of his own veins, incinerating the enemy.

It was just that there were so many Kaposi Cong, so many miles of tunnels to search and sanitize before Alfie could report that he and his fellow guerrillas had neutralized the threat.

The kitchen clock told Bo that it was almost two. Lib was not in the house. Nor, peeking through various windows, could he find her anywhere in the yard or near the barn. She had probably gone out to return Bossy to the company of the other cattle. Everything had been thrown off schedule, first by that heifer's appalling labor and then by hours of sheer bogglement in the video backwash from Little Ben.

Bo, feeling like flyblown horsemeat, dialed his old number in Pueblo. The telephone rang and rang.

His folks had gone out. But both of them at once? That wasn't like them. Usually, either Josey was out shopping and Nate was at home in his Archie Bunker recliner, or else Nate was sipping coffee in some two-bit café and Josey was filling up the house with Camel smoke. The last time they'd gone to a movie together may have been the year that Julie Andrews copped her Oscar.

Until six o'clock, Bo dialed every thirty minutes—with the same negative result.

He was dressed now and feeling more chipper, but neither Libby nor Sam had come home. What to do? Read? Get dinner? Gawk at Little Ben, where Albert Einstein might be barbecuing spare ribs, or Nancy Reagan and Raisa Gorbachev mud-wrestling, or Curt Gowdy long-bowing two-headed dragons over Hokkaido? (In fact, the set's only viewable channel was spewing soap operas and reruns of old sitcoms.) Bo felt paralyzed. If he stayed in this limbo too long, he would simply give up trying to . . . phone home.

At six thirty, though, he finally got an answer. "Nate? Is that you?"

"This is Theodore Gavin, his son. Who's calling, please?"

"Beaumont Gavin, his other son. The *first* one."

Ned made no reply. Bo could almost see him, the quintessential yuppie, staring at the handset as if it had burped.

"Where's Dad? Where's Mama? What're they doing?"

Said Ned preemptively, "You're at the Tipsy Q, aren't you?"

Bo, surprised, admitted as much, and their conversation went on from there. Bo learned that Papa Nate had just had multiple-bypass heart surgery in Pueblo. Mama Josey was in a waiting room near the ICU suites. She would not come home until she had seen Papa during the day's last visiting hour. Ned, meanwhile, had driven on to the house to see if she had laid in any groceries.

"Same old Mama. Same old Ned. Is Dad okay?"

"He's going to make it."

"I'm coming down. I've got to talk to him."

Visiting hours, Ned said, would be over soon and Bo would never make it if he tried to come tonight.

"Tomorrow then," Bo rejoined, but Ned said their mother blamed Papa's condition on the anxiety attendant upon finding out that Bo had acquired AIDS by buggering, or being buggered by, male lovers. So if Bo came to the hospital tomorrow, Mama would scream at him as if she were a death-camp survivor and he a Nazi prison guard only recently dragged in by the Israeli secret police.

"That bad? *Truly* that bad?"

"In Mama's eyes, you're a kind of mini-Mengele."

"Damn her. I'm driving down there."

"Why? To traumatize Mama? To hurl a monkey wrench into Papa's recovery?"

He's right, Bo realized. If I scramble down there against her will and upset Dad and her both, I'll only make things worse.

"What am I going to do, Ned?"

"Stay there. After I get Mama home from the hospital tonight, *I'll* drive up to the Tipsy Q to see *you*."

Ned could not possibly arrive before ten, but Bo surrendered to his suggestion. What else could he do? Get Lib's dinner? Yeah. As soon as Ned had rung off, Bo headed for the kitchen.

Libby wasn't ready for company. Sam had helped her haul hay to Abbot's Saddle and cut out three more heavy springers, but the work had gone slowly because a brand-new kar'tajan sighting had rendered the Ute altogether spacy.

Irritatingly, though, Sam would say only that a new batch of the critters had arrived on the Tipsy Q and that he had seen them above Naismith's Cabin last night after digging a grave for . . . well, the abomination.

"Where above Naismith's Cabin?"

"The mine."

"What were you doing up there so late, Sam?"

"Walking off the blues from that monster birth and your cousin Bo's finger-flipping meanness."

"Where did they go? The kar'tajans?"

Sam had shrugged, and Libby wondered if some lingering pique over her scolding him in front of Bo about that unicorn volume had made him so close-mouthed. She told him—to see what effect it would have—that she thought Bo, even though he still hadn't seen one himself, was beginning to believe in the kar'tajans.

"Such faith," Sam had disinterestedly replied, and she had felt rebuffed.

So why tell Sam about Little Ben's astonishing performance last night? He would think the old set's antics irrelevant to both the running of the ranch and the return of the kar'tajans.

Now, outright mundanity having reasserted itself, Lib was in no mood for a visitor. A glass of milk and a peanut butter and jelly sandwich—her dinner—had made her torpid. Midnight was only three hours off. Bo had slept most of the day, but if *she* didn't get some shuteye herself, she'd be absolutely worthless for ranch work tomorrow.

Have some compassion, she rebuked herself. Alfie has just been buried, Bo's AIDS isn't quite in remission, and Nate's recovering from bypass surgery. You ought to be glad Bo's semi-estranged baby brother thinks enough of him to warn him of his mama's wrath and to toddle all the way up here at night to talk to him.

I ought to be, Libby thought. But I'm not. All I want to do is sleep. Forever.

Ned Gavin drove a wide-bodied American car with a stereo radio, a tape deck, and electric windows. He got his mother back to the elder Gavins' tiny stucco house in northwest Pueblo well before eight, told her that a company client in Huerfano needed to see him "post haste," and went cruising down I-25 at better than eighty miles per hour. However, only the tachometer needle and the other vehicles drifting back toward Pueblo as he passed them clued Ned to his car's high speed, so smoothly did it glide.

Well, well, well, he thought. Our prodigal has made contact. And I . . . I should've sought him out long before now.

Ned pondered. Mama might believe that Papa's heart condition stemmed directly from his discovery that Bo was both a queer and an AIDS victim, but Ned knew that years of sendentary smoking, coffee drinking, and careless boozing, along with a cargo of suppressed guilt for rejecting Beaumont in his time of need, were more likely culprits.

As for Mama Josey, she lived for, and through, her clever sons' accomplishments—so long as those accomplishments had the cachet of Eisenhower Era innocuousness—and she would probably never forgive Bo for arranging to die in a way that not only called those values into question but flouted the very principles on which they were based. Bo was a "sinner." Ostensibly against God (whom Ned knew to be more forgiving than his folks), but actually against the idol of material success to whom they had both bowed down when it became obvious that Nathaniel was never going to make them wealthy and that only if their *sons* became "successes" would the elder Gavins ever spit in Mammon's fickle eye.

Stroking the Continental's plush seat, Ned smiled. That fickle deity had done okay by him. He was reaping not only its fortuitous bounty but also the love and approval of his parents for falling in the way of its largesse.

At twenty-four, Ned Gavin was the chief marketing executive for Zubrecht Products, Inc. This was a Denver-based firm specializing in various health-care items. It had been founded only nine years ago by his roommate's uncle, Everette Zubrecht, a connection that had allowed Ned to take a managerial position right out of business school. A promotion every six months had lifted him to his present eminence in the firm's hierarchy, and this catlike Lincoln bespoke the rapidity of his rise.

Luck may have arranged my first job with Zubrecht, Ned thought, but, once on the ladder, I made it to each higher rung by savvy and butt-busting work.

Chief marketing honcho at twenty-four! Usually, you made that kind of early mark on the corporate world only if the industry was a high-tech enterprise like bioengineering or computers. You went in with a head full of visions and the know-how to turn your dreams into marketable products. Ned, though, had come to Zubrecht with no revolutionary ideas—but his tenacity at work and the force of his personality had swept him past older men with more experience, and the ones who'd most resented his skyrocketing climb were no longer around to worry about it.

Bo, Ned told himself, is a lot like me. Except that, early on, he saw himself as an outlaw and our parents' way of life as a meat grinder of his hopes. So he rebelled and ran off.

However, from recent inquiries, Ned knew that his brother had been forging a notable career of his own. In fact, if Bo had not called him, Ned would have eventually telephoned Bo—for a woman named Carrie Plourde at Chattahoochee CommuniGrafix in Atlanta had told him over Zubrecht's Wats line about Libby Quarrels's rescue effort and Bo's return to Colorado, and Ned had long had the number of the ranch (which had once belonged to their first cousin Gary) on the Rolodex in his Denver office.

Absentmindedly, Ned extracted a cassette tape from the cabinet under the dash and clicked it into his player. It was a tape that he had put together himself, from a variety of old recordings, and the first song to come throbbing into the luxurious bell of his car was "Along the Sante Fe Trail" by the Glenn Miller orchestra, with a lovely vocal by Ray Eberle.

Appropriate, in a way. Stars were glittering tonight, and Ned was cruising past an old truckstop café (just off a side road west of the interstate), whose ruins suggested the tumbledown hideout of an outlaw gang.

In fact, as a tucktail teenager Bo had witnessed a holdup

and murder there, lying on his belly under a table. Ned recalled how his sixteen-year-old brother had told the story—Ned had been ten—and how the episode had seemed heroically Old Westish, as if Bo had wandered into Dodge City during a historic gunfight. But Bo had pooh-poohed that notion, insisting that all he could remember was being scared shitless and thinking over and over that the head-shot fry cook would never flip a burger again.

Eberle crooned, "I found you,/ And the mountains that surround you / Are the walls I built around you / Along the Sante Fe Trail," so sweetly that Ned sighed.

Today, a run on a moonlit ski trail was a far apter evocation of the West than that stupid slaying. Bo had been right—even back then—to scold him for finding romance in a sleezy little truckstop holdup. But wasn't that what Big Brother was for? To keep Little Brother . . . straight? To teach him the way of the world without creating either a Milquetoast or a Machiavelli?

Well, the time has come to repay Bo for his brotherliness, Ned thought. Maybe even to make up for the way I distanced myself from him during his time at Colorado Southern, when *I* could tell—even if our folks couldn't—that his true color was lavender and that he was merely pretending to be straight. Later, in Denver, I stood back because I didn't want the stigma of what he was evolving into to cut me off from our parents or to damage my career. But by then Bo was also busy distancing himself from *us* . . . so that he could pick up and depart for Dixie.

Fifteen minutes on, "I'm Beginning to See the Light" by Harry James and His Music Makers, with a Helen Forrest vocal, thrummed from the Lincoln's speakers. Ned was beginning to see the lights of Colorado City. By the time the final song on this tape started—"The Darktown Strutters' Ball" by the Benny Goodman orchestra—he'd be within hailing distance of Snowy Falls.

Ouray had not returned. Neither had the kar'tajans. Sam stood on the ledge fronting Naismith's Mine holding a big plastic-bodied flashlight. Then, pointing it into the shaft, he followed its beam along the ore-cart tracks toward the cul-de-sac where, last night, an alternative reality had exploded into view.

The way inward grew narrower and colder, just as it had on his earlier trip, but when Sam reached the rear wall, he was stymied by earth, rock, and shards of damp timber. The door to Elsewhere was closed. Sam knelt before it, his flashlight beam flickering over myriad embedded dice of feldspar, quartzite, granite.

"Crazy," he said, placing the palm of his free hand against the cold mountain. "I'm crazy."

Libby opened the front door, and there stood Bo's doppelgänger, although because he was so much healthier-looking than Bo, it was undoubtedly more reasonable to regard Bo as Ned's double than vice versa. Ned had nothing of the ghost about him; he was younger than her houseguest, stouter, and—if she could take this much from a quick perusal of his face—less given to melacholy. Of course, the fact that Ned had a high-paying job and Bo a life-threatening disease might have something to do with these contrasts.

"Hello, Elizabeth."

"I'm sorry about your father, Ned. Come in." Lib noticed that he wore a goatee, a blondish goatee. Otherwise, he was painfully cleancut, like an Air Force Academy cadet, and the glen-plaid suit he was sporting—which did nothing to slim him—had the nifty elegance of something from an *Esquire* ad.

But the goatee . . . well, it was the clincher. It proclaimed Ned's lofty self-opinion even more loudly than the suit. Did he mean it to give him either an exotic or a mysterious air? Too bad if he did. It made him resemble a callow Falstaff.

Bo stood up from the sofa and said, "Hey, Neddy. Nothing like a family tragedy to draw us all together again."

"There's been no tragedy yet, Bo. Dad's going to make it. His operation was fairly routine, as bypass surgery goes." Ned hovered just inside the closed door, appraising his prodigal brother, still uncertain of his welcome.

"Maybe Bo was referring to his AIDS," Libby said.

Ned colored. Ah. A man able to blush couldn't be as callously encased as a crocodile. Did the overdressed young Falstaff really care for Bo? Was there yet a chance that he would gather up his brother and cart him back to Pueblo or Denver? Ned *was* blood kin, wasn't he? No sense in Bo staying with her when he could go home with Ned and when Ned obviously had the wherewithal to take care of him. If this meeting led to a rapprochement.

"Maybe he was," Ned conceded. "But it wasn't tragedy—if an illness still being fought is a tragedy—that pulled me up here, Elizabeth. It was opportunity."

Bo said, "Opportunity doesn't pull, Neddy. It knocks."

"Come on, Bo. Don't start one of your—"

"Unless Opportunity's what you call your automobile. In which case you'd be the last person in the world to let it knock."

"—one of your damned trains of sarcastic puns."

"Actually, Opportunity's not a bad name for a train. Better than Bucephalus. Which is what I called my car until my ego was derailed—derailed by fate."

"Damn it, Bo."

Yeah, Libby thought, please. You guys will never reconcile if you stand here like a couple of swordsmen with drawn rapiers, each of you looking for an opening. And if you don't reconcile, I'll be stuck with Bo until . . . well, until the end.

Libby tucked her chin and bit her tongue. Shameful thoughts, but she couldn't help having them. Whatever Ned might represent to Bo—betrayal, selfish ego, rejection—to Libby he was a promise, although not a very hearty one, of liberation. This was the person who should care for Bo, freeing her to run her ranch without the added burden of caring for the doomed. Never mind that up until tonight Bo had pulled his own weight. Or that, but for a few bouts of nausea and fever, he rarely seemed indisposed.

"You want me to bear-hug you?" Bo said. "When you came up here to keep *me* from driving down?"

"That's only one of my motives," Ned said. "I've got three."

"All right. Let the other two shoes drop."

"Okay. First—I mean, second—a business proposition."

"Because you suppose me in the business of propositions?"

"Because I suppose the proposition I propose to propose will be of real interest. And therefore good for you."

My lord, thought Libby, they *both* do it.

"What kind of business proposition?"

"Patience, Beaumont. I'll tell you in good time."

"Patience is for the immortal. I don't qualify. In any event, release the third shoe."

Ned draped his handsome overcoat over one shoulder like a cape. Then he said, "Because you're my brother. Because you're my big brother, Bo, and I'm sorry you're ill."

The two men stood staring at each other. Libby fully expected Bo to mount a sardonic reply, but instead he walked to his brother, nudged aside his bulky overcoat, and embraced him with an intensity of feeling that charged the dry air. Ned returned this bear hug, the bear hug that Bo had just hinted he had no right to expect, and Libby stepped back, abashed by their show of emotion.

I don't belong here, she thought. This is *their* reconciliation. I should leave them to it. And so she excused herself and spent most of the remainder of Ned's visit sitting at her rolltop doing a neighbor's taxes.

For the next hour, all Libby could hear from the front room was conspiratorial whispering or raucous yucks. Then Bo knocked, poked his head in, and invited her to come out and hear Ned play his sax, which he had brought in his Lincoln's trunk. Band had been a major interest of his in high school, and, not long ago, he'd bought this expensive tenor sax to blow when he was listening to Ellington or Dorsey and found himself inspired.

Warily, Libby emerged from the bedroom to find Ned, elbows out and feet apart, ready to play. Standing beside the steamer trunk, peeled down to a crinkly linen shirt and a tie with spiral galaxies whirling across it, he looked legendary, a colossus. Bo gave him a get-it-on gesture, and Ned squeaked out a poor imitation of the sax solo in "Relaxin' at the Touro."

"Great," Bo said. "The house is really . . . semi-rocking."

"*Swinging*. Semi-*swinging*. Rock's a mere upstart."

"So are you. Except you really haven't started up."

"Listen, I do better if I play with a recording—the radio, a tape, something to give me direction."

How about directions home? Libby thought, but surprised herself by saying, "Try Little Ben again, Bo. Last night, that Swing Era station gave us Cab Calloway doing 'Hi De Ho Man.'"

"All it's been getting today, m'lady, is the regular mix."

"Yeah, but it's almost the witching hour. Try it."

Bo turned on the set. The Pueblo channel they usually got was a porridge of static, but a few more clicks of the knob brought in—fuzzily—the crazy channel on which the bands of Miller, Muggsy Spanier, and Duke Ellington had played. Tonight, Louis Jordan and His Tympany Five—dressed like an engineer, a conductor, and three porters—were camping up "Choo Choo Ch'Boogie."

Ned jumped into the sax part between choruses and blew until his forehead was beaded with sweat and his cheeks were puffed out like bullfrog goiters.

Bo played drums on the steamer trunk with a pair of pencils. Lib joined in with a jury-rigged kazoo.

But when the number ended, the Tympany Five faded from view and the Swing Era channel did likewise, as if it had aired merely to give Ned Gavin a chance to show off the one aesthetic talent that his marketing skills hadn't totally eroded. Bo kept flipping the knob, but Little Ben had shut down for the night—its screen was as slick and gray as if smeared with Vaseline.

Ned said her Bendix must have just picked up—by the magic of synchronicity—a PBS broadcast of some rare 1940s film footage. To discourage further conjecture, Libby agreed with him. No reason to let his visit mutate into *An Inquiry into the Strange Occurrences at the Tipsy Q Ranch*.

Thus stymied, Ned finally bid them adieu.

Bo, Libby saw, was not ready to see him go, as if meeting with his brother had resoldered a contact that this goodbye was severing again. But shortly after Ned's Lincoln had floated away, Bo's mood turned around. His pupils grew as big as a marlin's eyes. Giggles spilled from him as if he had just taken a snootful of helium. He hugged Libby (who couldn't believe that Ned hadn't offered to carry Bo back to Denver with him) and began to laugh.

Libby let Bo fall to the sofa with the boneless grace of a scarecrow. He kept laughing. The tears on his cheeks were little globes magnifying, and distorting, all the furnishings in her front room. His laughter abraded her eardrums, discouraging talk.

"What the hell is it, Gavin?"

"I still have family," he said. "I still have family!"

# 15

In the Sun Dance lodge, she found that she was one of sixteen ghostly dancers and the only female.

Was this the second or the third day? Or the fourth of one of those controversial four-day dances decreed by Alvin Powers in the late 1970s? No. She'd been a mere child then, and the year after Powers's heart attack sun-dancing with the Wind River Shoshones in Wyoming, DeWayne Sky had had a vision calling on the Southern Utes to go back to their traditional three-day ceremony.

But the young woman felt sure it wasn't the first day, for on the first day the center pole—the conduit of power from the Holy He-She—supported no buffalo head. Although the sun coming into the Thirst House struck so that she could not really focus on the totem lashed just beneath the crotch of the sacred cottonwood, she could see that *something* was there.

On the second day of the event, the tribal Sun Dance committee had tied it in place—an animal head now so halo-furred that she could give it no clear outline. She was praying to it, as well as to the Holy He-She, to channel water down the Tree of Life into her orphaned body so that she could do miracles. The miracles that she most wanted to do was the restoration of the health and dignity of her tribe. And of herself, too.

Which day is this? she wondered again. How much longer must I dance with these men?

In the path to the center pole next to her own path strutted Larry Cuthair. This was strange. Larry was between his junior and senior years of high school, a grade behind her.

It defied all logic that the Great Spirit had chosen Larry—in too many ways a quasi-Anglicized young man—to dance now. In fact, she would have bet that Larry was a decade or two away from such an honor, if he were going to attain it at all, and yet here he was dancing up to the Tree of Life and falling back from it in the path next to hers. She could smell not only his boyish sweat but also the chalky odor of the white paint smeared all over his belly and chest, his face, neck, and arms. The ceremonial skirt he wore, his beaded waistband, and the eagle feathers he clutched all gleamed white, too—in eerie contrast to the multicolored garb of the dancers at every other Sun Dance she'd attended.

This, too, was peculiar.

But then, looking around the dance floor of the Thirst House, she saw that all the other dancers—DeWayne Sky, Brevard Mestes, Timothy Willow, all of them—had powdered themselves in the same alarming way. Their skirts, ivory. Their waistbands, like bone. Their bare feet, chalk-dusted and ghostly.

The impression she had was of a room in an insane asylum for spendthrift bakers, men compelled to throw handfuls of flour into the air and then frolic solemnly in the fallout. But, of course, when she looked, she saw that she (though a woman, and the sort of woman who would pester a Sun Dance chief to admit her to a ceremony once exclusively male) had followed their example. Her own body paint was white. So were her doeskin dress, her sequined apron, her eagle-bone whistle, and every bead on every necklace and bracelet adorning her person. She had joined the crazy bakers in their floury celebration, and this Sun Dance would fail because its purpose was not just to acquire power but to appease the Old Ones already dead—to guide their spirits to rest in the ghost lands beyond the mountains. Its purpose certainly wasn't to mock the Old Ones by pretending to be an *ini'putc'* oneself.

"Why are we dressed like ghosts?" she cried.

Her cry went unanswered. The noise of the men drumming in the corral's arbor, the guttural chanting of the men and women around the drummers, and the shuffling and shouts of encouragement from the spectators opposite the singers—all these noises kept her from being heard. But maybe that was good. She knew that to talk too much while dancing was considered folly. It cut one off from the trance state triggered by the heat, the drumming, the chanting, the pistoning of legs, the prayerful flailing of arms.

And, she knew, it was this trance state that gave one access to God's Spine, the Tree of Life, the Sacred Rood at the heart of the lodge. For only through the center pole and the totems tied to it could one take the power that every dancer coveted for the sake of the entire Sun Dance community.

Maybe it was good that no one had heard her shout. Many of her neighbors already resented DeWayne Sky for letting her—a woman only recently out of high school—dance with the men. They would take great pleasure in telling everyone that she had been guilty of sacrilege, or at least of imperfect seriousness, while dancing, and that her behavior in the corral not only disgraced her and her dead mother, Dolores Arriola, but also destroyed the value of the dance for every Southern Ute. That was the more dreadful result, for all her tribespeople would ostracize her.

But so what? she thought. Ever since Mama D'lo shot herself, I've lived without their help. I don't need them and I don't want their approval. I want the Utes to be strong—to be better than they are—but if they turn their backs on me, so what? It's only what *I've* been doing to *them* since the night Mama spray-painted our walls with her brains. So I'm dancing today—my second day? my third? my fourth?—as a kind of apology for appearing not to wish them well. I *do* wish them well. I just don't want them to smother me with their fretful love.

Again, she shouted, "Why have we all made ourselves look like *ini'putc'*?"

But the shrill piping of eagle-bone whistles and the constant thunder of drums kept everyone from hearing her. Except, she soon learned, Larry Cuthair, who strutted up and rebuked her. Did she want to screw up everything? he growled. The Old Ones would think her questions out of place, disrespectful.

"The way we look is out of place!" she countered, dancing at Larry's side. "The way we look is disrespectful!"

Larry regarded her with something like incredulity. "DeWayne Sky told us to dress and paint ourselves like this—to pretend to be our own ancestors."

"We should honor them, Larry, not mock them!"

"But he only instructed us as he did because *your* dreams—the ones you had in the spring—showed us dancing this way. It's all your doing, Paisley."

"Horseshit," said Paisley Coldpony. She danced away from the center pole, angry at Larry for feeding her such garbage.

All her doing? How?

Yes, the Shoshones at Fort Hall sometimes used white body paint at their Sun Dances, one of which she had attended with D'lo three years ago, but it was idiotic to say that she had influenced Sky to tell every Southern Ute dancer to wear white dress and body paint because of *her* dreams. What dreams? And why would their Sun Dance chief go along with such a major change solely on her say-so? Some people believed that three or four dancers every year lied about their dream calls, saying they had had one when they really hadn't, and would-be dancers who went to Sky with a vision requiring novel alterations in the ceremony got looked at askance.

Besides, Paisley told herself, I *had* no dream like that. I had no such dream at all. But if not, what was she doing dancing with these men? They owed their tribe three days without food or water—solely in the hope of gaining the Great Manitou's curing powers, the repose of the dead, and their neighbors' respect. You couldn't dance without being dream-called, but Paisley had no memory of her summons. What was happening here?

Defiantly, she cried, "Why are we mocking our dead?"

An old man on the north side of the lodge shook a willow wand at her. Although Paisley had never known him to dance, he regarded himself as an expert on the ritual. The whites in Ignacio knew him as Herbert Barnes, the Utes as Whirling Goat. He had a face like a dry arroyo bottom and a voice like a sick magpie's.

"Do it right!" he taunted her. "Do it right or get out!"

Dancing toward the Tree of Life, half blinded by the sunlight pouring through its fork, Paisley shrieked her whistle at Whirling Goat, then gestured rudely at him. Another broken rule—but the old sot had provoked her.

"You don't know how!" he called. "You don't belong!"

"Stuff it, goat face," Larry Cuthair said, swerving out of his path toward the spectator section. Barnes retreated a step or two, pushing other onlookers aside, but halted when farther back in the crowd. From there, he croaked again for Paisley's removal—she was fouling the ceremony, turning good medicine to bad.

At that point, the gatekeeper and the lodge policeman decided that Barnes was the one "fouling the ceremony" and unceremoniously removed him. Many onlookers applauded.

"Forget him," Larry whispered when next they were shoulder to shoulder on their dance paths. "He's a woman hater."

Whirling Goat confirmed this judgment by breaking free of his escorts at the western door, stumbling back into the Thirst House, and yelling at her, "You foul the dance! You pollute the lodge!" He held his nose in a gesture implying that, against all law and tradition, she had entered the corral while in her cycle.

Many people jeered, but now Paisley couldn't tell if they were jeering Barnes or her. What hurt most was that she was clean, as her people still insisted on defining a woman's cleanliness. And Whirling Goat, a famous tosspot often as fragrant as a distillery, could not've smelled even Larry's sister Melanie Doe's overpowering styling mousse without having a ball of it stuck directly under his nose. In any case, the gatekeeper and the lodge policeman dragged him outside again.

Much aggrieved, Paisley told Larry, "He was lying."

"I know," Larry said. He smiled to show that he didn't mean to denigrate her entire gender, but the smugness of the remark ticked her off as much as had Whirling Goat's old-fashioned bigotry. She moved away from Larry, toward the backbone of the lodge. She tried to make the furry totem on the center pole resolve out of the sun's glare into a recognizable buffalo head.

Meanwhile, it amazed her to see that one dancer, Tim Willow, was wearing reflective sunglasses. His face appeared to consist of two miniature novas and a grimace. Surely, it couldn't be fair to sun-dance thus disguised, thus protected. Or could it?

Hours passed. Paisley's thirst increased. Her throat felt the way Barnes's face looked—parched. That was to be expected; it was a goal of the dance to empty oneself of moisture so that the purer water of Sinawef, the Creator, could flow down the cottonwood into the lodge and finally into one's dried-out body. Thirst was natural, a door to power.

What was *not* natural, Paisley reflected, was the sun's refusal to climb the Colorado sky. It continued to hang where it had hung all morning, forty-five degrees over the eastern horizon, so that its fish-eyed disk blazed down at a slant obscuring the bison-head totem in the Tree of Life. And without eye contact, how could she or anyone else receive the sun power mediated by Buffalo?

It's because we've made ourselves look like *ini'putc'*, Paisley decided. We're frightening the sun. It's afraid to move.

In spite of the sun's motionless fear, time passed. You could tell by watching the spectator section of the lodge. People kept coming in and going out, a turnover that would have distracted her if she hadn't been concentrating on her dancing. But, of course, she *couldn't* concentrate on it—her worry about the whiteness of the dancers and the stuckness of the sun prevented her.

Sidelong, though, she was able to make out the faces of some of the spectators. Two of the people were whites. Although her tribe had a public relations director in Ignacio and publicly encouraged tourism, many Southern Utes had little truck with white visitors at the annual Sun Dance.

Paisley's mother had told her stories about white cultists in the 1960s, drug freaks with more interest in peyotism than the Sun Dance. They had disrupted the event by speaking gibberish at the center pole or by dancing to the point of collapse on the first day. On the first day, no Ute would presume to charge the sacred cottonwood, seize it, and fall down in the grip of "vision." But the Bizarros—the cultists' own name for themselves—had done such things and worse, thereby defiling the ceremony.

One of this morning's white spectators looked like a refugee from the 1960s. She wore blue jeans, a T-shirt with Bob Dylan's frizzy head undulating across her breasts, and a leather hat with a peace-symbol button on the brim. She was pretty, sort of, but Payz could tell that she was at least twenty years older than she was—two decades, an entire generation. How did that happen to people? Old Indians, even a sot like Whirling Goat, seemed to have been born old, but old whites—even middle-aged ones—often seemed to have decayed into that state.

Next to the woman stood a man. He was too young, surely, to be her husband and too old, Paisley felt, to be her son and too unlike her in appearance, she concluded, to be her brother. What did that leave? Friend? Colleague? Stranger? Whatever the relationship, he was thin—starvation-thin.

He made her think of what an Anglo male with anorexia nervosa would look like if Anglo males were ever to buy into the grotesque lie that they could be attractive only if their bodies resembled those of famine victims. His eyes, which seemed too big for his head, were sunken in their sockets. Still, he had the kind of face that whites considered handsome—if only it had been less drawn, less pale.

In any case, he wasn't a hippie. His blondish hair was short, brushed back from his temples and forehead in a way that looked nostalgically hip. And he was wearing a long-sleeved jersey—much too hot for July—with the legend *Coca-Cola* right across its chest.

His female companion lifted her arms, and Paisley saw that she was holding a camera—one of those kind that pop the negative out and develop it right in front of you.

Paisley nearly stopped dancing. Cameras weren't allowed in the Thirst House. People who brought them in were expelled and told not to come back. True, the Shoshones at Fort Hall and Wind River allowed cameras and recording equipment, but the Utes never had, and Paisley couldn't imagine a time when they would. Such things were products of Anglo technology. Although not bad in themselves, they had no place in the sacred corral.

A flash bulb flashed, but the flash was obscured by the sun's pinwheeling brilliance. Paisley thought she heard the camera eject the developing print, but, given the din, that wasn't likely. She saw the print, though. The woman in the floppy leather hat passed it to her pale companion, lifted her camera again, and triggered a second flash.

She's taking my picture, Paisley thought, half panicked. But why? I'm nothing to her, and, besides, it isn't allowed.

Now the emaciated man was holding two prints for his companion, and she was taking a third photo. Her flash exploded impotently in the sunlight.

Someone noted the flash, though. DeWayne Sky, five dancers to Paisley's right, stopped strutting and waved his arms over his head like a man trying to halt traffic on a busy street.

It took a moment, but the Ute men at the drum, seeing their Sun Dance chief's gesture, lifted their sticks. Immediately, all the singers stopped singing.

For the first time since the ordeal had begun—whenever that may have been—Paisley could hear other noises from the camping areas and shade houses around the lodge: bread frying in skillets, children skylarking, adults playing the hand-and-stick game.

"Seize her," the ghostly-looking Sky commanded the gatekeeper and the lodge policeman.

Some of the Ute onlookers near the woman grabbed her arms as if she might try to run, but she stood like a stone. "I'm sorry," she said, embarrassed by the abrupt halting of the dance. "Have I done something wrong?"

No one spoke. An Indian man, a visiting Jicarilla Apache, took her camera from her and passed it to another man and so on all the way out of the lodge as if, Paisley thought, it were a bomb.

"Hey!" the skinny Anglo said, but the Apache who had seized the camera silenced him with a scowl.

"Not allowed," Sky said to everyone and no one. Then the woman was in the custody of the gatekeeper and the policeman, who began strong-arming her toward the Thirst House door.

Her male friend, although no one touched him or ordered his eviction, started to follow, but the woman said, "I'm the one who's broken the rules, Bo. You don't have to come with me."

"Not allowed," Sky repeated loudly. He padded across the dusty lodge to look at the man. He pointed his eagle-feather wand. "You can't stay either," he said.

Why? Paisley wondered, suddenly sympathetic to the visitors. I know that cameras aren't permitted, but what has the poor skinny man done, Chief Sky? Do you deem him guilty because he's here with the woman?

And then she realized that the man—"Bo"—was still

holding the developing prints. Ah, of course. It would be a sacrilege to let him depart with them.

Larry Cuthair ambled to the rail of the spectator section and thrust out his hand for the squares of solution-glazed cardboard. The skinny man surrendered them to Larry as if they meant nothing to him. Maybe they didn't.

"Now he can stay, can't he?" Paisley said. These words escaped her altogether unexpectedly. She was as embarrassed by them as she would have been if Whirling Goat had been right about her dancing during her period. Every pair of eyes in the Thirst House turned toward her.

"No, he may not," DeWayne Sky said imperiously. "He too has trespassed against the Holy He-She—he too."

"How?" Paisley challenged him.

"It's all right," the white man said. "I'll go with Lib. Just let me by."

No one moved—not the powder-white dancers, not the drummers and singers, not the onlookers. The gatekeeper and the policeman stood motionless at the gate, holding the woman who had brought the dance to a halt by taking photographs. Meanwhile, the stalled sun shone down on this tableau like a huge static flash.

"He's come here for a reason!" Paisley shouted. "He's come to us for healing!"

How do I know that? she wondered. Nevertheless, she did. She had simply intuited that this skinny Anglo had presented himself at the Sun Dance in humility and hope. He was a white, granted, but he was also a sincere candidate for shamanization at the hands of Sky or one of the other newly empowered dancers. So this must be the *last* day of the three-day ceremony. He had come on the third day to keep from having to endure the whole ordeal, an ordeal for which he lacked the strength; meanwhile, the woman, his friend, had accompanied him to provide moral support. It was just too bad that her curiosity—not malice or greed—had led her to carry in the prohibited camera.

"His reasons mean nothing," Sky said. "His crime is bringing moisture into the Thirst House."

"Moisture?" Paisley said. "His hands are empty."

"There," said Sky, pointing the tip of his eagle feather at the man's shirt. "Right there."

Paisley gaped. Sky meant the advertising legend on the young man's jersey—that inescapable soft drink. Even the name of the product, because the product was a beverage, was forbidden in the Thirst House. Paisley recalled that once she had seen a fellow Ute expelled because he was wearing a T-shirt advertising a well-known beer. On that occasion, though, the expulsion had seemed okay, for the man had known better. Later, wearing an unmarked shirt, he had returned to a fanfare of catcalls. But this man was a visitor, and his embarrassment would keep him from coming back.

"That's stupid," she said. "Anyone with spit in their mouths would have to leave."

"It's okay," the Anglo said. "I'm going."

DeWayne Sky glared at Paisley. "Spit is a part of who we are. *That*"—gesturing at the brand name on his jersey—"is not part of our bodies. It is *no* part of who we are."

You forget, Paisley mused, that there are soft-drink machines at the Ute Pino Nuche restaurant and motel in Ignacio. And you forget that right here on our campgrounds, there are motor homes with refrigerators full of canned drinks.

"What are you sick with?" Paisley asked Bo.

He hesitated a moment before saying, but when he said, everyone looked at him with new eyes—fear-filled eyes. People moved away from him, parting like that sea in the Bible.

"You can't catch it just by standing next to him," the woman in the floppy hat said. "That's not the way it works."

"Take him out," Sky commanded.

Neither the gatekeeper nor the lodge policeman moved.

"I can take myself out," the Anglo said. "Too bad, though—I've been kicked out of places a lot less interesting."

He walked the gauntlet of appalled and fascinated Indians. But as soon as he and the woman had left the Thirst House, ranks closed again. Sky waved for the drummers and singers to resume. Paisley watched the other dancers, including a subdued Larry Cuthair, begin to strut back and forth in their well-trampled paths to the center pole. So she began to jog-dance again, too. The sun still hadn't made any progress in its noonward ascent, and its fiery disk still blurred the animal head tied to the pole.

After a while, Larry strutted up beside Paisley and handed

her two developed prints from the white woman's camera. Paisley held them at arm's length, squinting at them as she danced. The images on the slick squares would not resolve any better than would the totem on the center pole. But a fearful uneasiness welled in her—not because the skinny man had a fatal disease but because Sky had not let him stay. It seemed to her that even though Bo was white, and whites had done little for her people but lash them more tightly to the follies of the past forty years, he owed it to *this* white man to try to heal him.

To Larry's surprise and dismay, Paisley tore up the photographs he had given her. The pieces fluttered to the floor of the Thirst House, where they were quickly ground into the dust by rhythmically shuffling feet.

After that, Paisley lost all consciousness of onlookers—they faded totally from sight. She was a spirit, a powder-white spirit, dancing with other such spirits, and she had the disturbing feeling that she was seeing the event not through her own eyes but, instead, through those of the emaciated, dying Anglo.

At last, the sun began to climb. As it did, Paisley, knowing herself on the brink of vision, approached the Tree of Life with more vigor. The other dancers recognized how close she was, and Tim Willow began to compete with her strutting, flailing his arms, making his mirrored lenses pinwheel dizzyingly.

Paisley ignored him. She was dancing faster, driving harder at the pole, urging herself to attack and touch. Only if she *touched* the sacred tree would the waters of the Holy Manitou flow into her, empowering her in ways that might one day benefit them all.

For her final run, she retreated to the backbone of the Thirst House. She lifted her eyes to the glittering eyes of the totem on the center pole. The sun had ceased to blind her, and what she saw hanging where a buffalo head should hang was not Buffalo but . . . something else. Paisley refused to flee. She screamed—not like a frightened woman, but like a warrior—then rushed the pole with such uncompromising fury that all the other ghostly dancers stopped to watch, shrilling their eagle bones.

"Mother!" she cried. "Mother!"

God's Spine staggered her with a jolt of power. She collapsed at its base.

The vacuum left in heaven by this discharge of power sucked her spirit up after it. High above Ignacio, Colorado, she eventually regained consciousness. Her cold body, however, lay far below, a small white effigy in the Thirst House.

How strange, she mused, seeing herself and being seen, dreaming herself and being dreamt.

# 16

Paisley could sense someone kneeling over her cold body, a hand on her brow. It seemed to be the skinny Anglo whom Sky had run out of the Thirst House for wearing a Coca-Cola shirt, just as he had banished that hippie woman for taking pictures.

But when Paisley opened her eyes, reflexively grabbing at this ghost, she found that she was lying on her pallet in her house five miles outside of Ignacio. It wasn't early July, the week of the Sun Dance, but April, and her wood-frame house was cold, just as it had been every night since her mother's suicide.

You've dreamed again, the young woman told herself. Your dream is a call. No one will want you to dance, least of all an old fart like Whirling Goat, and only a bit more a stiff traditionalist like DeWayne Sky, but you've got to face down their opposition. Mama D'lo's an Old One now—it's she who's calling you to dance.

Paisley didn't know the hour, only that it was the middle of a cold weekday night, near Easter. She had school tomorrow, but she couldn't wait until tomorrow to settle this matter. In the empty house, a shell of walls and doors, she dressed as warmly as she could and set off toward Ignacio. The nearby houses of the Willows and the Cuthairs, as ramshackle as chicken coops, brooded by the roadway in the windy dark.

As she walked, carrying her schoolbooks so that she would not have to return for them, she pulled her poncho tight and thought about her dream. This was the seventh time she'd had it, or a variation of it, since her mother's suicide. She couldn't ignore the fact that the Old Ones—or, at least, the Old One that D'lo had become—wanted her to dance this July.

That troubled her, for she had planned to leave the reservation the day after her high-school graduation to search for her father. A delay of a month—fourteen years after her parents' divorce—ought not to weigh so heavily on her, but just waiting until the end of school was proving harder than she'd thought. Another month or so would seem an eternity.

Coming into the commercial section of town owned by Anglo and Chicano business people, she strolled along Main Street past the drugstore, a café, the laundromat. The sidewalk was mostly dark and deserted, but as she neared the dim foyer of a bar, two boys—young men, if she wanted to be generous—fell out of the place, staggered toward her grinning, and spread their arms to make it hard for her to get around them without stepping into the street. She knew them as former classmates, moderately well-heeled dropouts with damn little to do.

"Hey, Payz, how 'bout taking a ride with Howell and me?"

"How 'bout *givin'* us a little ride?"

The dreariness of the confrontation, the stupidness of it, made Paisley's dander rise, but she replied only, "Let me by."

"No, missy. Can't do that," Howell said.

"You know us," Frank said. "We're not exactly strangers."

"You're too drunk to drive or ride, either one, Frank."

Frank cursed her roundly, but without viciousness, surprising her by staggering past as if she weren't worth another minute of their valuable time. Tall and burly, he was supporting the gangly, lean Howell in a way that reminded her of a bear trying to push a potted sapling along.

Grateful for their short attention spans, Paisley strolled on toward Pine River, the Pino Nuche motel-restaurant, and the diffuse Ute enclave north of town where DeWayne Sky lived.

But, a moment later, some sort of pointy-nosed sports car with flames pin-striped on its flanks pulled up beside her, Frank at the wheel. Howell, meanwhile, was lolling in the shotgun seat like a mannequin stolen from a tall-and-thin men's shop. Frank paced her up Main Street at ten miles per hour, his head half out the window and his mouth slurring a variety of one- or two-syllable activities that he seemed to think she would enjoy sharing with him.

Paisley wasn't amused. She had business in Ignacio. And she was tired of hearing Anglos throw around words like *papoose*, *squaw*, and *wampum* as if they were something other than clichés or insults, especially the way Frank was deploying them. She told him to fuck off and declined to speak to him again. At the next cross street, though, Frank blew his horn, turned directly across her path, and dialed up the volume of a song on his tape player whose lyrics were nothing but orgasmic grunts. The pulsing bass of this song put the empty street a-tremble. Even the besotted Howell came around long enough to open his mouth and pop his eardrums.

"Get out of my way!" Paisley shouted. "Move it!"

Frank replied with an elaborate pantomine involving his fingers and tongue. All she could think to do to show her outrage and contempt was to grab up an official city trash container at the end of the sidewalk and hurl it with her all might at Frank's car. It was a feat that, even as she performed it, astonished her—mostly because the four-sided receptacle, featuring a detachable metal top with a swinging door, had not been emptied recently and weighed at least fifty pounds. When it hit the car, it clattered, rebounded, and scattered debris, some of which spilled through Frank's window along with the dormered lid.

Frank shouted, Howell woke up again, and Paisley recovered the main body of the trash container for another assault. This time, though, she carried it, dripping vile liquids and moist pasteboard, to the front of Frank's car, where she wielded it after the fashion of a battering ram, repeatedly slamming one corner into the nearest headlamp. It took three whacks to shatter the glass, by which time Frank had managed to jettison the trach-can lid. Now he tried to halt her vandalisms by running her down. Paisley skipped aside, one-handedly bashing the container into his car again and knocking his rearview mirror off its mount.

A siren began to keen, and they all looked around to see Deputy Marchal Blake Seals come barreling into the intersection in one of Ignacio's two patrol cars.

* * *

Seals introduced her into the middle cell of five in the block at the rear of the marshal's office, and she was relieved to find that none of the others held prisoners. The drunk tank at the end of the damp hall looked exactly like a cave or the entrance to a mine shaft—a concrete grotto. For a time, Seals stood outside her cell, his pockmarked face like a big albino strawberry and his thumbs hooked in the pockets of his windbreaker so that it bellied out in front like a sail. He wasn't a cruel Anglo, just a pompous and partisan one.

"Sorry there's nobody in tonight for you to talk to."

"Couldn't you find any other Indians to arrest?"

"You were making a public disturbance, Miss Coldpony."

"I was the *victim* of a public disturbance. Those turkeys were drunk. Frank tried to run over me."

"The kid was just trying to depart the scene before you turned his Trans Am into scrap metal."

It was a temptation to renew their street argument, but they'd hashed out the details three dozen times already, in the middle of Ignacio, and Seals had sent the "kids"—friends of his—home to bed, promising Frank that the "perpetrator" would spend the rest of this chilly night "incarcerated."

Well, here she was, incarcerated. She would have cursed Seals for the fact that the jail stank of disinfectant if not for the linked fact that it would've reeked of something far less bearable if he hadn't earlier bothered to "sanitize" everything. That was one of the questionable bonuses of being deputy in Ignacio—you also got to be custodian.

"Sorry there's only that"—gesturing at the urinal—"if your bladder gets heavy. We don't have many female guests."

"Leave me alone, Deputy."

"I could bring you a bucket."

"Stick your head in it."

He grinned, mysteriously delighted by her retort. "Put my foot in that one, didn't I?" He returned to the office.

Paisley sat down on her grungy mattress, which lay askew on what looked like a pig-iron frame. She wouldn't be in for long, though. Her one phone call had gone to DeWayne Sky, who, although hardly overjoyed to be roused at four in the morning, had told her to hang on, he would vouch for her, put up her bail, or whatever was necessary. She was welcome to stay the rest of the night with LannaSue and him.

In the drunk tank down the hall, somebody or something coughed, a painfully congested hacking.

"Deputy," Paisley called, "I'm not alone back here."

"That's only Barnes," Seals shouted from the office. "I forgot about him."

Barnes. Herbert Barnes. Whirling Goat. Seals had shoved him into the cave and forgotten about him. The old man careened out of its bleak dampness, slumped against the bars with his arms hanging through. He was wall-eyed with cheap liquor or bread-filtered hair tonic, and his white hair tufted out from his temples in a way that made him resemble a great horned owl. Usually, reservation police took care of him, but tonight—last night—he had fallen to the efficient ministrations of Blake Seals.

"Hello, Alma." He sounded more weary than drunk. Maybe a nap had rubbed the nap off the velvet of his nightly stupor.

"Paisley," Paisley said. "My name is Paisley."

"Your mother called you Alma," the drunk lessoned her. "'Soul' in Spanish."

"I know what it means. But my father named me Paisley, Paisley Coldpony, and that's the name on my birth certificate."

"You lived with your mother longer than your daddy. Your name is Alma Arriola." He pulled some string out of the pocket of his dirty suede coat and, with his hands outside the bars, began making cat's cradles with it. He was remarkably dexterous for so old and alcohol-steeped a brave. Paisley found her irritation with his comments about her name softened a little by the web-weaving of his stubby fingers.

"Jackrabbit," he said, rotating the string figure so that she could see this two-dimensional creature loping across the blackness of the drunk tank.

"Arriola's a Spanish name too," he added pedantically, hacking her off again. Then he dismantled the airy jackrabbit and began a second latticework figure.

"And Barnes is an Anglo name, Whirling Goat."

Paisley knew that some of her hostility to the old guy was left over from her dream. She resented what he'd said to her in it and was sorry to find him—dare she even think the word?—*polluting* the cell block. (If, given the disinfectant fumes stinging her eyes, further pollution were even possible.)

"And this is a goat," he said, holding up the second figure and whirling it for her benefit. "When I was eight, I rode a goat for three minutes that none of my friends could even catch. My name—it comes from that."

"Which one of your friends had the stopwatch, Herbert?"

But neither this sarcasm nor her rude familiarity would provoke him. He ceased to whirl the goat and handily collapsed it, only to follow with several successive string compositions, all of which he was magically weaving for his own amusement. His equanimity put her off. She wanted to puncture it.

"I'm going to dance in the Sun Dance," Paisley told him. "I've been dream-called."

"What do you think of this one?" he said, holding up a figure that initially made no sense to her. Standing at the bars of her cell, she peered at the crisscrossing strings with real annoyance. Her world-shaking declaration of intent had slipped past him like a coyote squeezing untouched through a hole in a henhouse.

"What is it?" she grudgingly asked.

He coughed, but his preoccupied hands were unable to cover his mouth. "Kar'tajan," he managed.

"What?" The word summoned no resonances for her.

"Kar'tajan," he repeated. "But only the head, Alma—only the head and the horn."

Now Paisley recognized it. It was the head—the head and the horn—of a unicorn. She could not imagine how he had produced it with a single piece of looped string, but he had, and the awkward way that he held his hands to sustain the figure was justified by its fragile elegance. She'd never known that Barnes, a.k.a. Whirling Goat, had such a talent—or *any* talent, for that matter, beyond making a year-round nuisance of himself and sourly kibitzing every performer at every important Ute ceremony. But, so soon after the seventh repetition of her dream, the sight of the string figure—*this* string figure—gave her a decided pang. For it, too, seemed part and parcel of her summons.

"Why do you call it a kar'tajan?"

"Because that's its name. That's the name our Holy He-She gave it—before history turned the world inside out."

"It's a unicorn, Whirling Goat. There's no such animal."

"It's a kar'tajan, Alma. I've seen one."

From the office, Seals shouted, "He saw it drinking over by the Pine with this humongous herd of pink elephants!"

The deputy's words, and then his guffaws, dismantled the mood of balanced wonder and unease that Paisley had been experiencing in much the way that Barne's hands collapsed the string figure of the kar'tajan or unicorn. He stuffed the looped string back into his coat pocket and slumped more heavily against the bars.

"Can you do a buffalo?" Paisley felt strangely tender toward him. She hoped he wouldn't relapse into the stupor that had probably occasioned his arrest.

"Ain't nothing I can't do with string."

"Do me a buffalo, then."

Barnes coughed, more or less negatively.

Damn you, Blake Seals, Paisley thought. And then, as unbidden as lightning from a high azure sky, a memory bolt illuminating the headless corpse of her mother struck her. She was seeing again the clay-colored feet on the lounger's footrest, the dropped .12-gauge, and the Jackson Pollock brain painting on the walls behind the old chair. She'd just come home from a debate with the kids at Cortez, a debate that her team had won, and there was Mama D'lo, waiting to share the victory with her, messily at ease in the lounger, forever free of motherly obligation. Although maybe not.

"I've been dream-called," Paisley said. Defiantly, she looked at Barnes. "To dance in the Sun Dance."

"Good. Good for you." He hacked into his forearm.

Paisley stared at him. "Didn't you hear me? I've been granted a vision. I'm to dance with the men."

"It's what your mama wants." Barnes shifted against the bars. "She told me. That being so, you should do it."

"Told you? Why would she tell *you*, old man? When?"

"Tonight. A little time past." He indicated the impenetrable blackness behind him. "Pretty funny talk we had."

Seals lumbered into the upper end of the cell block. "Every talk you have while you're swackered is funny, Barnes. Chats with old Chief Ignacio. Arguments with John Wayne. Even a midnight powwow with Jesus."

"Get your butt out of here, Deputy," Paisley said. "Who asked you to horn in?"

Smirking, Seals raised his big hands as if to ward off physical blows. "Simmer down. I'm going. Just forgot for a minute we was running a hotel here." He backed out, closing the cell-block door behind him.

"You saw her tonight, Mr. Barnes? *Tonight?*"

"Yes. In here. I was on that pissy mattress"—pointing his chin toward it, a shadow in the dark—"and D'lo showed up, maybe from the San Juan Mountains. She stood over me, signing."

"Signing?"

"You know, hand talk."

"But why? To keep Seals from hearing?"

"That didn't matter. He was patrolling." Barnes hunched his shoulders. "Alma, that was her only way to talk. You see?"

Paisley understood. She had seen her mother's *ini'putc'* in the Cuthairs' station wagon on the day of her funeral, and the revenant, like the corpse, had had no head. But then the ghost had vanished, leaving Paisley to doubt what she had witnessed.

"What did she say? What did her hand talk mean?"

"Just what you say, Alma. That you must dance this year. That she desires it. That no one should hinder you, girl or no girl."

"It's not 'girl,' Mr. Barnes. It's 'woman.'" She told him as a matter of information, not to scold—for she was ready to forgive the old fart for his bad behavior in her dream.

A moment later, Paisley said, "But why did she visit *you*? Why did she come here to give you that message?"

"I have a reputation," Whirling Goat said proudly.

As a sot, Paisley silently chastised him, but she knew that he meant as an expert on certain ceremonial matters and so refrained from disillusioning him. Let Barnes claim for himself the dubious glory of an *ini'putc'* visitation.

"Also," he said, "Delores must have foreknown."

"Foreknown what?"

"That you'd be arrested tonight. That it would be good for me to give you my blessing."

"I have your blessing?"

"Of course. I gave it to you already. How many children do I show my string creatures?" He hacked again, magpie croaks.

"Not many," Paisley hazarded.

"Damned straight. Now, though, you're among with them."

Talk lapsed. Paisley wondered if her run-in with Frank Winston and Howell Payne had been providential. Yes, it probably had. But she had no time to mull the matter further, for Blake Seals entered the cell block again, this time leading a haggard-appearing DeWayne Sky and announcing loudly that she was "free to go." Her esteemed tribal councilman was vouching for her character.

"What about Mr. Barnes?" Paisley said.

"What about him?" Seals echoed her.

"He's slept it off. He isn't drunk any longer. You should let him out too."

"It's an hour or two till dawn," Seals protested. "He can get a snootful in five minutes, a sloshing bellyful in ten."

"Let Mr. Barnes out too," DeWayne Sky said. He was wearing khaki trousers with a turquoise belt buckle so large it made Paisley think of a chunk of the Colorado firmament for which the councilman's family seemed to've been named.

Not liking it much, Seals released the old drunk along with the unrepentant Trans Am basher. In the jail's front office, he called them over to a metal desk to reclaim their belongings. All Paisley had was her school-books, but Barnes had a small clutch of items—his wallet, his house key, a few salted peanuts, and some sort of foil-wrapped coin that Sky picked up and turned in the glare of the light bulb as if it were an extraordinary find.

"What the hell are you doing with this, Barnes?"

"He's a Boy Scout," Seals said. "His motto is 'Be Prepared.'"

Sky threw the coin back down on the desk. "Hell, man, you're eighty-something. And nine tenths of the time you're so stinking drunk, your carrot's got to have chronic droop anyway."

A rubber? Paisley speculated. Is Barnes, our oldest bachelor, actually carrying a rubber around with him?

"There's the other one tenth," the old man said, neither shamed nor amused by Sky's attack. He stuffed the battered coin into his pocket along with his other pocket fillers and moved to the door as vigorously as he paraded around the campgrounds at the Bear Dance in May and the Sun Dance in

July. Those were two weeks out of the year—maybe the only two—that he scrupulously laid off wine, beer, whiskey, hair tonic, everything but the old bucks responsible for organizing and running the dances. Paisley was proud of him for getting through the door upright, his dignity intact and that silly antique rubber in his pocket.

"What do you want to do?" DeWayne Sky asked her. "Stand here till Marshal Breault comes on duty?"

She didn't, so they left.

# 17

The Skys lived in a wood-frame house that, several years ago, they had remodeled in an unusual way. Around it, entirely around it, Sky had had built a conical frame whose summit rose better than forty five feet above the original roof. Sky's workmen had stuccoed the frame, windowing it at various places with huge rectangular sheets of Plexiglas to let in the sun. At night, spotlights lit the cone so that you could see it from several blocks away, a garish white tepee rising among the scattered tract houses like an advertisement for a Wild West amusement park.

The cone's huge stucco flap opened to the east, as prescribed for tepees by sacred tradition, but the door to the house inside the frame faced south. Thus, Paisley and her rescuer—once he'd parked his Ford Bronco in the driveway—had to walk an enclosed track between the house and the inside tepee wall to reach the *real* entrance to his living quarters.

Paisley felt decidedly weird following DeWayne Sky around this bizarre corridor, but she remembered that he had erected the fake tepee not just to pretend that he was still living in one, as most whites mockingly accused, but to avail himself of the power to call spirits that round houses—and only round houses—could impart to those living in them. A house with corners, a house with none of the circularity of earth and sky about it, preached DeWayne Sky, cut one off from the spirits and thus robbed one of power.

Although Paisley feared that merely masking a boxy house with a big stucco tepee was not the best way of persuading the gods that you were back in touch with both the earth and the Old Ones, she knew that in the years since erecting his cone, DeWayne Sky's power and influence among the Southern Utes had grown enormously. He'd spent a lot of money on his "folly," but he'd got all of that back, and a great deal more, representing his people at Indian caucuses around the country, presiding as the grand marshal in Frontier Day parades in various towns, and taking part in all five Shoshone-Ute Sun Dances, just like a true shaman. Now he was chairman of the tribal council and chief of the Sun Dance committee, and who'd have the sand to tell him that his big stucco tepee hadn't gotten him in good with the Great Manitou?

Not me, Paisley thought. Not on a dare.

LannaSue Sky handed her a cup of hot tea, sweetened with honey, and pointed her to a couch covered with a scratchy Navajo blanket. On the knee of her jeans, the teacup warmed a circle that Paisley couldn't help regarding as a tiny replica of the base of the tepee surrounding them.

When LannaSue returned to bed, Sky paced in front of Paisley in his boots, a stocky man with two tight braids hanging to his waist and a paunch decorated by that sky-blue belt buckle.

"What's the word, Alma? What's going on?"

"The word's Paisley," she corrected him.

He waved off the correction with angry impatience. "Tell me stuff I don't know. Tell me important stuff."

"Names are important. Names let us—"

"Okay. If I call you Paisley, you call me Papa Tuqú-payá, got it?" *Tuqú-payá* was the Ute word for sky, one of only a few dozen in her people's tongue that Paisley knew. "Understand?"

"Sure, Papa Tuqú-payá."

"Talk to me, Paisley. But only important stuff."

So she related her Sun Dance dream. Parts, however, she kept to herself, the parts that still frightened or unnerved her.

A lamp in the tiny living room relieved a little of the predawn gloom, but when she looked out its picture window, she saw only the interior wall of the fake tepee. A melancholy claustrophobia rose in her. Nevertheless, she kept talking, and when she was finished, she repeated that tonight's dream had been her seventh in the past five weeks. Therefore her visit to town.

"Women don't dance," Sky declared.

"Women *have* danced, Papa Tuqú-payá. At Fort Hall, they do it all the time. They've done it here, too."

"Twelve years ago, child. Two months later, one of them who'd danced, Theresa Eagle, took sick. The white doctors had no idea with what, but she saw the sacred water bird in the tube connected to her IV bottle and soon thereafter died."

"Mama told me that four other women danced. Nothing like that happened to them."

"No. It happened to other people. Our last Sun Dance chief, the one who let the women dance—his wife died of a heart attack that year. The aunt of the tribal council's last chairman—she died, too. I could make a list."

"None of that matters, Papa Sky. I'm being dream-called. If I'm not, why am I having this dream again and again?"

LannaSue Sky trundled back into the living room in her robe and sat down by Paisley. "Of course you're being called." She looked at her husband. "Who can sleep with this darling here?"

Sky tossed his braids over his shoulders—apparently, in this context, a gesture of disgust.

"Are you afraid to let Paisley dance? Afraid that, two months later, *your* beloved wife might die?" LannaSue briefly smothered a laugh, then gave up and released it. "Beloved wife, my ass. What he's afraid might die is his beloved *work-horse*."

"LannaSue—"

"Okay. I'll shut my silly mouth." She patted Paisley's knee, the one without the teacup. "For a while, anyhow."

The Sun Dance chief started pacing again, trying to recoup some of his pilfered authority. "If I let you dance, your dream says we must all paint ourselves like *ini'putc'*—ghosts."

"I don't know. Is that what it means?"

"I hope not. If we did that, Paisley, it would be like saying the Muache—we Southern Utes—are dead. Dead people can't ask the Creator to give them power."

"They can ask to be resurrected," LannaSue said.

Sky ignored this. "Forget that, for now. Why are there Anglos in your dream—the floppy-hatted woman, the sick man?"

Paisley shrugged. Even now, she could see them clearly—but she was fairly sure she had never met them in life.

"You haven't told me everything," Sky said. "Your dream scared you. It scared you so bad you're afraid to tell it all."

His keenness in this startled Paisley. Some of the Muache said that DeWayne Sky was a fraud—but he had never knowingly violated any ceremonial tradition, and his knowledge of her reaction to her own dream seemed to her a good sign.

"Tell me," he commanded her. "Tell me even what you're afraid to tell."

"Otherwise," LannaSue said, taking the empty teacup from her, "he won't be able to accept you into the dance."

Grimacing, Sky made a curt be-quiet gesture.

"I don't even know that I *want* to dance," Paisley admitted, her mind confusingly aboil again.

"Not your decision," Sky said. "My decision. Tell me so I can decide. If you *don't* tell me, the decision's out of my hands, and it's simple: 'No way, gal. No way.'"

Great, Paisley thought. That would keep me from dancing. And if I don't have to dance, I can leave that much sooner to look for my father. But then it struck her that if she didn't fully divulge the contents of her dream, the dream would continue to recur, and to vary with each recurrence, until it had driven her as crazy as Moonshine Coyote, a woman whose husband and three sons were all in prison and who often sat in a wheelbarrow near Highway 172 drinking cherry Kool-Aid and spitting mouthfuls at passing motorists.

"Come on," Sky said. "You're wasting my time."

"Yeah, you could be sawing logs," LannaSue tweaked him.

"There's three or four things," Paisley said. "The first is those pictures the woman took." Both Skys waited expectantly for her to go on. So she told them that when her dream self had looked at the developed prints handed her by Larry Cuthair, she found that they showed only the interior of the Thirst

House—no dancers, no singers, no drummers, no spectators at all. The people taking part in the event as pseudo-ghosts had become real ghosts when processed by Anglo picture-taking technology.

Which was just another variation, Paisley now realized, on that old cultural-anthropological chestnut about the camera's ability to steal the soul from a shy African bushman or an innocent Amazonian cannibal. From what Paisley knew of anthropologists, it seemed more likely that it was the people on the *taking*—not the *being taken*—end of the camera who forfeited their souls.

"That frightened you even in your dream," Sky said. "You tore the pictures up. You scattered the pieces."

"Yes."

"What else?"

She told him about the trouble she'd had focusing on the totem on the sacred cottonwood. The brightness of the sun, and the angle at which it shone down, had been the main culprits, but it was also likely that she hadn't *wanted* to see what was in the tree's crotch, knowing that it wasn't Buffalo but . . . something else.

"What?" Sky asked. "What was it?"

LannaSue gripped Paisley's knee, reassuringly squeezed it.

At last, Paisley told them: "My mother's face."

Having confessed this, she could *see* her mother's face again—not blown to smithereens as on the night of the suicide, but as it had been before that. Beaten-looking and imploring. Except that, in the dream, her face had been as large as a bison's head.

"Mama D'lo wants her to dance," LannaSue said. "D'lo's spirit is restless."

"Don't jump to conclusions, woman!"

"She has no son to dance her to rest, DeWayne. If it's to be done, Alma—Paisley, here—will have to do it."

Well, that was exactly what Whirling Goat had told her in the jail. It made sense. Mama D'lo's *ini'putc'* had visited Barnes in the drunk tank to ask him to assure her that she was doing exactly right in going to Sky with her seventh dream.

Sky, however, stomped out of the living room into another part of the house. Paisley was perplexed. Maybe LannaSue had so badly provoked him that he was washing his hands of both of them. Women weren't supposed to organize or dance in the Sun Dance, although they could support the men by singing or by bringing willow bundles to them during rest periods—and yet here were two women, his own wife and a teenage girl, one telling him how to interpret a dream and the other presenting herself to him as a would-be dancer. No wonder the poor old buck was pissed.

But a minute later, Sky was back, holding a red-cedar flute, an instrument that—he said gruffly, sitting down on an ottoman in the middle of the room—he'd made himself. Its song would help Paisley make sense of the two shredded photographs.

"How?"

"Shut your eyes. Hear my song. When it stops and I say you're doing something, do it. . . . LannaSue, turn out that lamp."

LannaSue obeyed, and the room, an hour before dawn, was so dark that Paisley felt better closing her eyes than sitting in it trying to find enough light to see by. Sky began to play. The melody was thin, broken, and not terribly pretty. But it altogether took her, snaking in and out of her mind as if seeking a hole to go into and hide. In fact, when the melody stopped, Paisley half believed that it had found this hole.

"A woman dancer in the Thirst House," Sky intoned, "bends down and picks up the pieces of two torn photographs."

That's me, Paisley thought. That's me he's talking about, me he's telling what to do. And in the darkness of her skull, inside the darkness of a boxy house inside the darkness of a stucco tepee, she saw herself clad all in white, powdered like a ghost, kneeling in the dust to gather up the scraps of treated pasteboard. As she did, Sky began to play again—the same monotonous but compelling tune. He kept playing until the white-clad avatar of Paisley Coldpony kneeling in the Sun Dance lodge of her own mind had picked up every single fragment of paper.

Said Sky then, "The woman carries these pieces to the drum and spreads them out on top of it."

The red-cedar flute crooned again, and Paisley performed in her head what Sky had just attributed to the neurological automaton—the day-dream stimulation—he called "the woman." To Paisley, it felt a lot like moving a computer figure through a two-dimensional labyrinth on one of the Apple monitors they had at school now; the sense of being two places at once was just that strong, as was her awareness that she could back out—albeit with a pang of real loss—at nearly any moment she wanted.

"The woman fits the pieces together—into two pictures. She takes all the time she needs."

Paisley took all the time she needed.

The flute ceased to croon.

Said Sky, "The woman speaks aloud. She tells everyone at the Sun Dance what the pictures show."

The obedient self-projection in Paisley's mind stared down at the puzzle-fit photos on the drumhead. In reassembling them, she had paid their images little heed, but now she was shocked to find that one was a picture of Samuel Taylor Coldpony—her father—standing next to the leather-hatted woman who had supposedly *taken* the picture. They stood side by side in the corral.

The other photo, meanwhile, was of an emaciated unicorn—or kar'tajan, as Barnes would call it—rearing at the Tree of Life in the Sun Dance lodge, its front hooves flashing like knives at the totem affixed to it.

Startled, Paisley opened her eyes on the dark.

"She *tells* them," reiterated Sky, "what the pictures show."

Reluctantly, staring at nothing, Paisley told the Skys what her dream self had just seen.

Laying the flute aside, her mentor said, "To find your father, Paisley, you must only find that woman."

"What of the sick unicorn?" she blurted. That Barnes had shown her a string-figure unicorn in the jail seemed not so much a happy as a monstrous coincidence.

"The unicorn and the sick Anglo in your dream," Sky said, "are different sides of the same coin."

Like the "coin" Barnes always carries? she wondered. But there was no way to ask Sky such a strange question, and she didn't yet know how a young man with AIDS and a kar'tajan with protruding ribs could mirror anything in each other but illness.

No matter. Sky had an explanation: "The parents of the sick young man have turned him away, just as you think your folks have done, Sam by never coming to see you and Mama D'lo by . . ."

LannaSue said, "She knows, DeWayne."

"That's why you saw D'lo's face on the Tree of Life. And why his unicorn is trying to cut up the totem with its hooves."

Suddenly, Paisley could stand no more. "You sound like one of those goddamn BIA psychologists! Chief Sigmund Sky of the Muache Shrinks' Association!"

She reached across LannaSue and turned on the lamp. The sudden light made everyone in the room—eyes narrowed, mouths pursed—look constipated.

The Sun Dance chief picked up his red-cedar flute, rose from the ottoman, and stomped off toward his tiny study. At the door, he turned and gave Paisley a bitter look.

"Maybe I do and maybe I don't," he said. "LannaSue, find her something to eat."

She ate scrambled eggs, to which LannaSue had added diced green pepper and jalapeño cheese. Her hunger surprised her. Ten minutes ago, eating had been the least of her concerns.

LannaSue was nursing a cigarette and a cup of coffee. "What do you want to be when you grow up?"

The question surprised her even more than did the extent of her hunger. "I *am* grown up, LannaSue."

"Okay. What do you want to do?"

"Finish school. Dance in the Sun Dance. Find my father." She couldn't think what else to add.

"You want to be a *po'rat*," LannaSue told her.

LannaSue Sky's absolute certainty on this score was yet another surprise, and Paisley halted her fork in mid-ascent. "How do you know that? Hell, *I* don't know that."

The Southern Utes had passed a quarter of a century without a real *po'rat*, or shaman. They had had leaders aplenty, chiefs and organizers and tribal councilmen, but persons with *powa'a*—supernatural authority from the One Above—well, the Muache had had to import such persons from the Navajos, the Jicarilla Apaches, or even the Shoshones, whose Sun Dance procedures were so lax that they let dancers suck wet towels in the Thirst House and had no ban on photography so long as the picture-takers were Indian.

Not even DeWayne Sky, tepee or no tepee, qualified as a

*po'rat*, although he had striven mightily to help maintain the integrity of the Bear Dance and the Sun Dance. On the other hand, not being a bona fide shaman, he hadn't tried to resurrect the *mawo'gwipani*, or the Round Dance, at which everyone danced to hold white diseases—smallpox, clap, polio—in check. Nor the old wedding rite in which a couple sat together in a smoke-filled tepee to prove their compatibility and faithfulness. Nor the ritual of laying a baby's birth cord on an anthill to bless the child with strength and good fortune. Sky's curing powers were beyond the average, but far from impressive in the old way.

For dynamic medicine, a true *po'rat*—a legitimate shaman—was required, and Paisley's people not only had no one qualified, they had no candidates. Why LannaSue would suppose that *she* might make a candidate, much less a full-fledged medicine woman, Paisley was unable to guess. No matter how often she claimed to be grown, she knew in her heart that she was still a schoolgirl, whose daddy had never visited her in all the years since his leavetaking and whose Mama D'lo had . . . done what she'd done. And here she was putting away scrambled eggs as if she hadn't eaten at school yesterday and gulping them down like a starved dog.

How can *I* be a *po'rat?* Paisley wondered. How can this kindly lady see me even as a *would-be* medicine woman?

"DeWayne!" LannaSue called, holding a smoked-down cigarette in front of her. "DeWayne, stop sulking and come here!"

A moment later, Sky propped himself against the doorjamb. "You should've married a poodle, not a man."

"DeWayne, Paisley's dream—it's calling her to be a *po'rat*, a medicine woman, a healer, not only a dancer."

"You've got piñon nuts for brains, LannaSue. If you open your mouth again, they'll rattle onto the floor."

"The sick man in her dream," said LannaSue, undeterred by this warning. Speculatively, she added, "The kar'tajan in the photo she pieced back together to your flute's song."

"What about them?" Sky said.

Paisley was confused again. LannaSue had just said *kar'tajan*, the very word Barnes had used earlier this morning. Moreover, Sky—despite his put-on disgruntlement—was clearly heeding his wife's words, trying to follow her reasoning.

"The Sun Dance is for earning power to heal with, and the Anglo with the deadly illness in her dream requires healing. So does the kar'tajan in her dream photo—it's angry and sick too, just like her stick-skinny white man."

Sky was noncommittal. "So?"

"Paisley calls for the man's healing. She wants to help him. But you say he's broken the rules, and you throw him out."

"He *has* broken the rules," Sky retorted, astonishing Paisley by talking about her dream as if it were an event of which he and his wife shared a real memory. "He brought in moisture."

"Only a name on a shirt."

"He brought in moisture, he brought in Anglo advertising, and he brought them with that picture-taking woman."

I only *dreamed* those things, Paisley thought, looking back and forth between the arguing husband and wife. And it was *my* dream. How can they argue about *my* dream?

But another part of her mind declared, Paisley, you dreamed it *seven times*. It's got to be seriously considered, and DeWayne and LannaSue are doing that.

"Fetch the god sheet, DeWayne."

"Christ, woman, that's only to come out at the end of the Sun Dance. Next, you'll be asking me to piss on the sacred fire."

"After asking for the healing of the man you threw out, Paisley had a vision. I think it means she's to become a *po'rat*. Fetch the god sheet. We'll see."

It looked for a minute that Sky might stomp off again, outraged and truculent. Paisley would not've blamed him. The god sheet, if that somewhat awkward term signified what she thought it did, was a piece of linen that the Sun Dance chief brought forth during the closing ceremonies to impress the Shoshones, Araphahos, Apaches, and Navajos who had come to take part, for only the Muache had anything so impressive to display at dance's end. That LannaSue was asking Sky to get it now, months ahead of time, for no other purpose but to determine her suitability for shaman-hood—well, it staggered Paisley. She finished eating, drank the last of her coffee, stared embarrassedly at her hands.

"He's getting it," LannaSue said. "Come on."

They found Sky peeking around his study door into the living room, holding something—the god sheet, Paisley figured—behind it out of sight. "Not a word of this to anyone," he said. "Not a word of this from either of you pathetically shy females to anybody outside this house. Got me?"

"Come on. Bring it out. I'll throw the rug back. You can lay it down right here." LannaSue tapped the floor with her foot.

"Blindfold her," Sky said.

"What? There's nobody here but us, DeWayne."

"Do it. Do it or I'll put it up. In this, I'll have my way. She's got to be blindfolded for the test to work. And turn that damn lamp out again."

Blindfolded? The lamp out? Was she going to get to see the god sheet or not? All the hocus-pocus—which she couldn't relate to the time-honored rituals of either the Bear or the Sun Dance—frightened Paisley. Hell, LannaSue's notion that she had *po'rat* potential frightened her. Before she could say anything, though, LannaSue had tied a clean dish towel around her eyes and further ensured her sightlessness by pressing a pair of Sky's sunglasses into place over the towel, before she turned on the lamp again. Blindman's bluff.

She could still feel, however, and when Sky billowed the sheet out and let it drift down like a provisional carpet, she felt the stirred air slap her like something wet. Moisture, when you were dry, was power, but she wasn't dry, and this whole business—now that she had told her dream and eaten—seemed peculiar. Still, she trusted the Skys, and if they thought this was the way to test her . . . well, it must be okay.

LannaSue sat her down, helped her remove her shoes and socks. Then she was standing behind Paisley, her large hands gripping her shoulders. Sky retreated and returned. When his red-cedar flute began to to play again (the same painful melody), LannaSue pushed her gently forward, telling her to step lightly on the god sheet.

"Try to make a crossing," she said.

A crossing? Paisley thought. I can make a crossing with my eyes closed—which was a joke almost good enough to laugh aloud at. But when LannaSue released her, all her fragile bravado fell apart, and she hesitated.

Legend had it that the god sheet—the sacred linen—was an authentic Muache relic. At some point over the past half century, a Ute visionary who had just successfully completed the Sun Dance went walking in the hills near the dance grounds and happened upon the footprints of a stranger. This Indian was wrapped in the sheet that he'd worn into and out of the Thirst House over the three days of the dance, and it occurred to him that these footprints—they were narrow and bare—were Jesus's. The Mormons claimed that the Indians were a lost tribe of Israel, after all, and that once upon a time Jesus had appeared in the New World. In any case, the Ute visionary laid his cloaklike sheet atop the strange footprints, and the sheet, according to legend, absorbed them into its fabric so thoroughly that no amount of scrubbing or detergent could lift them out again.

Now, the Sun Dance chief was the keeper of this holy relic, and Paisley stood at its edge, unable to see it, knowing that she must cross it to inherit to . . . well, an apprenticeship that might one day confer upon her divine power.

"Walk, darling," LannaSue Sky encouraged her. "Walk."

Paisley took a step. Sky's flute continued its balky crooning, and the young woman heard the music in the same way that she felt the god sheet—as a spiritual warmth. In fact, although the pine floor was cold and the sheet itself frigid, as she navigated the musty-smelling relic, Paisley noticed that the soles of her feet—step by careful step—seemed to absorb more and more warmth, more and more tingly energy, and it was tempting just to *dash* from one side of the linen to the other.

"The woman in the Thirst House goes slow," Sky said. "She goes slow and watches what there is to watch."

The flute resumed playing. Paisley overcame the urge to dash. Soon she found herself observing again her own ghostly automaton in the Sun Dance corral of her mind.

There before her self-projection's eyes, hanging from the holy cottonwood like Jesus on his Roman cross, was the skinny Anglo in the Coca-Cola shirt. He had been crucified on the center pole, his arms stretched out into unsupportive air and his feet nailed to the Tree of Life with splinters of antelope bone. The gaunt Anglo was saying something, mumbling aloud, but all that Paisley's dream self could make out was the end of his mumble— ". . . forsaken me?"—a phrase with the rising intonation of a question.

Whereupon the Anglo faded from her dream self's sight, vanished into the white air of the imaginary Sun Dance lodge, to be replaced on the center pole by another totem altogether—the head not of a buffalo, or of her own dead mother, but a taxidermically prepared specimen of a mythological beast that Paisley knew as a unicorn but Whirling Goat and the Skys as a kar'tajan, as if they all had some ancient knowledge to which she was not yet privy and on which she might never gain a steady grip. All the other dancers rushed the totem. Leaping, then falling entranced, all had visions, while Paisley's dream self watched from her own Sun Dance path, buoyed by the activity but confused by it too.

Then she saw that the gaunt Anglo, clad now only in an Indian breech-clout, stood beyond the Thirst House entrance. He looked at her peculiarly for a moment, then motioned her to forsake the lodge and follow him. Paisley could feel the soles of her feet—her real feet—growing warmer and warmer as she struggled to obey the mysterious Anglo's summons. It was pity that drew her, not quite conviction, and she knew that once she had seen what he required of her, she would return to the Thirst House to apprise herself of the contents of all her fellow dancer's visions.

Suddenly, the pine floor was cold under her feet again.

"You're across!" a woman's voice cried.

Paisley hoped that LannaSue would remove her sunglasses, untie her blindfold, and give her a look at the god sheet, but Sky, she could tell, was gathering up the sheet, hurriedly folding it and returning it to its hiding place in his study. Only when he had come back from this task did LannaSue remove the blindfold and hug her. Both she and Sky were beaming—as if she had just climbed Mount Everest or swum the English Channel. Paisley blinked at them, more confused than ever, her mind a jumble of images—some distilled from dreams and some from all that had happened to her since coming to town.

"I'm taking you as a Sun Dancer," Sky told her.

LannaSue said, "And for training as the new Muache *po'rat.*"

Toying with one of his braids, Sky nodded.

"But why?" Paisley asked them. "What did I do?"

"You walked where the Walking Man walked," LannaSue said. "On the sheet where *his* footprints lie, you put *your* feet."

Paisley looked at her mentor and her mentor's wife. She felt gratitude for their approval of her and of what she had reputedly accomplished, but also skepticism. All she had for evidence that she had done anything very significant was that odd warmth—which still just perceptibly lingered—on the soles of her bare feet. And, of course, the Skys' word that she had walked exactly atop the Walking Man's, or Jesus's, footprints. It seemed simultaneously a remarkable achievement and a con.

"Great responsibility comes with this honor," Sky said.

Paisley knew. Already, the responsibility had begun to weigh on her. Taking part in the Sun Dance would keep her from leaving to find her father until July, and her apprenticeship as a shaman would require not only her early return but a long sojourn on the Navajo reservation in New Mexico so that a true Navajo shaman could adopt and train her. Life seemed even more complicated than it had after Mama D'lo's suicide.

"It's wonderful," LannaSue said, chucking her under the chin as if she were a baby. "You'll bring us hope again—hope and pride and power."

Paisley slumped to the sofa. She looked through the picture window. The inside of the fake tepee was pinkly agleam, dawn light filtering through the hard plastic windows set high in its stucco cone. Was it possible that her dreams had led her to such a pass? Her private, impalpable dreams?

LannaSue hunkered in front of her, gripping her knees with her viselike hands. For a moment, she simply stayed there—Paisley thought that squatting so must be hard for her, she was by no means a petite woman—but then she abruptly said, "Some folks think that dreams aren't real, darling. Some folks think they're nothing but nonsense."

Sky grunted a derisive assent. The derision in it was for the people his wife was talking about, not for his wife. They were in harmony again. Paisley's walk had restored them to it.

"But dreams are of God, and dreams cause real things to happen, and you, a dreamer, are greatly blessed, darling."

"I—" Paisley began.

"Greatly," LannaSue said. She struggled out of her squat and looked at her husband. "When it's time," she said authoritatively, "DeWayne will drive you to school."

After school, Paisley mooched a ride from Larry Cuthair on his motorcycle. They didn't go home immediately, though, because Larry wanted to buy some notebook paper in Ignacio.

They rode into town together, Larry entered the drugstore, and Paisley sat at the curb on his bike waiting for him to come back. While she was waiting, she looked halfway down the block and caught sight of a man staggering out of the laundromat. It was Herbert Barnes, who'd probably spent most of the day in the Washateria with a bottle of cheap booze. He careened along, as if about to fall from the sidewalk into the street. Paisley ran to him and grabbed him by the elbow.

"Whirling Goat, are you okay?"

He cocked a bloodshot eye at her. "'Course I am," he croaked, patting the pocket of his coat. "Got me some spirits right here—some dandy Old Crow for a randy old Ute."

"Chief Sky says I'm accepted for the Sun Dance," she said. "He and LannaSue believe I've been dream-called."

"You're pretty?" he said doubtfully.

"Thank you," Paisley said, equally doubtfully.

"You're very pretty?"

"I don't know."

Barnes shifted his weight from one wobbly leg to the other. A look of obscene slyness came into the one eye that he was managing to keep open. "Your Mama D'lo told me you oughta take me home with you," he said. "You know, to watch over you."

"Yeah. In hand talk."

"I . . . s-swuh-swear," Barnes half hissed, half coughed.

Up the street, Larry shouted, "Paisley, come on!"

Paisley slipped the five-dollar bill that LannaSue had forced on her that morning into the old fart's coat. He'd only spend it on drink, but there was no way she could reform him in the next ten minutes, nor was she about to take him home with her. The money was guilt money, but it was also . . . well, a token of esteem for what once he had been. He believed he had seen a kar'tajan, and he carried in his pocket a foil-wrapped lucky coin—a talisman, both absurd and poignant, of hope.

"Paisley!" Larry Cuthair yelled again.

She kissed the smelly old sot on the cheek and ran back up the sidewalk to climb aboard Larry's motorcycle.

# 18

"What in Sam Hill?" Libby muttered, turning her pickup off the gravel highway and onto the Tipsy Q.

It was four o'clock in the afternoon. A delivery van with the legend ZUBRECHT PRODUCTS, INC. / DENVER, CHEYENNE, PHOENIX & SALT LAKE CITY stenciled on its side was backed up to her porch with its rear doors opened out like iridescent blue wings. Lib, returning from Arvill Rudd's with the wire-rolling machine that she borrowed from him every spring, had to maneuver her truck between the nose of the van and the edge of the scraggly aspen glade curtaining her house from the eyes of highway travelers. Ordinarily, this time of year, most such travelers were locals, but these fellows—minions of Zubrecht Products, whatever the hell *that* was—had come a long way to get here.

Blast the fuckers, thought Libby, steering her load to the barn and parking under its hayloft. Purposefully, she hiked back up to the house, pushed one of the van's doors to, and squeezed into her living room to find Bo talking with two men, one in coveralls and cap and one in a three-piece navy-blue suit.

"Welcome home," Bo said. "Is it okay if we remove the plywood cubbyholes at the back of your rolltop?"

Libby, staring around her, said, "Do what?"

"They'll come out in a single piece," the man in the navy-blue suit said. "Really, it's a module. All we need to do is take off the desktop, unscrew some screws, pull the shelf module out, and put the rolltop section back up on the desk."

As pleasantly as possible, Lib said, "I'm Libby Quarrels. This is my house, and I'd be really happy to meet you guys."

Bo nodded at the handsome Anglo-Hispanic who had just verbally dismantled her desk. "Libby, this is Darren Santaliz." Then he touched the arm of the man in coveralls, clearly the driver of the van. "And this is Gene Katt."

"Mr. Santaliz, I have no idea what you're talking about."

"Mr. Gavin said 'cubbyholes,'" Santaliz replied. "He means the unit of little boxes and shelves for storing envelopes and pens and stationery. We need to take that shelf module out."

"Why?"

"So we can put Mr. Gavin's computer on the desk. There isn't room with the shelf module in there."

"Well, that's tough, isn't it?"

"Libby, let's talk, okay?" Bo drew her into the kitchen, away from the perfectly-at-ease interlopers.

She was steamed. He had arranged this violation of her home without even bothering to consult her. Where did he get off? How could he invite these unctuous corporate hirelings to come in and field-strip the rolltop she'd bought years ago in Manitou Springs? An antique even then, it was an exquisite piece of furniture that she had bigheartedly—albeit reluctantly—let Bo use along with her study. What a betrayal of trust. It reminded her of his desertion of his lover Keith. Sort of.

"Tell those characters to beat it," Lib stage-whispered between fused teeth. "*Now!*"

Like a suitor, Bo knelt beside her chair and explained that he needed the computer for the freelance work he was going to begin tomorrow for Zubrecht Products, Inc. Ned had sent it. These men were simply here to install it, show him its operation if he had any questions, and hie themselves dutifully back to the firm's main offices in Denver. So why should she vent her spleen on them? The real cause of her anger and resentment was—Bo stopped talking and tapped himself on the chest.

"Why do they have to tear my rolltop apart?"

"I need that computer, Libby. Your house is so small there's no place else to put it. The kitchen won't do. That leaves the study, and your desk has the only surface large enough to hold all the equipment I'll be using."

"Why not work in the living room?" Libby said. "Then you could use the top of my plenty-goddamn-ample cast-iron stove."

Bo extracted a check from his shirt pocket. He unfolded it and spread it out lovingly on the Formica between Libby's elbows. She saw that it was made out to Beaumont Gavin for $10,000 and that it drew on the company funds of Zubrecht Products, Inc. Someone named Theodore Gavin had signed it.

"This is my retainer. Actually, though, it's yours."

Libby's mind masticated this news without absorbing it.

"I'm going to do an ad campaign for Zubrecht. Ned's their Boy Genius. He has total control of their marketing and advertising budget. Total. He's hired me. When I deliver a marketing package pleasing to *the* Mr. Zubrecht, I'll get another forty grand. Half of that will be yours too. I'd give you all of it, but there's taxes. And debts to my folks—abdicated responsibilities—that I need to reshoulder."

Numbly, Lib said, "Ten thousand dollars."

"Indeed." Bo endorsed the check over to her with a ballpoint. Then he folded it again, unbuttoned the pocket on her denim work shirt, and stuffed it with two quick fingers into this nest over her heart. "Here. All yours."

"This doesn't give you the right to destroy my rolltop." She removed the check, unfolded it, studied it. It seemed to be the real thing: a cashier's check on company funds. "I mean, you can't just *buy* me off."

"I'll finish the job in a month or so—maybe the last one I ever do. Then you can screw the 'shelf module,' as Mr. Santaliz calls it, back into the rolltop unit. Sam can probably do it by himself. Then we return the computer to Zubrecht. It's a loaner. A *loaner*, if you can believe it, on a fifty-thousand-dollar piece of freelancing."

Nepotism, Libby thought. "Why would they do this?" she said. "Isn't this a terrible risk for Ned?"

"He's my brother, Cousin Quarrels. My flesh and blood."

Santaliz came to the door, chagrined that the matter required a tête-à-tête between the lady of the house and a new comrade in the benevolent employ to Zubrecht. "Well?"

"Do whatever you have to," Libby told him. "Fast."

"Sure. Gene and I are as ready to get gone as you folks are to have us out of here."

That evening, Lib went into Bo's room and found him sitting at her rolltop in the padded swivel chair that Santaliz and Katt had delivered with the computer. Only the monitor's color graphics illuminated the room, firing migrating rainbows across Bo's face. The effect—dismayingly—was sort of keen.

"Do you know what you're doing?"

"StippleGenesis, the animated-graphics software, is new to me, but the computer's exactly the kind I had in Atlanta."

Libby removed her boots and sat cross-legged in the middle of the quilt on Bo's bed. The dovecote of shelves that the Zubrecht people had unscrewed from her desk balanced upright in the corner, rather like a fat ladder. Into the place that it had occupied, the two men had jammed the computer shell, its detachable keyboard, a modem, and a library of software packages. Atop the rolltop, next to the photographs of Bo's family, they had hooked up a twenty-one-color jet-ink printer that would permit StippleGenesis to make dazzling hard copies of Bo's art programs.

Although Libby had ten grand to console her, the way they had turned her old study into a high-tech command center rankled. The "shelf module," which, apart from her desk, resembled a piece of junk, needed to be stored somewhere, while the monitor Kodachroming Bo's face had as much business on a rolltop as a carburetor does in a covered wagon. They had traduced her house. In effect, they had raped her. She hated it, the oppressive aura of violation.

"Bo, why didn't Ned take you back to Denver with him?"

A myriad of cobalt-blue spirals coiled across the VDT. Bo turned his head. "Uh-oh. Is that question a prelude to my eviction?"

"To your answer, I hope. Why didn't he?"

"He saw, I suppose, that I was doing hunky-dory here."

"Did he make any inquiries about how *I* was doing?"

"No, he didn't. Like me, Cousin Quarrels, he assumed that you were offering me shelter for the duration."

"It never occurred to Neddy to question the appropriateness of our arrangement?"

"You mean, did he think, like Genghis Gary, that the neighbors would convict us of shacking up?"

"I didn't say 'propriety.' I said 'appropriateness.' He never once thought *he* might have the greater obligation?"

Bo swiveled, shut down the computer, yanked the limp diskettes from its twin drives. "Who else in the whole wide world would have given me a job worth fifty thousand?" Only the pale spillover from a lamp in the living room gave them any light. "Ned *can't* take me in. He's at work all day." Bo got up and walked to the door.

"I'm not here with you every minute, either."

"Then why is it so fucking difficult for you to tolerate me on the rare occasions you *are* around?"

"That's a red herring, Bo. The real issue is Ned's failure to meet his obligations—*not* my alleged homophobia."

"He's a bachelor. He's afraid taking me home with him will put his career in jeopardy." A distressed edge came into Bo's voice; calves unable to find a full teat sounded that way. "Neddy's doing what he can, Lib. He's doing what he can."

I doubt it, Libby thought. But I'm not in Neddy's shoes.

"I *could* hurt his career, Lib. The Zubrechts are country-club religionists. Ned's succeeded with them by working his ass off six days a week and flaunting a lukewarm Presbyterianism on Sundays."

"'Lukewarm Presbyterianism'? Isn't that redundant?"

Bo massaged his cheek. "Maybe. I don't know. But Ned can't afford to take any chances."

"Ah."

"And if Ned took me in, he'd be defying our parents—Dad with his operable heart disease, Mama with her inoperable."

"You're making excuses. Jokey excuses."

"Ha ha."

Cold silence intervened. Bo sat down again. Perversely, Libby imagined *Ned* settling into that swivel chair. How much deeper the leatherette cushion would sink.

Then Libby recalled the check in her pocket. Had she ever held ten grand this close to her heart before? The closest she had ever come was embracing Gary after one of his rare buckle-winning rodeo outings. But the purses were usually chicken feed, and it was even rarer that he'd come home, either pie-eyed or sober, to celebrate a bronc-riding victory with an intimate ride in bed. Why should he? Usually, would-be celebrants galore would show up right there on the manure-littered grounds of his triumph.

Change the subject, Lib advised herself. Or think about this unbelievable check. "I'd never heard of Zubrecht Products before," she said. "What do they make, exactly?"

"Health-related items," Bo said. "Ned calls them 'the goods.'"

"'The goods'? What sort of goods?"

"Latex surgical gloves. Protective garments."

"*Protective* garments?"

"Masks, booties, smocks—that sort of thing."

"But what for?"

"For handling radioisotopes or for pulling hazardous duty in nuclear power plants."

"Zubrecht wants you to work up ads for radiation gear?"

"No, m'lady. Not for that. For the goods proper."

"The goods proper?"

"Or improper. Depending on your point of view."

"What are you talking about?"

"Condoms," Bo said. "Prophylactics. Artificial fore-and-aft all-along-the-shaft skins. In short, m'lady, *the goods.*"

"You're kidding."

"But 'in short' is wrong. I could just as easily have said 'in long.' To be up and up about it, one size fits all. They're a lot like socks that way."

"Condoms?" Lib could feel a smile dawning. "You're telling me you're going to be doing an ad campaign for condoms?"

"It's great that one size fits all. Imagine your embarrassment if you had to go in for a fitting. Not 'you' personally. I was speaking generically—although more of gender than of genus. That, nowadays, is what I've a genius for."

It took a while, but Libby got him to cease his manic punning. Once he had, she found out that, yes, Zubrecht Products, Inc., had commissioned him to work up an advertising campaign—a television campaign—for a brand-new line of micron-thin, super-strength silicon condoms.

The company had already produced and electronically tested a proto-type—the protophylactic, Bo called it—hinting that here, at last, was an item of personal hygiene in tune with the changing health needs of a society in crisis. The Surgeon

General had gone on record in favor of advertising this sort of product on TV, and the three major commercial networks, intimidated by a public outcry against "sleazy programming" and the "hypocrisy" of a condom-ad ban, had begun to crawfish. Everett Zubrecht was certain that they would soon permit such ads on national—not simply discretionary local—TV, and that his firm would take the media lead.

"But this is the Reagan Era," Libby protested. "Do you really think Cowboy Ron will let that happen?"

"Remember the strange stuff you've seen on TV lately?"

"Interference from another solar system. Nonsense from our own subconsciouses. Fever dreams."

"Your kar'tajans too?"

"I don't know. But I can't imagine seeing condom ads on *Dallas* or *Miami Vice*." Libby stopped. "Wait. Maybe I can."

"Of course you can. It'll happen. That was one of the things Little Ben was trying to prepare us for."

And a major irony of this whole business, Bo went on, was that Nate and Josey were *un*prepared for it. They still didn't know that the most profitable commodity manufactured by Zubrecht Products was "the goods." Ned hadn't told them.

They knew about the medical gloves, shower caps, and high-tech radiation suits, but any notion that Ned shilled for items designed to facilitate the socially unmentionable acts of contraception and STD prevention lay beyond their imagining, and Ned wanted to keep it that way. A son fronting for a rubber maker—one unaffiliated with Goodyear or Firestone—was as shameful a parental mistake as a son dying of AIDS.

Another major irony of this whole business, Libby purposely did not remind Bo, was that he, like Alfie Tuck, would be fretting over and about condoms long after the effing, ineffable things could do him—personally—any good at all.

Bo's bedroom/study became his entire world. He regarded it as a kingdom, but also as a penitentiary cell.

A new snowfall, another melt, a fresh deluge of whiteness. But none of this weather meant anything, for the only window with a claim on his attention was his computer-monitor screen. Bo looked into it, or out through it, as a way to range *beyond* his illness. Ironic that his labors for a condom manufacturer should so absorb him. But gratifying, too.

Libby had put most of her $10,000 check in a certificate of deposit with a decent rate of return, and her mood of late seemed relaxed and centered. The money was partly responsible, but so was her daily involvement in the spring roundup, now going full tilt. Three of Arvill Rudd's hands, including Brooklyn Terry, Rudd's top wrangler, were helping Sam and her vaccinate, brand, and dehorn—assistance that she and Sam repaid on a day-to-day basis, as Rudd required—and this grueling work kept Libby out of doors, and out of Bo's hair, often until well after dark.

Trips to Huerfano for vinblastine shots and periodic checkups were welcome escapes from confinement, but Bo seldom made them last too long. Fresh air was fine for a while (especially now that violets, bluebells, and alpine forget-me-nots had embroidered the road to Snowy Falls with color), but the assignment from Zubrecht was top priority.

StippleGenesis was a versatile program that enabled Bo and his electronic mouse to summon, and to animate, an endless parade of images—realistic, geometric, abstract, what-have-you. But, like a starship pilot OD'ing on sensory riches, it was easy to space out on these patterns. Sometimes Bo had to yank himself back from the screen, murmuring, "This isn't it. Damn it, this just isn't it," and begin anew. In a week, he seeded and aborted a dozen different concepts—all of them somehow wrong for the classy marketing of a product as *sensitive* as a revolutionary new condom. So at times Bo felt that the dry heat in Libby's house, or the AIDS virus in his bloodstream, was decimating his brain cells.

Usually, though, his mood was upbeat. He was making progress, winnowing grain from chaff. As soon as he hit upon *the* structuring image to carry this campaign, it would all start coming easy. Part of the immediate problem was that Zubrecht wanted him to *name* this new line of "the goods," not just erect a scaffolding of images to publicize and sell it. Until Bo did that, all the dancing images powered up by him and StippleGenesis wouldn't mean diddly, and he'd be playing at this assignment rather than working at it. But, Bo believed, an assignment played at was more likely to turn out well than one joylessly sweated over.

So doodle, he encouraged himself. Sketch. Mouse around.

Ned telephoned nearly every other day to stay abreast of

Bo's progress, but Bo refused to send images over their computer link because he was unhappy with the ones he had so far come up with. *Soon,* he placatingly told his brother. A matter of days.

"You don't have all that long, Bo."

"Listen, I've got my purple freckles to remind me."

"You know what I meant. There's a giddy-up burr under Trail Boss Zubrecht's saddle blanket."

"Neddy, I called our house."

It took five or six long beats for Ned to respond. "Make you feel any better?"

"Mama knew my voice. She hung up."

"Well, sure. You expected?"

"So I wrote them a letter. Five single-spaced pages."

"I hope it was cathartic—because I can't imagine that it'll bring down anything but more silence."

"It hasn't so far," Bo admitted.

"Dad's doing okay," Ned said. "No need to sweat that."

After the call, Bo looked for the notes that he had laid aside to talk to Ned. Where were they? The slide-out boards on either side of the rolltop's chair well had him penned in, and he cursed his ridiculous genius for misplacing items in such a circumscribed area. Angrily, he flung sketches, stirred through Bic and Itoya pens, pressed down with his heel on the only drawer in the desk that Libby had not allotted him—a drawer locked ever since his arrival. Its handle splintered, and the drawer was driven deeper into the body of the rolltop.

Bo grabbed the handle. Hoping to get the drawer flush again, instead he jerked it completely out. It landed on his instep. A sheet of paper wafted to rest near his bed.

Bo yanked his throbbing foot clear, wheeled the chair back, and looked down, first at the drawer, then at the leaf of paper by the iron bedstead. The drawer contained dozens of these sheets. All, it seemed, were pencil or charcoal sketches of kar'tajans. (Damn it, *unicorns!*) Libby had drawn them in every possible posture—standing, running, leaping, lying down, climbing, and, in one truly tender portrait, copulating. Ignoring his hurt foot, Bo shuffled through the drawings with mounting wonder.

They were strange creatures, Libby's kar'tajans. Horselike and deerlike at once. Had she modeled them on horses? If so, she had ingeniously altered their bodies—as well as their hooves and heads–to intimate a bighorn-sheepishness that was lithe and powerful rather than meek and shamefaced. However, her kar'tajans had only a single horn, rising rapier-like from the brow. Further, in every sketch, these horns had the grooved twist and the obsidian sheen of Sam Coldpony's "letter opener."

Drawings from life? Libby would say so. It was just about the only eccentricity she allowed herself. Bo believed she cultivated it as a way of trumping the indisputable unconventionality of his homosexuality. If you're a fruitcake, then I'm a UFU—Unidentified Flying Unicorn—nut. Of course, the glaring flaw in this theory was that her drawings antedated his arrival and probably even her discovery of his . . . differentness.

Why kar'tajans, then? Because, as Libby outrageously claimed, they roamed her ranch? Or because she had a postadolescent equine hang-up that even her daily association with real horses hadn't yet resolved? No. These "answers" to the mystery of her fascination with kar'tajans were as bogus as his theory that she was trying to tit-for-tat, so to speak, his gayness.

When Lib came in that evening, she slumped into a chair at the kitchen table. Bo dropped a stack of kar'tajan drawings into her lap, a little bomb of accusation or ridicule. Neither of them knew which, but she could see an ambivalent sparkle in his eyes.

"Yours?" he demanded.

"I drew them, yes."

"Unicorns? Why?"

"Because my camera wouldn't take their pictures."

"Your camera wouldn't what?"

"Just forget it, Bo."

Bo shifted gears. "Unicorn Libby Quarrels. That's what I'll call you. The Roger Tory Peterson of mythological fauna."

"Knock it off. I'm seriously tuckered."

"Unicorn Libby Quarrels. With that monicker, you could develop quite a reputation as a colorful local character." Bo italicized the monicker with a blatantly faggoty gesture—except that he was ridiculing her, not himself. "Say, Unicorn

Libby Quarrels, aren't you a little past the age at which most girls go dippy over these chichi fantasy critters?"

Libby dropped the stack of drawings on the table and jabbed him with her finger. "Bo, I've told you they're real. Sam says you saw the alicorn he broke from the forehead of a dying colt. And, not too long ago, you and I watched a *Wild Kingdom* episode on which the Indian government was rounding up sick kar'tajans. So what's this 'fantasy critter' shit you're shoveling?"

Although startled by her vehemence, Bo said, "People who claim to've seen dragons on the expressway provoke my skepticism too."

"This is the Twilight Zone, remember? By your own admission."

"Hang on. I'm not finished. Sam's 'alicorn' could be a lot of things. Maybe even the narwhal tusk he said it was."

"And the kar'tajan roundup to which my Bendix treated us?"

"A fever dream. Your word for it. I mean, think of everything else we saw on your set. It must've been bunk, m'lady. Fascinating, mind-altering bunk." What else could it have been?

"Yep, a two-person 'mass psychosis.' Glad you figured it out. What about Brother Ned's witness the following evening?"

"A three-person 'mass psychosis.' More weird mind trips." But even Bo realized that this was unlikely.

Libby shook her head. "You didn't happen to make me a sandwich or fry me a piece of fish, did you?"

Bo sat down, nodded at the drawings. "You planted them, didn't you? You knew I'd stumble over them eventually."

"Planted them? I should've burned them."

"Just as Sam planted that so-called 'alicorn' in your pickup's glove compartment. For my benefit."

Libby was wearing shotgun chaps over her jeans. Her shirt was sweat-stained. She hadn't even bothered to take off her floppy leather hat. "Why?" she gently asked him. "Why would Sam and I do that, Beaumont?"

"To make me believe in kar'tajans. To bring about the deathbed conversion of a disillusioned, angst-ridden queer."

"You think Sam and I are missionaries? Sam'll like that. No one's ever accused him of being a missionary before."

"Oh, no? You're trying to turn my worldview upside down."

"Your AIDS has turned you into an upside-down paranoid. Word of honor, Bo—Sam and I aren't trying to save your soul."

"What are you trying to do, Unicorn Libby Quarrels?"

"Run a ranch," she said. "Keep you alive."

"Better stick to your first goal, m'lady. You'll never manage the second one."

Libby tossed her hat onto a chair in the corner and went to the sink to scrub her hands. Bo feared he had pushed her too far, that she wouldn't speak to him again. Of late, her work with Sam, Arvill Rudd, and Rudd's cowhands had led her to depend more on nonverbal communication—arm gestures, head nods, hat waving, a few vivid grunts—than on speech, and Bo sometimes felt that reasoned dialogue was no longer a variety of discourse interesting to her. She had turned cowboy on him, a subtle snub.

"Libby—" he began.

She returned to the table, picked up one of her drawings, and tore it in two. Then, with an alarming deliberateness, she ripped up all the remaining drawings in the stack.

"You think I planted 'em, huh? Well, now *you* can plant 'em, Bo Gavin. Preferably, up your twinky ass." And, without even having scrounged up a modest meal, she stalked out of the kitchen, leaving Bo alone in it, guilt-ridden and perplexed.

Aware of an alien touch, Bo opened his eyes. Sam Coldpony, who had not eaten with Libby and him for several days, stood beside his bed with the tips of three icy fingers on his throat. Still groggy from sleep, Bo feared the Ute was about to murder him. He lay motionless, staring up through the gloom into the implacable eyes of Lib's hired hand and wondering if maybe being slaughtered in bed wouldn't be preferable to dying slowly of AIDS.

"What time is it?" he said.

Sam withdrew his cold fingers. "You too sick to take a little hike with me, Gavin?"

"A hike? Where? What's going on?"

Sam said, "How fast can you get dressed?"

Bo turned his head. His clock radio's digital readout told him that it was 6:12. Libby had probably been up about an hour, but he usually slept at least two hours beyond her. Having Sam Coldpony act as an unexpected human alarm so far ahead of his own schedule was both irritating and spooky.

"Sam, didn't anyone ever tell you it was impolite to answer a question with a question?"

"If you're not too sick to come with me, you need to hurry. I can't promise that it ain't too late already."

A whole day had gone by since Bo's run-in with Libby over her unicorn drawings, and he dimly suspected she had put Sam up to this early morning harassment to get back at him for accusing her of planting them. Yesterday, she'd gone out of her way to avoid even a single face-to-face meeting.

Bo pushed himself to a sitting position. "Just what the fuck are you talking about, Sam?"

The Ute was wearing blue jeans, an old army-surplus jacket, and a baseball cap. "Get dressed," he said. "I'll wait out here." He retired to the living room, leaving the door partly open.

"Suppose I don't feel like getting dressed?" Bo shouted.

"Then you'll miss something you need to see. Get a move on. I should be helping Miss Libby with the roundup."

Exasperated, Bo got dressed, and a moment later, feeling tight in the gut and lightheaded—*is it the altitude or my attitude?*—he was skipping along behind the rigorously striding Indian, past Miss Lib's barn and up the trail snaking its way toward Naismith's Cabin on the high flank of Ptarmigan Mountain. *I suppose I ought to feel honored that Sam wants to show me his place,* Bo told himself, but instead he worried that the man planned to bludgeon him with a club and stuff him down an ore shaft in Naismith's Mine.

About fifteen minutes later, this worry was amplified when Sam led him right past the ancient cabin and along the steepening path toward the mine. Bo was already badly winded, and he resented his guide's refusal to stop, rest, and offer him something to eat, for he had not had breakfast yet.

On the other hand, his pride would not let *him* suggest halting, and when Sam kept trudging doggedly upward, Bo clamped his teeth and just as doggedly followed. However, it shook him again when Sam left the marked trail to lead them downslope through the pines and patchy snow to a clearing above the fog-filled, parklike meadow behind the Tipsy Q's ranch house.

Dawn light twinkled in the wet trees, uneven shadows purpled the foggy meadow, and Sam made Bo hunker in the lee of a weird crimson snowbank at the top of the triangular clearing. Squatting next to him on the twig- and needle-strewn slope, Sam smoothed several long pale strands of hair across Bo's thigh. They glittered against the dull denim; Bo knew that they would have floated off if Sam had not pressed them down on his jeans fabric.

"What's this?"

"Kar'tajan hair," Sam said.

"Palomino hair," Bo retorted, trying to catch his breath.

"It's kar'tajan hair, Gavin. I pulled it out of a pine branch on our hike up here."

"It's more likely you pulled it out of a currycomb a couple of days back. You could have shown it to me at the house."

Sam's mouth twisted like that of an ireful brave in an old John Ford Western, but he didn't try to rebut Bo's assertion. Instead, he nodded down Ptarmigan Mountain at a creek—Remuda Creek—flowing through the broad pasture. A distant wall of peaks gleamed in the early fog like a ghost barrier, while nimbi of steam surrounded the six or seven cattle loitering in a clump on the creek's near side. The willows on the far bank had the fairy-tale delicacy of mirages, and when Bo eased himself into the lotus position—so what if his jeans got wet?—he saw, or thought he saw, telltale movement among the cascades of leaves shimmering there.

"That wasn't . . ." he said.

"Just watch," Sam advised him.

Hugging himself, Bo watched. A great deal of time passed. His stomach rumbled, and his parched tongue felt as if it were about to split open.

"Nothing's happening," he finally complained. "And I'm thirsty enough to drain a goddamn rain barrel."

"Christ," Sam remarked. He duck-walked to the bank of crimson snow behind them, scooped a hatful of the strange stuff out of it, and duck-walked back to lay the hat in Bo's lap. "Eat this. It'll ease your thirst and maybe some of your hunger."

Bo peered skeptically into Sam's hat. He sniffed the red snow, which had a distinct but pleasant fruity smell.

"It's watermelon snow," Sam said, incidentally identifying the fruity smell for him. "Go on. Eat."

"Why's it red?"

"What other color should watermelon snow be? Go ahead and eat it."

Overcome by both thirst and the enticing aroma, Bo obeyed. He at the whole hatful, crunching the tasty snow and then extending the hat to Sam for a second helping. Noncommittally, Sam fetched him another. Bo downed this batch too, sucking each icy mouthful of its flavor and satisfying his thirst so thoroughly that it was no longer a burden to sit there waiting for whatever it was Sam wanted him to see.

"Watermelon snow," he mused. "Watermelon snow."

"Look," Sam said, pointing toward Remuda Creek.

Two kar'tajans were walking side by side there, like deer at an early forage. They nibbled grass. They nibbled leaves. And the larger of the two animals—not quite so large as an adult horse—nibbled the cheek and throatlatch of the smaller. They were misty animals in an evanescent landscape, but Bo felt certain that as the day wore on, they would grow more substantial, sharpening against the whetstone of noon, trailing signature odors as pungent as those of any other animal. But for now, they were quadrupeds of carven, deliquescent ice. They would flee like eidolons or burn away like fog. Bo struggled to hold them in view, and his foremost thought was that Libby, in her heartfelt sketches, had almost managed to do them justice.

This thought intensified when the larger kar'tajan mounted the smaller. Their coitus occurred over a stretch of time that seemed measurable only by the slow dispersal of the ground fog. Watching, Bo could not move. He wanted to look over at Sam, to see what Sam was experiencing, but he didn't, for he wanted even more to file this fragile epiphany with all his best memories—as, for instance, his childhood meeting with the naked man in the bathhouse at a swimming pool in Pueblo.

So he watched until the animals had separated, and the mist was gone, and sunlight was shuttling through the willows' branches like singing copper thread.

Then Sam's shadow fell across him. "You've found out, Gavin. You've found out they're real."

Bo looked up as if Sam were awakening him from sleep again. It was true. He had just found out that unicorns—kar'tajans—existed in fact and that they were among the most beautiful animals he had ever seen. Unicorn Libby Quarrels, no doubt about it, was truly Unicorn Libby Quarrels.

"You owe Miss Libby an apology," Sam said. "Come on. Let's go back down."

Bo was happy to obey. He would gladly apologize to his cousin-in-law. And he would return to his computer with an enthusiam that he hadn't felt since signing on with Chattahoochee CommuniGrafix well over a year ago. How, though, could he hope to concentrate on his work? How? He was an eyewitness to a miracle, the copulation of a pair of fantasy animals, and the sight of them would remain in his mind—in his inward vision—forever.

It was as if God had arranged the constellations over Colorado to spell out, in English, the unequivocal declaration, "I AM."

At seven o'clock that evening, exhausted from the branding and dehorning, Libby entered her house and called Bo's name.

"Here," he answered feebly.

He was exactly where she thought he would be—in the bathroom linking their bedrooms. At their midday chuck, Sam had assured her that Bo would have need of that facility.

"Kar'tajans," Bo said from beyond the door. "You were right, m'lady. You were right."

"I'm glad you finally saw them."

"So am I. They're . . . they're . . ." Apparently he had no words to describe what they were.

"Are you all right, Beaumont?"

"One AIDS symptom is diarrhea. I've spent the last two hours, on and off, in here." Wan chuckle. "On, off. On, off."

"This isn't an AIDS symptom, Bo."

"What?"

"Sam said he'd taken you to see the kar'tajans. He also told me he fed you some . . . watermelon snow."

"Yeah, he did. Why?"

"He was hacked off at you, Bo. Watermelon snow takes its color from algae living in the unmelted banks. If you eat it, it usually has a laxative effect."

No reply from beyond the bathroom door. Libby wondered if she should break it down. Then Bo began to curse.

"Remember the kar'tajans, Bo. Remember the kar'tajans."

"To hell with them! As soon as I'm able to get off this pot, I'm going to de-dick a two-timing Injun!"

Libby, smiling, thought, Serves you right, Beaumont. It sure as shooting serves you right. . . .

# 19

Libby couldn't believe that she was wearing panty hose, a dress, a tailored jacket, a neck scarf, lipstick, heels. But she was, and she felt . . . not herself. Bo sat beside her at the wheel of his Mazda. In his pin-stripped suit, he looked like a male mannequin—pale, faceless, unreachable.

They had zipped from the Tipsy Q to the outskirts of Pueblo in just over an hour, primarily because Bo had traveled seventy on the four-lane. And, as on their much longer trip from Atlanta to Snowy Falls, they had hardly spoken to each other.

"Are you going to the house or directly to church?" Libby finally asked.

"Ned told me not to come to the house."

"He told you not to come to the *funeral*, Bo. If you ignore him in that, why not in the other?" Libby winced as, a few blocks from I-25, Bo flipped on his right-hand signal, then swung left across a busy intersection. He'd been doing back-asswards crap like that the whole way. Fingering the radio's volume knob when trying to find a new station, turning on the windshield wipers when wanting to start the heater.

Stupid crap. But why not? Bo's father had died suddenly,

of a stroke apparently unrelated to his heart disease, and Ned had asked Bo over the telephone to consider Josephine's need's and to refrain from attending either the service in their old Presbyterian church or the brief ceremony at graveside. Libby was welcome to come, but Bo's attendance at either site might prove an embarrassment to the family.

"Hypocrite," Bo said. "I'm family too, and Ned's a two-faced son of a bitch." He had spoken maybe three times since leaving the ranch, but only to curse his brother.

"Easy, Bo."

They were going not to Bo's parents' tiny stucco house (Lib realized with relief), but to the church, and soon they had come in view of an ivy-tangled stone building across the street from a park not yet fully green, where two sable squirrels with tufted ears ran up and across a rusted metal merry-go-round. So many mourners had already arrived that it took Bo fifteen minutes to park.

Walking from the Mazda to the sanctuary, Lib kept wishing that he'd worn a hat, a cape, a muffler—anything to help hide the fact that he was the Gavin family black sheep. But Bo refused even to hunch his shoulders. Blessedly, his pale gauntness was at least as effective as a disguise.

In the dim church itself, however, Libby and Bo sat down in a rear pew—his lone grudging concession to Ned's request that he make himself inconspicuous. Here, eyes adjusting, they soon could see his father's bier in front of the altar. The "family"—minus Bo—hadn't entered yet, and mourners were filling slowly past the open casket to view the body.

"I'm going up," Bo said. Libby's heart misgave her. She had come to honor the uncle of the no-account to whom she had once been married and to offer Bo some moral support at a funeral he'd been asked *not* to attend. She hadn't come to witness a dramatic clash between a mother and her estranged and bitter son.

Bo got up. Not having seen his father, alive or dead, in more than five years, he knew that this was his last chance—at least in this life—to look upon the features that had provided half the template for his own. Ned had wanted to steal that chance from him, and Mama Josey . . . well, she seemed to want to believe that he had died *before* Papa Nate, that he was now even less real than her memories of her husband.

At the bier, Bo gazed down. What he saw was a waxen caricature of the man who had fathered him, a figure even more wasted by his illness than was Bo by the depredations of his—a wizened mummy of the athlete who had once made acrobatic dives from the high board of any public pool where he could attract an audience.

Fumbling in his pocket, Bo's fingers closed on the inescapable pewter unicorn. Should he place this figurine in the coffin beside his father? Nate had always preferred whiskey to whimsy, and it would horrify him to be packed off to God with a toy once valued by an AIDS-stricken stranger. Bo decided against.

"You okay?" Lib asked him when he sat back down beside her.

He nodded dully.

Eventually, the family filed in and sat down in a small section of pews near the altar but perpendicular to the seating in the nave proper. Lib was at first startled, and then relieved, to see that among the family members were Gary and his mother, Pamela Fay. Ned had already helped Mama Josey to the front row, while remaining pews filled with aunts, uncles, cousins, in-laws.

Two ushers closed the casket. Ned came forward from the family section, took up his saxophone from behind Papa Nate's bier, and played on it a hymn that Bo could not remember as a favorite of his dad's. (Papa Nate had enjoyed polkas, marches, and "funny" songs like "Dance with me, Henry" and "The Purple People Eater.") Bo couldn't remember him even politely moving his lips to a hymn, much less singing one, and yet here was Ned making "The Old Rugged Cross" echo like Beale Street blues through their old Presbyterian church, his sax crying and heartbreakingly catching its breath.

Josephine Gavin was convulsed with sobs. Gary held her to him and spoke directly into her ear. But Mama Josey didn't stop weeping, and all Bo could think was that Gary had no right to be sitting there and that his mother had already begun to resemble a Greek widow in smutty-black mourning weeds. How long before she started rocking back and forth and keening?

Ned returned to the ribboned-off pews to sit on their mother's right, and the service ceased to interest Bo. Recitation, eulogy, weepy organ music. He felt true relief when the pallbearers—men he only vaguely recognized—toted the ice-gray casket outside, slid it into the hearse, and slammed the ebony hatch.

In the cemetery, fifteen minutes later, Libby and Bo skulked on the far edge of the thinned-out crowd, watching with hooded eyes as the pastor concluded the graveside service and even close relatives began to wander away.

"Let's get out of here," Libby said. "You've done your duty. Stay any longer and we're tempting fate." She was afraid that Gary would spy her and come sashaying across the damp grass—it had just begun to drizzle—to say hello, betraying their presence to Brother Ned and Mama Josey and triggering the kind of set-to that she had been dreading ever since Ned's call.

To her angry consternation, Bo shook his head and went walking straight toward the awning that the funeral home had pitched above his father's grave. His pinstripes had the pale verticality of the drizzle itself, and Libby half believed he would melt like a ghost before reaching the tent.

As for Bo, he had decided not to dissolve so passively. He wanted his mother to acknowledge him, and he wanted her to do so—whether with forgiveness or outrage—in front of those friends and family members still tarrying on the grounds.

"Bo, don't!" Lib half whispered, half cried.

He turned and peered at her. The chilly spring mist was like a curtain of transparent beads.

"You said we'd stay out of everyone's hair, Bo."

"If Mama and I make up, m'lady, I'll be out of *your* hair—for good. Isn't that worth the risk of a flushed face or two?"

"No. No, it isn't."

"Sure it is," he said. "Sure it is."

And he resumed his march on the rain-stained green awning. His mother, flanked by Ned Gavin and Gary Quarrels, saw him coming and waited with the stolidity of a Brahma bull determining when best to attack and horn-toss a rodeo clown. That she didn't simply stride away surprised Bo, for she had hung up on his telephone calls and pointedly ignored his letters. She didn't want to acknowledge him, not at all, and yet it must seem to her that he'd chosen the day of her direst vulnerability to press the issue of their relationship, to lay out the claims of his Gavinhood.

Ned said, "Bo, go on back to Snowy Falls."

Gary Quarrels looked down. If he had not told his ex-wife that the Gavins were turning their backs on Bo, Bo would probably still be in Atlanta. Gary had wanted to help his cousin, but not for him to take up lodgings with his ex-wife or to disrupt this funeral by waylaying Aunt Josey at graveside.

Then Gary saw Libby stepping gingerly over the grass, gliding among the tombstones as if they were pylons. His stomach dipped. When had he last seen her so gussied up? At an anniversary dinner, maybe. Despite Libby's outfit—she looked damned good—a familiar resentment began to pulse in his gut, and he unwittingly fisted his hands.

"Got another black eye for me, Gary?" Bo said. "Or maybe you want to retouch the old one."

Nonplussed, Gary said, "Sorry about your daddy, Bo," and he and Ned, at Josey's bidding, retreated over the lawn to the limousine provided by the mortuary for family members.

Lib came under the awning, gripped Bo's mama by the shoulders, kissed her on the brow. Josey politely returned this peck, fished about in her pearl-crusted handbag for her cigarettes, shakily lit one, then blew a disintegrating plume of smoke into the moist air. Her eyes were puffy, her lips gravity-weighted.

Bo looked for another face under her lacquered mourning mask—the face she had worn twenty-odd years ago—but all he could summon of it was the aggrieved flicker in her eyes. A signature.

"I didn't cause this," he said.

"You didn't stop it, either, did you?" Mama Josey came up to his sternum but seemed taller. She was mastering her grief—*real* grief, Bo saw—to face him, and suddenly he felt defensive, intimidated. He'd been a bad boy, and Josey was doing her maternal duty by pointing out to him exactly how.

"I deserved to be here today, Mama. You should've asked *me* to sit beside you—not Gary."

"How sick are you?" Her interest seemed clinical.

"Not sick enough to give what I've got to anyone here."

"You're twice sick. A sickness you didn't have to have bought you the second one you can't get rid of."

"Mama, that's wrong. Part of what you say is simply wrong. In any case, I'm who I am—namely, your and Dad's son." Bo stepped toward her, wanting to embrace her.

She raised her cigarette, wordlessly deflecting him. Then she said, "You can hug me when you begin to try to get over your first sickness, Beaumont—the one you didn't have to have."

"Mama, I'm gay. I was gay even when you thought I wasn't—virtually from the beginning."

Libby said, "Josey, it's a part of who he is. He can't help it any more than I can help having hair this color."

"You could dye it," Josey said. She sipped at her cigarette—languidly, infuriatingly.

"I can't keep pretending not to be what I really am, Mama."

"Why not? Maybe we're every one of us murderers pretending not to be. Maybe it's only by pretending as hard as we can *not to be* that we don't end up killing each other and becoming what we really are underneath."

This speech stunned Bo. His mother had independently concluded that willpower could overcome a tendency to homosexual behavior—or, in fact, to any kind of behavior deemed unacceptable by society at large. Denying these unacceptable natural impulses would reduce the ranks of the deviant and/or the criminal by subtracting oneself from their number.

"Mama, do you think *you're* a would-be-murderer?"

"I know I am. And I'm honest enough to admit it. But I'm not a *real* murderer because I don't do what I sometimes want to."

Original sin with a sinister twist, Bo thought. Aloud he said, "Have you ever considered murdering me, Mama?"

"Lots. Nathaniel's laying dead there because you couldn't pretend any better not to be what you *think* you are." She gestured at the casket, still on its rollers over the unfilled grave. "He started going down right after that last time we called you."

Well, Bo thought, temples throbbing, he'll make it all the

way down when we beat it out of this boneyard and let the undertakers finish their job.

"That had to be just coincidence," Libby said, touching Josey's arm. "Nate was riding for a major heart attack—or something—even before Bo went to Georgia."

"That may be. But he didn't have it, did he, until Bo told us he was . . . what he says he is."

"My friend Carrie phoned you to say I had AIDS. I wasn't happy about what she'd done, but when you and Papa called me back, I had no choice but to tell you the truth."

"Punishment for not pretending better. You'd never gotten what you've got, Beaumont, if you'd just pretend harder."

"Because we're all murderers pretending not to be? Except for whoever doesn't pretend hard enough to keep from *really* murdering someone and so has to pretend to be pretending to keep from ending up in the electric chair?"

"I'm going home, Beaumont. You go home too."

"I'm your son, Mama. That's why I call you mama. Is your home my home?"

"You're as dead to me, as your daddy. I don't want to be there when the Lord makes it official. I don't deserve that, I've always pretended harder than most, and you've been sent Elizabeth, a damned good pretender, because God is Merciful."

Bo's mother dropped her half-smoked cigarette on the turflike carpet beneath the wet canopy, then rubbed it into the furry pile with her toe. This callous disregard for the property of others—even though Bo didn't give a damn about the carpet or the funeral home that had sent it—irked him unreasonably. He had to pretend very hard that he didn't want to yank her about and slap her.

But he couldn't pretend hard enough to keep from saying, "Have you ever thought, Mama, that murderers—bona fide killers—may just be people pretending really hard not to be as good as their natural impulses would lead them to be if it weren't for this silly mandate of yours to avoid at all cost doing what would be truest to our God-given selves? Does that ever occur to you?"

Josey had started walking toward the glistening limo in which Ned, Gary, and Gary's mother sat. But she stopped and looked back at Bo. "I don't know what you're talking about."

"I mean, maybe heterosexuals are really born gays, or lesbians, who've overcome their true wishes by pretending very hard to prefer members of the opposite sex. Maybe Dad was a queer with so much willpower no one ever suspected him of faggotry, and maybe you're a lesbian of such self-denying courage you kept making it with Dad even though the act itself turned your stomach."

Libby caught his sleeve. "Bo, don't."

"*You* turn my stomach," Josephine Gavin said. "I wish *you* were in that casket. I wish just pretending would put you there."

Libby restrained him bodily, but Bo continued to rant. "Just think about it. Maybe child molesters are simply well-disciplined necrophiliacs. Arsonists are brave souls defying their unreasoning terror of matches. Embezzlers are generous folks who—"

"Bo, stop it!"

"—have to fight like crazy to resist the impulse to give all their worldly goods to charity. Liars are people with such a deep respect for the truth they always decline to speak it. Chain-saw murderers are wimps sickened by the sight of blood who nevertheless commit spectacular carnage. Drugs dealers are— "

"*Damn it, Bo! Shut up!*"

He fell silent. His head felt balloonlike, detached. People all over the cemetery were staring at him—funeral goers, passerby, groundskeepers.

Ned opened a rear door of the limousine for Josey. Before stooping to enter, she looked at Bo across the damp, marker-studded lawn as if he were a manifestation of some repellent supernatural force. Her eyes scorched him, cigarette-lighter coils held to the tender flesh of his identity.

"You're evil, Beaumont," she told him. "So evil you can't even pretend any more you're not. You've forgotten how."

She ducked into the pearl-gray limo, Ned waved it on, and the car left the cemetery by a gate beyond which the smoke-stacks of the city's defunct steel plants rose up in the rain like swollen black tree trunks. Nearer, real junipers waved wet boughs.

Ned came walking over, rolling across the grass as if he

were Captain Bligh and the lawn were the main deck of H.M.S. *Bounty*.

"I told you so," he said, his eyes red-rimmed.

"There's a new one for Bartlett's."

"Just consider what your greater wit has wrought, Bo, and maybe you'll see why lameness like mine still has its appeal." His hands deep in his trouser pockets, Ned nodded distractedly at Lib.

The throbbing in Bo's temples had grown worse. He sat down on one of the cold folding chairs and put his head between his knees. "I've lost them both," he said. "For good and all."

"You've still got me, Beaumont," Ned told him.

Lib said, "Yeah, a hundred and fifty miles up I-Twenty-five in Denver." She sat down next to Bo and stroked the nape of his neck with two fingers. She still felt not herself, and having to keep her knees together because of this salmon-colored polyester dress added to her uncomfortable self-estrangement. The only good thing that had happened today was that Gary had ridden off with Mama Josey and Pamela Fay without trying to talk to her—no sledgehammer-subtle badgering about her lawyerly "theft" of "his" ranch.

Ned was standing legs apart, shoulders thrown back, as he had stood while playing his saxophone solo. "If you're jealous of the fact that I'm Mama's alpha-and-omega son and want to take some cheap revenge on me—no, make that *expensive* revenge—all you have to do, Bo, is bollix up the ad campaign you're doing for us. The Big Boss himself will have my scrotum for a dice bag." He smiled sheepishly. "I beg your pardon, Elizabeth."

Wanly, Bo looked up at his brother.

"Are you at all close to being finished?" Ned asked.

"Yeah. I'm real close," Bo said listlessly.

"Shoot it on up to me when you are. We want to get this thing into production. ASAP."

Bo lowered his head again.

Ned blew a fingertip kiss toward their father's casket. Some men in khaki jumpsuits came under the awning to begin folding and stacking chairs. Ned kissed Lib on the forehead, shoved his hands into his pants pockets, and ambled across the wet lawn to a second limousine, in which Papa Nate's pall-bearers sat patiently awaiting his arrival.

Once again, Bo put his head between his knees.

"You all right?" Libby asked.

"No," he said. "But I can pretend."

# 20

Snowy Falls nestled half a mile down the mountain from Libby's ranch. More a village than a town, Snowy Falls took its focus from Mrs. Thrower's boardinghouse.

In fact, Mrs. Thrower's was three structures in one on a raised Western sidewalk that always made Libby think of the sets on old cowboy TV shows like *Wanted, Dead, or Alive*, (Except that there was no livery stable or saloon on this set, only a few adobe hovels, a garage, two churches, and a bodega called the Cove.) The buildings making up Mrs. Thrower's were the U.S. Post Office, Gina's General Merchandise, and the boardinghouse proper—with a flashy tin roof that reflected the languid bodies of magpies and the hurtling ones of red-winged blackbirds. The chickens pecking about beneath the boardwalk spent half their time darting under it to escape circling hawks and the predatory shadows of willow branches and afternoon thunderheads.

Two gas pumps—regular leaded and regular lead-free—guarded the front of Gina's General Merchandise. Libby reckoned them the costliest, orneriest self-service pumps in Colorado. Only rarely did vehicles fuel up at them. In fact, Lib usually had Sam buy gas for the pickup in Huerfano. When she did gas up at Gina's, it was almost a small bribe to ensure the old lady's goodwill.

At noon, Libby parked her truck near some boulders thirty yards above the boardinghouse. Bo had just finished his marketing assignment from Zubrecht Products, Inc., in Denver, while Libby and Sam, along with Arvill Rudd's cowhands, had just concluded a spring roundup that had run long because of some tricky weather, the death of Bo's daddy, and the roundup going on concurrently at the Rudd place. The three of them sauntered down the road to Gina's. A goat chewing forbs near an adobe hovel bleated at them, and several mistrustful chickens went scurrying.

Once on the weathered planking, Libby herded Sam and Bo into the boardinghouse, gave Amy the cashier twelve bucks, and, noting her guests' reticence, took them directly into the dining room. Here, postmaster Ernest Waldrop and Arvill Rudd's top hand Brooklyn Terry were sitting at table bantering and heaping their plates. Bowls of cooked vegetables, canning jars of corn relish, and dozens of cups and dishes ranged across the oilcloth.

Waldrop stood up, announced Lib's entrance with a fist trumpet, and bowed the newcomers into the vacant chairs opposite Terry and him. Libby laughed, but Sam and Bo were poker-faced, as if afraid that Waldrop—a decent guy—was openly mocking them.

"Hoooeee!" Brooklyn Terry cried. "Didn't think you'd let Gina feed you, Lib, till you'd won yourself a Publishers' Clearing House sweepstakes. Guess you're aging into generosity."

"Gentlemen, meet my cousin Beaumont. Bo has just wrapped up a big ad job for a major company in Denver. And Sam and I finished branding, vaccinating, and dehorning our final stray dogie about"—she checked her watch—"an hour and seventeen minutes ago. That's why I'm treating these hard-working devils to the goodies here at Gina's, and I hope to hell you greedy chowhounds had the decency to save us some greens and corn bread." She made a dramatic survey of the bowls and platters on the oilcloth. "Just as I feared—you've already done a number on everything."

"Castrating calves always makes me hungry," Brooklyn said, then shouted into the kitchen, "Hey, Gina, bring us a few more mountain oysters!"

Waldrop laughed uproariously.

Libby leaned into Bo to whisper, "And Gary liked to call *me* a ballbuster." She anticipated a smile, or at least an ironically raised eyebrow, but Bo poured himself a tumbler of tea and sipped from it as if he hadn't even heard. Sam, who had worked closely with Brooklyn Terry for several weeks, was equally narrow-eyed and unforthcoming.

Out of the kitchen came the queen of the Thrower complex, Gina Thrower herself, a tall woman with arms like old ropes and a face like carved granite. "There's plenty left," she said, setting down a bowl of chicken-fried steak and another of mashed potatoes. Then she eased her long body into the chair next to Waldrop's. "No need to fret."

Dishes got passed. Amy brought hot biscuits from the kitchen, and a Chicana girl carried in bowls of green beans and coleslaw. A moment later, she returned with a golden wheel of corn bread, and Amy was back with a platter of fried pies bursting with cinnamon-brown sweetmeats.

Waldrop and Terry took third and fourth helpings that in no way diminished the newcomers' fair share. Bo never ate much, anyway, and Sam limited himself today to one piece of steak and a mound of potatoes. It disturbed Libby that, of the three of them, *she* was the patron taking greatest advantage of Gina's all-you-can-eat-for-four-bucks menu.

Brooklyn, a sandy-haired guy with squint lines and heavy mauve lips, said, "What kind of ad work were you doing, Bo?"

"Something for Zubrecht Products, Incorporated."

"Yeah, but what?"

"A health-care product."

"Toothpaste? Mouthwash?"

"Go easy," Libby said. "It's like a writer finishing a book. Read the book. Don't ask Bo to tell it to you."

"What goddamn book are we supposed to read," Brooklyn said, "if he won't even tell us the goddamn title?"

"It's a condom ad," Bo said. "The first ad for a condom you see on national TV . . . well, it'll probably be mine."

"Pardon me for saying so," Waldrop told him, "but you may be smart to keep *that* news under your hat."

"Holy shit!" Brooklyn said. "How in the hell do you go about advertising a rubber on TV? Animation?"

Bo said, "There *is* some animation—computer animation."

"Fucking sex-education stuff? Sperm and ovaries and bunches of fucking little mobile arrows to show what they do?"

"It's really more a metaphorical approach," Bo said. "Which is all I feel free to tell you about it right now."

"Like this?" Brooklyn said. "'I dreamed I met Miss September in my Love Muscle Latex'? Or: 'Mother, *please*, I'd rather put it on myself'? Or: 'Steel-belted Goodfeels, for when the rubber hits the rufus road'? How about it? Am I in the ballpark?"

"You're out of line," Lib said, but she was smiling so broadly that Brooklyn said, "Hoooooeee!" again and plopped another scoop of mashed potatoes on to his plate.

"Is Sam all right?" Gina Thrower said, unexpectedly diverting everyone's attention from Bo.

"I'm okay," Sam said, his hooded eyes instantly alert.

"Well, those're the first words you've muttered since coming here," the sinewy old lady said. "Did you know that?"

"Just busy eating, I guess."

"You're a Muache, aren't you, Sam?" Gina asked him. "From the Southern Ute Reservation down by Ignacio?"

Guardedly, Sam admitted that he was. Libby wondered why Gina, who could sometimes put on a grouch and rub even her best patrons' sensibilities raw, was quizzing Sam.

The old lady leaned forward. "Sam, do you know DeWayne Sky?"

"Yes, ma'am. He's the head of our tribal council. Wasn't when I left. Is now."

"Ever talk to him?"

Sam, Lib saw, started to say no, but reconsidered and mumbled, "Yeah. Sometimes."

"When?" Libby asked. "You haven't gone back to the reservation since coming to work for Gary and me."

Sam took a bite of steak to camouflage his perplexity.

"You gonna talk to Sky any time soon?"

"Why?" Libby demanded—even though, technically, it was none of her business. "Why are you asking Sam these things, Gina?"

The lariat-lean old gal turned a what's-it-to-you? eye on Lib. "Our quadrennial Pioneer Days is coming up," she said. "I'd like Sam to recruit this Muache chieftain—this DeWayne Sky fella—to be our grand marshal. We'll be having the high-school band up from Huerfano, a pay-as-you-go barbecue, a few nifty prairie schooners, and a bunch of other floats, and we need a real Native American to head up the festivities."

"Then why not Sam, Gina?"

"He's not a chief. He's got no grand-marshal experience."

"Sky's no chief, either," Sam said. "He's the chairman of our tribal council."

"Chief. Chairman. Same difference. I've looked into it. Sky did a parade down in Angular last year and cut a handsome figure."

"Snowy Falls gonna pay him?"

"Two hundred bucks, Sam. Plus travel expenses. Not to mention all the free barbecue he can put away."

"Then I'll get him for you. That ought to about do it."

"When? When can you say for sure? If he won't show, I'll need to get somebody else. An ex-miner, maybe. Or a war hero."

"Is a week soon enough? I'll talk to him next week."

"That's the outside limit, Sam. If you're not back to me with Sky's acceptance by next Friday, I'm after somebody else."

Outside on the boardwalk, Libby got in front of Sam and grabbed him by the wrists. Bo was already on his way down the steps.

"How is it you'll be talking with the chairman of your tribal council next week, Sam?"

He gently shook his hands free and laid them on her shoulders. "Hon," he said, "I've got to be in Ignacio next Friday anyway—it shouldn't be too hard to find and talk to Sky."

"Why do you have to be in Ignacio?"

"Because my daughter—my daughter Paisley—it's her graduation, Miss Libby. I have to go."

Lib stared hard at Sam. She had known about his daughter—that he had one—but until this moment she hadn't realized that the girl was now a young woman. Sam seldom talked about Paisley, and then only when pressed, and because all his memories were of a child caressing stuffed animals or sitting in his lap looking at picture books, these were the images he had communicated to Libby and therefore the ones she had absorbed.

"I *can* go, can't I? Roundup's over, and I'll be back a couple of days after she's picked up her diploma."

"Sure you can," Bo said. "Our mean old Boss Lady wouldn't keep you here on your daughter's graduation day."

Sam threaded his arm through Libby's and walked her

down the steps. "I'd like to leave Thursday. Catch a bus in Huerfano, get down there that evening."

"I'll take you to the bus station," Lib said, pleased to note that Bo had developed a real regard for Sam after Sam had taken him to see the mating kar'tajans.

As for Sam's muteness in Mrs. Thrower's—his disinclination to talk with anyone—that wasn't hard to explain. He'd been worrying about making arrangements to get to Paisley's graduation.

Back in the truck, returning to the Tipsy Q, the three of them sat shoulder to shoulder, gamely enduring the shocks imparted by the washboard roadway. Lib, wrestling the wheel, was aware that their dinner at Gina's had been a pretty lame celebration. To make up for it, they should be singing songs and cracking jokes, and yet they were riding in silence—never mind the relentless banging of the pickup—as if on the way to their own hangings.

Bo, however, reached deep into his jeans pocket and withdrew a key ring. "You won't have to take a bus to Ignacio," he told Sam. "I want you to take my car."

"Why, Bo, bless your heart," Libby said.

"In fact, just keep the car."

"What?" Sam said.

"Keep the car," Bo reiterated. "I'm giving it to you."

Bemusedly, Sam hefted the key ring. "Why?"

"So you'll have transportation to and from Ignacio. What am *I* going to do with an automobile?"

Damn it, thought Libby. More intimations of mortality.

But Sam smiled. "Thanks," he said, pocketing the key ring. "I mean it, white eyes, thanks a load." He patted Bo's knee and made an upbeat clucking noise with his tongue.

In the Denver offices of Zubrecht Products, Inc., Ned Gavin led his boss, Everett Zubrecht, and four other company executives into a soundproof presentation room on the fifteenth floor.

Ned was nervous. Outside, he recalled, a late-spring inversion layer had settled upon the city, holding a thick dun haze in place; now and again, anomalous eddies would perturb this haze, giving it the look of smoke in a huge brandy snifter.

A perfect description of Ned's emotional state—hazy and perturbed.

If Zubrecht and his catty yes-men don't like what Bo has sent us, he told himself, I'll have made a fifty-thousand-dollar fuckup, and my ongoing climb to the top will have suddenly encountered an obstacle. Not that any of these bastards, Peter excepted, will regard my comeuppance, and subsequent comedown, with anything other than great inward glee.

Peter Zubrecht was Ned's former college roommate and the nephew of the only man in the room whose opinion truly counted. Peter sat down next to his uncle in the front row of the tiny theater, while the other three ZP Inc. officials lowered themselves into chairs on the conspicuously elevated row behind it. When two of these men began to confer in whispers, Ned suspected that they were debating his fate if Bo's pilot ad failed to excite their CEO.

Sean Broiles, vice-president in charge of products research and the older of the whisperers, abruptly faced front. "Why isn't your brother here, Ned? This *is* his work, isn't it?"

The implication was that Ned had only *ostensibly* farmed out to a relative an ad-campaign proposal that Ned had actually prepared, thus helping himself to some company money otherwise unavailable to salaried employees. The charge stank, but Broiles had leveled it so indirectly that Ned would have been an idiot to react to it with either indignation or aggrieved bitchiness.

"Beaumont Gavin is ill," Everett Zubrecht said. He was wearing chocolate-brown slacks, a suede jacket, and hand-tooled leather boots, which were stretched out into the lane between the front row and the semicircular stage on which Ned was waiting for a chance to begin Beaumont's presentation. "He's *deathly* ill," Zubrecht went on. "Ned says we're fortunate he was able to finish."

"Deathly ill with what?" Broiles asked.

"Meningitis," Ned lied. He'd be an utter nincompoop to tell that Bo had Kaposi's sarcoma, that the AIDS virus was waging merciless guerrilla war against his immune system.

"Sorry to hear that, Ned," Broiles said. "Please go on with what your brother—at some personal cost—has sent us."

"All right," Ned said, looking straight into the eyes of the man who mattered. "Everyone here understands that Mr.

Broiles's division has created a condom superior in both sensitivity and protective capability to nearly all those made by our competitors, and that we intend to tout it nationwide this summer on late-night broadcasts of ABC's *Nightline* and on reruns of the CBS cop show *Cagney and Lacey* and the NBC comedy *Cheers*.

"Gentlemen, we'll be making history. We must inform without offending, merchandise without haranguing. No easy task. However, I believe that the independent agency of Gavin Graphics has succeeded admirably in these aims. I further believe that you will come to feel as I do. But there's no way to know for sure until you've seen the stunning pilot ad from Gavin Graphics."

A large wraparound video screen dominated the rear wall. With a handheld remote, Ned dialed down the lights and activated the VCR unit on line to the screen. Immediately, the room seemed ten degrees cooler, as if a blanket of gelid air had wafted in along with the steadily infiltrating darkness. The pads of Ned's palms felt like shifting lenses of ice—only a cold sweat, but as he eased himself into the seat next to Peter, he blotted his palms on his pants legs.

Bo's computer-animated ad pilot materialized on the wraparound screen: a matrix of swirling blue-white mist out of which a single unicorn stallion came galloping in dreamy slow-motion. This mythic creature came straight at the viewer, scything its horn and growing larger as it came. Behind its image, evocative music swelled, a melody that Ned had earlier recognized as the Glenn Miller theme, "Moonlight Sonata," but here imparted an exotic tango flavor and played on guitars.

Suddenly, the viewer zoomed away from the galloping unicorn and rocketed skyward so that the animal was seen from on high, running through mist-hung trees and alongside sudden pools of diamond-blue water—until in a glade of white birch trees it encountered another unicorn, smaller than itself, and the viewer was whirled dizzyingly to ground level again. Then a panther—an inky apparition—leapt from the fog-draped woods. Startled, the stallion reared, flashing its hooves, and the cat fell back, disappearing as if vacuumed into shadow. The unicorns—as the ad's point of view rotated and rose—trotted off through the virgin snow, touching muzzles and leaving their cavern hoofprints on the whiteness.

"*Kar'tajans,*" a serene male voice intoned. (Ned had dubbed the voice of a professional actor over Bo's somewhat reedy narration.) "*For intimacy. For security. For love. Kar'tajans. A peerless protector in a new time of peril. Kar'tajans.*"

The ad concluded with a superimposed closeup of a package of the condoms, featuring a unicorn head against a blue background and an identifying line of print: *One dozen technologically advanced condoms with a special viricidal lubricant.*

Ned sat nervously in the dark, waiting for Trail Boss Zubrecht, or Peter, or the always semihostile Broiles to comment.

"Screen it again," Everett Zubrecht said.

Ned did. It took thirty seconds. The silence afterward was as biting as the air-conditioned darkness.

"Pardon my French, Mr. Zubrecht," Al Pettigrew from sales and promotion said, "but what the hell does *kartajans* mean?"

This question blew the lid off a Pandora's box of questions, the addressing of which—once Ned had dialed the lights back up—settled his nerves by triggering his innate combativeness. Back in front of the group, he explained the word's origin. He argued that *kar'tajans* was sufficiently exotic to pique yuppie curiosity and sufficiently relevant in a metaphorical sense to justify using it as a brand name for their product.

"Do female unicorns have horns?" Broiles asked. "I mean, both the unicorns in this thing have horns. That suggests—"

"Homosexuality?" Ned said, enjoying himself. "That Zubrecht Products is cynically targeting gay males rather than responsible heterosexual couples?"

"Exactly," Broiles said. "Exactly."

"The size difference between our animated unicorns is meant to suggest sexual dimorphism—the male larger, the female much smaller. We're covered. But if a certain portion of our product's likely consumers choose, even subconsciously, to interpret the fact that both unicorns have horns to mean that they're both male—well, so be it. We could benefit from that too. It isn't intentionally misleading, it's just . . . happily ambiguous."

More questions followed. Was the phallic imagery too

obvious? Was the name *Kar'tajans* too esoteric to fly? Was that apostrophe in the word really necessary? Did the ad play too much on public fears? Would blacks object to having the AIDS epidemic—or VD in general—represented by a sleek ebony panther? Would the use of unicorns inadvertently make the ad a must-see for underage fantasy-gamers and teenybopper horse lovers?

"Will the networks let us get away with a unicorn's head on our packaging?" Broiles asked.

"Why wouldn't they?" Ned said.

"Frankly, Gavin, that's like sticking an angry foot-long dick in their faces. Subtle, this isn't."

"There's a famous perfume ad where the shadow of a jet plane flies between the legs of a woman in a backless bathing suit. By comparison, we're as chaste as nuns."

"Whatever you finally do, Gavin, that lousy apostrophe has to go," Pettigrew said. "It's pretentious and confusing."

"Fine," Ned said. He didn't mind. Making a concession or two demonstrated one's reasonableness.

Warming to the battle, he refuted every other objection. The eyes of Everett Zubrecht—who kept a kingly silence—imbibed light from the overheads, growing brighter and ever more roguish as they drank. The Big Boss was enjoying Ned's performance as much as Ned was. He was having himself a fine time.

"Kartajans," Zubrecht said at last. "Minus the apostrophe."

The hush in the room had a raw, concupiscent edge.

"Otherwise," he said, "we'll go with it exactly as it's been screened. It's lovely."

Standing in the middle of her cramped living room, Libby, Sam, and Bo touched wineglasses. Bo had just spoken long-distance with Ned, who had conveyed word of his ad's success with the founder and CEO of Zubrecht Products, Inc. Great, Libby thought. This news gave them a second chance to celebrate, and although they might have flubbed their noontide party at Mrs. Thrower's, they wouldn't drop the ball tonight.

She had found a spiderwebbed bottle of cold duck in a kitchen cupboard—cached there in the second or third year of her failed marriage—and had splashed it into these glasses, along with some freezer-furred ice cubes, to mark Bo's triumph.

"So tell us about the ad," she said. "Now that Big Everett has accepted it, there's no jinx in talking about it."

"It'll be a bigger kick if you wait and see it on TV, m'lady."

"You Took Advantage of Me" by the Paul Whiteman orchestra, with a vocal by Bing Crosby, was playing on Bo's jam box. While sipping their cold duck and turning about one another more or less in time to this music, the three of them became conscious of a noise out beyond the barn. Lib picked it up first. It was Bounty, the aged gun dog, barking frantically and apparently drawing nearer the house as he barked. What was wrong? They had been home all afternoon, nobody had turned into the drive, and, at last check, Bounty's food bowls were brimming with dog chow and tap water.

"I'll go see," Sam said. He set his stem of cold duck on the Bendix and went outside.

A few moments later, he was back. "Maybe you guys should come too," he said. They obliged him, and when they stood in the drive facing the barn, Bounty madly barking, Libby saw the kar'tajans—stallion and mare—poised between flight and defiance in the chapel of the barn door.

Bo, who had felt a bit tipsy even before drinking Libby's cold duck, gaped. Were these the the same kar'tajans that Sam had shown him from the clearing on Ptarmigan Mountain? He was a good two hundred yards nearer the creatures now, and although they were in shadow, he could see them clearly. The twisting ebony horns. The tufted ears, pasterns, and cannons. The sapphirine eyes. It was like seeing ghost—no, *two* ghosts.

Abruptly, Libby angled past the aspens toward the animals, who observed her coming with what struck Bo as an insane calm. Insane kar'tajans and a crazy lady ranch owner. Didn't Lib realize that the stallion—hell, the mare—could disembowel her with a stab of its horn and a lightning-quick follow-through?

"Don't!" he shouted. He had already lost Keith and Papa Nate. He was in no hurry to see Lib follow them. "Do something," he told Sam. "Stop her!"

Sam was stunned. Except for that time in Naismith's Mine when eight of them had paraded past him as if he were invisible, he had never been so close to these visitors from

Elsewhere, and he could not believe that they had dared to approach Libby's ranch house—a human settlement!—as they had. Briefly, he was unable to move. Then he shook himself, shouted, "Don't, Miss Libby!" and trotted awkwardly after her.

The kar'tajans, to Libby's surprise, stood their ground. She felt her courage bottoming out. No matter. She marched toward the barn (Sam skipping at her side, telling her how stupidly she was acting), whereupon the kar'tajans refusal to budge became not just a disconcerting but a menacing phenomenon, and she slowed.

The male—as Sam had reported of other mute visitors from their impossible dimension, and as Lib could see for herself tonight—was sick. His ribs protruded. Magenta sores spotted his flanks, legs, and throatlatch. His nostrils, repeatedly widening and narrowing, heartbreakingly puffing his fatigue, were lined with scarlet. On the good side, however, the spike spiraling up from the stallion's forehead had the innate utility of a tire iron and the stark beauty of a burnished gun barrel. He had a beard like a goat's.

As for the mare, she was huddled against the stallion's flank, eyeing the approaching humans with both hope and apprehension—if, Libby cautioned herself, she were reading the mare correctly. She decided that she was, shushed Sam Coldpony, and hiked straight into the barn. There, holding the sick male's head, she began stroking him between the base of his alicorn and his nostrils, rubbing his bony head with wonder-stricken pity, amazed to be doing so.

"See there?" she told Sam. "What do you think?"

Bo came up last. He sat down on the bottom step of the rickety stairs to the loft. "What *I* think," he said, "is that here we have proof positive that those old tales about its taking a virgin to catch a unicorn are absolute bullshit."

"Up yours," Libby said mildly. The animals beside her gave off an odor like those of ripening fruit and musty carpets, and she was gratified to have finally drawn near enough to embrace a kar'tajan, not merely to sketch one. Maybe it was from Elsewhere, but it had real bones, an honest-to-God aroma, and a coat that sloughed hairs onto your fingers when you touched it.

"Now what are you going to do?" Bo demanded from his

perch on the ramshackle loft step. The victory he had earned with Zubrecht Products, Inc., had already begun to seem hollow. He couldn't look at these two unicorns—real kar'tajans—without feeling the rotary movement of an intangible blade through his belly and gut.

"Bed them down, I guess." Libby looked toward the manger where she and Sam had midwifed the two-headed calf. "Over there ought to do." By hooking her knuckles under the beast's chin, she was able to coax him through the dark barn to the birthing stall. His mate came too, following placidly, trusting in Lib to do right by both of them and sidling into the cramped crib with a gracefulness that was at once preternatural and fillylike.

Sam ambled to the stall. "Whatever that stallion's got could be catching. He could infect your horses, hon."

"What do you want me to do?" Libby said. "Shoot him?"

"A solution often proposed for PWAs," Bo said, standing behind Sam now and peering in.

The stallion, as trustful as his mate, had collapsed into the hay featherbedding a corner of the manger. Libby knelt beside him, stroking the taut line of his cheek and scrutinizing the burgundy lesions that glistened under the cobwebbed 100-watter like overripe strawberries. The mare stayed on her feet, a four-legged blockade across the upright seam of two walls.

"That's not my solution," Lib said. "Why don't we do what we'd do with the horses, Sam, and call in the vet?"

Sam could think of a thousand reasons why that was a piss-poor solution, including the obvious one that a vet from Huerfano would probably know damn little about the illnesses of imaginary equines from a transdimensional reality, but because *Sam* knew nothing about caring for sick kar'tajans, and because he understood that his boss wasn't going to sit still while the beast's condition deteriorated, he walked back to the house to telephone Dr. Preston Brinkley.

Even though it was past eight o'clock, Brinkley came. He lived and worked in Huerfano, and it took him nearly an hour to make the drive up Highway 69. He believed he had been summoned to look at Libby's favorite quarter horse, Telluride, and he came thinking that Telluride was the victim of a peculiar sudden-onset palsy that he had never treated before.

Once on the Tipsy Q, he was disabused of this notion by his first sight of the animal lying on its side in the stall, and his first reflexive act was to grip the alicorn in his meaty fist and use it as a lever to lift and reposition the creature's docile but dead-weight head, a trophy that Bo could imagine every sportsman in the world willing to die for. Even the female's shorter, somewhat thinner spike would have provoked universal bloodlust.

"My God," Brinkley said. "Where in fuckin' glory did you folks come across these babies?"

Bo was fascinated by the vet. He was the biggest *old* man that he could ever recall beholding, a jut-jawed polar bear of a fellow with massive shoulders and a hip as high as Bo's rib cage.

It took Brinkley five minutes to bend down and fifteen to stand up. The female took fright and darted out of the stall into the equipment-crowded runway between the loft and the saddle sheds. There, she paced. Brinkley had driven her out—by his bulk, by his ponderousness, and by a voice so resonant that even his whispers suggested a laryngitic grizzly growling into an oil drum.

"What's wrong with this poor creature?" Libby asked.

"Besides the fact that he shouldn't exist?" Brinkley shot back, one big hand on the heaving pale flank.

"Yes."

"I can't say, Mrs. Quarrels. I don't have a lot of experience diagnosing these here fellas."

Bo remembered the weird-ass broadcast of Mutual of Omaha's *Wild Kingdom* on Libby's Bendix. "Swamp fever?" he said.

"If this were a horse, maybe," Brinkley said, squinting up at Bo skeptically. "Being as this is . . . something else, it could be most anything. Measles, fantasy flu, you name it."

"But what if it were a horse and you suspected swamp fever?" Bo said. "What then?"

"I'd draw blood and try to confirm my diagnosis with a Coggins test—an immunodiffusion laboratory test for sick horses."

"Do it, then," Libby said. "Go ahead and do it."

"No results until tomorrow afternoon," Brinkley said. "That

soon enough for you? Or were you hoping I'd goose old Lancelot here back into the woods tonight?"

"It's soon enough," Libby said. "But don't spread this around, Dr. Brinkley. We've got a secret herd of them here on the Tipsy Q, and I'm afraid of what'll happen if word leaks out. I'm afraid of what's going to happen anyway. Sam says *several* of the ones he's seen are sick. He's already watched one die."

"A long yearling," Sam said. "Just below Abbot's Pate."

"What if your Coggins test says it's swamp fever?" Bo put in. "What do we do in that case?"

"With horses, Mr. Gavin, pretty fuckin' little." Brinkley was using a syringe to draw blood from the kar'tajan's throat, and the stallion, although still occasionally blowing, was making no other protest. "They either outlast the virus or get steadily punier and pass on. There's no cure, only nursing and hope."

"You won't spread this around, will you?" Libby said.

"What? Equine infectious anemia? Shit, no. Not me."

"You know what I mean."

"Listen, Mrs. Quarrels, if I breathed one goddamn word of this down in Huerfano—*unicorn*, for Christ's sake!—Covarrubias and the other greedy shysters would pack me off to the funny farm. Did Sam call because you folks trusted me or because I was the handiest horse doctor in the fuckin' phone book?"

This question, Bo could tell, abashed Libby, who had called on Dr. Preston Brinkley dozens of times over the years. He was a good vet, bearlike and blunt, and he kept his own counsel.

And so, having advised them to close the stall and to go in and get a little sleep, Brinkley left.

The next afternoon, he telephoned from Huerfano to say that the Coggins test had proved positive for equine infectious anemia, a.k.a. swamp fever, and that the Tipsy Q horses were indeed at risk if the unicorn were not isolated and if the virus peculiar to its unlikely species could infect "regular horses," too.

Because Libby and Sam were in the barn seeing to the kar'tajan stallion and his restless mate, Bo took the call and wrote down the pertinent information. What he had done for

Ned kept crowding into the foreground of his consciousness, and he rang off from Brinkley feeling that his AIDS, the unicorns' swamp fever, and the marketing ploy he'd devised for ZP Inc. were all inextricably tangled in ways that would condemn him—if there were a hell—to everlasting fire. He ached in every sinew.

# 21

In Bo's Mazda, driving U.S. 160 southwest out of Huerfano, Sam remembered the jaunt he had made going the other way in a jury-rigged elk-drawn buggy. That trip had concluded with his arrival at the Tipsy Q, where, against all expectation, he had come to feel almost as welcome as he ever had on the Southern Ute reservation on the New Mexico border.

In fact, after the Quarrelses' divorce (and that tail-chasing Gary's retreat to a ranch in Texas), Sam had almost, but not quite, convinced himself that he would never return to Ignacio. He had occasionally entertained the bozo notions of slipping back to woo Dolores again or to rescue Paisley from the boredom of reservation life—but D'lo's suicide had shown him how late in the day it was, and he'd never really believed that a reunion with Payz would end in spontaneous avowals of mutual esteem.

For these reasons, and others, Sam had subconsciously begun to regard the Tipsy Q as home, and although he had prayed to the Great Manitou to reunite Paisley and him through the mystic offices of the kar'tajans, he had forgotten that the Holy He-She would first resort to the mundane ploy of graduation ceremony.

Driving, Sam was nervous and full of guilt. He realized that he would almost rather be arriving naked in Grand Central Station than coming back to Ignacio fourteen years after abandoning the girl. He owed her his presence at this event, the most significant to date in her life, but he feared the one-on-one face-off that paying his debt would entail. He wanted to see and embrace his daughter, yes, but he wished he had found some way to let her inevitable resentment diffuse a little. He hadn't. The roundup, his fears, and the sudden appearance of those kar'tajans in Miss Libby's barn had prevented him.

An hour from Snowy Falls, Sam reached the top of North La Veta Pass and swung into a horseshoe-shaped overlook to breathe in the sharp air and to think. At the speed he was going—about fifty, slower on the upgrades—the trip would take four more hours.

Sam had left the Tipsy Q at noon, after taking a final look at the sick kar'tajan. The day after Brinkley's visit, the female had banged around the stall so insistently that Sam had let her go. Bounty barking at her from a safe distance, she had trotted into a draw on Ptarmigan Mountain and vanished amid the granite outcroppings and the silent evergreens.

The stallion, her mate, was holding his own, without markedly improving, but Sam could not forget that the kar'tajans, over the past three years, had established a pattern of showing up around Christmas and migrating out by early July. Was it almost time for them to retreat again? If they stayed true to form, yes. But more had been fleeing their desert Elsewhere through Naismith's Mine (and maybe a hidden portal on Abbot's Pate) than ever before, and Sam was starting to suspect that their secret migrations were going ahead with greater urgency. Were they transferring en masse from that peculiar reality to this one?

If his suspicions were correct, this was a crucial time on the Tipsy Q. Maybe he shouldn't be running out on Miss Libby and her not intolerably fruity cousin-in-law right now. Parked high on La Veta Pass, Sam considered turning around and going back to Snowy Falls. Then he heard Dolores say, "That'd be just like you, Sam Coldshoulder—running out on Alma again."

Sam sat up behind the steering wheel to search for the source of this voice. Was it only memory, or had that doggedly vengeful woman's *ini'putc'* shown up again to torment him? He had not seen her ghost since the midnight it had led him to the door into the spirit realm in Naismith's Mine and then hurtled off into the dark on Ouray's back. In fact, he hadn't seen the great elk Ouray since that night, either. He sat outraged and trembling in the little Mazda.

"Only a piss-poor excuse for an hombre would cut and run on his baby girl twice," D'lo accused. Sam knew that he had heard rather than remembered *this* disembodied voice. He yanked the door handle and jumped out onto the overlook's cracked pavement.

A beige and white RV pulling a Chevy Cavalier was struggling up La Veta Pass. Its driver glanced over at Sam as if at a madman. Being seen by him was embarrassing but also reassuring. How could a ghost talk to you in the middle of such a quiet afternoon? When the RV began its descent of the western grade, Sam found himself staring across the forested abyss beneath him at two figures on the opposite hillside: an elk with a rack far too big for early June, and a sun-haloed rider in buckskin and beaded leggings.

Ricocheting sunlight made it hard to assess the reality of this double apparition, but Sam knew that for him it was real. He dove back into the car and squinted through its windshield to see if his dead ex-wife and the magnificent wapiti were still there. They were. D'lo broadcast again from the car's radio speakers: "Those two damn Anglos are all right. Go to Alma's graduation!"

"I will," he said. "That's what I was doing."

"If not just for Alma's sake," the radio speakers went on, "then because you told Gina Thrower you'd talk to DeWayne. There's important stuff to do in Ignacio."

"Okay," Sam said, trying to turn the radio off but finding that its knobs had no say-so over this broadcast.

"For once, just once, do what's right for *somebody else*."

"Okay!" he cried, peering across the abyss. "Now get off my back! Ouray's, too! What business do you have riding him?"

"This business," D'lo said, her last words to him. She turned the elk with her knees—sunlight winking off her beaded leggings as if the beads were minute Christmas-tree bulbs—and rode him down a path behind a jagged border of ponderosa pine and Douglas fir that hid them from view. Sam kept peering, but they were gone, and he was in doubt again about their reality. His last glimpse of D'lo's *ini'putc'* had shown it to be—as dictated by the grim character of her suicide—headless.

Yet again, Sam realized, he had an erection, this one bent by his jeans and by his posture behind the wheel. Yet again, he was ashamed and confused. He had loved D'lo, but in hating what *she* loved—the reservation—he had let her divorce him and had forsaken his birthplace and his family. Maybe his humiliating physical ache was as much for his lost past as for D'lo's ruined spirit body.

Sam twisted on the seat, closed his eyes, and sat waiting for the starch to go out of him. When, finally, it did, he jammed the car in gear and ran it through the counties of Alamosa, Rio Grande, Mineral, Archuleta, and La Plata, into the proud but bitter heart of a private Indian Territory.

In Ignacio at last, in the brass heat of the afternoon, Sam had sufficient loyalty to register at the Pino Nuche motel, a Ute-owned and Ute-run facility in the northern part of town, not too far from DeWayne Sky's grandiose tepee.

The desk clerk at the Pino Nuche was a young Muache unfamiliar to Sam, thank Inu'sakats. However, almost every Ute under the age of twenty would be a stranger to him, and he had already decided not to go looking for people who would remember him—Joey Cuthair, old Herbert Barnes, the parents of Benjamin Elk. Running into such people would only lead to questions, the questions to fussing, and the fussing to fruitless arguments.

He had come to see Paisley receive her diploma (exactly as D'lo had commanded him on La Veta Pass) and to depart without causing a ripple in the sluggish stream of reservation life. At Paisley's graduation, of course, he would be unable to sidestep the gaze and the questions of old acquaintances, but he planned to do all he could to ward off talk, pleas to return, all controversy. Maybe he *could* sidestep such things.

At the Pino Nuche, he signed the register as Samuel C. Taylor, an inversion of the truth that put a blister on his heart.

The clerk, an acne-blemished brave wearing pigtails and a Grateful Dead T-shirt, examined Sam closely. "You Indian?"

"Not enough," Sam said. "Only about an eighth, I guess." This was the tack he had decided to take, to deflect any questions about his identity that his looks might provoke.

Indian, but not Indian; too few *red* blood cells to satisfy BIA computations.

"I only ask," the kid said, "because there's a nice discount if you're Ute, Jicarilla Apache, Navajo, or Hopi."

"I don't qualify," Sam lied. "My blood's Capote Ute, but it's just not thick enough."

"Tough," the kid said sympathetically. He showed Sam the rate schedule and gave him a key.

"Is there a phone in the room?"

"Sure. This is a modern place."

"Yeah. It's been modern a long time. How much d'you put on my tab if I make a phone call?"

"Fifty cents if it's local. That plus whatever you run up with A.T. and T. if it's long-distance."

Sam nodded and found his room. After a hamburger in the motel restaurant (where all the cooks and waitresses, like the maids at the inn, were Anglos or Anglo-Hispanics because too many Utes still thought themselves above such low-level tasks), he returned to his room, checked the telephone book, and dialed the false-front tepee of DeWayne Sky. Even at fifty cents, this would be a cheaper call than the one he'd placed from Tío Pepé's back in March.

LannaSue answered. "Sky's residence."

Sam asked for the "man of the house"—even though he had always liked LannaSue and was briefly tempted to say hello to her just to hear her musical spunky-jolly voice rumble at him again.

Sky's wife spoke again, anyway. "Who is this?"

"Does it matter?" His attempt at a vocal disguise failed.

"Sam," LannaSue said. "Sam Coldpony. You here to see Payz get graduated?"

"I'm calling long distance, LannaSue. I wish you'd put DeWayne on before this really begins to cost me."

"Will you be here tomorrow? If you will, come to the football field. There's gonna be a reviewing stand, and a band, and—"

"LannaSue—"

"It begins at seven thirty. If you're in-state, you got plenty of time to make it. Start driving early."

"I can't. I'm in—" Sam wanted to say Wyoming or Montana and to name a ranch on which he'd worked in the mid 1970s, but realized that asking DeWayne to grand-marshal a Pioneer Days parade in Snowy Falls, Colorado, would probably undermine his lie.

"Sam, your daughter's here. Want me to put her on?"

"God, no, LannaSue!" Sam cried. "Don't even mention it's me. Just let me talk to DeWayne, I'll say my say and get off."

LannaSue's receiver banged—not as if she had slammed it into its cradle but as if she had let go of it in disgust and it had hit the tabletop. "DeWayne," he heard her say, "some sorry pecker wants to talk to you."

A minute went by. If the call had really been long distance, Sam would have fidgeted even more frantically. At last Sky picked up the handset—*clunk, clunk*—and barked, "Okay, talk to me."

Sam identified himself and outlined the grand-marshal proposal from Mrs. Thrower.

"Snowy Falls?" Sky said. "That where you calling from?"

This time Sam refused to lie; he remained mute.

"I'm assuming it is. And I'll do it—be your grand marshal, Coldpony—because I'm assuming so. We'll have us a good long one soon as I get there. When are these Pioneer Days, anyhow?"

Sam told him.

"That's less than a week before Sun Dance, you renegade apple, and I'm the goddamn Sun Dance committee chief."

Which meant, Sam knew, that DeWayne would have to lay out the Thirst House and supervise the ritual, sunrise to sunup, for each of three grueling days. He would also dance. So maybe he wouldn't be able to come. In a way, Sam hoped not—he had no strong desire to sit down for a "good long one" with Sky in Snowy Falls.

"Hell, I'll squeeze it in," the Sun Dance chief finally said.

"Full regalia," Sam said hurriedly.

"I've done this before, Coldpony." A silence intervened. Then Sky said, "I told you I'd pipe buckshot up your wazoo if you came down here before Alm—uh, Paisley's—graduation, but tonight, if I could, I'd boot you in the ass for *not* being here to see her take honors in front of all the Anglos. Did you know she's her class's goddamn salubratorian?"

"Salutatorian," Sam said. "Not salubratorian."

"Okay, whatever. Maybe she got *some* of her smarts—hard

as it is to believe–from her daddy. Don't you want to talk to her? I could fetch her up from the basement."

Not a chance, Sam thought. He set the receiver down, stranding DeWayne Sky amid the hissing buzz of telephone limbo.

How could he attend his daughter's graduation if he wasn't even willing to talk to her over the phone?

Simple. He would go in disguise.

He examined the contents of the cloth suitcase that Miss Libby had loaned him: a new pair of jeans, a new shirt, a pair of shades, and a red acetate scarf for either an ascot or a bandanna. Bo had given him all these items. It wasn't much, but after fourteen years, how fancy would his disguise have to be to fool the Anglos who had never paid him any mind or the Ute parents who would be watching the events marking their darlings' supposed transition to adulthood? Nobody at tomorrow's ceremony would notice him, not even the Skys, Paisley's self-appointed foster parents.

Sam pulled another item from the bag: the alicorn broken from the forehead of that long yearling up on Abbot's Pate. Protection, Sam told himself, against a reappearance of D'lo's *ini'putc'*. If it could show up at Naismith's Cabin or on elkback in La Veta Pass, it could even more easily appear in an Indian place like the Pino Nuche.

And a final thing, another gift from Bo, a talisman he had pushed into the watch pocket of his jeans: a pewter unicorn to remind him of the living kar'tajan in Miss Libby's barn.

Sam sat down in the only chair in the room, holding the alicorn in one hand and the tiny figurine in the other. Oddly, he began to fancy himself a *po'rat*, objects of power at his disposal and the ability to communicate with wayfarers from the spirit realm already a proven part of his identity.

Trouble was, Sam didn't want to be a shaman. He didn't want to have to protect himself from D'lo's angry *ini'putc'*, or to regard himself as a benefactor of Kar'tajans, or, for that matter, to go to Paisley's graduation dressed like the sick Anglo who'd given him the makings of his disguise. What he wanted was to be both a bona fide Ute and the person he had become during his long self-exile. He wanted to bring the two types of experience together and begin the process by reclaiming his daughter.

Show me how, Inu'sakats, Sam prayed, squeezing the figurine and lazily brandishing the alicorn. Jesus, show me how.

Unable to sleep, Sam got in his car and drove into the Skys' neighborhood. It was easy enough to find. You took a bead on the apex of the spotlighted stucco tepee and headed toward it until a cross street led you directly to the monstrosity itself. It had not existed in the days of Authentic Ute Handicrafts in Ignacio, but Sam had once seen it depicted in a grainy photograph in the *Rocky Mountain News*.

Sam drove past this kitschy landmark, inscribed a U and crawled by it again, then returned and parked across the street. The Skys' gigantic "round house" was as tacky in reality as it had been in the photo, and yet it exerted a powerful pull on Sam—a pull not wholly stemming from his knowledge that Paisley was sleeping in one of the rectangular rooms inside that towering cone.

No, it was the flamboyant extremism of DeWayne Sky's commitment to his Indianhood that fascinated Sam—the sense that Sky was not just exploiting the legacy of his blood for publicity and monetary gain but, rather, trumpeting his allegiance and laying claim to his heritage. Sam couldn't do it as Sky had; on one level he suspected the man's motives but on another admired him for his willingness to risk ridicule for the sake of such a bravura proclamation.

As Sam sat studying Sky's "folly" and thinking, a patrol car turned onto the street and came prowling down it toward him. His gut tightened. Although a grown man with money in his jeans, Sam mistrusted cops. Ever since leaving his people, he had felt both guilty and childlike around them. That was how he felt now—as if, simply by sitting here, he was breaking a law. Maybe he was.

As it drew alongside, the prowl car slowed, and its driver—a hulking shadow—slashed at Sam with his flashlight. Then the beam centered, and Sam had to protect his eyes to keep from having his vision scooped brutally from his sockets.

"What're you doing here?" the shadow demanded.

"Never seen such a big tepee. Couldn't get over it."

"Anywhere else but this featherhead ghetto, it'd've been yanked down long ago. . . . Kinda late to be sightseein', ain't it, Tonto?"

Sam explained that he was a guest in the Pino Nuche and that he hadn't been able to sleep.

"You Ute? Or a *real* goddamn Indian?"

Despite the stinging flashlight, Sam dropped his arm. "Both. My daughter's Paisley Coldpony, senior-class salutatorian."

"Payz is a smart gal," the deputy marshal said, "but a real troublemaker." He nodded at the Skys' tepee. "That's where she's living. If you're her daddy, how come you ain't staying there, too?" Mercifully, he clicked off the flashlight.

"I'm her estranged daddy. She doesn't know I'm here."

The deputy's cratered face was like an off-center moon. "You ain't thinking of kidnapping her, are you?"

"I'm here for her graduation. That's all."

"Better get some sleep, then. Take your pick—the Pino Nuche or the famous Paisley Coldpony suite over in our jail."

Sam picked the former and drove back to his motel. The deputy, a bigoted klutz, was one of the reasons he had left Ignacio—not this deputy per se, but other powerful Anglo authority figures too much like him to make a forelock's difference.

Paisley began to rise higher in Sam's estimation. She'd pulled time in the slammer presided over by that lunkhead!

Delivering her salutatorian's address from the bunting-draped bandbox on the football field, Paisley saw a figure standing in an aisle between two bleacher sections. He was listening hard to her speech, which, although not ringingly eloquent, *was* heartfelt.

Its themes were the responsibilities that attended fulfilling one's dreams, bettering one's community, and challenging entrenched power structures that could keep you from attaining the first two goals. Uncontroversial stuff—except for that generic "entrenched power structure" business—but true, and a kick to lay out for the middle-class Anglos and Chicanos, who usually failed to see that the Utes were victimized as often as they were helped by the largesse of the state and the paternalism of the BIA.

Last night, in the basement rec room of the Skys' wacky house, Payz had practiced this speech for Larry Cuthair, her voice echoing impersonally off the moist cement. Afterward,

Larry had drawn back as if sniffing something vaguely—but only vaguely—rancid.

"Traditional commencement-speech bullshit," he had said. "When it isn't, it pulls too many punches."

"The words aren't as important as who's saying them."

"Hail, Muache Ute woman."

"And what I'll be wearing, Larry. Everything I say is going to be underscored by what I'll have on."

This evening, then, she was conscious—as everyone else in the bleachers and the folding chairs on the football field had to be—that she was the only member of the senior class (including twelve other Utes) clad in Indian garb. Her classmates wore disposable gowns of crinkly pleated paper and crooked mortarboards; they gazed up at her as if at a character in a historical pageant. For Payz had worn a buckskin dress and a pair of leather leggings that Mama D'lo had beaded for her for this occasion. Moccasins slippered her feet, and from the tassel button on her graduation cap fluttered an eagle feather given to her by Papa Sky. So *she* was the statement, and her salutatorian's address little more than an official excuse to stand up before this gathering to make it.

But as she spoke, Paisley's eyes kept finding the queer figure at the back of the bleachers. His clothes, given the prevailing masculine attire of suits and ties, were too casual. He stuck out like . . . like a man in Bermuda shorts at a funeral.

The Coca-Cola jersey he was wearing reminded Paisley of her dream-calling and the skinny Anglo who had been swallowed by an identical shirt in her vision. In addition, this man was sporting mirrorshades, a red bandanna, and some brand-new wheat jeans.

But it was the Coca-Cola shirt that had first drawn Payz's eye and that still teased it. She stumbled over a line in her speech. Checking her notes, she recovered, but her gaze—as if ensorceled—went right to the superannuated hippie in the soft-drink jersey.

A sudden intuition: *The guy in that shirt is your father!*

Stunned by this thought, Paisley faltered again, recalling that either Mama Lanna or Papa Sky had told her that if only she could find the woman in her Sun Dance vision—the woman expelled from the Thirst House for taking photographs—she would then find her daddy too. Well, that woman hadn't come to see her be graduated, nor had the AIDS-stricken Anglo thrown out for bringing "moisture" into the lodge—but, rather, a stranger in the same kind of jersey that had gotten the sick blond dude in trouble. How peculiar dreams were, and how mysterious—even backasswards—their fulfillment.

Paisley glanced sidelong. The principal, the valedictorian, and the state senator engaged to deliver the primary commencement address were regarding her with half-puzzled, half-solicitous looks that struck her—even in her confusion—as patronizing.

All the faces out front—classmates on the field, relatives and teachers in the stands—appeared impatient or embarrassed. They were waiting for her to get past this bad spot and to wrap up her remarks with an applaudable flourish. She had a reputation as a debater; this fumfutzing was not what folks expected from her.

All right, Payz told herself. So your daddy's shown up. Don't let him shake you. You've *earned* this moment, and if you let him spoil it, the fault'll be yours, not his. Finish your speech and finish it looking that lousy piker straight in the eye.

Self-admonished, Paisley recovered. Without another glance at her notes, she swept through the remainder of her talk, leaving her audience murmuring approval even during Mr. Hackett's introduction of the valedictorian. While speaking, though, she had stared right into the silver lenses of the stranger's—her daddy's—sunglasses, and her boldness had plainly discomfited him.

Three or four times, he had lowered his head. Then, flustered, he had crossed behind a bleacher section, briefly disappearing, only to reemerge at the top of the next aisle down (no more or less conspicuous than before), where Payz had zeroed in on him again.

By the end of her talk, the confused joe—although game enough not to flee—was hugging himself, turning his Coca-Cola jersey into a kind of straitjacket. That was his posture as she walked in mild triumph to her chair on the speakers' stand. In fact, he seemed to be one of the few people purposely *not* applauding, and his refusal to applaud simply confirmed for her his identity. So did the fact that, although trying to hide behind some latecomers clogging the upper aisle section, he stayed to hear the other speakers and the beginning of the alphabetical handing out of diplomas.

Payz, meanwhile, kept returning her eyes to his fidgety person and locking them on his sunglasses, simultaneously thinking, Daddy, they've just turned on the stadium lights, you don't *need* those things now, and knowing he'd worn them (and the shirt with the billboarded logo) for a disguise. The ineptitude of his attempted ruse was touching, almost endearing.

"Coldpony, Paisley Coldpony," Mr. Hackett, the principal, said, "our salutatorian."

She stood, crossed the platform, grasped her diploma.

Folks were applauding again, Ute friends like Larry Cuthair and Gloria Mestes standing up and whistling as if she had just canned a long one in B-ball game against Cortez. DeWayne and LannaSue Sky were also up, beaming; Payz had the sense that everyone—Anglos and Chicanos too—admired what she had accomplished. If there was added sympathy for her as a result of her mama's suicide—well, she deserved it. Her daddy, though, was not among those emanating good vibes. Having seen her accept her diploma, he had begun an abashed and solitary retreat to the parking lot.

"Crutchfield," Mr. Hackett said. "Guy Crutchfield."

Paisley, unencumbered by a gown, tripped down the steps of the reviewing stand, darted through an aisle of folding chairs on the threadbare football field, and pushed herself into the crowd at the base of the bleachers. The Skys—she noted peripherally—appeared as amazed as if she had bolted from her own wedding.

"Daddy was here," she told them, "but he's leaving!"

She went pelting up the steps of the bleacher aisle, reached the grassy summit, and spied her father juking and dodging through the dusty vehicles in the parking lot.

It was not that he knew she was in pursuit, but rather that her unflinching examination of him during her talk had told him that he was not welcome. And so he was hustling to get away—not fleeing, exactly, but hustling to re-remove himself from her life.

"Sam Coldpony!" she cried, running. "Samuel T. Coldpony, you'd better not leave Ignacio without talking to me!"

Behind her, DeWayne and LannaSue Sky, heavy people accustomed to only occasional strenuous exertion, came galloping after.

Silhouetting the press box and bleachers as sunset had earlier silhouetted the roller-coaster ridge of the San Juan Mountains, the stadium lights—like immense owl eyes—laid a slippery liquid sheen on every car and truck in the parking lot.

And Paisley's father, hearing her shout, halted, squinted back toward the stadium, and reluctantly permitted her and the lumbering Skys to overtake him.

Sam was appalled by the sweatiness of his palms, the headlong canter of his heart. He had ridden wild ponies—had sidestepped yearling bulls—with far less apprehension.

His grown daughter was approaching, dressed like one of her nineteenth-century ancestors. How she must despise him to have drilled such fiery holes into him during her speech. Would she vilify him in front of the Skys? If so, he had no choice but to stand before this handsome girl and absorb her anger. He hadn't deserted her—his leavetaking had come hard on the failure of his marriage—but he had, granted, held himself inaccessible for far too long. She had a right to call down the gods' anger.

Resignedly, Sam took off his sunglasses. He untied the acetate bandanna and stuck it into a pocket of his borrowed jeans. What a dumb-ass disguise. He'd've done better to rent a tuxedo.

"Papa!" Paisley blurted. The two of them were five feet apart in a narrow corridor of cooling cars and pickups.

"Paisley." He waited. He waited for her to erupt. There was a stand of cottonwoods along the lower margin of the schoolyard—grotesque, gnarly trees that he wished he could hide among—but she would find him there, just as her eyes had repeatedly found him in the stadium during her address.

DeWayne and LannaSue appeared—DeWayne with one braid over his shoulder and one on his chest, LannaSue carrying a cigarette that she had lit in the stadium. Even though she had been trotting, she took a deep drag and exhaled a shadowy cloud. Payz conferred with the couple, who retreated at once to their Ford Bronco. What power the girl already had.

"Okay, Papa, why did you come?"

Sam's tongue felt like a slab of calf's brain, only not quite so smart. "Because I'm . . . like you say . . . your papa."

"You've been that as long as I've been me." Which was true, of course, and she gave the truism a twist that bitter or angry people always give their accusations. "Why now?" she went on. "Why come back now? Because I've done something that reflects credit on you for"—cruelly mocking him—"*siring* me?"

"Graduation, I knew about. The salutatorian thing, no."

"Or because I've had a birthday and got my 'eighteen money'?"

As he had suspected, she hated him. Dolores had poisoned her against him; maybe the Skys had too. Sam crammed his hands into the pouch on his jersey and drew in the dirt with his shoe—whether to divert Payz's attention from her righteous wrath or his own from the coiled spring in his bowels, he didn't know.

"Where are you living?" Paisley demanded.

Sam told her.

"How long have you been there?"

He told her that too.

"That's not far. You could have come to visit us. You could have come to visit *me*, Papa." One hand was holding her diploma as if it were a billyclub.

Sam dared to look her in the eye. "Come back with me now."

"No!" she shouted. "I can't!" Her face contorted, then took on the blankness of false calm. "I'd've been happier, Papa Sam," she said evenly, "if you hadn't come at all."

Sam could not think. All that registered—beyond the fact that his daughter was striding away from him—was an awareness that Mr. Hackett had reached the *M*'s: "Mabry, Martinez, Mestes . . ."

The weird double echo of the P.A. system reverberated like the voice of a Hollywood alien. Bats swooped in scattershot squadrons, piping strident melodies.

DeWayne and LannaSue approached, shapes at once grizzlylike and graceful. They halted near Sam, and DeWayne said, "There's more to your daughter than just salubratorian shit, Coldpony."

"She's been dream-called, Samuel," LannaSue said. "She's going to dance Sun Dance with the men."

Sam did some quick calculations. The dance was in early July. Payz couldn't leave Ignacio until she'd participated in it. Maybe, after Sun Dance, he could convince her to join him on the Tipsy Q. The way things were going, Bo might not be around much longer, and Paisley could live with Libby in the ranch house. Miss Libby would welcome another pair of hands. Wages were a problem, but the girl did have her "eighteen money." Room and board would suffice until the Tipsy Q's beef-on-the-hoof production began to climb.

"What LannaSue's trying to tell you," DeWayne pointed out, "is that Payz has obligations. She'll *never* be able to join you—not anywheres off the reservation, at least."

"She's going to be a *po'rat*, Samuel."

Before Sam could reply, DeWayne turned and impulsively kicked dirt on the hubcap of a nearby truck. "You bastard. You were in town last night. You were here."

"What can I do, Tuqú-payá?"

"Fuck you, Coldpony," DeWayne barked. "You don't deserve that girl." He strode off through the dusk toward his fancy all-terrain vehicle—Paisley a wraith beside it, an *ini'putc'* with a diploma.

LannaSue came to Sam. Hugging him like a sister, she smelled of cigarette smoke and a faint cologne. "Didn't even bring her a graduation present, did you, Samuel?"

"Money isn't what I'm made of."

"Nor smarts, either. You could've given her a flower—you'd've looked cheap, but not like the puckered asshole you do now."

Mr. Hackett had reached the *W*'s, and a few folks came filtering out of the stadium, hoping to beat the inevitable clot of traffic once the last diploma was handed over.

Sam tried to sight past a pickup's rearview mirror at the Skys' vehicle, but the darkness was finally too thick to make out either Paisley or her indignant pigtailed guardian.

Then he remembered something. He dug into the watch pocket of his jeans, pulled out the pewter figurine, and handed it to LannaSue.

"Give this to her," he said.

LannaSue rotated the metal beast between the ball of her

thumb and her forefinger. "Kar'tajan," she murmured respectfully. "Sam, this'll do. Inu'sakats be praised, but you may've just saved your scrawny buns." She pecked him on the brow, then began her stately one-person pavanne back across the lot to the Bronco.

"Will Tuqú-payá still come to Snowy Falls?" Sam called. Or had last night's lie and tonight's unhappy encounter with his daughter soured Sky on the proffered grand marshalship?"

LannaSue halted, looked back. "He'll come," she said. "We can always use the money."

# 22

A week after Sam's return, Libby was in the barn currying the stricken kar'tajan and marveling at the pale delicacy of the long strands adhering to her comb. Could a creature with such a silken, incandescent coat really be sick?

Apparently so. The stallion's sores and listlessness belied his healthy pelt. Moreover, Dr. Brinkley's lab test had revealed what *appeared* to be a unicorn-specific variety of equine infectious anemia—unless, of course, the viral agent could infect horses native to this reality, too. Somehow, no matter how foolish it seemed, Lib was reluctant to believe that. She had refused to stable her handsome Telluride and Sam's favorite mount Crip (a.k.a. Cripple Creek) elsewhere. So far, even given that the incubation period for equine anemia was usually three or fewer weeks, neither horse had shown any sign of the disease.

Without neglecting her ranch work, Libby cared for the animal. Three times a day, on Dr. Brinkley's recommendation, she force-fed him a slurry of dehydrated cottage cheese, dextrose, electrolytes, and dehydrated alfalfa meal with a dose syringe. She used a garden spade to clean his cream-colored stools out of the stall, and at least once a day she replaced his soiled hay with fresh. Currying the kar'tajan seemed to soothe them both, so she spent as much time as she could kneeling beside the creature, whom she had named Pete, pulling nonexistent burrs from his coat and fingering the strands of his mane.

Pete's mare—whom she had christened Phyllis or Phylly—had not deserted him. She came down from Ptarmigan Mountain, or maybe out of Remuda Creek Meadow behind the house, every evening at twilight and stayed outside his stall until dawn. Often, other kar'tajans would come with her.

On the evening of Paisley's graduation in Ignacio, Libby had stepped outside to find eight of Phylly's friends bunched together outside the horse trap, as if waiting for Phylly to pay Pete their respects and to report back from the barn with any news.

Bullshit, Libby had scolded herself. An example of . . . well, what? The pathetic fallacy? Something like that.

Anyway, in crossing over to the paddock, she had startled this covey of kar'tajans, who had fled like so many equine fireflies, trailing a weird bioluminescence and vanishing into the hillside's night-entangled trees.

Similar episodes had subsequently occurred. Last night, three more kar'tajans had herded down, but at Libby's first approach had bolted like the others. Phylly, however, remained faithful to the stallion, and Pete . . . well, Pete was going nowhere at all.

Neither, of course, was Bo. He had fallen into a funk after completing his ad assignment for Zubrecht. He seemed to think—and, granted, he had compelling reasons—that he'd just wrapped up the last public endeavor of his life. Chemotherapy, visualization therapy, and every other kind of therapy aside, Bo's condition was steadily and markedly deteriorating.

Symptomatically, he spent his days vegetating, seldom even reading a magazine or working a crossword. The only activities that truly amused him were tottering out to the barn to look at Pete, with whom he had felt a powerful kinship from the start, and sitting in front of the Bendix between midnight and five watching the grainy sepia videos of Swing Era music that the set would still filter miraculously out of the ether, as if exclusively for him. Over the past three days, his visits to see

Pete had grown less frequent and his after-hours TV habit even more obsessive. The latter was driving Libby bonkers.

"Pete," she said, numbly plaiting several strands of shimmering mane, "I'd almost rather *he* died than you."

It was six o'clock in the afternoon, and she was sitting beside Pete nervously anticipating Dr. Nesheim's arrival from the medical center. Although Sam, since his return, had been trying to nurse Bo as well as do his ranch work, Libby was almost ready to hand her morose houseguest over to professionals.

That was why Nesheim was coming. That was why she was trying to center herself by fiddling dreamily with Pete's mane. Nesheim planned to discuss with Bo the advantages—to everyone concerned—of his transferring to the hospital in Huerfano.

Murmured Libby under her breath, "Even saints wear out." (The animal's sapphire eye rolled white; he puffed a phlegmy bubble from one nostril.) "Even your basic goddamn all-purpose saint."

Outside, near the aspen grove, gravel was churning. A vehicle had galumphed off Highway 69 into her drive. Maybe two.

Libby eased herself free of Pete and walked to the barn door. What she saw was not Dr. Nesheim's expensive Porsche but a van bearing on its side panels the legend ZUBRECHT PRODUCTS, INC. / DENVER, CHEYENNE, PHOENIX & SALT LAKE CITY. Behind the van, a sleek, pantherine Lincoln Continental.

My God, thought Libby. It's Brother Ned and those bastards who dismantled my rolltop.

Then, behind those vehicles, Nesheim's Porsche appeared too, and Libby trotted back to shut the door to Pete's stall and to tell the enfeebled kar'tajan to behave.

After brushing herself off, she pinched up the shoulders of her yoke-collared blouse, so that it would settle as she wanted it to, and walked back out to confront what was starting to resemble the vanguard of a Pioneer Days parade.

Inside, on the bed in Libby's former study, Bo was lying in his jogging-suit pants and a T-shirt—*OUR* BRAVES WERE HOME BEFORE *YOUR* BRAVE EVEN HAD A FLAG TO WAVE—that Sam had bought for him in the gift shop at the Pino Nuche motel. He felt lousy, but

Sam was in the room too, subjecting him to another bout of Ute remedies, most of them more amusing than helpful.

"Sam, for Christ's sake. I don't *want* to wear a potato on my forehead."

"You told me you had a headache." Sam had cut an Idaho potato in two and threaded one half with a piece of nylon cord. Now he was tying the potato half to Bo's brow.

"I've had athlete's foot, too, Samuel—but did I rush to carve myself a pair of shoes out of cantaloupes?"

"A potato cures headaches. It sucks the pain into its flesh so *you* don't have to suffer."

Bo teetered between angry tears and hysterical laughter. Sam's earnestness was both a trial and a hoot. He had been this way ever since returning, semirepudiated, from Ignacio. Old Ute cures for the trots (flour paste), smelly feet (sagebrush in the shoes), and chapped lips (skunk grease) had come crawling up through an inside-out pocket of his Muache soul and, once up, demanded that he locate some hapless orphan to use them on: namely, Bo, who could respect Sam more for feeding him watermelon snow than for strapping a spud to his forehead.

"Look at this," Bo griped. "As a kid, I *played* with Mr. Potato Head. Now, I *are* one."

"Wear it an hour. If the pain leaves you, thank the One Above for giving us this cooling earth fruit."

"Who gets credit for my headache? My nausea? My diarrhea?"

"Hold on." Sam went to the door, looked back as if to admire his handiwork. "I've got something else for you."

Oh, no, thought Bo. He could hear Sam opening and closing a storage-cabinet door on the porch just off the kitchen. Then Sam was back, holding a plastic squeeze bottle of shoe polish with a felt applicator, carrying it as if it held holy water.

Bo flinched. "What gives, Samuel? And don't try to tell me there's an ancient Ute cure based on liquid shoe polish."

"This is just the container." Sam unscrewed the cap with the felt applicator and thrust the bottle at him. "Smell."

Bo recoiled. "Gaaaghh." He rubbed the back of his hand under his nose as if ammonia fumes had gassed him.

The Ute smiled mysteriously, replaced the applicator cap, and pulled a straightback chair up to the iron bedstead.

"Christ, Sam, that smelled like piss. It *isn't*, is it?"

Sam's smile faded. "What do you care what it is? So long as it works, use it and bless the Holy He-She."

In one motion, Bo tore Sam's unorthodox headband from his brow and hurled it across the room. "Thank you, Holy One, for piss and potatoes? That's what you want me to tell the blessed Entity who gave us mosquitoes, and the AIDS virus?" Although hampered by his bed's narrowness, he tried to scramble away from Sam. "Tell me what it is," he said, nodding at the squeeze bottle and taking a reflexive swipe with his forearm at the starchy potato slime still glistening on his brow. "Tell me!"

"It's horse urine."

"*Horse urine!*"

"For your sores. It'll pucker 'em and make 'em break."

"You're out of your fucking head, Coldpony! These are lesions, not unpopped pimples. Piss is full of bacteria. Bacteria cause infections. Infections have to be fought. And, Samuel, my body isn't capable. Are you *tired* of having me around? Do you want me to shuffle off my shiftless mortal coil a couple of weeks ahead of schedule? Why didn't you just truck a load of watermelon snow in here and pack me in it up to my eyelids? That'd get rid of me just as quick , and it'd be a helluva sweeter demise."

Sam kneaded Bo's leg. "Calm down. It isn't horse urine."

Bo's ireful passion collapsed. "What?"

"It isn't horse urine."

"A joke, then? Is that it—an unfunny practical joke?"

"Actually, Bo, I got it from Pete. It's kar'tajan pee. Let me use some, just a little, on a couple of those sores."

Anger, exasperation, relief, incredulity, more anger: Bo was unable to keep up with his feelings. "Oh, you mean, it's not *plain* old horse urine, it's the liquid waste product of a *diseased* animal about whose physiology we know almost nothing? And that's supposed to make me want to rub down with the nauseating stuff?"

Sam frightened Bo by slamming his fist on the bed and booming, "Damn it, Bo, this is something to try!"

Bo, heart pounding, rolled over, got up, and stared across the quilted coverlet at the fiery-eyed Ute as if across a battlefield. "Samuel," he said quietly, "I'm not that desperate yet—not enough to let you rub kar'tajan piss on me from a shoe-polish bottle. It would *scare* me to let you—more than I'm scared already."

Earnestly fuming, Sam said, "All right. Okay."

"And I'm not your daughter, Samuel. I'm sorry, but I'm not."

Sam shook the bottle like a tomahawk. "The old remedies work. We've forgotten, but they do. That animal out there—even sick, he's magic. Even dying, he's full of the ancient *powa'a*."

Then, realizing how futile it was to be standing in Bo's room with a bottle of kar'tajan piss in his hand, he made a bemused face and left. He went through the living room into the kitchen and out the back door to the paddock. There, where nearly three months ago he had buried the two-headed calf that had so upset Miss Libby, he dug a hole for his spurned remedy.

As Sam went out, Libby came in the front door at the head of a motley parade. She saw Sam going through the living room into the kitchen, carrying a bottle of shoe polish, but he was intent on his own business and did not see her. Bo, standing wraithlike in the backlit rectangle of the study door, saw her, however, and also the people crowding into the house behind her—Ned Gavin, Dr. Nesheim, Darren Santaliz, and Gene Katt. He appeared as startled to see this crew as she had been to have them converge simultaneously on her ranch.

"Company," she said simply. Why had Ned and the Zubrecht boys shown up exactly when Dr. Nesheim had? Hadn't their mamas taught them you were supposed to telephone ahead?

"Hello, Bo," Dr. Nesheim said. "How're you feeling?"

"Full of piss and potato peels," he said, stepping aside as the two employees of ZP Inc., with embarrassed half smiles and almost imperceptible nods, brushed past him into his room.

Santaliz and Katt, the computer man and the van driver. Their coming felt to Bo, as it had once felt to Libby, like an invasion—especially in light of their unapologetic blitzkrieg on the various units of his computer setup. No, *their* computer setup. It had been on loan, after all, and they were here to recover it and take it back to Denver.

"Good to see you, Bo," Ned said. "They won't be long, and then we've got a gift for you. A bonus, that is."

"A bonus for what? I've already been paid."

"For effort above and beyond. Under trying conditions."

Libby gestured at the sofa and the room's only sittable chair, urging her guests—or, at least, Ned and Dr. Nesheim—to sit down. Would they like something to drink? They declined. Libby and Bo fetched dinette chairs for themselves from the kitchen.

In the study, Santaliz and Katt were picking up computer gear—monitor, mouse, keyboard, jet-ink printer, along with the auxiliary drives and the portable software library. It had been weeks since he had even booted up a video game, but Bo, hearing their activity, felt empty. The last piece of work he would ever undertake was over. He had guilty regrets about its substance, but he resented these men for dismantling his command center. It felt as if he, too, were being . . . well, *deleted*.

Ned had sunk, like a water buffalo into quicksand, into the sofa behind the steamer trunk. "Didn't think there was an American M.D. alive who still made house calls," he told Nesheim.

"This is something of a social visit," the doctor replied. "I wanted to see how everybody was getting along."

Libby glanced gratefully at Nesheim. It would be impossible, or at least unpleasant, to talk to Bo about moving to the hospital while Ned and his Zubrecht co-workers were here. The Tipsy Q could go a month without a single visitor and then the whole Red Chinese army would show up and bivouac on her front stoop.

"Well," Bo said, "I feel like refried frijoles. I'm tired of doing without sex, safe or otherwise, and I'm afraid to die."

This speech silenced everyone. Libby was ready to offer drinks again when Katt came out of the study carrying the computer module and Santaliz the keyboard and the software file. But because the sofa had a death grip on Ned, it was Nesheim who opened the front door for the two men.

"What Mr. Zubrecht has sent you," Ned said, hurrying to change the subject, "is a television set."

"We've *got* a television set," Lib said. Offering Bo a new

TV, when he spent most of his midnights worshiping her Bendix, would be like trying to get Iacocca to buy Japanese.

"Not like this one," Ned said. "This is a large-screen set with a directional antenna. When Mr. Zubrecht heard how lousy your reception was up here, he thought Bo—you too, Elizabeth—might like to see *Cagney and Lacey* minus fuzz and interference lines."

"We don't watch very much TV, Ned."

"You'll want to see *this* show, even though it's a return. Bo's ad will be on it—three times. Catch it again on *Nightline* if his minimasterpiece grabs you like it does me."

Santaliz and Katt returned, gathered up joysticks, disk drives, and the electronic mouse, and traipsed back out to the van.

"Katt'll put up the antenna. Just give him twenty minutes."

"I don't want it," Bo said. "The set, the antenna, or a chance to see my 'minimasterpiece.' None of it."

In his boots, Sam had soft-shoed it back into the kitchen. He leaned against the doorjamb and said, "If you take the new set, Bo, I could maybe use Miss Lib's up in Naismith's Cabin."

"Reception might be better there," Libby said. "The mountains wall this house in, put it out of signal range."

When Santaliz and Katt returned again, Bo began to feel walled in himself. Ned was going to give him—all of them—a new TV, and Katt would put up the rotary antenna so that Lib and Sam, watching his ad, could see how he had back-stabbed them. As he had betrayed his lover Keith in Atlanta. As he had repeatedly sold out his own identity by pretending to be straight.

Dr. Nesheim said, "Libby, would you rather I came back some other time? If so, I will—but since Ned is here, I'd like to go ahead. Family *ought* to be in on a discussion like this."

"A discussion like what?" Bo said.

"Darren, Gene," Ned said from the escape-proof sofa, "go on and put up the new antenna. Careful of the power lines."

Libby watched the two men troop out again, but her thoughts were on the rule change that Nesheim had just effected. Bo needed to be hospitalized before he became a total invalid. Summer work— fence mending, windmill repair, and, now, prowling for kar'tajans—would occupy much of her and Sam's time as the hot days rolled by. If Bo lasted until fall, he would be alone a lot while they mounted another roundup and prepared to market their stock.

Having Ned here complicated things. On the other hand, maybe the bastard could be made to see—especially now that his boss had sent Bo a pricey gift—that he, Ned, had responsibilities too, and that only a bigot would brand him a fruitcake if he finally got off his fat butt and assumed them.

"Okay, Dr. Nesheim," Libby said. "Go ahead."

Nesheim said, "Bo, let's lay it on the line: I think you should relocate to the medical center."

Bo looked at Libby. He felt as if he had been bludgeoned. He had been half expecting it, however, and so the blow, telegraphed, glanced off. Who was betraying whom? Who adhering better to the immemorial Brazen Rule, "Do unto others before they do it to you?" Why, Unicorn Libby Quarrels, his ever-loving landlady.

"No!" Sam said. "He doesn't want that."

Libby was startled by the outburst. "Sam, it's Bo decision."

Said Bo, "You mean, if I refuse to be relocated, I won't be?"

An aluminum ladder clanged against the rain gutter. Gene Katt began slip-sliding down the roof. Libby cringed. Those shingles were old. Too much putzing around up there would ruin them.

"I won't ask you to leave if you don't want to."

"But what do *you* want?" Bo said. "Why is the good doctor here telling me I should change my address?"

"Because he thinks it's advisable," Ned piped up. "So why not give Elizabeth a break and take that advice?"

"Why don't you give everyone a break and butt out?" That from Sam, whose insolent tone secretly tickled Bo but made Libby wonder if she really had an ally in the Muache.

On the other hand, hearing Brother Ned jump to second Nesheim's suggestion, when he knew nothing about the hospital in Huerfano or the character of her relationship with his brother—well, *that* gave Libby pause. She didn't want to be like Ned. Maybe Bo, even if ultimately doomed, was simply at the bottom of a mood trough from which a little tenderness would free him. His midnight thralldom to her Bendix was maddening, yes, but not unbearable.

"Look, Mr. Coldpony," Ned was saying, "if there's anyone whose nose doesn't belong in this business, it's yours."

Nesheim stood. "Bo, you've seen our medical center. You know what we can do there. Until you're too sick to take advantage of it, you'll have as much freedom as we permit any other ambulatory patient. That's the gist of my message."

"If I got in, I'll come out the same way Alfie Tuck did." The scraping overhead reminded Bo of a Christmas when the patter of icy elm boughs, cracking and falling on their house in Pueblo, had made him think—actually believe—that Santa's sleigh and eight prancing kar'tajans were up there. (No, not kar'tajans—reindeer.)

"Well, if you've decided to stay," Nesheim said, "I'll drive up here every other week to give you your vinblastine shots. Libby, call me if there's anything else either you or Bo needs. I think the two of you should be able to manage."

"The three of us," Sam corrected him.

Long after Dr. Nesheim and Ned's cohorts from Denver had left, Ned was still at the Tipsy Q. The wide-screen television that Katt had installed—after Bo had unplugged and disconnected the Bendix, only to lug it to his room as if it were a pirate's treasure chest and its contents stolen Aztec gold—so thoroughly dominated Libby's cramped living room that she was still out of sorts.

They had had to move the sofa from the east wall to the west wall to make room for the set in the southeast corner. Then they had rearranged all the other furniture—except for the bolted-down wood stove—to accommodate the repositioning of the sofa.

"Thanks for the wide-screen," Libby told Ned. "But maybe old Ev should've given us a bigger house to hold it."

Ned laughed. "Maybe he should have, Elizabeth."

Sam popped Black Diamond popcorn in a pressure cooker—he and Ned had reached a tacit truce while moving furniture—and brought it out in four one-pound butter tubs so that they could all have their own while watching TV. Bo, whose appetite was unpredictable, declined his. Sam dumped it back into the pan on the floor atop a copy of *Western Horseman*. The bouncy theme music of *Cagney and Lacey* began to play, and the opening credits appeared over a picture as clear as spring water.

"The first ad's scheduled at half past," Ned said. "CBS

wants to hook its audience—if a rerun can do that—before throwing it a controversial condom ad."

"I'll be in there," Bo said, nodding at his room. "I don't like cop shows, even if the cops are female."

"Especially if they're female," Ned said, smiling above his popcorn like . . . well, like a boar at a trough.

Bo stared at Ned. Any retort at all would lend legitimacy to the nitwitticism. Libby and Sam had already drawn back, radiating disapproval, and Ned could sense that he had blundered.

"A stupid joke, Bo. Don't you want to see your ad?"

"I'm intimately familiar with it."

"But this is network television—you're making history."

"I'll be in there," Bo repeated.

He withdrew, leaving his door ajar, and slumped into his swivel chair. The rolltop-minus both the computer setup and the shelf module that Katt and Santaliz had taken out to make room for it—seemed as bare as Old Mother Hubbard's cupboard.

Bo spied the Bendix sitting on the floor, got up, carried it back, and set it on the desk. The effort cost him. It had been a long day; all he could think to chalk up on the credit side of its ledger was that he had escaped having kar'tajan piss applied to his sarcoma lesions.

Now, to cap off everything, Sam and Libby were going to see his animated betrayal of Pete and all the other kar'tajans. Twenty-two minutes to go. Nineteen. Fifteen. Twelve. Ten.

Mary Beth Lacey—through his cracked door, Bo could hear random snatches of dialogue—had just been taken hostage in some sort of metal shack in a city rail yard, and Chris Cagney, her partner, was trying to talk the psychotic bad guys into releasing Mary Beth and surrendering. Bo had seen this episode back in Atlanta—he liked an occasional cop program as well as the next guy—but then, of course, Zippy Inc. hadn't been one of its sponsors and he hadn't had to worry about how his landlady would react to a clever little condom ad of his creation. Tonight, he was worried.

He was still worried when the ad aired. "Moonlight Sonata," played on guitars. Hypnotically spoken, the brandname Kartajans floated into his room. (The announcer repeated the word twice). Afterward, a brief silence, followed by the abrupt resumption of soundtrack noises.

Ned gave a war whoop. "If Mama ever saw that," he called in to Bo, "if she ever learned you and I teamed up to do it, wouldn't she just *shit*? Bye-bye, prune juice!"

Libby took the remote unit from him and clicked off the set.

"Wait, Elizabeth. It'll be on again two more times."

"Beautiful," Libby said. "For an ad for silicon rubbers, it was about as beautiful and moving as anyone could hope."

"But—"

"Another viewing would disrupt my mellow mood, Ned. Why don't you get started back to Denver? Tomorrow's a workday."

Bo sat at the rolltop in Libby's study, fiddling with the knobs on the Bendix and straining to hear what everyone was saying. Sam, for starters, mumbled a curt good night and left via the kitchen and back porch—maybe for Naismith's Cabin, maybe for the barn.

Libby, meanwhile, herded Ned outside, hoping to have him leave without intruding again on his brother. But as soon as he reached his automobile, he remembered something, keyed open its trunk, and lifted out a pasteboard carton of Kartajans. A gross, apparently, twelve packages to the carton, one dozen "technologically advanced silicon condoms" per package. He then insisted on returning to the house and giving this carton to the man responsible for naming the product and devising its witty marketing strategy. Ned was puffed with bullfrog pride, but, hardly reprehensibly, his pride—Libby could tell—was focused on the "historic" accomplishment of his dying brother.

Bo looked up when Ned barged through the door. He watched his brother set a pasteboard carton on his bed's coverlet. He saw Lib standing hipshot in the door and wished he could dematerialize from his reality. He had so often abused its truth that maybe he no longer had the vision to recognize it.

"Free samples," Ned said. "If you need more, just holler."

"Make a delivery every month. That way you'll almost manage to keep up with me."

Ned swaggered over to pinch the nape of Bo's neck, then

leaned down and kissed the crown of his dry, blond head. "Mama's a hard case," he said, "but she may still come around. I'm sorry to leave you here with Elizabeth again, but . . ."

"Yeah," Bo said. "I know."

Then Ned went away, and Libby came into the darkness. She say down next to the carton of Kartajans, and the two of them—in Bo's peculiar conceptualization of the moment—occupied the study as if first one were oscillating into it from another continuum and then the other. Their presences in the study coincided only by chance, and they were alone in spite of their apparent proximity.

"I'll call Nesheim in the morning," Bo said. "I'll ask him to reserve me a room in his antiseptic Hotel Thanatos."

"Cut and run, eh?"

"That's what *you* want, isn't it? At this stage, I should take Brother Ned's advice and do what's easiest for you."

"Nifty ad."

"But—"

"For an accurate self-portrait, Bo, spell *but* with two *t*'s."

"Merci, m'lady."

They sat in their places, unmoving and unspeaking, immaterially oscillating in and out of each other's presence. Finally, Libby said, "It *is* a nifty ad. We so often sell out what we most love that we don't quite realize we're doing it."

"You think that's what happened to me?"

"I don't know. We can't see the sacred even when it's a hand's-breadth away. Everything's grist for our money mills. We believe we're imbeciles if we ever get weak and bypass the main chance."

Bo gave a wan laugh. "Stop it, okay? Don't generalize from Bo Gavin to the moral bankruptcy of the nation."

"Sorry."

"What I want to know is, would an apology do any good?"

"In my case, sure. In Sam's, God knows. Kar'tajan is one of his sacred words. Now the whole country's going to associate it with your tony yuppie eelskins."

Bo swiveled, nodded at the carton on the bed. "They make great party balloons. Just ask Dr. Nesheim. We—"

A fierce, ghastly cry came outside, a cry halfway between a bleat and a strangled whinny. Bounty began to howl, and chills ran up and down the backs of both Bo and Libby. Oscillating into synch, they jumped up like telepathic twins.

"He's dead," Sam said when they had reached the birthing crib. "He gave that terrible holler and kicked out."

Bounty was huddled on a broke bale, shaking uncontrollably, no longer howling. Phylly, who had arrived only a few moments before, was trotting back and forth in the runway outside the stall.

When Libby and Bo knelt beside the stallion, his nostrils were already cold, and the rime of phlegm coating the veins in them had taken on a frosty look. His eyes, still open, suggested nothing so much as fissure-traced glass balls.

"We need to get him out of here, Sam. To bury him. I'll help you this time. We'll put him out there beside the calf."

"Don't need to do anything, hon, but wait. In the meantime, though, grab his horn."

Libby obeyed, placing her hand around the hard spiral edges of the two-foot-long alicorn, jogging it, and feeling it break off in her hand as if it were set not in the firm base of the creature's skull but rather in an impalpable matrix that partook more of Sam's Elsewhere than of Remuda County.

"It'll stay," Sam said. "The rest of him won't. He'll be gone by morning. At the latest, tomorrow afternoon."

"What about the others?" Bo asked, aware that Sam had expertly avoided making eye contact with him. "Are they doomed too?"

"I don't know. Lots are sick, though. They're passing through from the mine. And maybe from a cave over on Abbot's Pate."

"What do they do once they're through, Sam?"

"They hook up in Remuda Creek Meadow. Nighttime, they're with your cattle, eating grass and giving off their shine. During the day, they fade off into fir strands and aspens and such, where they get dimmed down by shade and high sunlight."

"How many? As a guestimate."

"If it keeps up, hon, you'll have more of them—kar'tajans—than Herefords, and it'll be impossible to keep 'em secret."

Saying *kar'tajans*, Sam looked at Bo for the first time since he and Libby had entered the barn. Trembling, Bo returned his gaze.

Libby hefted the horn. Where it had snapped from Pete's brow, there was a diamond-shaped hole with smooth bone underneath and, at the edges, a welling of velvety blood. The alicorn was heavy. It had a lethal potentiality, but holding it intensified her sense of helplessness. She began to weep.

Back inside, Bo found that Santaliz and Katt had left him the computer's extention cord. He pulled it up through the hole that Katt had drilled near the back of the writing surface and plugged in the Bendix. He clicked on the set. A storm of telegenic gauze—flickering, fading out—lit the dimness.

A picture resolved out of the phosphor-dot chaos, and sound out of the static. There was the legendary blues singer Bessie Smith walking about the kitchen of a Hollywood mansion peering into pots, checking out the refrigerator, and flirting in a touchy-feely way with a muscular black cook who went about his business as if she were nothing more than a starved cat rubbing against his shins or clawing pitifully at his trousers. The song Bessie was singing was "Kitchen Man":

> *Oh, how that boy can open clams,*
> *No one else can catch my hams,*
> *I can't do without my kitchen man.*
>
> *When I eat his doughnut,*
> *All I leave is the hole.*
> *Any time he wants it,*
> *Why, he can use my sugar bowl.*
>
> *Oh, his baloney's really worth a try,*
> *Never fails to satisfy.*
> *I can't do without my kitchen man. . . .*

"All right!" said Bo. Inexplicably, the sachems of the Otherworldly Broadcasting System—OBS?—ran Bessie's "Kitchen Man" video two more times. The Kartajans on Bo's bed—an entire complimentary carton—were there either to mock or to sanitize the pleasure of the flesh, Bo wasn't sure which, but ol' Bessie was doing nothing but celebrating them. Bless her.

So, the new TV notwithstanding, how could he give Lib's Bendix to Sam? Maybe he *owed* Sam the set, for exploiting the kar'tajans in that condom ad, but right now it was just about the only thing in the world keeping him sane.

Bo, you're out of it. The Bendix proves you know as much about sanity as the Rockefellers do about poverty.

The Swing Era station faded out. Bo changed the channel. An around-the-clock news program appeared, running a story about the kar'tajan die-off in the Great Indian Desert. A panning shot of a parched ocher landscape littered with equine corpses filled the screen, as a Hispanic correspondent—Che Guevara—reported that the World Veterinary Council had no idea what to do.

In the morning, Sam, who had spent the night in the barn, awoke to find that Pete had completely demanifested. All that remained of the animal was a depression in the hay, a few silken strands of hair caught on the rough planks of the stall, and a vague memorial odor. The alicorn that Libby had broken from the stallion's brow was propped in one corner like the handle of a custom-made fishing rod—an idiosyncratic but not impossible artifact.

Phylly, Pete's mare, was pacing the runaway outside the birthing crib. She was blowing mucous bubbles, her eyeballs were filmed, and red lesions had appeared on her nostrils, her lips, and the insides of her ears. She was so wobbly that Sam feared that she would fall over. He put one arm around her neck and guided her into an open space under the hay lofts.

Here, he broke open a clean bale of hay and bedded her down, fearful that exposing her to the crib where Pete had died might be to hasten the progress of her own disease. He understood, however, that Phylly had been infected some time ago and that he was being overpicky in introducing her to another stall.

Somewhat later, Lib called Preston Brinkley, who drove up from Huerfano pulling a horse trailer behind his pickup. Both Sam and she were astonished to learn that he intended to take Phylly back down the mountain to his clinic on the outskirts of Huerfano. They argued with him. None of the kar'tajans emerging onto the Tipsy Q from Naismith's Mine or the hidden doorway on Abbot's Pate, Libby said, had ever lived anywhere in this reality but on her ranch, and removing them might be an immediate death sentence.

"What're they under now?" Brinkley said. "I can't babysit this fucking four-footed mirage up here, and you've got worries aplenty without having to nurse a dying unicorn."

"Down there, Dr. Brinkley, someone's sure to see her."

"Only me. I'm not looking to encourage other worrywarts with imaginary animals to start ringing me up. Think I want a fucking practice based on griffins, yeti, and jackalopes? Shit, no. It's almost more than I can do to treat lame cow ponies."

"But where will you keep her?"

"In the storage shed behind my clinic. It used to be a stable, anyway. I got rid of all my help last year, thinking to retire, so Phylly here"—nodding at the kar'tajan— "won't have to put up with anybody but yours truly."

"What are you going to do to her?" Sam asked.

"Observe her. Treat her. Swamp fever's incurable, supposedly, but these sad-sack mothers haven't infected your horses, and they're from some other fucking dimension. It may be they'll respond—over here, so to speak—to a course of treatment that wouldn't quite get it in the whereabouts they hail from."

Finally, despite their misgivings, Libby and Sam let Brinkley have his way. He jackknifed his horse trailer up to the barn, got Phylly to her feet by cutting off her wind with the palm of one enormous hand, and walked her into the trailer like a medic limping a wounded soldier to a field hospital.

As soon as she was in, he dropped a Navajo horse blanket across the tailgate to keep prying eyes from seeing her, touched the brim of his hat to bid Libby and Sam farewell, and headed back down the mountain to Huerfano.

# 23

DeWayne Sky sat in the only bar in Snowy Falls, an adobe hovel called the Cove, drinking the worst margaritas he had ever tasted. In front of him, half eaten, his fourth barbecue-beef sandwich of the afternoon—all four of which Ernest Waldrop's son Stevie had fetched him, one after the other, from the pits laid out under a blazing-hot corrugated-tin awning on the grounds of the Snowy Falls First United Methodist Church.

Part of the bargain: all the barbecue he could eat. Having already led the Pioneer Days parade through Snowy Falls on Highway 69, DeWayne was cashing in. The sandwiches cost everybody else two bucks, but DeWayne had ridden his horse Otus Asio—Screech Owl—at the head of a procession of band students, VFW members, Boy Scouts, Girl Scouts, ramshackle covered wagons, make-believe gold rushers, make-believe coal miners, and four county riding clubs, and he had been photographed two million times. He had *earned* this grub. The barbecue was great, but the margaritas—a pay-as-you-go item—went down like bleak blends of cod-liver oil and kerosene.

The Cove was packed. Cowboys from several of the ranches above and below Snowy Falls crowded the tiny mud-daubed bodega, as did tourists and adult representatives of many of the groups that had marched in the parade. Gina Thrower had warned DeWayne about the Cove, pointing out that mostly riffraff frequented the place and that during Pioneer Days a patron could count on having his whiskey watered and his tab pumped up. But Mrs. Thrower had a motive for badmouthing the Cove. As a teetotaler, she deeply resented any establishment, especially a local one, that sold spirits.

For which reason DeWayne had sought out the place: you couldn't buy booze at Gina's, and ever since setting foot in Snowy Falls, he had had an angry thirst.

"This seat taken?" a woman asked.

DeWayne turned toward an attractive auburn-haired woman in blue jeans and a Western shirt. He sized her up as a tourist, although a wicked knowingness about her mouth and eyes caused him a moment's doubt. "It isn't if I can buy you a drink," he said. Hospitality, he told his mental picture of a disapproving LannaSue: nothing but innocent hospitality.

"I don't drink, chief."

"In here, that's smart. Why'd you want this seat?"

"It's news time." She nodded at the portable television in a high niche beyond the bar. "I'm addicted to the news."

"Why?"

She smiled. "I'm Karen Banks. And to answer your question—because I work for the news department of the CBS affiliate out of Pueblo. News is my livelihood."

The bartender, a good-humored Chicano, was talking with a trio of cowboys at the other end of the bar. "Hey," DeWayne hailed him, "lady here wants to see the news."

Karen Banks named a channel, and the bartender, never ceasing to smile, dialed it in and turned up the volume.

The anchor on the Pueblo station was the sort of semihandsome video clone you expected to see on the local news. "Denver-based Zubrecht Products, Incorporated," he was saying, "is riding high, buoyed by strong initial sales of the first line of condoms to be advertised on national commercial television."

Replacing the newsman's earnest face was a shot of Zubrecht's headquarters in Denver, followed by a shot of Everett Zubrecht, the company's founder, climbing into a limousine, and by a soundless clip of the animated ad for Kartajans that had been running every night for the past two weeks on *Nightline*.

"Company spokespersons claim that this imaginative and colorful spot for their new product has not only upped Zubrecht revenues but has begun to echo in the minds of the American people in a way that few ad messages ever do," said the clone in a voice-over. "They make comparisons to the Marlboro Man campaign of the fifties and early sixties but are quick to emphasize that Zubrecht Products, unlike cigarette manufacturers, are hyping goods designed to *preserve* life and health. They further claim that the condoms—called Kartajans, apparently from a Sanskrit word for unicorn—are the end result of three years of intensive research and testing and that letters and telephone calls to the networks about their controversial animated spot are running about two to one in its favor."

Kartajans, DeWayne mused. He hated the ad. He hated the fact that someone had lifted the mysterious word *kar'tajan* from a secret Ute vocabulary—to hell with that Sanskrit crap—and slapped it on a product that men of *his* generation would never have talked about in mixed company. Well, it was the men's turn. Women were already putting up with those sappy feminine-hygiene ads.

DeWayne glanced at Karen Banks—whose image, to his surprise, suddenly bloomed on the bar's TV set. "I'm here in Denver talking with Theodore 'Ned' Gavin, head of marketing for Zubrecht Products, Incorporated," her televised self said "At twenty-four, Gavin is one of Denver's—in fact, the entire West's—fastest-rising and most admired business prodigies. He has been profiled in *Fortune*, *Business Week*, and *Harper's*, and it was Gavin who commissioned the independent advertising agency responsible for the famous—some would say infamous—Kartajan campaign that has touched off so much recent debate."

"That's you," DeWayne told Karen Banks incredulously. Nearly everyone in the Cove had turned toward the set, although only he of all the bar's patrons seemed to realize that they had a celebrity, not counting himself, in their midst.

"Shhhh," Ms. Banks said. She touched one of his graying braids and redirected his attention to the TV set. Now appearing on the screen was the man she had interviewed, a broad-faced Anglo with a sandy tuft of whiskers. His beard reminded DeWayne of the goatee on the kar'tajan head on the dark blue package shown in close-up at the end of the infamous ad.

"What independent agency did you hire?" Ms. Banks's voice asked the unsmiling image of Theodore Gavin. "Insiders have told us that you involved a close relative—your brother—and that Zubrecht Products provided him with all the computer equipment and software necessary to complete the project."

"The information you've been leaked is right on target."

"Why 'leaked,' Mr. Gavin? Does it upset you that some Zubrecht employees regard your hiring of your brother as nepotism?"

"It upsets me that colleagues of mine are airing this matter in public—as if Mr. Zubrecht hadn't known from the beginning that my brother was the brains behind Gavin Graphics. Besides, Beaumont—my brother—worked up this entire project in a thoroughly professional manner for far less than it would have cost us if we'd gone to some brand-name Manhattan agency. The publicity generated by Beaumont's work and the sales figures currently coming in prove he's done just what we hoped he would, and I have no regrets about our having engaged him."

"What was his fee, Mr. Gavin?"

"That's a private business matter. I'll say only that it was a great deal of money to him but not all that much to us."

"Where are your brother's offices, Mr. Gavin?"

"That, too, is a private matter. Beaumont retired from ad work immediately upon completing the Kartajan project. All he wants now is rest and privacy."

Down the bar, a cowboy shouted, "I'd do without before I'd wear a goddamn rubber! It ain't natural!"

"From what I hear," a comrade retorted, "neither's your bedroom technique. So why sweat bullets over going in barefoot?"

Karen Banks's brow knitted in annoyance and renewed concentration; otherwise, the banter among the bar's less inhibited patrons had no effect on her.

"It would seem to me, Mr. Gavin," her video image said, "that in the wake of your brother's popular ad for Kartajans, this would be a foolish time for him to retreat from the business."

"My brother has all the money he needs," Ned Gavin said. "He took this assignment because he believed in it, and we at Zubrecht Products are grateful to him, not only for creating a memorable ad but also for helping us address the current health crisis in a way that's both tasteful and informative."

"What hypocritical bullshit," the real Karen Banks said.

"It's rumored that your brother is ill," her videotaped self said. "And that his illness explains his unwillingness to accept either accolades or new ad assignments."

"He has meningitis," Gavin said tightly.

"Not AIDS, as some rumors suggest? The irony of an AIDS victim programming an ad for a new condom is . . . well, provocative."

"There's no truth to those rumors."

"Mr. Gavin, we've done some sleuthing, and so far we've found no record of a Beaumont Gavin hospitalized with meningitis anywhere in the Rocky Mountains."

"He *is* hospitalized." The young man with the sandy goatee was sweating, visibly. "But not in this state and not under his real name. Now, if you'll forgive me, I have work to do."

"An outright lie," the real Karen Banks said.

"Thank you, Mr. Gavin," her videotaped persona said. "Back to you, Richard."

"A *transparent* outright lie," the real Karen Banks said.

Richard, the anchor, proceeded to discuss the impact of the "current health crisis" on the condom industry in general. Several cowboys and VFW types began to heckle his impervious talking head. Karen Banks no longer cared. Her three minutes of glory were over, and when DeWayne next tried to buy her a drink, she indifferently accepted a highball glass of soda water.

"Hope this doesn't hurt your feelings, chief, but I didn't come to Snowy Falls to watch you lead this morning's big parade."

"Didn't, huh?"

"We taped that interview yesterday in Denver. At noon today, we aired it on *Colorado Almanac*. As soon as it was over, we got a call from a woman named Josephine Gavin. She asked for me. I was editing some unrelated news footage but stopped and talked to her. She told me that no matter what anyone thought, she *wasn't* the mother of either Theodore or Beaumont Gavin. What they were doing for Zubrecht Products was immoral. She was ashamed that two men with the same surname as her late husband should be involved in any way with such a vile product. She hoped no one at our station would do anything to try to connect her or her dear husband with these revolting characters."

"Kartajan," a man in camouflage fatigues at one of the cramped booths yelled. "You know what that is, don't you? An ad man with a bad case of hoof-in-mouth disease."

"It's a yuppie eelskin," somebody else shouted. "The same way Häagen-Dazs is a yuppie ice cream."

"She sounds crazy," DeWayne prompted Karen Banks.

The newswoman ignored the barflies and her relentlessly yakking colleague to continue her story. "Of course, Josephine Gavin was—is—Beaumont and Theodore Gavin's mother, and her sons were native Pueblans. I'd missed that in earlier research, but as soon as I was off the phone with Mama, I confirmed it in five minutes. Found out from neighbors that Bo, the older, had moved to Atlanta a few years back. Learned through our Atlanta counterparts that he had worked for a small ad agency there until March, and that he'd since come back to Colorado to recuperate from an unspecified illness. A woman at his Atlanta firm refused to divulge either his disease or his whereabouts. Said she'd already got herself in trouble telling tales out of school and was probably doing the same thing again. Had no doubt that Bo had done the Kartajan campaign, though, and was glad to hear he was still alive."

"So why are you in Snowy Falls?" DeWayne said impatiently.

"Some additional snooping revealed that Beaumont's up here on a ranch that once belonged to his first cousin, Gary Quarrels. It's pretty evident he has AIDS. As soon as that blockade north of Mrs. Thrower's gets moved, Frank and I are going to drive up, shoot some context footage, and talk with him." She nodded at a table next to the unplugged jukebox, where her cameraman—Frank—was sitting with a draft beer and a napkin piled high with pretzels.

DeWayne had still not laid eyes on Sam Coldpony, who had gotten him this grand-marshal gig, but he knew from Mrs. Thrower that Sam was working on the Tipsy Q. "Why not just telephone the place?" he asked, uneasy with the newswoman's revelations.

"I did. Libby Quarrels answered, but when I told her who

I was and asked if someone named Beaumont Gavin were living with her, she said 'No comment' and hung up."

"Did you hear about the deaf moron?" a bearded man immediately to Karen Banks's left asked the bodega at large. "He put a rubber on each ear so he wouldn't get hearing AIDS."

"Why're you telling me all this, lady?" DeWayne said. It was clear that she had not squeezed in beside him simply to see herself on TV or to hit on a paunchy old brave in buckskins.

"A Ute named Sam Coldpony works for Libby Quarrels," Ms. Banks said. "You're a Ute too, chief. Frank and I were hoping if we paid you a little something, you'd give us an introduction to help us get past Ms. Quarrels so we could talk to Gavin."

"An introduction?"

"Let's not beat around the piñon tree. This is a scoop that'd put us on *The CBS Evening News*, right up there with Rather. 'AIDS victim in Colorado spends last few months of his life preparing ad for revolutionary new condom.' With that kind of story, we'd be shoo-ins for a network feed. Understand me, chief?"

In Ute, DeWayne said, "Screw you, squaw."

"An insult, no doubt. Never mind, then. Frank and I will find our own way and make our own introductions."

The condom segment on the news was still on. The screen showed a panning shot of the interior of the factory in Greeley, where most of the workers were white-smocked women. Following this was a close-up of an elaborate display of twelve-packs bearing such names as Feelings, Halberdiers, and Good Nudes.

"Anybody hear about the queer-baiter who claimed to have a cure for AIDS?" shouted the cowhand next to Ms. Banks. "Swore he'd have the poor suckers back up on their knees in no time."

Someone in the bar inflated a balloon, or a condom, and burst it with the tip of a lit cigarette. Its explosion caused laughter, startlement, a brief but intense argument. Outside, two little boys labored past the Cove dragging a shoat on a chain. Across the highway, the tuba player for the high school band was *oom-pah-pah*-ing the chorus of a monotonous Top Forty song.

"Wait a minute," DeWayne said, full of misgivings. It would be terrible for this lady and her cameraman to barge in unannounced at the Tipsy Q. "You want an introduction? I'll give you one."

"How much?" Karen Banks asked, turning back to him.

"What'd you have in mind?"

She glanced at Frank, who shrugged. "Twenty-five dollars?"

"Done," DeWayne told her.

"Okay, Frank," Ms. Banks said. "Onward to the Tipsy Q."

Hearing this, the bearded man who had been cracking jokes said, "You people going to see Bo Gavin? Poor bastard's been real sick. Didn't even make it to the parade."

DeWayne watched Karen Banks turn to the man. "Are you a friend of his? Do you know him personally?"

"Name's Hoke Gissing, ma'am. Not exactly a friend. I've seen him at Mrs. Thrower's place a couple times, though. Pretty regular dude for a fruitcake."

"We're trying to do a story on him," Karen Banks said. "Would you take my cameraman and me to the Tipsy Q to see him?"

"Sure," Gissing said. "My pleasure."

The newswoman gave DeWayne a look of scornful dismissal. You blew your chance, her eyes told him.

But Gissing, who was wearing shotgun chaps and boots, surprised Ms. Banks by vaulting up onto the bar and waving his arms over his head. "Hey!" he shouted. "We're putting together an expedition to go see Bo Gavin. He was too sick to make our parade this morning, but this kindly TV lady thinks we should take part of our parade up to the Tipsy Q. If Muhammad can't go to the mountain, the mountain will go to Muhammad. You know the saying."

"Wait," Karen Banks said. "Wait a minute."

"We've even got our grand marshal right here in the Cove, and he's agreed to lead us up that way if we can round up enough folks to make the trip worthwhile. How many of you boozehounds here are willing to go? You'd be brightening up a poor dying fella's final days, believe me."

"To the Tipsy Q!" one of the Gissing's drunken companions shouted, lifting an amber bottle.

"To the Tipsy Q!" a dozen voices inharmoniously chimed.

Soon, almost everyone in the Cove was trumpeting Hoke

Gissing's suggestion of an impromptu charity march on the Quarrels place, and DeWayne gave Karen Banks a look that said, I didn't blow my chance, you're *still* going to owe me twenty-five simoleons, and look at all the company we're going to have.

Gissing jumped down from the bar, waved one arm over his head like a cavalry officer, and led half the people in the Cove—maybe twenty—out into the town's makeshift midway. Karen Banks, Frank, and DeWayne squeezed out right behind this enthusiastic mob, which grew by accretion as Gissing told other celebrants what was going on and as the motley procession gimped past Belucci's Repair Shop, the clapboard Methodist church and its smoking barbecue pits, and Gina Thrower's little empery.

At a hitching post in front of the post office, DeWayne placed his eagle-feather war bonnet on his head, mounted Screech Owl, and goaded the obedient gelding to the front of the crowd.

Gissing and several other men began breaking up the blockade of buckboards, painted prairie schooners, and parked cars above the boardinghouse, all of which the local constabulary had positioned there to turn an in-town stretch of 69 into a temporary mall, and Karen Banks and her cameraman climbed into the lead buckboard, with Gissing, to start the bumpy ride to the Tipsy Q.

DeWayne, looking over his shoulder, figured that at least forty people, most either cowhands or skylarking teenagers, were now part of this train. Although it was a pretty ragtag affair compared to the highly organized event that morning, he found himself puffing out his chest and making Screech Owl prance sidelong exactly as he had done at the real thing.

The sun was going down, the Sangre de Cristos to the southwest loomed like a serrated wall, and a dusky coolness had begun to settle. No one in the calvacade seemed concerned. They were headed for the Tipsy Q to cheer up the local AIDS patient.

Although DeWayne knew that Karen Banks had wanted an exclusive interview, not a parade, she now appeared content to let events carry her along. Why not? She and Frank were at the center of a human-interest story almost as bang-up as the one she had set out to report. Even if she couldn't get it on

Dan Rather, she had an entertaining piece for her local station, and that was probably about all the CBS affiliate in Pueblo expected of her.

# 24

Brooklyn Terry had a streetside room on the top floor of Gina Thrower's boardinghouse. On his bed, sprawled naked, luscious butt upward, lay seventeen-year-old Placida Garcia, whom he had enjoyed thoroughly an hour ago and whom he intended to screw cross-eyed again as soon as he could rouse her from the deep doze that so many sated females her age seemed to fall into.

Mrs. Thrower throught Plácida had gone to Huerfano to visit her senile great uncle. Brooklyn knew that, to stay on the old lady's good side, he would have to sneak Placida out in the middle of the night. Well, fine. Every reckless minute—the uncertainty, the flouting of rules—was hugely more exciting than getting skunked at the Cove or trying to pitch vinyl doughnuts over beer bottles at one of those cheap midway booths. Besides, the pillowy Placida had lost her cherry at twelve or thirteen, and he sure as hell wasn't contributing to the delinquency of a minor by plowing her a few times. What he mostly seemed to be contributing to was her beauty sleep.

A commotion in the street drifted up to Brooklyn. He stopped stroking Placida's satiny ass and tilted his head. The noise got louder. He swung his feet over the mattress's edge and placed them on the floor so that he was facing the window overlooking Highway 69. Between his thighs, the Kartajan condom that Placida had made him wear hung like the distended skin of a baby rattlesnake. He removed it as carefully as he could, but still managed to snag a couple of short hairs. On his way to the window, he dropped the gluey sheath in the tin basin on his chest of drawers.

What Brooklyn saw, gazing down, was a mob of people shouldering covered wagons, buckboards, and old cars out of the blockade set up earlier by Neville Fuller, Snowy Falls' chief of police. To the wagons without dray animals, they were hooking up horses or mules. Some members of the mob were brandishing beer bottles; others were pumping walking sticks up and down like clubs. Nearly everyone was chanting or shouting.

Brooklyn ducked behind the curtain, peeked around it again, saw that the mob was now moving—clattering—up the highway toward the Tipsy Q. Now why in blazes were they doing that?

Only one reason occurred to Brooklyn. They were on their way to demonstrate their unhappiness with the fact that Miss Libby had brought an AIDS patient into their county and put him up in her own home. Also, someone down there (Brooklyn recognized Edgar del Rio and Henry Martinez, as well as Hoke Gissing, from Ray Hilliard's ranch, all of them potted) may have found out that Libby Quarrels's houseguest was the same son of a bitch who'd done the controversial Kartajan ad. (In fact, that ad had suckered Placida, a Catholic girl, into buying a box of the damned things.) Not many Chicanos would wink at such blatant impiety; condoms encouraged premarital sex and illicit connubial birth control, and Brooklyn feared that Hilliard's boys were leading a vengeful horde up the road to give Bo a hands-on lesson in seemly religiosity.

Christ. You damnfools can't do that.

He looked toward Placida's dreamy body, but his mind's eye kept seeing Bo Gavin hanging lifeless from a willow bough. Frightened, Brooklyn fumbled through the pockets of his jeans, which he had thrown on the floor, for change. He clawed out some coins, put his arm into the sleeve of a threadbare bathrobe, and let himself into the upstairs hall of the boardinghouse. At the head of the Stairs was a pay telephone. He looked up Libby Quarrels's number, slotted in a coin, and dialed. After five or six rings, a voice—female—said, "Yes?"

"Miss Libby, this is Brooklyn. You've got trouble."

The voice laughed at him. "So what else is new?"

"You've got trouble *coming*. Right now." He told her about the hostile parade rollicking up Highway 69 toward her ranch.

"My God, Brooklyn. Get Neville for me, would you?"

"Yes, ma'am. He's patrolling the midway, though, and I'll have to get dressed to do it."

"Dressed? At this time of day? You sick, Brooklyn?"

"Right now, ma'am, you betcha. Get ready. There's a slew of angry peckers coming. Neighbors, some of them—but they're either drunk or sunstruck. I can't begin to guess what they'll do." He could, of course, but he saw no point in waxing graphic.

Back in his room, Brooklyn stared wistfully at Placida—by God, her buttocks were wonders!—but dutifully pulled on his clothes and tramped down the stairs to find Neville Fuller.

On Mrs. Thrower's Wild West sidewalk, he paused to look after Gissing's vigilantes, but they had already gone around the abrupt bend above Snowy Falls and were no longer visible. Apparently, no one else in town had paid any heed. All up and down Highway 69, festival goers queued up around, or dawdled past, game booths and fast-food stands. A country-western combo on the church grounds was savaging "Ghost Riders in the Sky."

Bo was breathing loudly in the coverted study, already a waxen effigy of himself. Libby, shaken by Brooklyn's telephone call, ran out her back door.

"Sam!"

She saw him high up on the galvanized angle-iron ladder of the thirty-foot windmill behind the horse trap. He was repairing the motor of this contraption, using nothing but a pair of pliers. He looked toward the house. Libby plunged across the yard, stooped under a rail in the horse trap, and went dashing up to the Remuda Creek Meadow side of the enclosure, where, gasping, she clutched a fence post and looked up into the fading sunset colors against which Sam was dramatically backlit.

"A mob! A drunken mob's coming up here from Snowy Falls!"

"What the hell for?"

"For Bo, I think. Maybe for us too. They may be thinking to hurt somebody, Sam."

"That'd be stupid. Bo's already hurt, and I'm liable to hurt one of them before they manage to hurt us."

"Who said booze ever increased anybody's IQ?"

"You've got a gun rack, honey. Pull out that old twelve-gauge of your ex's and go stand in the front door."

"Hey, I don't want to gut-shoot anybody."

"You may have to."

"I may not be able to. I don't think I've got any shells."

"Fake it, then. Got to the porch and poke that shotgun barrel at whoever makes as if to come inside."

"What're you going to do?"

"Give me a few minutes to think."

"From what Brooklyn just said, you haven't got that many." Lib pushed away from the creosoted post and ran back to the house. The hasp on the gun cabinet in her bedroom had rusted. She rattled the glass doors, grabbed up her Bible, shattered the left-hand window. It still was no lark getting Gary's .12-gauge out, but she managed, breaking more glass and virtually unhinging one of the doors. She brushed diamondlike fragments from her arms and strode to the front porch, clutching the oily Remington.

Atop the windmill, Sam gazed across the roof of Libby's house—past her brand-new rotary antenna and through the tops of the aspen trees clustered in the median of her horseshoe drive. He could see part of the highway from Snowy Falls and, narrowing his eyes, the ghostly images of the first few people and wagons belonging to the mob that Brooklyn had seen gathering. They seemed to be floating, but, for all their muzziness of outline, they scared the holy shit out of Sam. He closed his eyes, hoping they would go away.

They didn't. Sam said a prayer to Inu'sakats: "Merciful one, deliver us from evil." The dusk got thicker, and the sky behind Ptarmigan Mountain bled from dove gray to violet and from violet to a luminous indigo. The safety lamp on the pole beside Libby's barn came on, and rods of her new antenna hung there like X-rayed finger bones. Time was briefly suspended, and Sam thought—against all other evidence—that he had eons with which to work. Dizzy, he looked down.

Ouray was standing at the foot of the angle-iron ladder. His antlers were so big that dozens of nuthatches, camp robbers, and magpies could perch among their twiggy points all at once. So big that hunters would mistake them for migrating trees.

The antlers had enlarged tremendously just since Sam's last sighting of the elk on the ridge opposite North La Veta Pass.

Then, his old buddy had struck Sam as half apparition, but this evening the bull elk seemed wholly mythological—a beast from Sam's own subconscious, or maybe that of his dying people. An animal at once primeval and everlasting. A focus of divine *powa'a*.

All Sam had to do was imagine that the final days had come and a thundering explosion of white buffalo would burst from the seams of the Sangre de Cristos and everything would be changed forever, all the griefs and indignities of both the unhappy present and the shameful past trampled under the hooves of these redemptive albino bison. Ouray would trumpet, and they would come forth like woolly behemoths—crimson-eyed, unswerving.

Sam climbed down the ladder, leapt to Ouray's back, and put his fingers through the creature's heavy shag. The elk trumpeted his daunting call through rounded lips. A shiver, a dozen shivers, snaked down Sam's spine. Suddenly, the woods behind the house—all the fir and ponderosa pine on Ptarmigan Mountain, all the poplars and water birches in Remuda Creek Meadow—were ablaze. Fire on the mountain. Cold flickers in the grass. A hundred conflagrations in the secret uplands.

"Thanks be to Inu'sakats. All praise to you, Son of Mary."

Ouray began to trot. The fire coming in quicksilver packages down the mountain and out of the lush grass of the meadow, Sam saw, glancing back, was the fire of maybe seventy kar'tajans responding to Ouray's summons, breaking from their hidden retreats.

They surged like molten pewter, three or four separate flows of bioluminescent animal flesh, all of which united a hundred yards or so behind the paddock and the windmill into a whinnying river of flame. Ouray lengthened his stride but, once past Libby's house, could not outdistance the flood. Kar'tajans had surrounded them—stallions, mares, even yearlings. In relationship to these other stampeding animals, Sam saw, he and the elk were steadily drifting back. So what? They were a torrent pouring down Highway 69, and if a river of fiery kar'tajans could not turn back a drunken mob, Sam knew that nothing else could either.

* * *

Without prompting, Otus Asio began to prance sideways. Then the horse snorted, whinnied, reared.

Trying to calm his pinto, DeWayne Sky saw that a vast fireball was rolling down Highway 69 toward him and all the other members of his parade. Water, he thought. A dam near a top-secret nuclear-power plant has collapsed, and millions of gallons of radioactive water are spilling toward us from the break.

Next, holding Screech Owl by the mane and digging in his knees, DeWayne imagined that one of Remuda County's road crews had worked some sort of cordite mixture into the asphalt coating the highway and that this evening someone had lit the mixture: 69 was burning toward them like the wildest combustible fuse ever engineered. When it reached Snowy Falls, the whole damn town would explode.

"My God!" Hoke Gissing cried, poised over the buckboard's seat like a dude over an outhouse hole. "Would you look at that!"

It was neither a radioactive flood nor an immense burning fuse, DeWayne realized, as Otus Asio reared and reared again. It was a stampede of spirit creatures, kar'tajans. They were stampeding, he deduced, to punish the white eyes for stealing both their name and their image in order to market, yes, rubbers. But I'm not a white eyes, DeWayne inwardly protested. Why am I being punished along with these mercenary Anglos and Chicanos?

As his pinto pirouetted on its hind legs, whinnying and shaking its head, DeWayne saw many of those who had marched out from Snowy Falls hightail it for cover or jump from their wagons and run off the highway to escape the oncoming juggernaut. They scrambled into the wildflowers below the asphalt or into the fractured boulders and lodgepole pines above it. Many were screaming, and many others were duck-walking or crawling, as if staying close to Mother Earth would save them.

Meanwhile, either ignorant of or indifferent to the fact that Gissing's parade was well-intentioned, the kar'tajans kept coming. They had eyes like red glass, their pale haircoats rippled with white or blue-white fire, and their hooves struck sparks from the asphalt. The noise of their approach filled up the roadbed like thunder, and their ebony alicorns glinted like the shouldered rifle barrels of an infantry brigade.

DeWayne took one hand from Otus Asio's bridle and raised it in greeting. This wasn't punishment, he decided. This was a gift of the Holy He-She. How many mortals, either European or native, had ever seen so many four-legged *ini'putc'* at one time?

Gissing leapt from his buckboard and ran, but the mules pulling it halted and began struggling against each other, one fighting to back up, the other to turn downhill. As they seesawed, Karen Banks pointed at the kar'tajans and demanded that Frank capture them on tape even if doing so put their lives in jeopardy. Frank obeyed. DeWayne watched as he jumped from the buckboard and staggered up a flat-topped boulder at roadside. There, he trained his Portacam on the animate conflagration now engulfing them.

Flickering packets of silver fire swept between the abandoned wagons in the highway—one after another, over and over. DeWayne, on Screech Owl, was swarmed by kar'tajans, repeatedly encircled and released. On the buckboard behind him, her hair lifted by the wind and the heat of the kar'tajans' passage, Karen Banks was shouting, "Get it, Frank! Dear God, it's fantastic! Can you believe it? My God, it's unreal!" Frank, crouching low, pivoted to record as much as he could. At last, most of the unicorns having slid around and past the stalled wagons and frantic dray animals, Frank was aiming his Portacam down 69 toward Snowy Falls and the torchlike tails of the hallucinations that had just overrun them.

"Great!" Karen Banks shouted. "Absolutely sensational! Like being visited by God!"

In the middle of the highway, DeWayne was alone at the head of Hoke Gissing's routed parade. Otus Asio did a nervous dance under him, and some of those who had fled—including Gissing, Edgar del Rio, and Henry Martinez—began returning, gingerly, from the flower clumps, ditches, and pine stands where they had been lying doggo. The stampede had lasted less than a minute, but during it DeWayne had done a year's worth of furious cogitating.

"I didn't have *that* damn much to drink," Gissing told the folks gathering again at the wagons. "Swear to God."

"It was real," Karen Banks reported, her face glowing as if sunburned. "I mean, it was *unreal*, but it really happened."

A bulky shadow up the highway drew DeWayne's attention. The shadow moved toward him—until DeWayne was able to see that a big wapiti with a rack like two Christmas trees was edging down the asphalt. This creature was no *ini'putc'*. It was a living being. Its pelt undoubtedly harbored ticks, fleas, mites. Another living being—this one a man—clung to the elk's back with a ferocious but fearful resolution. When the wapiti was only twenty yards away, DeWayne recognized the man: Sam Coldpony, Payz's father, the sorry renegade who had come to see her graduate without even telling her that he was there.

Seeing what DeWayne saw, every member of the routed parade fell silent again. Frank pointed his Portacam at the newcomers. He was going to immortalize everybody present.

"Come no farther," Sam said.

"We want to see Beaumont Gavin," Karen told him.

"I know you do. He's sick. Leave him be. Have some pity. Go back to Snowy Falls."

"We were overrun by unicorns," Karen said. "Did you see them?"

"We *sent* them," Sam said. "As a warning."

"If we go back to town," Hoke Gissing said, "we'll have to wade through that whole damn herd—unless they're still running."

DeWayne cocked his head and squinted at Sam Coldpony. This man had given Paisley a kar'tajan figurine. Now here he was, elkback, acting as a sort of guardian to a small herd of the creatures. Had he recently acquired the powers of a shaman?

"What do you want me to tell your daughter?" DeWayne asked.

"To come see me. Here on the Tipsy Q."

"Ask her up, then." DeWayne would have said more, but the elk trumpeted and this call silenced him. When it hallooed again, Sam waved his arm at the roadsides, indicating—DeWayne figured—that those would be good places to hunker when the gist of the wapiti's bellowing was finally understood.

"It makes me sick you'd be a part of something like this," Sam scolded DeWayne. "Get ready—the kar'tajans are coming back." He nudged the elk about and loped it up the highway in a canter that was funny to behold. But DeWayne's amusement was short-lived. The beasts that had just swooped down on them were swinging around and massing for a return assault, summoned by the rough yodeling of an elk with an entire lumberyard on its poll.

In fact, there they were. The lower corridor of 69 burst into blue and blue-white flame, and the pounding of their hooves sent quakes through the pavement under every stalled wagon in Gissing's cavalcade. People ran for cover again, and DeWayne, wondering why the hell Coldpony had rebuked him for taking part in this goodwill march, yanked Screech Owl off the road and watched the kar'tajans—a flickering apocalypse—come galloping back.

"Get it again, Frank!" Karen shouted. "My God, get this one, too!"

Libby, the unused shotgun in her arms, stood in the center of her gravel drive. She saw the kar'tajans returning. The herd had slowed from a headlong gallop to an easy trot; their incandescent pelts had ceased to glow as brightly as they had on their outward journey. Now, in fact, the beasts gave off the workaday sheen of quarter horses that have been run to a healthy lather. Although still awesome, they no longer seemed supernatural.

Reaching out, Libby touched the first seven animals that came trotting down the drive. She inhaled the high muskiness of their sweat and noticed the lesions and shaggy coat patches endemic to nearly every creature from Bo's Elsewhere. The animals refused to dally for any pensive fondling. They were returning to Ptarmigan Mountain or the lush glades in Remuda Creek Meadow.

Sam rode into view on Ouray. It had to be Ouray, but how the elk could hold his head up under such a fantastic rack, Libby could not guess. Willpower, maybe, or a primeval wapiti pride. He was at once magnificent and comic, a creature—for now, at least—more imposingly mythological than the kar'tajans.

"Forget that shotgun," Sam said. He slid off Ouray and walked over to her. "No need for it tonight, hon."

Ouray ambled into the aspen stand and was briefly eclipsed from view. Reappearing, the elk picked his way up the mountain toward Naismith's Cabin. Trees swallowed him again—whereupon Bounty came slinking from the barn, tuck-tailed and quavery, as if he had just outlasted a brutal beating.

"What a baby," Libby said, chucking the dog under the chin and tugging at one of his ears. Then she stood back up and handed Sam the .12-gauge. "Glad I didn't have to threaten to use it."

Lib and Sam walked to the house together. Although Brooklyn's call had frightened her, making her fear the unpredictable wrath of a gay-baiting mob, she had held her ground without flinching. She had watched the kar'tajans stream past, she had hefted her unloaded shotgun as a potential bluff against every vigilante who finally showed up, and she had done these things without surrendering to a persistent urge to barricade her doors and hide. She had slid her fear into a hip pocket and ignored it.

Now, though, she was trembling—as Bounty had been trembling a moment ago. Remarkably, Sam was trembling too.

There, on her front porch, Libby placed the palm of her hand on Sam's chest—his work shirt was dappled with sweat—and peered into his ebony eyes. Did those eyes harbor either a smile or a humane hint of perplexity? Hard to tell. Did it matter? It should, Lib thought. I should have at least a glimmering of his state of mind before vamping him. Shouldn't I?

"Let me hold you," Sam said.

Gratifying words, which contradicted the black indifference of his eyes. Aloud, though, she heard herself respond, "Sam, you're nasty. Come in and get a shower."

"I don't have any clothes here, Miss Libby."

"For Pete's sake, stop calling me that." (Never mind that she had never objected to this manner of address before.) "After your shower, you can put on an old robe of Gary's."

Sam propped the shotgun against the wall under the front window and took her by the shoulders. "You're nasty too."

"What does that mean?"

"What does it mean that *I'm* nasty?"

"Nothing," Libby said. "Hold me, okay? Just hold me."

Sam pulled her to him, and they stood embracing on the shadowy porch. After a while, they went inside together.

* * *

At the CBS station in Pueblo, Karen Banks and her cameraman found that none of their potentially spectacular footage of the unicorns was usable. It all seemed to be horribly overexposed or shot at the wrong speed to render the beasts distinct. None of the standard remedies that they tried was of the least benefit. A pal of Frank's, another cameraman, told them they were probably spending too much time investigating Zubrecht Products, Inc., and watching *Nightline*. "Up yours," Frank retorted. As for Karen, she left the station an hour before lunchtime, went to a bar, and let a complete stranger buy her a double Scotch.

# 25

On Costume Night at the Cove, Bo was prancing in his Sun Dance garb, a breechclout and a pair of moccasins. The track lights on the pole at the center of the dance floor—the phony Tree of Life atop which real Sun Dancers would have wedged a buffalo head and a medicine bundle—shone straight into the dancers' faces. Bo ducked and squinted sidelong to identify the dancers next to him. To his right strutted Alfie Tuck, clad in his Vietnam battle gear, while to Bo's left, chanting and crossing himself, shuffled Father Oskar Zinzalow, the padre who had given last rites to Alife in the midst of an armada of ballooned-up condoms.

*We may not worship the sun*, said a bodiless amplified voice, *but no one makes better use of it than Heliodyne*.

Maybe this wasn't Costume Night at the Cove. No sane gay would have ever set foot there, anyway. No, this was a private bar and a weekend reunion of the folks—actors and support personnel—who had helped him do his CCG ad for Heliodyne. Bo lifted his head and sighted through the track lights' interesting beams. Opposite him high-stepped his former boss, Jimbo Watling, in a kilt with a tartan plaid like those manufactured by another CCG client, Piedmont Mills.

Dancing next to Watling was a figure in billowing black robes. Bo was finally able to identify him as Keith Jory. His robes were graduation robes, and on his head he wore a computer disk the size of an academic mortarboard. Keith was Sun Dancing for Emeritus Software, a show of unwarranted loyalty that made Bo's legs turn to Vaseline. The jukebox was thrumming "Sugarfoot Stomp" by the Benny Goodman orchestra, and everyone on the floor—save Bo—was doggedly advancing on and retreating from the center pole to the rhythms of this hokey number.

Keith's hands were sheathed in black. His feet were invisible because the track lights did not shine that low. One of his black hands flipped his mortarboard into darkness; the other unzipped his robe. When the robe had fallen open, Bo's dead lover gazed at him from empty eye sockets, then shrugged aside the garment to show not his disease-wasted body but the skeleton that had undergirded it in life. None of the other Sun Dancers noticed, but Bo, stung by this sight, swallowed air.

The club blew away. All the other dancers on its floor were snatched up like puppets and hurled off into nothingness. Desert swept in, an arid geometry of yucca and sage buoyed the night, and the living head and picked-clean skeleton of the lost Keith Jory jumped astride a passing kar'tajan and galloped vengefully down on Bo like very death.

The nearness of annihilation awoke him, and he slipped from his bed to find the sun—the real sun—spilling through the door to his room like radioactive water and no one else around to measure or to bring down his anxiety count. Until, that is, he staggered through the connecting bathroom and seated himself on a metal kitchen stool on which, yesterday morning, Libby had stood to replace a burnt-out hundred-watter.

"Well, well, well," he said.

He felt woozy, but his wooziness stemmed not from his worsening immune deficiency but from hunger. He had had only some toast and tea yesterday morning, but today—a new day—he wanted a scrambled egg, maybe even a slice or two of bacon. The reality of his hunger cheered him. Dead men didn't eat; they were eaten.

"Well, well, well."

Libby looked up first. She had her head on Sam's naked chest, another sight that stirred a familiar hunger in him. The Indian's pectorals were well defined, scarred but hairless, like the dented bronze chest guard of a veteran Roman centurion. When Sam's eyes opened, both people in Libby's bed were staring at him staring at them. Neither of them seemed able to move.

"Well, well, w—"

"Shut up, Bo," Libby said.

"Sorry. Just surprised, I guess. And jealous. I figured you guys were too hung up on employer/employee mind games to indulge in . . . ah, egalitarian hanky-panky."

"So did we," Libby said. "Up till now."

Sam looked trapped, but when he reached for the bathrobe at the foot of Libby's bed, she put her hand on his arm. The Ute desisted and fell back, and Bo thought that in this leisurely compliance Sam was laying claim to his right to be there.

"Coldpony here saved your life," Libby said, knuckling Sam on one of his bronze pectorals.

"A wasted effort," Bo said. "I won't make it through August." He smiled. "And that's being optimistic."

Libby sat up against the iron lyre of her headboard, drawing the sheet with her to keep from exposing her breasts. Propped that way, she told him a story—in Bo's view, almost a fairy tale—about a bunch of would-be gay baiters from Snowy Falls and the kar'tajan stampede that had sent them home in humiliated disarray. Evident in her tone was the pride she had taken in her own pluck and the greater satisfaction she had derived from Sam's resourcefulness and courage—just as if the Hollywood stereotype of the Strong Silent Hero had worked its loopy magic and she had tasted the uncommon joy of not being disappointed in a man.

Her narrative embarrassed Sam. He seized Gary's robe, shook it out before him, hid his nakedness behind it, and rocketed from bed to bathroom in a single Superman-ish bound altogether in sync with the story Bo had just heard. The bathroom door slammed. It opened again. The Ute's arm shot out, and he asked Bo—if Bo didn't mind—to gather up his clothes and pass them in to him so that he could start taking care of pressing ranch business.

"What's pressing right now," Libby said, "is going to Ignacio to invite Paisley to the Tipsy Q."

"She won't come," Sam said from behind the door. (Bo heard the Ute's belt buckle clatter on porcelain.)

Libby argued that she would. That although Sam had botched his own mission to Ignacio, she, Libby, would act now as his proxy, and her presence at the Sun Dance—her intercession with the headstrong girl—would count for plenty. Besides, once Payz heard how DeWayne Sky, her mentor, had thrown in with a lynch mob, her allegiance to that charlatan would crumble and a reunion with Sam would seem the logical alternative to studying for the shamanhood under Sky. From all that Sam had told her, Lib knew that Paisley had character, and character would out.

"Sky's not a nigger-knocker," Sam said. "He thinks his farts smell like roses, and he's got everybody in Ignacio buffaloed, but he's not a nigger-knocker."

"Last night, Sam, he was well on the road. Literally."

Bo felt an intense excitement. Libby was planning to attend the Utes' annual Sun Dance in order to fetch Sam's daughter back to Snowy Falls, and it struck him like a slap that the only course for him was to go with her. He hadn't done that Heliodyne ad, and all the research leading up to it, just to make CCG and himself a few bucks richer. He had done it because it had felt right, and it had felt right because he had had a subliminal precognition of the trip that he and Libby would eventually take. This morning's dream, so horrible on one level, was in fact a kind of call, an id-delivered letter of acceptance. "M'lady," he said, "I'm going with you."

Libby stared as if he had offered to grow a tail and swing from a loft rafter.

"It's my car," he insisted, "and I'm going. Even if it's truly the last thing I ever do."

"You gave your car to Sam," Libby reminded him.

Inside the bathroom, a boot thumped the veneered surface of the hollow door. "Suppose I deed it back to Bo?"

"Then I'll take the truck," Libby said.

"I need the truck," Sam said. "And if I'm outside prowling and seeing about the stock, who's going to take care of him?"

Bo could smell victory. "If I cash in on the way, m'lady, just shove me onto the road for the coyotes and the crows."

"As if they'd have you," Libby said, disgusted. But she wasn't really unhappy with the prospect of his going. They both knew that whatever its outcome, this would be his last road trip anywhere—at least while clad in the flesh—and why shouldn't Libby allow it for his sake and why shouldn't Bo insist upon it for hers?

Sam emerged from the bathroom, dressed in the same clothes he'd worn during his heroics. "Sounds like a bang-up idea to me."

It did to Bo too. He was convinced—although he didn't bother to say so aloud—that the reason he felt so good had everything to do with last night's stampede. Sam's magic animals flashing by the house in the early dusk, and then hurtling back past it only ten or fifteen minutes later, had generated a kind of electromagnetic flux that had realigned his out-of-kilter somatic molecules and infused him with a healing energy that had triggered an overnight remission of his AIDS. Or, if not a true remission, an undeniable abeyance of the syndrome. Which had happened so that he could accomplish one last thing—one last positive thing—during the days remaining to him: namely, help his cousin-in-law help her spanking-new lover reconcile with Paisley. Which was why he felt peppier than he had in over a month. Hell, in over *two* months.

"I'm going to fry up every last strip of bacon in the kitchen," he said. "One of you guys make some juice."

The story that something outlandish had occurred on the first day of Pioneer Days on Highway 69 between Snowy Falls and the Tipsy Q began to slither around among the bunkhouses, bodegas, and pool halls of Remuda County. This was natural. More than forty people—ranch hands, construction men, denim-clad teenagers with packages of Tarletons rolled up in their T-shirt sleeves—had seen the fiery unicorns driven toward them by Sam Coldpony and that bodacious elk, and two or three of these people talked.

DeWayne Sky, however, was one witness who remained mum. He spent the night in his upstairs room in Gina Thrower's (bothered by occasional muffled thrashings and ecstatic vocalizations from the next room) but checked out early the following morning. There had been talk of his dedicating, on Sunday afternoon, a statue of a Sioux princess given to the town by an itinerant wood carver, but because DeWayne's primary duties were over, he elected to return to Ignacio in his all-terrain vehicle.

Otus Asio rode behind him, in the attached trailer, but indulged in such frequent and violent bouts of van fits—troubled even yet, DeWayne figured, by his recollections of six dozen equine brothers stabbed in the foreheads with pikes, draped with popcorn strings of invisible Christmas-tree bulbs, and savaged into headlong flight by a rabid wapiti—that he had to stop three times before reaching La Veta Pass. There, he tranquilized his horse, waited for the drug to kick in, and then headed on home with his gelding comatose in the trailer.

I don't much blame you, DeWayne thought. He knew that Alma's—Paisley's—father had done something extraordinary last night, but that it had happened because the fool had misconstrued the motives of those marching on the Tipsy Q. Gissing and the others (leaving out that newswoman and her cameraman) had simply wanted to cheer up the AIDS patient befriended by Coldpony's boss, but Sam had chosen to believe that they were coming for blood and that even he, Papa Sky, was a partner in their imaginary mischief-making. But, then, Coldpony was a meathead.

On the other hand, driving those kar'tajans onto the road and having that motherhumper of an elk bugle them back again had been a stroke of strategic genius—if only there had been a real threat to counter—and DeWayne had to admire Coldpony for pulling it off. It further proved that Paisley's daddy had unsuspected powers and that letting the girl take part in this year's Sun Dance—now only three days away—had the wholehearted blessing of the gods.

For the remainder of his drive, Screech Owl down and out in the van, last night's stampede playing in his memory like stirring but muted background music, DeWayne turned his attention to practical Sun Dance matters. Where would he put the Thirst House? Who would he appoint to the first shifts of singing and drumming? Plenty to think about. One item of concern was what to tell Alma—Paisley—about what her daddy had done to reassert his Indianness and how his unorthodox assertion could possibly make for him a doorway back into her affections.

Just as DeWayne Sky drove into La Plata County, Hoke Gissing was eating venison and beans at Ray Hilliard's chuck and trying to get Martinez and del Rio to cool it about the alleged events of the previous evening. Hoke believed that they had seen *something* on the highway below the Tipsy Q, but probably not unicorns. (Christ, definitely not unicorns!) He was inclined to attribute the seeming stampede to a riot of living creatures, probably ponies or bighorn sheep, and to overimbibing at the Cove.

The overimbibing had turned the ponies or bighorn sheep into fantasy animals. Every other explanation that Hoke could come up with branded him and his pals a queer species of UFO crank, for it seemed more likely to him that aliens would descend on Earth than that unicorns would run amok in the Sangre de Cristos.

"You saw them, Hoke," the hotheaded del Rio accused, viciously assaulting his steak. "Claimed you hadn't drunk that damned much, either."

"Everybody saw them," the wiry Martinez said. "Unless we were hypnotized or dreaming, it goddamn well happened."

Added del Rio, "I'm going to work up a petition. Every hombre who went with us last night will sign it."

Hoke saw reason for panic. "Yes, sir. Run it in the *Huerfano Warrior*. Two weeks from now, we'll be the laughingstock of every cattle outfit in the Rockies."

"Then there'll be no petition," Ray Hilliard said.

Hilliard, who had been the president of a Michigan real estate firm before buying his ranch in Colorado as a tax shelter, sat in the cinderblock bunkhouse with his crew. They were arrayed around a Ping-Pong table that the cook had covered with a sheet of plywood and a blue oilcloth. Hilliard visited the table once a week during his summer sojourns in Remuda County to testify to his camaraderie with the hands, but Hoke was aggrieved that the skinny old coot had picked out today, even as Pioneer Days ground on in Snowy Falls, to settle in for a plate of pan-fried venison and a side dish of nutty talk about yesterday's . . . happening.

Hilliard wasn't a pea brain, not by any twist of the term,

and he had listened to the bulk of their babbling—sensibly enough—as if his good-old-boy cowpokes were having him on. Just in the past few minutes, though, the relentless sincerity of Martinez and del Rio, the heat of their impatience with Hoke, had begun to persuade him that, yeah, they really had seen something peculiar near Libby Quarrels's place.

"I believe you fellows," Hilliard told them.

The other two Anglo cowhands at chuck, neither of whom had gone on last night's march, immediately stopped making fun of the three men who had. Hoke, however, suffered an intense, unremitting pang in his lower bowel. Things were going gronky fast.

"And if you saw what you say you saw," Hilliard said, "they've still got to be up here somewhere."

"On the Quarrels place," Eddie del Rio said. "Sure."

Ray Hilliard had his own light aircraft, a Beechcraft Bonanza, which he hangared on a scrubby airstrip near Huerfano, and he told his men that first thing tomorrow morning he intended to take it up and overfly Remuda Creek Meadow, Ptarmigan Mountain, and every acre of the Tipsy Q visible from the air. He could transport two or three brave souls with him (the mountains, Hoke knew, were a real hazard for amateur pilots), and whoever chose to accompany him would earn a full day's wages, just as if they were bucking hay or setting new fence posts.

Hoke begged off, but the two Hispanics committed, and Hilliard grinned his harmless death's-head grin.

Riding with Sam in the battered pickup, Bo was gratified by how good he felt. He might still resemble a concentration-camp victim, but over the past four months he had adjusted to that aspect of his deterioration, and neither Sam nor Libby ever tweaked him about his looks. However, the Southern Ute Sun Dance would not begin for two more days, and a condition that Libby had placed on his going along—a non-negotiable condition—was that he continue to show signs of feeling top-drawer. If the merest hint of depression or weakness or nausea claimed him over the next forty-eight hours, his trip to Ignacio was automatically forfeit. She had also warned him against trying to con her by pretending to feel better than he really did. She was on to that sort of numbskull scam, and he would forfeit not only his trip but also any further lien on her trust.

Stung by her reference to trust, Bo had agreed. This morning, however, he and Sam were riding up through Remuda Creak Meadow not just to demonstrate that he was feeling good—although he did feel good, astonishingly good—but to throw a couple of bales of hay in among the cattle and kar'tajans. Some of these animals—going by their droppings—were still falling victim to the sweetgrass runs, more common in the spring, and Libby had decided that a little hay might be just what her Herefords needed to stiffen their stools and put them right again. It hadn't rained in several days. The wheel ruts through the meadow were like long rusted beams of reinforced steel, and the peaks walling them in on the southwest wore wreaths of threadbare cloud. Sunlight ran along the vapory filaments like electricity. Water birches and poplars gleamed.

Even over the pickup's familiar *wheeze-and-clunk*, Bo could hear the drone of a small airplane. He thrust his head out the window and twisted his neck to get a good view of the robin's-egg-colored sky in which that machine had to be operating. He saw its shadow ripple over the meadow, evergreens, and mountain flank, and heard the growly Dopplering of its engine, without once catching sight of the aircraft itself. Then he didn't see the shadow or quite hear the engine any more, and Sam boot-soled the brakes and brought them to a rocking halt.

"That's Ray Hilliard's plane," he said.

"What's he doing?"

"Spying. If I were a Russian, I'd throw a ground-to-air after the skinny son." Sam opened his door, hung by its top edge outside the pickup, and tried to draw a bead on the departing aircraft. But it was already gone, and he slid back in.

A few minutes later, Bo and Sam began distributing hay along a well-grazed stretch of Remuda Creek. Hilliard's Beechcraft came back from the opposite direction, saluting them with a wing tilt or maybe just orienting its pilot and passengers for a better view of the park.

If they were kar'tajan-hunting, Bo mused, they weren't getting their money's worth. Save for fifty or so cattle and the hay-laden truck, the meadow seemed to have been set aside today for the wind, the quicksilver creek, and a vista so unsullied that the red pickup slashed into it like a switchblade. No matter. The Bonanza flew over Remuda Creek Meadow two more times.

Still later, as Sam goosed the truck over the drive between the house and the horse trap, Hilliard's aircraft was joined above the Tipsy Q by a helicopter with a cockpit bubble and two rubbernecking mannequins for occupants. This tiny machine—the ruckus it made was a disproportionate one—skimmed perilously near treetop height but surged up under Hilliard's airplane with such nimble aggressiveness that Bo briefly feared they would collide.

"Did someone order up an air show?" he asked Sam.

Sam stopped the truck and pulled his door-hanging stunt again. Bo played monkey-see. From the markings on the copter's tail, they discovered that it belonged to a radio station in Pueblo and was ordinarily used as a scout for morning and evening traffic reports. What it was doing among the risky environs of the Sangre de Cristos, Bo could only guess. He guessed that it was doing what the Beechcraft was doing: flying a reconnaissance mission and giving its suddenly frightened passengers a better-than-average go at spotting a unicorn.

"Thank God they didn't bump," Sam muttered. Bo sensed that Sam was less concerned for the people in the two air machines than for the property and wildlife that so much plummeting debris would have destroyed or traumatized, and he too was happy that the jerks had not collided. Apparently, they had terrified the whiz out of each other, though, for neither the light plane nor the Eye in the Sky helicopter returned (even though the latter had made but one pass), and Bo imagined that over their radios the pilots were bawling each other out for reckless endangerment.

Walking back from the barn, Bo and Sam saw an open-topped Jeep parked on the highway above Libby's drive. Four people sat in the vehicle—or half sat, half stood, for the figures in the back seat, trying hard to peer through the aspens, had raised themselves into crouches to do so—and they all seemed to be young, scarcely old enough to shave. Sam tapped Bo on the shoulder and said, "Come on." They cut through the tiny aspen grove and emerged onto 69 in front of the Jeep before the teenagers aboard it could react to the fact that they had been both seen and stalked. Belatedly aware of their presence, the boy at the wheel did a double-take and fumbled to restart his engine.

"Don't," Sam said. "Don't even try."

Bo tried to distinguish among the four kids, but although they all had their own physical quirks—blond bangs, or acne blossoms, or knit-together eyebrows, or a fleer of smarmy hipness—none came across as either attractive or sensitive, and all were united by an unappealing age-specific gawkiness. Even the heavyset blond kid at the wheel had this gawky quality, as if the plumpness of his upper arms and the inner tube of flesh around his middle might suddenly go elastic and thin out, giving him the stereotypical teenage gauntness of his broomstick buddies.

"What are you doing here?" Sam asked.

"Nothing, really," the driver said. "Talking."

"About what? And why here?"

"About when unicorn season starts," said the smart aleck in the back. "About how much the license costs."

"Shut up, Whisenant," the driver said.

"I've snapped all of your faces," Sam said, making a snapping motion alongside his right eye. "Any time I want to see you again, all I've got to do is close my eyes and flip through the album in my head. So now you'd best beat it."

"You're the guy with the lethal disease, aren't you?" said the kid with the unbroken eyebrow ridge, addressing Bo.

Bo looked more closely. There was a subtle hint of personhood under this kid's wan gawkiness, some authenticity he was struggling to put on. "Fatal disease," Bo corrected him. "Not lethal." But he had to laugh—most people regarded his disease as both.

"We're sorry," said the wan kid with the unbroken eyebrow. "We wanted to tell you that the other night."

"We're on your side," the driver said. Lifting his left hand, he revealed emphatically crossed fingers.

"Be on it someplace else," Sam told them. "There's nothing to see up here today. You've already seen it."

The driver turned the ignition key, gunned the Jeep's engine, and sped the vehicle away from Bo and Sam in reverse ("Fuck you!" shouted the punk in the back seat. "Damn it, Whisenant," the kid with acne cried, "shut up!") Then the Jeep spun about, backfired, and squealed off toward Snowy Falls just ahead of an audible stench of tire rubber.

As soon as this squeal had died, Bo thought he could hear the drone of a light aircraft again, but it was hard to say, and Sam had no interest in pursuing the matter. "I hate the way the world keeps trying to break in," he said as they walked back to Libby's house. "The goddamn 'modern' world." Bo knew he didn't mean technology, he meant instead an attitude, but it was hard to figure what to say to him by way of consolation, and in any case Bo probably wasn't the person to say it.

# 26

I've got a lover and a traveling companion, Libby thought, but they're not the same person.

She was driving Bo's, or Sam's, or whoever-the-hell's Mazda—the car seemed to be community property—and she and Bo were headed for the Southern Ute reservation for the annual Sun Dance, which, said Sam, would have its opening ceremony this evening.

First, though, they had to stop west of Huerfano at Brinkley's Sangre de Cristo Veterinary Clinic to get word—straight from the kar'tajans mouth—as to how poor Phylly was doing and if there was any hope for her equally ill conspecifics. This, just now, was a matter of some urgency. Ray Hilliard and the buttinskys from that Pueblo TV station had seen nothing out of the ordinary on their flyovers, but that same afternoon Bo and Sam had chanced upon nine animals in the woods below Naismith's Cabin, all nine of them lying as if exhausted among the pine needles and snow buttercups.

Every kar'tajan had a fever, a bloody nasal discharge, swollen joints, sores on its nostrils or throatlatch, and protruding ribs. They looked so much like death that at first the two men supposed them dead, and in one case—that of a long yearling—they had been right. The others were dying. Already sick and susceptible, they had gone even further downhill, Sam believed, as a direct result of their stampede. Racing down and back up Highway 69 had aggravated their sickness, and it seemed likely that many other kar'tajans on the ranch were similarly done in. In fact, Sam suspected that some of the others were crossing back through spirit doors to their home reality—which would account for the trouble that he and Libby had had in locating the creatures of late.

Lib felt like a traitor leaving Sam to cope with the situation alone (while she and Bo ran their nifty errand to Ignacio), but Sam told her not to fret and that he now believed it essential that she fetch his daughter back. He had stuff to tell her, love to offer. And vice versa, he hoped. Meanwhile, time was running out, and all the Sun Dancers in this year's dance must try to rechannel its flow along the course that the Holy He-She mandated.

This sort of talk, welling up from mystic depths unfamiliar to her, disturbed Libby. Could it actually mean something?

Bo rode shotgun wearing the Hawaiian shirt that she had bought him in Atlanta. He looked as well as she had ever seen him look—post-AIDS, at least—and although they did not have Dr. Nesheim's official blessing for this trip, Libby could not imagine the doctor putting a leash on Bo when he was radiating so much hope and enthusiasm. He'd been talking virtually nonstop since leaving the ranch—half an hour, so far—first about earning Keith Joy's forgiveness and then about forgiving his own mother as a step toward that first goal.

To Lib's surprise, this wasn't a gloomy recital, and she could not help contrasting it with the long silences and the cynical bon mots typifying his behavior on their trip home from Atlanta. Even so, cruising Huerfano's chief strip, staring out the windshield at the dilapidated red-brick façades of its offices and stores, Libby found it easy to shut out most of his talk and to satisfy him that she was listening by occasionally saying "Uh-huh" or "Yeah." Thus encouraged, he would motormouth on, as full of goodwill and resolve as an aluminum-siding salesman, and she would rotate her mind back to either the kar'tajans or Sam.

Actually, it was Sam, and Sam's face, that popped up most

often in the windows of her mind's overactive slot machine—but never in jackpot sequence. How long had they been acquainted? Five years? Six? As the beginning, though, she had been Gary Quarrels's wife, while he had been hired help, only hired help, and an Indian to boot. A renegade Ute with a semimysterious past and a crackerjack way with animals.

Later, after her divorce, Sam had been essential to her running the ranch—she would have failed in two months without him—but she had never ruminated on him in a romantic or a lustful way, probably because some hidden part of herself—a self-destructive and stupid part—had been hoping that Gary would castrate himself bronc-riding and come crawling back, *cojones* in hand, so that she could put both his manhood and their marriage back together.

Ha. It hadn't worked out that way, and she'd gradually come to see that it never would. Meanwhile, she continued to regard Sam, an untiring worker in early middle age, as a two-legged barbed-wire stringer *cum* haying machine *cum* branding-iron manipulator. He was good to talk to—to act, really, as a sounding board for either her worries or her bitchy dreams of revenge—but the idea that he might have his own fears and dreams, or that he might have more business in her bed than some of the self-reputed hard dicks who worked for Arvill Rudd and who promised her Kingdom Come if ever she said them yea, that idea had never come wholly clear. It swam around in her subconscious like a rainbow trout, too slippery to grapple with. Now that she had it out on the bank, though, she was stunned by the promising iridescence of its scales.

They had spent one night together. That was all. Libby had asked Sam to move in with her, to abandon Naismith's Cabin to the pine martens and the gray jays. He had refused. His rationale was that she had one man to take care of already, and another in the house would open her up to the kind of gossip Gary had feared when he realized Bo was sleeping in the bedroom next to hers. The argument that no one gave a damn about such arrangements any more, that the Sexual Revolution had not come and gone entirely for naught, held no water with him. He went back to his cabin the night after their ravenous whoopee-making not as if it had never occurred but more as if it had been either indiscreet or immature, and the only reference he'd made to it since was a muted comment on the long-term sadness of Anglo-Ute marriages (even given the joy of the wedding day itself) because they thinned the ancient blood and channeled it toward oblivion.

You have a child, Libby had wanted to say, and a full-blooded one at that. As for me, my blood is off to oblivion whether I opt for total celibacy again or turn my body into a bounce-back doll for every horny oaf in Remuda County.

But she hadn't said that. And what seemed in retrospect most noteworthey about Sam's remark was not its complaint about thinning blood, or its emphasis on sadness, but the fact that he had segued from unthinking passion in her bed to postcoital contemplation of marriage. In other words, he had respected her in the morning—it was half a joke and half a miracle.

"Elizabeth!" Bo said, bracing against the dashboard. "Pretend you're still among the living, okay?"

She had just about rear-ended an Airstream trailer at the last stoplight in Huerfano. Bo's cry had saved them. For apology, she offered an abashed grin, then eased through the light and continued on out the La Veta Highway toward Brinkley's veterinary clinic. On their left, to the southwest, the twin peaks called Huajatolla, or Breasts of the Earth, showed off the same poetic "purple mountains' majesty" celebrated in song. It was amazing, really, and it would have moved her, Libby thought, if she hadn't had so frigging many other things to worry about.

A mile outside of town, they came upon the clinic. It had been built into and around the remodeled shell of an old truck stop and grocery store that had gone bust during the Ford administration and a particularly severe inflationary spiral. The gas pumps had been taken out, and two rectangular planters made of creosoted railroad ties occupied the islands where the pumps had been.

The flowers in the planters were wildflowers that Brinkley had brought down from the high country—moss campion, alpine forget-me-not, and Indian paintbrush—and Brinkley himself was irrigating some of these transplants with a garden hose. The hose, Bo noted, was exactly the color of unpackaged hot dogs.

After greeting his visitors, Brinkley draped the hose over

the topmost railroad tie and led them around the converted truck stop to his outbuildings—a prefabricated storage shed and a cinderblock hovel that he had ordered built and that he now referred to without irony as his "stable." It had a Chinese-hat roof with a screened opening under the eaves only partly concealed by the overhang. Bo saw that tiny birds—sparrows, chickadees, finches—had homesteaded various blocks around this ledge, using dried grass from the nearby fields as a prime nest component.

Brinkley worked the combinations on two heavy padlocks, cracked the swinging metal doors, and nudged his visitors into the hayey gloom ahead of him. Inside, he clanged the doors to.

"Come on, then," he said in his characteristic booming whisper. "Come on, then, Phylly."

Bo, waiting for his eyes to adjust, heard a skittering on the concrete floor and turned about to see a ghostly shape whirl toward him from the last crib on the stable's right. He also caught the ebony-blue glinting of the creature's alicorn. His first impulse was to charge back through the rusty doors. But Libby and the vet stood fast, and Phylly stopped directly in front of Brinkley with the tip of her forehead spike touching his monogrammed brass belt buckle. He grabbed the alicorn and made as if to break the mare's neck by thrusting the spike from side to side. In fact, he was giving a lot of English to his elbow but moving the creature's head hardly any. A charade of roughness. Some playful tough-guy/tough-gal sport between friends.

"This baby's okay!" Lib said. "What did you do, Dr. Brinkley? You've got Phylly up and running."

The vet took a piece of candy and let the kar'tajan nibble it off his palm. Bo could smell the liquor in this confection even before Brinkley identified it for them as a rum ball, and he was as astonished as Libby to find Phylly eating—especially candy—when a few days ago both her appearance and her behavior had suggested that she would soon be as dead as Pete.

Said Libby, "Tell me, Dr. Brinkley. Give."

He took another rum ball from the pocket of his suede jacket and extended it toward her. She made an unpleasant face and folded her arms. Brinkley shrugged, popped the rum ball himself, and sucked it noisily. Remembering himself, he also offered Bo one, and when Bo likewise declined, he handed it to Phylly. "But two's plenty," he told the animal using her horn to push her out of the way—and Bo was reminded of a man fending off an overeager puppy.

"What did you feed her while she was sick?" Libby asked.

"That same sour shit you forced down Pete," Brinkley said. "I don't know how anyone, human or horse, can tolerate cottage cheese, dehydrated or otherwise, but Phylly here managed." The vet made a smacking noise at her. "Didn't you, girl? Didn't you, now?"

Phylly, who had been given the run of the building, backed off a few paces, shook her head, and went prancing sidelong toward her stall. There was something about the way she carried herself—the mischievousness of her movements—that put Bo as much in mind of a goat kid as of a young horse, and the wispy, almost invisible beard under Phylly's chin heightened this impression. She vanished into her crib but looked out again with a sapphirine eye and then just as quickly ducked from view.

Munching on another rum ball, Brinkley escorted them back to a partitioned-off work area containing a green army-surplus desk, an aluminum examination table for small animals, and several tiers of cardboard filing cabinets dating, Bo imagined, back to World War II days, if not earlier. Bo hoisted himself—nimbly, he thought—onto the examination table, while Libby sat down in an office chair next to the particle-board divider and Brinkley sprawled into the swivel chair behind his desk.

"You couldn've told me on the phone that she was better," Libby said. "That much, at least."

"Listen, Mrs. Quarrels, I don't fucking talk about the care and treatment of *unicorns* over Mountain Mama Bell. A policy of mine from all the way back to my oat-sowing days—when I didn't but half believe . . . in either unicorns or telephones."

Libby brought her irritation to heel. First things first, Bo imagined her telling herself. "Phylly *looks* like she's well," she said. "What's your long-range prognosis?"

Brinkley popped another rum ball, grabbed the edge of his desk, pulled himself into its chair well. "Outstanding," he said. "Her prognosis is outstanding."

"She's got infectious anemia," Libby reminded him. "It never goes away. She'll have it the rest of her life."

"Ma'am, it's true that in recovered horses—visibly recovered horses, I mean—this goddamn disease goes subclinical on us and the viremia that's diagnostic for it continues to exist and will always and ever be there. On the other ha—"

"Viremia?" Bo said.

"Bugs in the blood, Mr. Gavin. Bugs in the blood. Any horse that's 'recovered' from EIA—equine infectious anemia—still has the virus circulating. You've got to shut the horse up during fly season, 'cause flies are the primary vector; and you can't breed the horse again, unless you're a crazy son of a bitch who gets a charge out of spreading the fucking disease via virus-laden spit and gism rather than a swarm of bloodsucking horseflies."

"Fucking disease?" Bo echoed the vet.

Brinkley rocked back and looked at Bo with unabashed—but not, Bo told himself, unkindly—amusement. "My late wife never approved of colorful language, Mr. Gavin, but the only truly serious reason I can see for going pussy and cleaning up my act is maybe that one right there—nonfunctional ambiguity."

Impatiently, Libby said, "A minute ago, you started to say, 'On the other hand.' On the other hand, what?"

The vet took all the remaining rum balls from the pockets of his suede coat and arranged them on his desk blotter—seven in all, each one about three quarters on the size of a golf ball and all of them lightly dusted with powdered sugar. Brinkley rolled the rum balls around under his palm for a few seconds, then popped two at once, licked his fingers, and leaned back.

"On the other hand, I ran another Coggins test on Phylly a day or two ago, and the fucking thing showed her—the way I read it, at least—virus-free. She's come out of her viremia not as if she'd had EIA, but as if she's had EVA, equine viral arteritis. Another bunch of bugs entirely."

"What sort of bugs?" Libby asked.

Brinkley explained that equine viral arteritis was a disease— more common than often supposed, since an animal could be infected without showing any outward signs—that in clinical cases, bad ones especially, presented such symptoms as fever, discharges from the nostrils, breathing difficulties, general weakness, weight loss, depression, and so on.

"Sounds like EIA," Libby said.

The big vet begged to differ. The symptoms might be similar in some respects—although only in some—but most cases of arteritis had a happier ending than did most cases of infectious anemia. For one thing, the clinical illness itself was usually mild. (Only one type of the EVA virus led inevitably to death.) For another, once recovered from it, the lucky survivor had earned lifelong immunity and could go on to interact safely with its stable or pasture mates in all the immemorial down-and-dirty horsy ways. Even though he'd first fingered Phylly as an infectious-anemia victim, Brinkley now had a strong hunch that she could return to her conspecifics on the Tipsy Q without reacquiring the virus or infecting any animal that had so far escaped infection.

"What about Pete?" Libby asked. "What was wrong with all the other animals—unicorns—that didn't pull through? And what about the ones that're sick right now?"

"Fuck if I know," Brinkley said. "They were further down the road than Phylly was. They weren't as tough or as immunocompetent, and getting over here from wherever the hell they were before took all the piss and vinegar out of them."

"Which is why they came," Bo said. "To find a place where they could beat the disease that was bumping them off in their home reality."

"But over the past three years," Lib protested, "they only stay until late June or July and then vanish again. Sam suspects they may be migrating out now—it's time. But why return to a reality where there's only death?"

"There's no place like home," Brinkley said, poker-faced. He picked up another rum ball, flipped it into the air, caught it in the slack pouch of his mouth. "Actually," he said, "that *is* their goddamn home territory. Why *not* go back to it? You don't see many fucking kangaroos in the goddamn Pyrenees, do you?"

Continued Brinkley, "There's probably a vector for the kind of anemia they contract that's really bad—in season, I mean—during the months they toddle over our way. But this vector—an insect, a nematode, maybe a plant spore—is probably in a dormant phase of its cycle when Phylly's kind gets this itchy blood sense that it's all right to go back.

"Which is why they take off, even though for all their instinct they're still just dumb brutes. So they *fail* to sense the disease agent will pop up again, just like the bloody fifteenth of April, at which time there'll be taxes to pay and the only way for them to ante up is to do the goddamn mortal-coil shuffle."

"Can't figure out what the vector is?" Libby asked.

"How? Shit, Ms. Quarrels, from what you good souls've told me about your sockdollager late-night Bendix broadcasts, even the smart people who live in your lousy beyonder dimension haven't been able to do that. How am *I* supposed to do it?"

"Can't you examine Phylly? Take microscope slides? Something like that?"

From his vantage on the examination table, Bo could look over the L-shaped partition dividing the main floor of the "stable" from Brinkley's walled-off office. Now he saw Phylly emerge from her stall and come tiptoeing over the concrete toward them. When she wished to make no noise, it seemed she made none; both Libby and the vet were surprised when she poked her head into his office and strode straight up to Brinkley's desk.

"I could've done an autopsy," the vet said, quickly adjusting to Phylly's arrival, "if she'd been thoughtful enough to die. but, as you can see, the pretty biddy didn't die."

"Thank God."

"On the other hand, maybe it wouldn't have done that damn much good, anyway. I can pluck hairs from her tail and count them, or pull blood samples and do an immunodiffusion test—but Phylly won't X-ray and she shows up in a mirror the same fucking way vampires're supposed to. Not at all. So just what the"—he lent a highfalutin spin to the word— "*kar'tájan* infectious-anemia vector is remains a mystery to me, and I'm a big enough son of a bitch *not* to feel like a complete failure just because it does."

Phylly lowered her muzzle, extended her neck, tilted her head to one side, and, with her alicorn, began pushing around the four rum balls still on Brinkley's desk.

"Stop that," he warned her.

The mare ignored him. She was never going to be able to

spike one of those candies. Even if she did, Bo could not see how she planned to get it off her horn and into her mouth. For the moment, though, she was content to imprint Brinkley's lavender ink blotter with trails of confectionary sugar. Eventually, she pushed one rum ball over the edge of the desk into the vet's lap. He grabbed at his crotch to retrieve it, but instead squooshed the candy against the inner thigh of his khakis. His arms went up.

"You pestiferous prickhead!" he boomed. "Beat it!" The noise of this cry, and its basso-profundo echo, succeeded in frightening the kar'tajan—she backed out of Brinkley's makeshift office at wicked speed—as well as some of the sparrows and finches nesting on the tops of the building's walls. These birds hurtled up and careened away. In fact, Bo himself started.

Libby, who was wearing her floppy leather hat, pulled its brim down on both sides so that it was covering her ears—but too late to muffle Brinkley's last megaphone blast. Although the vet didn't shout again, Libby was slow to release her hat brim, and when she did, she did it slowly, regarding Brinkley as if he were about to try to deafen her for life.

"Instinct pushes them over here," he said, speaking in a normal voice, "and instinct calls them back when they get this blood sense that the vector's dormant. But the impulse that drives them over here's a pretty fucking reliable one and the other's just flat-out fucking bad news. I'm talking survival here, of course, and I'd say it looks pretty good for them if we can keep them from heeding that bad-news instinct every summer."

"Even the ones who are sick as Pete was?"

"Probably not, Mrs. Quarrels. Only some of them. We just have to save the treatable ones—let them earn their lifelong immunity—then keep them from blowing our whole goddamn mercy effort by going back to their cattywampus otherworldly Death Valley."

"How do we stop them?" Bo asked. "And how do we treat the ones that are sick and haven't crossed back over? Usually, it's hard to find them. The nine that Sam and I ran up on the other day—that was something of a fluke. And if we *do* find all the unicorns that are sick—there could be as many as fifty—well, how do we care for them? Lib had all she could handle looking after Pete. Trying to feed fifty with a dose syringe would be a herculean task. Maybe an impossible one."

"It's pretty fucking stupid to tackle an impossible task, isn't it? So don't do it. Just do what you can."

"But what do *you* think's possible, Dr. Brinkley?" Libby asked.

He was silent a moment. Then he admitted that he thought they would do well to save four or five of the animals. To answer Bo's question, he had no idea how they could stop the beasts from going back to their native reality. Maybe everyone on the Tipsy Q should give a little thought to that problem.

Urgent now, however, was locating, stabling, and force-feeding, either via nasogastric tubes or surgically implanted esophagostomy tubes, as many of the animals—"kar'tajans," Brinkley enunciated, finally saying it without mockery—as possible. He would help. If they saved four of the animals, two of each sex, that might be just enough to preserve the species, over here if not in their fucked-up beyonder reality, and maybe, a few years on, advanced cloning and farsighted husbandry programs would provide a means to establish the weird buggers over here permanently. Kar'tajan would replace kangaroo in all the fucking alphabet books written in these United States, and unicorns would be real at last: "Great Gawd Amighty," Brinkley intoned, "real at last."

"Then we've got to go back up to the Tipsy Q and help Sam," Libby said. "It's too much for him to tackle alone."

"No," Bo said. "We have to go get Sam's daughter."

"Go after the girl," Brinkley said. "I'll drive up to Snowy Falls to help Sam. We'll throw you folks back into the effort as soon as you're home."

"But what if your kar'tajans are slipping away through spirit doors right now, Dr. Brinkley?"

"You'd be too late to catch them, wouldn't you? Let me do the worrying, okay? I'll take Phylly with me. If she'll do a little stalking-horse work for us, we'll make out like bandits."

Libby was only reluctantly persuaded to go on to the Southern Ute Reservation, and Bo, who knew that to miss the Sun Dance would be to woo a small disaster, inwardly thanked Brinkley for calming Libby, even with a bedside manner more profane than grandfatherly. Bo would have kissed the vet if assured that the old guy would not have rapped him in the teeth.

(And if . . . well, just "and if.")

"Something else," the vet said as he saw his guests through the stable's swinging metal doors, and as the kenneled dogs in the main clinic began to bay like bloodhounds.

"What?" Libby said.

"I'm not that all-fired busy nowadays. In my spare time, I'm going to try to isolate that suckbutt arteritis-anemia vector—even if it is from some other cattywumpus dimension."

"Good," Libby said. "Good."

But as their Mazda pulled out of the clinic's parking lot onto the highway, Bo noticed that Brinkley had picked up his hose and resumed watering the flowers in the tar-gummed planters. The vet recognized the urgency of the kar'tajans' situation, of course, but even during a crisis, you had to water your flowers.

# 27

Paisley rocked cross-legged on the floor of her mother's house, trying to empty her mind of all but Sun Dance thoughts. She would enter the Thirst House this evening and not come out again until Monday afternoon. When she did, she would be brand-new, a vessel of power transformed by the Holy He-She, particularly if she were found worthy of vision, a gift seldom offered first-timers and not to be regarded by them as their due.

Still, she would emerge from the corral like an infant from the womb, and maybe it would be good to lay aside the name Paisley and take up the one that her Mama D'lo had preferred. After all, Mama D'lo's spirit was still restless, and if Payz accomplished nothing else during the next three days, maybe she could buy peace for her mother's ghost.

During Paisley's sojourn in Ignacio with the Skys, vandals had broken out the windowpanes in Mama D'lo's house. They had stolen Buffalo, the bison head that had hung on the wall near the recliner in which Mama D'lo had shot herself. Missing, too, was the effigy of the Walking Man, Jesus Crucified, that had once made sacred the dwelling's threshold, simply by its nearness to the door. The door itself had been hacked down by thieves with axes, and the emptiness of the house—emptier than it had ever been, even emptier than the ritual giveaways of Coldpony and Arriola property over the years had made it—keened in Paisley's ears like the mountain wind and the ratchety leg music of locusts.

She was alone today because ever since Papa Sky's return from Snowy Falls (an adventure about which he had told her only that he had seen real live kar'tajans and that her father had been riding an elk among them), the men dream-called to this year's dance had been purifying themselves in the sweat lodge behind his tepee. They had voted on whether to let her take part in the ritual with them, and the vote had gone against her.

So what? The men stripped down to breechclouts, Jockey shorts, or maybe just their sheet-wrapped butts, and some of the older ones had so much greasy flab that the chance to gaze upon it was hardly a privilege. Also, for modesty's sake, she would have had to cover herself, maybe in buckskins, and the temperatures generated by the steam boiling off the hot stones and the weight of her own sweat-soaked garments would have made her ordeal greatly more severe than that for any but the most blubber-bound of the men.

So she had come home to purify herself. For the week prior to her three-day total fast, she had eaten nothing but saltines and fried bread. Her friend Larry Cuthair—who, to his family's happy astonishment, had been called to Sun Dance by a series of dreams in May—had helped her stick to this diet not only by eating with her but by bringing her other permitted foods: beef-jerky sticks from a local saloon and crunchy peanut butter for the crackers.

After all, Larry said, the idea wasn't to make yourself too weak to dance, but to become worthy of the honor by purging the mind and body of evil poisons. Protein wasn't a poison, it was an essential, and the jerky and peanut butter would give them the necessary energy and stamina for the twelve dance sets required to attain that empty purity of mind—the openness to *powa'a*—leading to vision.

Well, this afternoon, Larry steamed in the sweat lodge with the men. She had asked him not to separate himself from them solely to show a narrow solidarity with her, when the important thing now was tribal solidarity. Reluctantly, then, he had joined the chauvinist assholes. Good. He didn't need their contempt.

Paisley had no hunger in her at all any more and only a residue of bitterness against the pigs who had voted against her. Ute men were often as bigoted and petty as Anglos, but their failings upset her more because they so often boasted that they were superior to whites in spiritual matters. But never mind. Once the Sun Dance began, the people *would* be united. All the crass hypocrisies and jealous infighting of their desperate lives would vanish under the prayerful tread of the dream-called.

Paisley's head was floating. Could it be that the hunger she denied, and the bitterness she was trying to repudiate, had already weakened her so much that she would fail in the dance?

It seemed possible, for her body was floating too—her body as well as her head. She was levitating above the filthy floor of her mother's oft-vandalized house.

No, she thought. My lightheadedness is playing tricks. But for a moment, trick or no trick, she was the victim of this strange floating sensation. She had no ground in the age-old basics. Her awareness of this lack terrified her. Even the sunlight streaming though the broken kitchen window intensified her sense of dreamy floating. She reached toward the sun just to see if her hand would make an eddy in the coppery motes.

At which moment Mama D'lo materialized among those motes. She hovered in the kitchen's ruins. Mama D'lo was still headless, but her dowdy burial clothes—no one at the funeral had seen them—had turned to doeskins, beaded leggings, moccasins.

Mama D'lo windmilled through the chilly house toward Paisley, stopping perhaps six feet away, a restless *ini'putc'* whose motives were unguessable, and the daughter wondered for the thousandth time if she had driven her mother to suicide or if any of her subsequent behavior had been displeasing to the dead woman.

No, she thought. Unh-uh. On the night that Blake Seals jailed me, Whirling Goat said that Mama D'lo wanted me to dance with the men. And it was my mother's spirit that sent the seven dreams that called me to the dance, that gave me the power to walk blindfolded across the god sheet as proof of my worthiness.

Mama D'lo's ghost seemed to grow denser the longer she hovered in place. Soon, the afternoon sunlight had ceased to shine through her, and she was standing on the floor like any other living human being without a head. Mama D'lo had substance.

Now Paisley sat in a band of shadow so wide and black that she shivered. Shivering, she reached for the object at her throat—one of the last items of personal property other than clothes remaining to her—to reassure herself of her own solidity. This object was the pewter kar'tajan that her father had given LannaSue to pass on to her as a graduation gift. Paisley had paid to have a tiny metal ring soldered to the figurine's withers so that she could wear it on a chain. She held the kar'tajan up so that Mama D'lo could see it. Or rather so that her mother, who no longer had eyes, could drink in something of its aura.

"Daddy came to see me get my diploma," Paisley told her.

The *ini'putc'* stepped closer.

"Earlier this week," Paisley continued, "he asked Papa Sky to ask me to visit him in Snowy Falls. There are kar'tajans where he's working, Mama. Living ones. I need to go see them. Mostly, though, I have to go see my father."

The *ini'putc'* leaned forward, grasped her daughter's necklace, and yanked down on it. The chain snapped. The pendant broke free and spun across the floor into the rubble near the door.

Paisley aggrievedly began to rub her neck. Her mother's sudden ability to act upon material objects reminded her of the glorified Christ's like ability in post-crucifixion appearances. Of course, her modus operandi didn't really gibe with the risen Savior's. It scared Paisley, and it pissed her off. She knew that Mama D'lo's anger was meant for Daddy, not for her, but it was still a pretty sorry stunt. She was bemused and disappointed that the dead could transport all the negative emotional energy of their lives into the spirit realms. If the dead weren't *better* than the living, well, they were nothing at all.

Mama D'lo read Payz's mind and spoke to her in hand language: *I'll get better when your father gets better. Dance him to his duty, Alma, and you'll dance me to everlasting sleep.*

"He's already doing better," Paisley said.

*That's because, even before I killed myself, I afflicted his no-account ass with memories. Sam Coldpony, the haunted, is a much better man than Sam Coldpony, the devil-may-care. It's the way men are, Alma. It's the way they are alive, and it's even the way they are dead.*

"Daddy's changed," Paisley said. "The kar'tajans prove it. He would've never seen them if he hadn't changed."

A figure materialized in the front door of the Arriola house, a compact male figure wearing a Pendleton shirt in a night-watch plaid and a Navajo hat with linked turquoise stones for a band. As soon as he appeared, Mama D'lo's revenant vanished. Stupidly uncertain, the man in the doorway said, "Alma?"

"My name's Paisley, goddamn it! What do you want?"

The man stepped inside. He stooped and picked up the kar'tajan pendant. When he straightened again, she saw it was Whirling Goat, old Herbert Barnes, the sot with whom she'd once spent some bizarre but quality jail time. He looked spiffy today—barely even recognizable as Ignaico's most devout drunk.

"What the hell do you want?"

"I'm the gatekeeper," Barnes said proudly. "Sky appointed me a week ago. I've come to take you to the Thirst House. It's time, Alma—time for the dancers to gather."

Paisley was stunned. She had been sitting in the middle of her mother's house for nearly ten hours. It was evening. The air was cold. The sunlight had ruddied and thinned. Barnes was visible to her because angelic radiance poured from his face. He lighted his own way inward and handed her the kar'tajan pendant.

Then, outside, Barnes led her through scrub brush and Joshua trees toward the dance ground. It was a ten-minute walk from Mama D'lo's, much closer than Ignacio. On the dirt road leading to it—a big open field with heat-singed grass—a line of autos, pickups, and camping vehicles was creeping forward, and an amber veil of dust hung in the evening air.

Whirling Goat, a dozen paces ahead of her, marched toward that veil. His purposefulness was funny. Also funny, although not in a way to prompt laughter, was the sight of a piece of string hanging down from one of the pockets of his plaid shirt jacket. About six inches hung down. Paisley tightened her grip on the kar'tajan and stepped gingerly after the old fart.

One of the cars on the dusty road belonged to Bo Gavin. Libby Quarrels sat at its wheel, inching it along behind the hundreds of other people, mostly Indians, who had come for the Southern Ute Sun Dance. She saw license tags from Wyoming and Utah—as well as from Colorado, Arizona, and New Mexico—and Bo told her that this meant that Shoshones from Wind River, Wyoming, and Utes from Fort Hall, Utah, were among those gathering.

In some ways, the press of people and vehicles struck Libby as daunting, especially here in the wilderness, but then she recalled that even Huerfano's high-school football team drew larger crowds, and she understood that the Utes—Muaches, Weminuches, Capotes, Uncompahgres, and all the rest—were a people numerically on the wane. Because the Sun Dance was an attempt to bring themselves back up to strength, by spiritual rather than sexual efforts, the ugly looks thrown their way by some of the hostile Indians in other vehicles derived from their shared conviction—hard for Libby and Bo to dispute—that Anglos had no business here.

What, after all, did Anglos hope to achieve at this ceremony? They had no right to dance themselves, for there was nowhere for them to use the power they acquired if the One Above granted them power, and their presence as spectators registered with many of the Indians as a kind of voyeurism—as if they had stumbled into the wedding tepee of a Ute couple and then invited themselves to kibitz the nuptial screw. Of course, you could pretend to be a cultural anthropologist or a reporter, but Anglos of those persuasions were maybe even more despised than the voyeurs in Bermuda shorts, Argyle socks, and penny loafers. Nearing the dance ground, Libby began to feel more and more uncomfortable.

"Why did you have to wear that shirt?" she asked Bo.

"I thought you liked it. You bought it."

"I do. It's just that it's sort of touristy-looking."

"My God, the lady's embarrassed."

"It's not that. It may resemble a desert out here, but we're six thousand feet up. You're going to get cold."

"I'm not wearing denim, and you're embarrassed."

"No, I'm not."

"Yes, you are. We're surrounded by angry redskins, and the guy riding shotgun for you looks like he's binged-and-purged after a holiday luau."

"I'm *not* embarrassed."

"You lie, m'lady."

"All right, damn it, I'm embarrassed. You look touristy. You look . . . square."

"The old-hat goddess of sixties hipness has spoken. Hey, I'll grab a sweater or something if I get cold."

Bo's "old-hat" remark stung. "I look more Indian than you do."

"So what? I look more dead than anything else."

"Stop it."

"On the other hand, if the only good Injun's a dead Injun, I'm a gooder Injun than you, m'lady. Looks-wise."

"Would you shut up, please?"

A wooden sign on a stake said SUN DANCE GROUNDS, and the arrow pointed off the dirt road to the left. Libby wrestled the car into the turn, and a young Muache wearing a navy-blue T-shirt under a fringed blue suede jacket put up his hand to halt her. Around the upper sleeve of the jacket was an armband identifying him as one of the Southern Ute tribal policemen—although Libby had the idea that he had assumed the role just for the duration of the Sun Dance and its inevitable short-lived influx of visitors.

Beyond him, Libby could see the apex of a leather tepee and a few of the cottonwood shade houses erected around the perimeter of the grounds by visiting Indians and the relatives and friends of the dancers. There were pickups with built-in campers, recreation vehicles, and big vans with drop-down windows from which vendors were selling food items. To the east, away from Ignacio, the San Juan Mountains seemed to absorb and then to shift subtly under the salmon-shot rays of the sunset.

"What's your business?" the brave in the suede jacket asked, leaning toward Libby but keeping his hands behind him.

"We came to see the Sun Dance. Isn't that allowed?"

"It's a free country," he replied, smiling. "Did you bring any weapons, cameras, or alcoholic beverages?"

"No. No, we didnt'." Sam had told them not to.

"Mind if I check? You folks don't have to let me, but I'd feel better about you if you did."

"Let him," Bo whispered. "We need to get through."

"Do you check Indians too?" Libby asked.

"Only if I don't know them."

Discrimination, Libby thought. Despite his comment about its being a free country, the reservation was a de facto foreign land, with an agenda and regulations all its own. "You don't exactly welcome whites with open arms, do you?"

"Ma'am, we're happy you're here. It's the Weminuche—the Ute Mountain Utes—who don't like Anglos at their dances."

Bo, whispering, again urged Libby to obey the guard.

"What if I refuse to let you look?" she said.

Hands behind his back, the Ute shrugged. "I'd wonder what it is you're so uptight about, lady. That's all."

"Damn it, Libby," Bo insisted. "We've got nothing to hide."

Libby clambered angrily out, forcing the Ute to step hurriedly back. Bo go out on his side. The three people met at the trunk, and Libby keyed it open while another tribal policeman waved the next vehicle in line around them.

"I'm Kyle Smalltree," the Ute said. "Thanks for cooperating."

Only a single suitcase occupied the trunk. Libby had thrown it on Bo's bed last night and asked him to fill it with enough clothes to see them through the next three days, keeping in mind that they would probably be sleeping in the car or on the ground, if they got to sleep at all, and pulling stuff straight from the bag.

Kyle Smalltree unzipped the soft-shelled case and felt

about among the clothes inside it. He did so discreetly, trying, Libby thought, not to look at the garments themselves but to detect by unassisted feel the presence of, say, a flask or a handgun.

"What's this?" Smalltree's hands came out of the suitcase with the heavy but delicately spiraled spike of an alicorn. The horn was better than two feet long and as black as midnight, and Libby understood that it had belonged to the stallion she had called Pete. Both confused and outraged, she glared at Bo.

"Sam told me to bring it," Bo said.

"Is this some sort of weird dagger or spear?" Smalltree turned the alicorn as if working it on a lathe.

"Why did he do that?" Libby demanded of Bo. "What for?"

"As a gift for DeWayne Sky."

"After the bastard led a lynch mob on the Tipsy Q—a lynch mob that was out after *your* neck?"

"Sam thinks we got that all wrong. He thinks it was a joyous crowd coming our way, not a rabid and hateful one."

"Why didn't you tell me you'd packed that? It hurts like hell to see it here, Bo." It did, too. Her gut ached.

Said Smalltree, "You've given me a problem. A dagger and some harsh words about Chief Sky."

Bo turned to him. "Hey, that's a gift for Sky. Libby's 'harsh words' don't mean diddly-squat."

"But what is it?"

"It's the horn of a magnificent animal called a kar'tajan."

"You mean a unicorn? That animal they're trying to sell . . . well, condoms with?" Kyle Smalltree, congenital redman, contrived to blush. Libby began to like him a little more.

"Exactly," Bo said. "It's a unicorn's horn."

Smalltree's face stayed red, but now Libby believed that he was embarrassed on behalf of the Anglo in the Hawaiian shirt who wanted him to accept this beautiful but murderous human artifact as the appendage of a creature that did not exist now and more than likely never had. "You folks," he said, "will have to pull your car over and come with me."

Libby saw that Bo was shivering. "Better get that sweater."

Numbly obedient, he rummaged in the suitcase. As he did, he argued with Smalltree, informing him that the object really was a kar'tajan horn, that a Ute named Sam Coldpony—the father of one of the dancers—had sent it as a gift to the Sun Dance chief, and that Coldpony wanted Chief Sky to mount the alicorn on the center pole along with the bison head, the hide stuffed with sweet grass, and the colored scarves intended as gifts for the people's ancestors. In fact, argued Bo, pulling a beige jersey from the suitcase, this summer's Sun Dance would be a real flop if they *failed* to tie the alicorn to their sacred cottonwood. The Holy He-She would refuse to give the dancers sufficient power for their own or the people's needs. Sam Coldpony, Paisley's father, had told him so.

This story tickled Smalltree. In turning the alicorn, however, he had sliced his palm on one of its helical ridges. Blood oozed from the cut even as he chuckled.

"Maybe we should strap an AK-forty-seven to the Tree of Life," he said, taking out a handkerchief to wrap both his hand and the horn.

His equanimity amazed Libby. He had made a semisarcastic joke, sure, but he hadn't cursed them, and now he was calmly gesturing Bo and her toward the dance ground with the alicorn again.

Then Libby saw that the jersey in Bo's hands was the same lousy Coca-Cola shirt about which they had argued in Atlanta. "I thought you gave that to Sam," she said accusingly.

"Guess he gave it back. That pose a problem?"

Before Libby could offer any objection, Smalltree nodded at the jersey. "You can walk the grounds in that, but don't wear it into the sacred corral."

"What's wrong with it?" Bo asked. "Too commercial for a Sun Dance shindig?"

"It's just inappropriate attire for the Thirst House."

"M'lady," Bo said, "these people have a dress code."

"No dress code. You figure it out, man—'inappropriate attire for the Thirst House.' It's simple."

Smalltree, for the first time, appeared to be nearing the edge of his patience, and Libby was embarrassed for Bo, not because his Hawaiian shirt was too touristy-looking but because his fatigue and his chip-on-the-shoulder feistiness had him acting like a real turkey. She feared that Smalltree would confiscate the alicorn and have them booted off the reservation.

"Okay, okay," Bo said. He stuffed the Coca-Cola jersey

back into the suitcase, withdrew a navy-blue cardigan, re-zipped the bag, and slammed down the Mazda's trunk lid.

Smalltree, his handkerchief-bandaged hand around the alicorn, shepherded them across the field toward the Sun Dance corral. Libby wondered if the way she felt now was similar to the way that white settlers kidnapped during the nineteenth century had felt when prodded into a ring of tepees far from their own set-ablaze ranches or ransacked sod houses.

DeWayne Sky was overseeing last-minute adjustments to the lodge in the center of the grounds. All those dream-called to dance this year, Paisley included, had entered the corral. Each dancer waited on the inner circumference of the lodge in the spot where, tomorrow morning, their seconds would help them prepare the stalls to which they would retire between dance sets. The older dancers had chosen paths to God's Spine beginning on the north side, where, during the day, exposure to the sun was nearly constant. The newer dancers—Paisley, Larry Cuthair, and two or three others—had the remaining, sometimes shaded pathways and therefore prayed to the Great Manitou for full sun and vision-spawning heat.

Whirling Goat, this year's gatekeeper, entered the lodge and beckoned to DeWayne. The old man had not been a popular choice for this prestigious position. Even LannaSue had jumped on DeWayne for selecting him, and DeWayne had been too embarrassed to admit to her that he had named Barnes gatekeeper to keep Barnes from making as ass of himself as a spectator.

DeWayne still remembered what Payz had told him about her dream-calling, and he was determined not to let the old billy disrupt the Sun Dance, or upset his only female dancer, by leveling the charge that she was unclean. Paisley had already told Lanna Sue that she was not in her cycle; therefore, no one could legitimately deny her entrance by arguing that she was. DeWayne's strategy in regard to Barnes, then, boiled down to this: "If you can't squelch the crazy coot, coopt him."

Now DeWayne's heart misgave him. As gatekeeper, Whirling Goat was supposed to begin the Sun Dance by offering the first prayer to the sacred cottonwood. But Barnes had not entered to do that. He was standing in the gateway, grimacing and clawing urgent get-over-here gestures at Sky. This was not only nonliturgical behavior, it was the kind of nose-thumbing shit you would expect from a pimply-faced kid. But DeWayne swallowed his put-upon pride and walked over to the old man.

Outside the lodge, he found that Barnes was standing with Kyle Smalltree and a pair of Anglos—one male, one female—whom he had never seen before. Somehow, though, the nervous whites managed to seem familiar to him. Uncannily familiar. They were the Anglos from Paisley's Sun Dance dreams. Their lives were interthreaded with that of the girl's father, Sam Coldpony. The woman was Sam's boss, and the skinny, washed-out-looking man was the AIDS patient she had brought to live with her.

DeWayne looked at the man—Beaumont Gavin, Smalltree had called him—realizing that, only a few nights back, some revelers in Snowy Falls had set out to do Gavin a good turn, first by recruiting Sky to lead them and then by parading a portion of their Pioneer Days celebration up the road toward Libby Quarrel's ranch. A farcical misreading of the intentions behind this parade had led Coldpony to break it up in a way that DeWayne was still unable to forget. He had witnessed a kar'tajan stampede.

Now, here stood Smalltree balancing in his hands, almost as if it were a rifle, the lethal-looking spike of one of those animals: proof, DeWayne saw, that the stampede had actually occurred and that Paisley's presence in this year's Sun Dance was god-ordained and portentous. An exhilarating curve of wind from the San Juans filled his chest.

"They say this is a—" Smalltree began.

"They speak the truth, Kyle."

"They say they want you to tie it to the Tree of Life."

"That's exactly what he must do," Barnes butted in. DeWayne was glad to have him as an ally, not a boozy antagonist.

Smalltree gave up the alicorn, incidentally tearing his bloody hankerchief on one of its fluted ridges. DeWayne patted him on the shoulder and told him to go back out to the road.

"What else do you two want?" he asked the Anglos.

To watch the dance, they said, as much of it as Chief Sky would allow them. And to act as seconds to Paisley Coldpony, for they had a message for her from her father and believed it important for her to receive it.

"Let these people into the spectator section any time they come to your gate," DeWayne told Whirling Goat. "Understand?"

"Sure," Barnes croaked. "What the hell. You think I'm a dummy or something?"

## 28

In the Sun Dance lodge, she found that she was one of sixteen ghostly dancers and the only female.

This was the final day of the three-day ordeal, and although no one had fallen to fatigue, sunstroke, or heat cramps, no one had achieved vision, either. All the dancers—just as in her dreams—resembled ghosts. Their skirts, waistbands, moccasins, and willow wands were powdered white, as white as bone. Although the sky was bright blue and full of pinwheeling haloes, a milky haze hung over the Thirst House, the dance grounds, the arid reservation— in fact, the whole world—and Payz could feel herself bobbing as if afloat in the primeval whiteness before Creation. She and the One Above were on the verge of breakthrough, she felt, but the kaleidoscopic events of these past few days had pooled in her joints like poison, and it was hard to keep going.

On her first evening in the corral, Paisley had been surprised to find the two Anglos from her dream-callings watching from the spectator area: the hippie woman pushing forty and the blond young dude with AIDS. And these visitors weren't junk quirks of a hyperactive imagination, either.

As she stood listening to Whirling Goat's inaugural prayer and then intently regarding Papa Sky's invocation of the gods and his performance of the pipe ritual to the four cardinal compass points, she realized that these two people were stand-ins for her father—who, she was certain, would have been present if not taking care of compelling business of his own.

Then the sacred fire was breathed to life in the fire pit, and Barnes told everyone that although nondancers must leave now, they could return at dawn for the sunrise ceremony that would introduce the actual dancing.

Papa Sky came to Paisley to say that she had Anglo well-wishers in the crowd. They had offered to help LannaSue furnish her rest stall with bundles of cooling willow branches and poplar leaves and to act throughout as her attendants. Paisley accepted their offer because the Cuthairs were the only people, other than LannaSue, who had proposed to help her, and the Cuthairs would have plenty to do looking after Larry, just as LannaSue would have her hands full helping her husband.

The first day's dancing dragged. But the two Anglos lined her stall with greenery and tied colored scarves to its frame. During rest periods, they told her about her father, themselves, even the kar'tajans on the woman's ranch. They seemed genuinely to wish her well, but what they had to say was so interesting—so distracting—that each time the chanting began again, she was unable to drive herself as deeply into "dance trance" as she wanted, and time, like the sun, hung fire.

The second day was better. Her body slipped naturally into the rhythms of the chants. Time rushed past in a flood. The dancers had daubed their bodies white and chalked their faces, and contact with the spirit realm seemed, at least to Paisley, imminent.

Late that same afternoon, Papa Sky came out of his rest stall to exhort the singers to sing more enthusiastically. He chastised the dancers who'd been hotdogging it—jogging in place like a bunch of yuppies in an aerobics class and thinking less about obtaining a vision than about buying a cold beer back in Ignacio.

Were they Indians or white eyes? Did they want to obtain power or surrender to weakness? Whatever they most wanted, Papa Sky told them, just that would they receive.

Suddenly, ritually pepped up, all the people in the corral—chanters, drummers, dancers, even spectators—were afire with both energy and the exhilarating zeal of would-be martyrs. Paisley danced into the sweat-drying cool of the sunset without noticing that night had begun to draw down.

In fact, on that second evening, she approached the center pole to see the silver fingernail of the quarter moon caught in the fork of the Tree of Life between Buffalo's horns. It was balancing on the point of the kar'tajan spike that Papa Sky had strapped to the holy cottonwood with a belt that had belonged to the late Sun Dance chief, Alvin Powers. Piñon fires rioted on the edges of the dance ground—Paisley could taste their bittersweet smoke— and spectators hugged Navajo blankets or colorful woolen shirt jackets as close to their bodies as they could.

And now the third day of the dance was upon the corral, and the sun had already sculled westward over three quarters of the shallow ocean sky. Papa Tuqú-payá was yelling even as he danced, imploring everyone to exert themselves fully, waving a flabby arm at the men playing drums, commanding them to step up the cadence and so propel the dancers headlong into vision.

The drummers obeyed Sky, and the singers followed the drummers' lead. Soon, Paisley was careening helplessly out of her own path, staggering toward the center pole and then lurching back from it, all the while half deafened by the relentless screeching of a dozen or more eagle-bone whistles. Finally, Paisley knew that the Spirit had brushed her with an invisible feather and that all the other dancers were retreating to their stalls to allow her a clear attack on the pole.

To her left was the fenced-off spectator section of the lodge, and as she pistoned forward, circling on herself even while dancing ahead, she again caught sight of the Anglo couple who had come to represent her father. To Paisley's mounting wonder, they had shown up in the corral every morning, staying until the end of the day's dancing both to watch and to urge her on. What astounded the girl about their faithfulness was the obvious fact (obvious even to one struggling to keep in mind the ultimate purposes of the dance) that although the man had grown weaker and weaker over the past three days, he had stubbornly refused to let his woman friend make him quit the scene.

During an early rest period, Paisley had discovered that

they were sleeping at night in his car—not a lot, though, because the windy mountain cold, the narrowness of the car seats, and the noise from all-night poker and two-card monte games prevented them. They were amazing, this couple, and Paisley had inevitably come to see them as beyond-the-call-of-duty allies.

But how much longer can the poor man last? You've got to hurry to reach your vision, Paisley warned herself. For his sake as well as for your people's. There was something wrong with this pattern of priorities, she knew, but there was also something right about it. The old days were dead.

Although Papa Sky undoubtedly wished her to become a *po'rat* to rekindle some of the old magic, she must change even as the times themselves were changing. She must earn her rise to shamanhood by drawing a circle even larger than the base of the Sky's ridiculous false-front tepee. That circle must expand to take in Ignacio, La Plata County, the state of Colorado, the American West, the United States, and all the countries and peoples shone upon by the Sun to which she was now so feverishly dancing.

Abruptly burying these thoughts, Paisley Coldpony charged the Tree of Life. Then she retreated and charged it again.

"Mother!" she cried. "Mother!"

The One Above hurled a jolt of power. She was lifted from her feet, held parallel to the Thirst House floor, and slammed down so hard that everyone gasped: Paisley's was the true unconsciousness funneling into vision. All drumming, chanting, and dancing ceased so that Papa Sky could kneel beside her and shamanize her with both his prayers and his hands. . . .

Bo heard the spectators inside the Sun Dance lodge gasp as if the sun itself had exploded—like a hundred-watt bulb popping when its wall switch is thrown. Darkness fell for him at the same time that it fell for Paisley. Carried to the edge of his endurance by willpower and orneriness, he sank to his knees among a crowd of fretful Indians. The heat from their fire pit blew over him.

"Bo!" Libby cried. She caught him under the arms and tried to keep him from sprawling headlong. Even in his private darkness, he understood that few of the spectators had noted his collapse. They were watching Sam's daughter—God, how hard she'd fallen!—and he could hardly blame them. Paisley's fall was the sacred event for which they'd been waiting all year, and it had been as spectacular as his own had been feeble.

If he, Bo Gavin, pitched forward and ate dirt, so what? He was finally dying, but, slipping toward oblivion, he could tell himself that he was going out in the midst of life, not belted down and intubated on a hospital bed, a bond servant to death every time he sucked air, spilled fluid, or leaked wind.

"Bo!" Libby shouted again. "Damn it! Help me, someone! Your dancer's not the only one who's fallen! This man needs help too!"

There was no room to lay Bo out, the spectator section of the lodge was that packed. Consequently, Libby had to stoop behind Bo with her arms through his armpits, levering upward with her elbows and all her upperbody strength to keep him from sprawling.

At last, somebody noticed. Several somebodies. The first was Whirling Goat, a.k.a. Herbert Barnes, the gatekeeper, who demanded in a voice like a rusty meat grinder's that the men around her relieve her of her burden and carry Bo out the gate and into a shade house near the concession vans. The men who obeyed Barnes included three Utes and a nattily dressed Navajo.

Over the past few days, these men and others had become nodding acquaintances of the two Anglos. They knew that Bo had AIDS. They knew that many people feared the infection could spread from simple contact. But persisting in the belief that Libby had brought Bo to the Sun Dance to be healed, they had no overt qualms about picking him up and carrying him to the shade house.

Nor did the people in the shade house object to their laying Bo out on a big terry-cloth towel with the words NEPTUNE BEACH printed on it. Libby knelt beside Bo—on the burnt grass, not on the towel—and the matriarch of this clan, a woman named Evangeline Mestes, wife of the dancer Brevard Mestes, put a cold rag on his forehead and arranged willow saplings at his flanks to draw out his fever and bring him back to consciousness.

Asked Libby, "Is there a doctor here, or a hospital in town?"

Bo opened his eyes. The Mestes woman's willows had done half their work. Bo still had a fever, but the saplings, tucked next to his sides like limber spears, had revived him from a state akin to death. Libby was grateful. She leaned over him to report that she intended to drive him into Ignacio in search of a doctor. This was what she had feared all along, the sudden resurgence of his disease and his complete collapse. She had been a fool to let him come; he had been a fool to insist upon it.

"What do you mean, sudden?" Bo managed to object. "Three and half days. Closer to four."

Libby ignored him. She asked the men who had toted him nearly fifty yards from the Thirst House if they would mind carrying him another hundred yards or so to Bo's parked automobile. But, there on the NEPTUNE BEACH towel, Bo moved his head from side to side, a weak but unmistakable no.

"Not if Paisley's still down," he said.

"If she's really got her vision," Evangeline Mestes said, "she could be out a long time."

"How long?" Libby asked. She looked back at the Thirst House and saw hundreds of figures clustered around it. What were they doing? What was going on inside the corral?

"Three hours," the Mestes woman said. "Maybe four. One who's been vision-struck—he goes off honky-tonking with the spirits."

"She," Libby corrected.

"Yes, miss, she. Well, that's what she's up to. The spirits will teach her things. New songs. New dances. New ways to make sick people well. It takes awhile."

"I don't want you hauling me anywhere," Bo told Libby, "until Sam's daughter has come back from her . . . honky-tonking."

"But you could die."

"I'm *going* to die. Not until Paisley's had her vision, though, m'lady. Which is why we came. Partly, anyhow."

As unhappy as Bo's insistence on staying made her, Libby gave in to it. Bo's glad to be here, she thought. And who knows what kind of help I can get for him in town? The AIDS epidemic hasn't hit full force down here. How much can they know?

So they gave Bo something to drink and let him lie back again. For the next two hours, he slept between his willow saplings with his hands folded on his breast and a husky wheeze in his throat that sounded to Libby too damn much like a practice run for a death rattle.

Paisley looked up. She was lying alone in the center of a huge white field—so huge it had no margins. The sky above her was white, too, as were the mountains encircling the plain. She lay on her back, motionless, and eventually saw above her the beginnings of a tiny black hole in the middle of the glowing whiteness. This hole was fascinating because it was different from everything else in the world. It suggested that the mountains she believed she saw on the edge of her edgeless white field were there only because she chose to see them and not because they were genuinely distinct from the plain.

However, the black pinprick above her *was* distinct. It became more so by extending its circumference into the whiteness around it, like a fire ring in a sheet of paper enlarging itself by burning—although this dark hole seemed to be a cool one. In fact, Paisley thought, Snow! when white motes began sifting down on her out of the hole. These particles piled up around her, still indistinctly white. Her eyes closed, a nameless animal wheezed, and she opened her eyes again to see her mother's face—a face as big as the Holy He-She's—staring down through the enlarging hole of heaven at the uncreated world and its waiting blankness.

As Mama D'lo watched, the whiteness around her dream daughter began to shape itself into hard-edged living forms. White buffalo arose from the papery snow, as did white bears, white elk, white deer, white pumas, and so many albino birds that the hole through which the One Above observed Creation was briefly eclipsed by the pale chaos of their wings. Paisley had to stand to escape being battered back to lifelessness by the newly forming creatures. Once on her feet, she walked among them as lightfootedly as she could, touching them on their heads or flanks or wings—to identify them in her own mind and to give them names.

After walking all day, during which time colors filtered out of the hole and the hole shrank again to a pinprick, Paisley came upon a herd of one-horned creatures that now so dominated the landscape they seemed to be the only animals to have survived the coming of color. They were white themselves, but white with such a fierce sting of fire to it that Paisley knew no other animal in this new creation would be able to stand against them in the eyes of the two-legged beings that *she* represented. To give other animals a chance to win humanity's love, she would have to hide these radiant ones. For a time, anyway.

Kar'tajans, Paisley called them. Lords of the desert. Lords, she understood, of Mama D'lo's unfinished reality.

Eventually, she came to the front of the herd. On a red-cedar flute, she played a song for the lead stallion. Her song soothed him enough for her to mount him. Then she directed this stallion, and so every other kar'tajan, over the white desert toward a far horizon. Meanwhile, such colors as ocher, umber, and sienna were seeping into the ground. Distant mountains, too, were taking on an earthtone vividness.

Paisley looked up. A ptarmigan in winter white was flying east ahead of her. It was approaching the mountains, but slowly. She was able to trot the stallion, and so the entire herd, after it. For a long time, the herd ran behind the white bird, a vast cavalry of kar'tajans, the sound of a million hooves like a crescendoing boom of rifles and the reddening dust of their passage like a high unending hemorrhage. The ptarmigan disappeared into a draw between two mountains.

Paisley goaded the stallion into the boulder-strewn V of this draw, and the herd followed. A vertical seam opened at the rear of the pinched V, disclosing a world already fully formed in the vast bowl beyond it. Paisley jumped from the stallion and slapped him on the rump to get him to pass on through. She scrambled away to avoid the thousands of animals following him and saved herself by kneeling behind a rock wall next to the luminous seam. Hours and hours later (as many hours, perhaps, as Mama D'lo had devoted to Creation), all the kar'tajans had gone through.

Paisley rose to her feet and peered through the tall opening in the rocks. The territory beyond her own world was red rather than white, a wine-colored landscape ripening to both scarlet and purple at its edges. The one-horned animals that she had herded into this territory were milling on its barren scarlet plain like *ini'putc'*. In fact, they seemed to be melting into the red light even as she peered down on them through the spirit seam.

Even more interesting was that, far beyond them, pinpricks of light glittered in the otherworldly mountains ringing their desert, and Paisley decided that people—dead or uncreated people—had made their homes in those inaccessible places; as a direct result of her concern for the well-being of less handsome animals, these people would have the glory of the kar-tajans all to themselves. Paisley briefly regretted what she had done, envying those into whose world she had driven the radiant creatures and wondering if the brothers and sisters whom Mama D'lo eventually made for her would look upon her act as evil. She had exiled magic in order to bestow that very quality on creatures that might not seem to have it.

Suddenly, the spirit door into this crimson dimension began to close. Rocks tumbled from the tops of the mountain flanks squeezed together to form the narrow draw, and Paisley had to retreat from the booming avalanche to keep from being crushed. Her back to the tumult, she ran. She ran until she was standing again in the midst of the white blankness that was now a beige and umber desert. She realized, standing there, that Mama D'lo was no longer looking down on her and she was just as lost in this painted desert as she had been earlier in the edgeless whiteness . . .

Bo opened his eyes again. The men sitting in lawn chairs or on metal coolers around the Mestes shade house were almost all wearing shirt jackets. These woolen shirt jackets reminded him of the work he had done for Piedmont Mills at CCG in Atlanta. For a moment, in fact, he thought he saw a sheep with a tartan plaid fleece standing next to the piñon fire beside the shade house—but this colorful fleece was actually the back of a brave hunkering next to the fire and poking it with a willow branch.

Peering hard into the darkness, Bo saw that Libby and the old man who had been serving as gatekeeper were sitting next to each other in aluminum chairs. The geezer was chatting with her in a voice so low and throaty that Bo wondered if he were talking Ute. He had taken part in all the sunrise rituals in the lodge and had conscientiously overseen the admission of visitors to the spectator section, and yet he looked to Bo about as decrepit as a human being could look this side of the Styx. Which was pretty funny, wasn't it? That old cad sparking Libby, and Bo, a third the geezer's age, courting nothing but oblivion. It was hilarious, the counterpoints life could throw at you.

"She's still out," Evangeline Mestes told a woman from another shade house. "It's been two hours." What the other woman said, Bo was unable to hear. He was listening to the gatekeeper growl and watching him weave complex string figures among the fingers of his stubby hands. Already, Bo had seen—unless his eyes were playing tricks on him—string portraits of a barking dog, a flying eagle, and, yes, the head of a kar'tajan.

The gatekeeper stopped talking when he held up the kar'tajan head for Libby's inspection, and so did she. In fact, there was a lull in everyone's conversation, and the branches of the saplings atop the shade house rattled in a gust of wind. Bo shivered uncontrollably but refused to advertise his discomfort. After all, what the hell was there to say?

The color in the primeval landscape refused to set. Whiteness kept creeping back in. As she stood in the middle of this desert, waiting for rescue, she saw the mountains and the mesas lose their earthtones and blanch like boiled turnips. Everything was edgeless again. She was alone at the center of the edgelessness.

Much later—myriad circlings of the sun—three *ini'putc'* came walking out of the void to counsel with her: Alvin Powers, DeWayne Sky's predecessor as Sun Dance chief; Dolores Arriola, who appeared not as the One Above but as a grisly suicide victim; and, finally, the young Anglo man with AIDS.

Paisley was surprised to find this last ghost in the company of Powers and Mama D'lo, not because he was not a Ute but because she hadn't known that he was dead. In any event, she sat down on the white hardpan with these ghosts for a powwow. They taught her new songs, new dances, new cures, and forgotten wisdom. It took a long time. She had to sing the songs, stand to do the dances, memorize the healing techniques, and age into the wisdom.

Then the three wise ones vanished, and Paisley was alone again in the middle of nowhere. She sang to herself. She danced a small white bird out of the air. She healed its broken body with a kiss, held it aloft in cupped hands, and shooed it off into the expectant blankness of the world. Then she sat down on the hardpan, crossed her legs in front of her, and waited.

The desert acquired color again. So did the mountains. Mama D'lo's primeval creation was taking on fresh life. As it did, so did Paisley. She was waiting expectantly for the reappearance of mystery, and her hope was not disappointed, for a solitary figure appeared on the plain at the head of the mountain draw into which she had once driven the kar'tajans, and this figure came walking toward her like a shaggy *ini'putc'*.

This man, she saw, was nearly naked, wearing only a breechcloth and some sort of animal skin over his head and shoulders. As he drew closer, she realized that his robe was the glowing hide of a kar'tajan. The head was still attached to the pelt, and the man coming toward her was wearing the kar'tajan's head on his own as if it were some kind of luminous helmet. The alicorn that should have risen spearlike from the dead animal's brow, the walking man held across his body like a rifle.

When the *ini'putc'* reached Paisley, he had nothing to say. He gave her his hand and pulled her to her feet. She found that there was blood in the palm of her hand and that it had come from a spike hole in the hand with which he had lifted her. His other hand had been similarly pierced. The man ignored these wounds. He gave the oddly ridged alicorn to her as if it were a weapon or a magic staff, and his eyes smiled.

Then the walking man vanished. Although Paisley could see his footprints burned into the hardpan across all the distance that he had walked to reach her, the *ini'putc'* himself had ceased to exist in the world that the heavenly Mama D'lo had made. Paisley lifted the alicorn that he had given her, pointed it at the mountains, and spoke a single word: "Move."

They did.

Libby felt a hand on her arm, gently shaking her. "Come on," Evangeline Mestes said. "The girl's come out of her vision, and DeWayne Sky wants everybody down there."

The sun had been down a long time. Libby looked across the field at the Thirst House, a twelve-posted, open-topped polygon given a wacky off-centeredness by the night, the quarter moon, and the sacred fire flickering in the pit near the spectator section. Dozens of people were outlined against the rest stalls visible to Libby from the Mestes shade house.

"What about Bo?" she asked, sitting up.

"Him too," Evangeline said. "That girl asked for him to be there. She asked especially."

Before Libby could protest that Bo might be too sick to move, some men appeared with a collapsible wheelchair that they snapped open and speedily hoisted him into. Bo gave Libby a wan grin, and a hulking Muache—impossible to identify in the dark—floated this chair over the bumpy field to the corral entrance on the east. The gatekeeper—his name, Libby had learned, was Herbert Barnes—had returned to his post, after using Paisley's drawn-out trance as an excuse to sit down and gab with her, and he not only passed Bo into the spectator section but cleared a path for him right out onto the dance floor. The Ute acting as Bo's attendant wheeled him to the center post and parked his borrowed chair so that he was sitting directly under the eerie visage of Buffalo. Libby wanted to go out on the floor with him, but Barnes restrained her.

"The healing session's just for him," Barnes told Libby. "Alma asked for it the minute she came out of her vision."

"Alma?"

"Okay, *Paisley*. Sam Coldpony was a scatterbrained fella once, and he gave her a stupid name."

Libby knew what a healing session was. Sky had presided over several such sessions between dance sets over the past three days, at which times all the dancers came forward to help diagnose and treat those presented to them for cures.

Every earlier session, Libby remembered, had taken place during the day, while the sun was still high. She and Bo had witnessed the healings—whether real or fake, whether lasting or fleeting—of an epileptic teenage boy from Fort Hall, a madwoman named Moonshine Coyote, a local girl who stuttered, and a mixed lot of middle-aged men and women with problems ranging from bursitis to alcoholism to plantar's warts. In each case, the designated shaman (not always Sky, who was not a full-fledged medicine man) cured the ailment by sprinkling dirt from the sacred cottonwood on an eagle-wing fan and pressing the fan down hard on the supplicant's head.

Libby and Bo had not been tempted to enroll Bo for one of the sessions, and the constant piping of eagle-bone whistles during the shamanizing had just about put their eardrums out. Now, though, Bo had been *recruited* for the honor.

Watching from the spectator area, Libby saw Paisley come out of her stall and walk directly to Bo. Looking like a person made from white mud, Paisley put her white hands on Bo's shoulders and lifted her gaze past the vertical alicorn on the Tree of Life, past the glittering eyes of Buffalo, and on up to the moon. The singers in the lodge chanted, the drummers drummed, and the other dancers, Sky among them, blew their eagle-bone whistles.

Libby knew—as Bo himself knew—that this would never work, but the healing session went ahead anyway. At its end, after Paisley had knelt before Bo and pressed something into his hand, she and the other dancers retreated to their rest booths, and Sky walked to God's Spine to announce the end of the dance.

In turn, he "cemented in" the *powa'a* the dancers had earned (by pressing down hard on their heads), led the bestowal of blessings, showed the sacred items owned only by the Southern Utes, including the god sheet, and asked the water chiefs to tote in the ten-gallon vessels containing a bitter mixture of water and white clay. The dancers, then the spectators, would drink from these pots, and the Sun Dance would be over again until next year.

Before any of these wrapping-up rituals began, Bo was wheeled back to the spectator area. Libby was surprised to see that he was more alert than he had been all day and that all that had happened tonight—hours after the dance should have ended—had amused and maybe even invigorated him. Almost absentmindedly, she reached down and massaged the back of his neck.

As the closing ceremonies wore on, however, Libby became aware that Bo was relapsing. He held on as gamely as he could, clutching the arms of the wheelchair and noisily gritting his teeth, but the past three days' events, and the pitiless inroads of his AIDS, had destroyed his ability to keep fighting back.

Libby kept bending down to ask Bo if he wanted to try to find a doctor. During the water ritual, when she asked him for maybe the twelfth or twentieth time, he tilted his head back and hissed, "Stop it, Cousin Quarrels. This is what we came for. This is what I'm staying to the end of."

Libby, at once angry and hurt, straightened to watch the last half dozen spectators go forward for a drink of bitter water.

"Don't worry," Bo said. "I'll go last. That way, nobody will have to drink after me."

Bo went last. Libby pushed him over the moccasin-pummeled dirt floor to the center pole, and Sky gave him a dipper of clayey white liquid that Libby had already found to taste more like a potter's slurry than water. Bo, hands trembling, sipped at the stuff with the twisted-up face of a kid taking cod-liver oil, then dropped the dipper, staining the lap of his dirty pleated trousers, and lolled, at best semiconscious, against one arm of the wheelchair. By this time, Libby hated him for being so mule-headed and persnickety and herself for not simply overruling him in his singlemindedness—by main force, if sweet reason or threats wouldn't do. If the turkey died out here, she would have to live the rest of her life with the guilt of her wimpy negligence.

Paisley had been sitting cross-legged in her stall for the past forty minutes. She reappeared on the near-empty dance floor, her chalk- and water-streaked face aglow in the moonlight, and knelt in front of the chair as she had done during the healing session. She tipped Bo forward, received him on her shoulder, and then carefully rolled him onto his back at the base of the Tree of Life. Then she stood and told Sky to bring her the god sheet.

"The god sheet? What for?"

"Get it," Paisley said. "I'm going to take this man home in it, Papa Sky. I'm going to go see my father."

There was an argument. There were threats and counter-threats. Sky was offended (outraged, Libby would have said) that an upstart dancer, even one who had received a vision, would demand custody of a sacred artifact like the god sheet, especially for the intended benefit of an Anglo stranger. Sam's daughter countered that this Anglo, this stranger, was a friend of her father's—he had a right to die in his own home. She would bring the sheet back to Ignacio once she had seen Bo home to Snowy Falls in it, and she would give it directly into Sky's hands to lock up for another year in his Sun Dance trunk, where no one could take any benefit from it until he dragged it out next July and displayed it around again—like a mink stole paraded for others only on Easter.

"You'll dirty the sheet," Sky said. "The sacred linen bearing the Walking Man's footprints— you'll defile it."

"I'll wash it," Paisley snapped. "In a strong detergent like Tide or something. If the Walking Man's footprints are part of the material now, as you and Chief Powers always claimed, they'll still be there when it's washed. And if they aren't, well, these people brought you that"—she indicated the alicorn on the Tree of Life— "and that's a straight-up trade, Papa Sky."

In the end, to Libby's surprise, Paisley won the argument. Her trump card was the threat not to return at all if Sky refused her this use of the sheet, for if she didn't come back at all, on Sky's head would fall the blame for chasing off the first real candidate for *po'rat* to come among the Southern Utes in half a century. The sheet miraculously appeared. Libby watched as Sky, Kyle, Smalltree, and Larry Cúthair, a friend of Sam's daughter, placed the delirious Bo on the god sheet and wrapped him up in it.

"K.S. stands for Kyle Smalltree," Bo said, talking to no one in particular. "K.S. stands for Kaposi's sarcoma."

Lord, thought Libby, he looks like a buritto, a *burrito grande* from the Prairie Schooner Café.

Sky stalked off into the night. Smalltree and Cuthair eased Bo—Bo the Burrito—back into the wheelchair and helped the two women trundle him across the bumpy field to his car. They laid Bo in the back seat, Libby keyed the ignition, and Paisley, smelling strongly of sweat, grime, and body paint, got in on the shotgun side.

"My mother's house is off that way," she said, nodding into the darkness. "Let me wash up and get some clothes. Then we can go. You don't mind driving at night, do you, ma'am?"

"'Libby,' not 'ma'am.' No, I don't. Not at all."

And in thirty minutes' time, Bo blathering on about kar'tajans, condoms, his family, and too many other subjects to make sense of, Libby was driving northeast toward the Sangre de Cristos and the father of the intense young woman sitting to her right.

"Paisley, there's something I haven't been able to tell you up to now: I'm in love with your daddy."

"I figured you were," Sam's daughter said. "Does he love you back?"

Libby had to think. "I don't know."

"The bastard. He better."

# 29

On Monday morning, Al Pettigrew entered the boss's office with a folded newspaper. "Thought you might like to see this, sir." He placed it on the desk as carefully as if it were a breakfast tray, laying it down so that the headline he had circled in red would be immediately visible. "Sure as hell one of the screwier articles to come from all the Kartajans hoopla."

Zubrecht was wearing a tan hunting vest with a blue shirt and white linen trousers. He glanced at the headline. "Thanks, Al," he said and went on working.

Pettigrew, disappointed, withdrew.

The headline *was* something, Zubrecht decided, but he had been studying a report about his firm's chances of securing a government contract for providing U.S. enlisted personnel with condoms, and he had let Pettigrew come in only because he had an open-door policy to all his department heads. He wanted no one at management level to be able to accuse him of inaccessibility. However, the headline in that funny hick newspaper kept drawing his eye.

The newspaper was the *Huerfano Warrior*, a semiweekly journal of "news, events, history, and entertaining commentary." The logo on the masthead featured the twin peaks known as Huajatolla, and the circled headline declared PUNCHY COWPUNCHERS AT SNOWY FALLS PIONEER DAZE/"SEE" UNICORN STAM-

PEDE BUT GET TRAMPLED BY SKEPTICISM. Finally, Zubrecht's curiosity took over, and he picked up the newspaper and began to read. The story turned out to be a column by somebody named Julio Covarrubias, identified at the end of the piece as "a Huerfanovian attorney who writes an occasional column of idiosyncratic observation for the *Warrior*":

> Our neighbors up in Snowy Falls had such a good time at their Pioneer Days festivities last week that some of them "saw" unicorns running up and down Highway 69. Not pink elephants or flying mules or two-ton canaries, but a herd of unicorns.
>
> Sadly, the response to this sighting hasn't been joy or amazement but ridicule and disbelief. Henry Martinez, an old friend who cowpunches on Ray Hilliard's place, says he's "sick up to here" with the catcalls and derision that have dogged him and some of his saddle mates in the wake of their run-in with these animals.
>
> "Lots of people ragging us," Henry says, "are saying stuff like, 'They were smashed. They're dumb cowboys. So when they sat they saw unicorns, it's really just booze or cow-manure fumes talking.' Well, horsefeathers to that." (Henry didn't really say "horsefeathers," of course, but this is a family newspaper.)
>
> Hey, I know Henry. He may take a nip now and then (I've shared a few with him), but he never gets more than a sheet or two to the wind, and a cowboy who can't handle the hardships of cowpunching, up to and including close association with cowpies, isn't going to be a wrangler as long as Henry has been. So I believe him when he insists that this unicorn claim has nothing to do with any alleged intemperate bibbery.
>
> I believe Henry. I believe Eddie del Rio. Why, I even believe the incredible Hoke Gissing, known far and wide as both a big talker and an even bigger bibber than his saddle mates. I believe Henry and Eddie because Hoke, who could conduct a talk show from horseback, has clammed up tighter than a scared stoolie. My theory is that a man who talks when nothing has happened will only shut up when something really has.

And Hoke ain't talking.

Q.E.D., the unicorns that Henry, Eddie, and a crew of imaginative youngsters from Snowy Falls and environs say they saw—these unicorns, going by Hoke's uncharacteristic lockjaw, *must somehow exist*. Hoke enjoys being laughed along with, but not at, and not even an outrageous truth will out when it seems to Hoke that folks are leaning more toward "at" than "along with."

All right. If there really are unicorns up around Snowy Falls—which there must be, given that Henry isn't an intemperate bibber and Hoke would only say there were if there weren't—how did they get there? Unicorns are ordinarily as rare around here as undiluted whiskey at a couple of Huerfano's chintzier watering holes.

I have another theory. A Pueblo newswoman has lately claimed that the fellow who did that artsy-smartsy unicorn ad on TV for a controversial birth-control and disease-prevention product lives on the ranch known hereabouts as the Tipsy Q. My theory is that hormone-tormented cowboys and teenage males have such products on their minds more often than on their private appointments, and that all the media hype about the ad's creator living in our area has created *unicorns of the mind* in the noggins of my friends from Hilliard's spread.

You could maybe call it the Kartajanization of Remuda County. But, shoot, we're all being Kartajanized, whether we're a target market for this product or not, and the most innocent among us—cowboys and teenagers qualify, I think—are always prone to fantasy flights.

Yesterday, I asked my friend Henry Martinez what he thought of my theory.

"Horsefeathers!" he said.

Which leaves one alternative. Maybe this AIDS victim and reputed ad person on Libby Quarrels's place is calling up computer images of unicorns and sending them down the road as mobile, four-legged billboards for that big Denver company he's reputedly working for. Teenagers and cowboys are always suckers for an imaginative ad.

This morning, I asked my friend Henry what he thought of this alternative theory.

I won't repeat or even clean up what Henry said, but allow me to tell you that after cussing me out, he did say that both my theories were just the sort of verbal fog bombs that cowhands anticipate from a lawyer. And for all their "braininess"—his word, folks, not mine—they failed to meet head on the Big Truth of his and his saddle mates' most powerful Pioneer Days experience.

"And what was that, Henry?"

"We *saw* those unicorns. A herd of them."

Well, I like a committed man. And I hope for all our sakes that Henry is committed soon. Along with, mind you, all the avaricious souls responsible for the Kartajanization of our state and nation.

Zubrecht read the story, or editorial, or essay, or whatever it was, a second time, folded the paper, and walked down the long hall to young Ned Gavin's office, with its imposing picture window and its stainless-steel worktable. At which, reassuringly busy, Ned was going through some photographs and making notations on a large sheet of graph paper.

"Have you seen this?"

Ned was surprised when the boss came up behind him and slapped a copy of the *Huerfano Warrior* on his worktable. He set the photo proofs aside and read the piece under the red-encircled headline—because, he could tell, Zubrecht expected him to read it. Having the company president at his shoulder made it hard to concentrate, but Ned made a deliberate focusing effort and so managed to get a grip on the author's heavy-handed irony.

"This isn't the first time I've seen this rumor, Ned."

"That there are unicorns in Remuda County?"

"That the creator of our Kartajans ad is an AIDS sufferer."

The copy of the *Warrior* in Ned's hands had begun to rattle. He clutched it harder to keep the vibrating pages from betraying his nervousness.

Said the persistent Zubrecht, "Does your brother have AIDS?"

"Yes, sir." Ned loosened his grip on the paper to see if that would work. The rattling got louder.

"You told us it was something else."

"Meningitis." Ned set the paper down and shoved his hands into his pants pockets.

"A lie, in other words."

"Yes, sir."

"Did his AIDS come about from . . . homosexual activity?"

"It looks that way. Yes, sir." Where was this interrogation heading? Were Zubrecht's questions ones that he had either legal or an ethical obligation to answer?

Zubrecht ambled over to Ned's desk, sat down in his chair, and swiveled it so that he could gaze out toward the mountains. "How's your brother doing, Ned? Who's he staying with? How's your mother reacting?" Ned answered with the truth, insofar as he knew it, and Zubrecht said, "Why isn't Beaumont living with you? Shouldn't he be here in Denver rather than down there in the sticks?"

Their conversation proceeded. Ned gave the answers that he had long since formulated for himself. Bo preferred the Tipsy Q to the city. For his personal physician, he had an expert in oncololgy who specialized in the treatment of AIDS. Papa Nate was dead, and Mama Josey was distraught. Otherwise, everything was about as far under control as you could expect, given the nature of Bo's sickness and the unpredictability of people's responses.

Including yours, sir, thought Ned. For he had no idea what the man was driving at or what Zubrecht would do if he regarded AIDS as a latter-day variety of plague.

"Are *you* a homosexual, Ned?"

"No, sir." Ned wished that he had declined to answer, but his reply was out before he could recall it. Besides, taking the fifth could incriminate you simply by making you appear too weak-kneed to acknowledge an incriminating truth.

"You're not married," Zubrecht pointed out.

"I'll be twenty-five at the end of the summer. My age gives me a little elbow room, don't you think?"

"I was nineteen when I got married."

Maybe if you'd had a Good Nudes or a Halberdier in your wallet, you wouldn't've had to get married. But Ned was too canny to voice this sarcasm; instead, he noted that many good men put off marrying until they were established. Bachelorhood wasn't always a marker for . . . what some supposed.

"That may be," Zubrecht said. "But I suspect you. I started suspecting you as soon as those first rumors about Beaumont's being an AIDS victim hit the news."

"But why?" Ned knew that Zubrecht, although not a gay baiter, had tacit company policies against hiring homosexuals and against retaining them if their orientation were disclosed after they had deceitfully come aboard. Legal ways to get around these policies might or might not exist, but the policies themselves derived from Zubrecht's religious beliefs and so were unappealable.

"I think you refused to take in your brother, Ned, because you were afraid that if you did, my finding out that he was living with you would upset me. It would have, I admit, but I'd've admired you for standing beside your brother in his time of need."

"But I've done that. I got him the assignment that led to the Kartajans campaign."

"A way to assuage your guilt for not taking him in. Which you didn't do because you really are a gay man, Ned. You were trying to do what *I* thought would be the right thing for you to do—when a real man would've said to hell with my misread opinion and taken in his dying brother anyway. The only reason you didn't do that is that you *aren't* a straightshooter. You're what you thought I would assume you to be if you'd brought your brother home to Denver with you—even though that *isn't* what I would've assumed at all. If you follow me."

How could anybody follow such twisted "reasoning"? It was so tangled and thorny that even a pair of pruning shears couldn't have cut through it to a stripped-bare logic. It had none. It was what old Ev did silently in his head and aloud during company meetings and brainstorming sessions. It defied diagramming. It took you, Escher-like, up a set of stairs that brought you down to a level above the one where you had started. . . .

Ned was trembling. He put his thumb and forefinger

under his chin and pinched his sandy goatee. "I don't know what to tell you, Mr. Zubrecht, except that I'm not gay."

"Well, I have no proof. Only a suspicion."

"Your suspicion's off base and out of line, sir, even if you are my boss."

"That may be," Zubrecht conceded.

"It is, sir. Ask Peter about me. Ask him about our wild times as roommates in college." He stopped.

But Zubrecht said, "Been in touch with your brother recently—within, say, the last week or so?"

"I get no answer when I call. The medical center says Bo isn't there, though. He and Elizabeth are probably out of town."

"Drive back down there and see."

"Why?" Ned realized that he was still in the outfit, although under both sufferance and scrutiny.

"Bring me that newspaper." Zubrecht nodded toward the chromium worktable and the copy of the *Warrior* atop it. Ned fetched the paper, and Zubrecht swatted the essay by Covarrubias with the back of his hand. "What if there were really unicorns, or something moderately like them, down there? Wouldn't it be a sin not to find one of the animals? We could supplement Beaumont's animated spot with . . ." He smiled.

"Live appearances?"

"Right. Go see about your brother. Tomorrow."

It'll be a pleasure to get out of here, Ned thought. To absent myself from this menagerie of egos, assholes, and loons. It struck him that maybe he qualified under all three of these pejorative headings, but he salvaged a scrap of pride by refusing even to nod his head. Bo's the faggot, old man. Not I. Not once in this life has Theodore Gavin lusted after a fellow male.

# 30

Sam saw the mountain lion before Brinkley did—before, in fact, Telluride, the vet's mount, or Crip, Sam's own, or even Phylly, the kar'tajan dallied to Sam's pommel horn on a length of rope, caught scent of the big cat.

The puma was lying at the base of the rocks making up the pika colony under Abbot's Pate. Sam was certain that it had seen them riding up the saddle toward it, but it hadn't moved—it had simply lifted its compact head and roared soundlessly. Now it lay gazing at them over the rim of a small white boulder.

A delayed ripple of startlement rushed through Sam as he reined in Crip and tried to give Brinkley a warning tap on the arm—even though the vet was a little too far away to reach and Phylly had just become aware of the mountain lion herself. She began pulling back on her rope. Meanwhile, Brinkley, looking like Paul Bunyan astride a chihuahua, continued to urge his own petite mare up the mountain.

"Whoa," Sam said. "Dr. Brinkley, stop." The big vet bridled Telluride and looked at Sam, who nodded toward the pika hotel and the cougar. Brinkley peered, blinked, peered again. His vision was lousy. Then Crip and Telluride sensed the cat's presence, and Telluride did a sideways stutter step that the vet had to counter with a quick tug on the bridle. "There's a cat up there," Sam told him. "Look close and you'll see it."

Brinkley, giving Telluride no slack, squinted, blinked, peered more narrowly, "Yes, ma'am. I see the bastard."

Was that "ma'am" for him or for Telluride? Sam was too busy trying to keep Crip from bolting and Phylly from pulling all three of them down to worry the matter. He encouraged

Crip in whispers, and the pony dug in against both its own fear and the tugging of the kar'tajan.

"Let her go," Brinkley said.

"She'll run off," Sam said, astounded by this advice. "We'll lose her help tracking down the others."

"Let the little cooze go!"

Sam loosened the dally-tied rope, hopped off Crip, and worked the noose around Phylly's head free. He expected to have to fight her while he did this, but she stood still for him. In fact, she lowered her head so that he could slip the noose over the wicked spike of her alicorn.

Once free, Phylly trotted downslope about thirty yards, then circled back up the saddle to the men's right, sixty or more yards from the spruce forest paralleling the left-hand arm of the saddle's inverted V. It was hard to believe that, given her original panic, Phylly was now *approaching* the pika colony and the mountain lion looking warily downslope.

The pikas themselves had retreated to their rock holes, but the close-cropped grass around their boulder pile told Sam that they'd already begun stockpiling fodder for the winter. One pika popped from cover, whistled an annoyed protest against either the cougar's presence or the men's and then, perhaps seeing Phylly on the trot toward it, vanished again.

Oh, shit, thought Sam.

It had been a hard three days. He didn't relish seeing Phylly get belly-slashed so soon after Brinkley had worked his heinie off saving her from anemia, arteritis, or kar'tajan plague. Besides, Phylly had helped them find and escort back to Libby's barn all six of the enfeebled animals down there now. Without her, they'd get little more done in the way of kar'tajan rescue, and if others, who were *bad* sick, didn't come around, they'd've lost every magical creature from Elsewhere given into their—his and Libby's—keeping by the Great Manitou. Which would be a black spot on his soul that maybe no future act of his could ever remove.

"What the hell's your 'little cooze' doing, Dr. Brinkley?"

"Responding to a fucking instinct."

"An instinct? What instinct?"

"Look closer, Coldpony. You had me give that big feline mother a good going-over. Now you do it, man."

Stroking Crip's throat, Sam narrowed his eyes and looked

harder at the pika colony. And saw that the small white boulder in front of the cat was actually the capsized body of a kar'tajan. Despite their approach, the cat had refused to slink away. It was guarding its kill, daring them to take from it what it had earned by stealth and brute strength.

Sam regarded the old vet with quiet surprise: His vision *isn't* lousy. It's better than mine. You just have to whack him with a two-by-four to get him to use it. But, Jesus, that kitty will tear Phylly up. What are we lollygagging here for?

"Come on," he said, swinging up into Crip's saddle. He flicked the reins and set off toward the pika colony. Brinkley didn't tell him to stop. In fact, Sam heard the old man cluck Telluride into a trot behind him.

The closer they drew to the cat, which had begun to glance back and forth between the men on horseback and the prancing kar'tajan on the edge of the spruce forest, the more Sam could tell about its features. Its markings may have been beautiful once, but today the black fur tipping its ears and outlining its squat muzzle resembled cheap, crudely applied mascara. The fur itself had a scruffy nap. One ear had been bitten nearly in two. When the puma yawn-snarled again, as it did now, it revealed either badly worn teeth or liver-colored gaps. Its voice was so stingy that Sam could have mistaken it for a constipated house cat's.

From two or three lengths back, Brinkley cried, "He's like me—an *old* son of a bitch. Phylly can probably handle him."

As if to justify the vet's confidence in her, Phylly slipped into the wedge of forest to her left. Sam believed that she was using the trees as a cover for her single-minded advance. But not wanting to go to her aid alone, he reined in Crip and waited for Brinkley to catch up. Meanwhile, the puma got slowly to its feet, keeping its amber forepaws on the snowy flank of the kar'tajan that it had killed. It sniffed the air. It yawned another terrific but soundless yawn. Then it miaowed a couple of times. Sweet Jesus, thought Sam, you're just a pussycat, aren't you? A lamb in lion's hand-me-downs.

"A goddamn Mexican lion," Brinkley said, once again at Sam's side. "You should have brought a rifle up here."

"You just said you thought Phylly could handle him. Why do we need a rifle?"

"Look, that's the cat world's Preston Brinkley—an ill-tempered old tom with two or three spoonfuls of fight left in him. Leave it to them to find the easiest pickings they can. But leave it to 'em to claw your balls off if you cross them, too."

"Mountain lions are protected, Dr. Brinkley."

"Not if they're fucking trying to *kill* you, they aren't, and I wish you'd brought a rifle."

But what Sam had brought was rope. They'd found rope useful in rounding up the kar'tajans that Phylly had helped them find, and a rifle—even in a saddle scabbard—would have been in the way. Now, though, this blasted cat had showed up.

Sam had no intention of getting close enough for it to claw his balls off—he had just discovered a use for them again. However, if Phylly was fool enough to put herself in jeopardy, he'd have to do something to help. Like intervene. Libby had entrusted a task to him, and even if it was a task about twelve times too big for a rifleless Indian and a foul-mouthed old horse doctor, well, Sam had made up his mind to attempt it anyway.

Phylly broke from the woods near the pika colony. She lowered her head, sprinted up the slope, and, simply by bursting from the trees at breakneck speed, flushed the startled cat out from behind the torn body of the dead kar'tajan.

Under the boulder pile, however, Phylly stumbled in gravel, and the cougar, ears back and tail peevishly twitching, took a powerful swat at the thigh of her hind leg as she foundered by. The miaow out of the cat's mouth was louder and nastier than ever before, and Sam knew that if Phylly fell, it would be all over for her, alicorn or no alicorn.

By playing deft mountain-goat tricks with her feet, she managed not to fall. Cautiously, she doubled back under the rock tiers to meet the cat head on, scything her alicorn so that the backpedaling puma couldn't take cover behind the kar'tajan corpse again. Thus, Phylly worked the cat craftily down the saddle—away from the pika colony and into the roomier meadow.

"The two men were half a football field from the action, but Sam kept goading the nervous Crip closer. If things got out of hand, he wanted to be able to bring up reinforcements quickly. What he *didn't* want to see was kar'tajan guts—no matter how briefly they might exist before dematerializing—

strewn across the summer grass like the reeking contents of a fisherman's creel.

But now it was obvious that the cat was in bad shape. Despite its recent meal—one it hadn't had time to finish—its ribs showed. Its responses to Phylly's dashes and feints were clumsy and off-speed. Clearly, it had killed the dying kar'tajan not so much through stealth and brute strength as through sheer good luck in catching it out alone. Which was why the miffed cat wouldn't retreat from its kill and why it was do-si-do-ing with Phylly even though it was overmatched. That kill had been a long time coming, and it would rather die—if big cats reasoned about such matters, which Sam felt sure they did—defending this dinner than trying to run down the next one.

But Phylly made the puma change its mind. She galloped from a dead standstill right at the cat, swung her head at the animal as it leapt awkwardly aside, and marked it from shoulder to rib cage with the red beginnings of an alicorn scar. The puma's yowl echoed down the saddle like the cry of a restless *ini'putc'*.

Phylly, almost like a ballerina, caught herself up, whirled, and came cantering back. Playfully, Sam thought. She was having a grim good time, but, of course, the ill-tempered old tom had killed a dying kar'tajan and perhaps some sort of instinct was driving her to defend even its corpse. Maybe she wanted to give the poor dead beast time to disappear from this reality—time for its spirit to make a final trip from Over Here to Over There.

Anyway, the puma had had enough. It began to run. But not up into the rocks or off into the spruce forest. It ran straight at the horses, its arthritic forelegs reaching out and sweeping back like pistons—so that the forty yards between the men and the puma were consumed in six or seven breathtaking bounds.

Sam couldn't believe the cat was moving that fast, but his mind was actually elsewhere. As Telluride reared and Brinkley yelled, "Whoa!" and the puma raced between Brinkley's horse and Sam's, he lifted his lariat, swung it over his head in an expanding loop, and flung it at the cat in a near-perfect heel shot.

The honda of the lariat closed up like a tourniquet on one of the puma's hind feet, and the cat went sprawling on its chin.

Crip reared and whickered, but Sam dallied the end of his rope on the pommel horn, yanked the bit into Crip's mouth, and had his feisty cow pony back up against the struggling cat—a damned funny-looking dogie—so that they were able to drag it on its belly six or seven feet up the saddle.

"What the fuck are you doing?" Brinkley cried from somewhere far away. "What the holy fuck?"

The cat, snarling and spitting, twisted, pulled like a cripple with its forelegs, and gimped into an outraged three-legged stance whose potential for death-dealing Sam saw at once. For the first time, he asked himself why he was playing rodeo with an animal this dangerous. Blood rushed through his temples like water into the vaults of a hydroelectric plant.

The cat leapt clawing at the only thing in its vision hindering its escape—Crip and the two-legged creature astride Crip. Sam let go of his lariat so that the length dallied around the pommel could unwind, then watched in dismay as the puma boxed the rearing Crip in the underbarrel, staggering the panicked horse and knocking Sam himself right out of the saddle.

Sam rolled over and over, blood and disaster drumming in his ears, and scrambled to his feet only when he figured that he could dare to. Crip, hindquarters cranked as low as the trunk of Benny Elk's first jalopy, went pelting down the meadow toward the cattle grazing along a distant fence.

Then Phylly came galloping so hard at the puma that it had no time to growl, much less veer aside, before her horn went straight through its neck, plowing a furrow in the grass as it drove the writhing cougar downslope, away from the men and horses that had brought her up here today.

Sam was numb. He could only watch—while Brinkley stood by shaking his head, restraining Telluride, and letting an occasional disgusted "Fuck!" or a disbelieving "Shit!" explode from his lips. "What the holy fuck were you doing, Hopalong? Whatever it was, it got Crip slashed and that goddamn curmudgeonly cat killed. Way to go, Coldpony. Way to fucking go."

The vet was shooting holes in Sam's numbness. He could feel anger oozing up to caulk them: "You're the one who wished we had a rifle."

"Only in the event of attack. We wouldn't have *needed* a

gun if you'd let the poor mother run on by. Jesus *God*, that was about the stupidest fucking stunt I've ever seen anybody pull."

"It could've gone after the cattle," Sam said. "The Tipsy Q's better off without an old gummer like that slinking around."

"Yeah? How many head has the old gummer taken off, pray tell? Come on, Coldpony. How fucking many?"

Sam watched the cat's jaws open and close and its legs kick in reflex as Phylly held it to the earth. He had to admit that he and Libby had never found the corpse of a puma-mauled Hereford on her ranch. Of course not, Brinkley said. That was because puma liked deer better and tried to stay away from populated areas. This one had crept onto the Tipsy Q only because it was old, hungry, and klutzy, and because it had found an incompetent hunter's paradise up here with so many disease-weakened kar'tajans for prey. Hell, the one that Phylly had just kept from becoming puma meat may have been the only kar'tajan it had ever killed.

"Okay, okay," Sam said. "Who knows why I threw that rope? It was out of my hands before I could even think." He was sorry, but there was nothing he could do to revive the cougar now and Brinkley was a prick to gig him when all he'd done was react instinctively to a crisis that Phylly's instincts had called down. Forgive and forget, Sam thought. For God's holy sake.

The cat had stopped twitching. Phylly's poll was down on its neck, her horn straight through the fur, muscle, and sinew of its neck into the ground. She put a forefoot on the cat's shoulder and pulled the alicorn out. Blood geysered from this wound and gushed from the old tom's mouth. Phylly pawed the grass, jumped over the cat, kicked it with her hind legs, and trotted a semicircle around it. Out of a sky more blue than gray, rain began to fall, and fat drops thudded like bullets into the cat's scruffy hide.

Brinkley remounted Telluride, pulled a rum ball from a jacket pocket, and whistled. "C'mere, Phyl. C'mon to Daddy, now." And Phylly redrew the circle she was inscribing so that she could stop near the vet and nibble the rum ball from his hand.

Sam walked down to the puma's corpse, loosened his heel shot, carried the rope back up to Phylly, and slipped the noose over her head—including her bloody alicorn—as easily as dropping an inner tube over a Coke bottle.

"Let's go see Phylly's friend," Sam said, nodding at the mauled kar'tajan below the pike hotel. Already, three or four pikas were perched on the rocks whistling at them.

"What about your horse?"

Sam stayed mute. He didn't think Crip was really crippled and figured that the gelding would graze with the cattle until they finished their business under Abbot's Pate and went back down the saddle to check on him.

The puma's kill, the two men found, was a mare with a crooked alicorn, inflamed eyeballs, and viral lesions on the throatlatch and withers. The cat had torn several mouthfuls of meat from its hindquarters, and this flesh—a reddish gold that looked more like the flesh of a nectarine than it did animal meat—had drawn flies. Sam let go of Phylly's rope and squatted beside the corpse.

The smell wasn't bad, more like that of overripe fruit than of rancid meat, but even the wound's high peach color couldn't keep the sight from nauseating Sam. He wondered if mutilation on such a scale would keep a dead kar'tajan from dematerializing as all its predecessors had done. Maybe Phylly had been so set on rescuing this kar'tajan because she realized—deep in her semihorsy self—that mutilation cut off the spirit's sure migration home.

"Should we bury her?" Sam asked Brinkley.

"With what? You got a fucking shovel in your back pocket, or do we start digging with our fingernails?"

Usually, the vet's cantankerousness was easy to take. Lately, though, the poisons of his bulk seemed to have contaminated his behavior—he'd become a bear to get along with as well as to look at. Of course, Sam reminded himself, he's had damned little sleep these past three nights, and he's old, and he's been riding a horse back and forth across the Tipsy Q, and those stomach-tube cuts he did on the kar'tajans in Libby's barn—esophagostomies, he called them—well, they took something out of him too. He's got a foul mouth, but his disposition doesn't ordinarily bend that way, it's been . . . well, *wrenched* in that direction.

"Forget burying her," Sam said. "Let her lie."

Although Telluride was whinnying, troubled by the strange

smell coming off the dead animal, Phylly had already forgotten her. She leapt onto the lowest of the pika-colony rock tiers, sending even the most reckless of whistling hares scampering, and balanced there as prettily as a mountain goat.

In fact, just now, she looked more mountain goat than horse, and Sam thought that maybe she was the alicorned version of one of those lizards that turn green on an oak leaf, beige on a rock, and gray on a tree stump. She adapted to whatever place she happened to be. She was very adaptable. It was just that even a kar'tajan had to fight to adapt to a world where an unknown disease vector ran—or grew, or crawled—amok.

Sam said, "Dr. Brinkley, couldn't that cougar have made itself sick eating . . . ?" He nodded at the dead kar'tajan.

"Sure. If animals from this reality are susceptible to viruses from Over There—as hasn't been proved yet, and as I'm fucking well inclined to think doubtful, anyway."

Phylly bounded to the next highest tier of boulders, tightroped along its edge, then leapt down—out of the men's sight—so quickly that Sam was alarmed. He had dropped her rope without even knowing it. She had come back to Brinkley for a rum ball, but there was no guarantee that she'd come back again. Anyway, this was the second place—the other was Naismith's Mine—where Sam suspected that the kar'tajans sometimes passed between metaphysically abutting worlds, and he was afraid that she would disappear through that doorway, if one existed, and never return. He told Brinkley so.

"Go after her, then. *I* can't clamber up and down those damned rocks. *You* do it."

Sam hoisted himself to the first tier, nearly slipping on some crystallized pika urine and wet rocks. He then pulled himself up another level. A glance down Abbot's Saddle showed him a rainy blue-green vista of grass, forest, and mist-enshrouded mountains. Straight below him, Brinkley, his upturned face glistening like a waxed melon, made an impatient get-going gesture, and Sam scooted on his hands and boot toes over the rocks until he had come to a jumping-off place—where, steeling himself against the inevitable ankle crunch, he jumped off.

He crouched in a tight defile of boulders angling up toward the slatey dome of Abbot's Pate. He had never explored this corridor before, but Libby had said there were caves in here, and Sam didn't doubt it. In fact, this had to be another point of both entry and departure for the kar'tajans, and if Phylly had come this way—he didn't see her—they could probably just kiss her a mocking *hasta la vista*, for they wouldn't lay eyes on her again, if at all, until next December.

The defile was so tight that Sam was protected from most of the rain. He clambered up it, pushing off the rocks on either side and noting that some of the crevices were mortared—even in July—with unmelted ice.

A five minute climb, during which he hallooed Phylly's name or whistled beckoningly, brought him to a wider alley, which, when the sun broke through a coal sack of afternoon clouds, was abruptly awash in both rain and ricocheting light. Sam jumped from boulder to boulder, as if dodging these glowing arrows, and there, another twenty feet ahead of him, reared Phylly.

The kar'tajan's pale back was to him. She stood like a unicorn on a coat-of-arms, her forefoot against the leading edge of a rock spill so vast that Sam understood that he had been climbing through and atop its litter. No, not a spill—an avalanche. There'd been an avalanche up here, the consequence of ice expanding in the rock seams, frozen soil thawing at midday, and the whole pebbly surface shifting from the temperature changes and sliding upon itself like a load of potatoes on an underlayer of . . .

Sam tried to think. *Piñon nuts.* Right, piñon nuts. And the result was tons of stony rubble and a doorway to Elsewhere forever slammed shut on the loveliest creatures ever to use it. Sam could feel relief and disappointment contending inside him, much the way that Phylly and the cougar had fought.

It took awhile, but after some stumbling around and a lot of coaxing, he was able to grab Phylly's rope and lead her back down the defile to the pika colony. Here, she had to find rock steps to the surface of its lowest tier, but eventually she did that, and from there both Sam and Phylly were able to leap down to the upper slope of Abbot's Saddle.

Brinkley smiled to see her—the first time in a day and a half, Sam figured, that the vet had put on a smile. It made him look at least a year younger.

# 31

When they got back to the Tipsy Q, Sam saw an unfamiliar yellow truck parked near the aspen stand at the heart of Libby's drive. This truck glistened in the relentless drizzle, brutally informing him that he and Brinkley had made a bad mistake leaving the ranch unguarded by anyone but Bounty.

"Who the fuck's that?" the vet said.

Sam didn't reply. He flicked Crip's reins (still relieved that the damned puma had only scratched the gelding), yanked on Phylly's lead, and rode straight toward the barn. Brinkley goaded Telluride forward after Sam, and their party passed between Libby's GM pickup and Brinkley's jackknifed horse trailer. Sam dismounted, strode into the barn pulling Phylly with him, and came face to face with a woman.

Unlike her truck, the woman looked slightly familiar. She had a camera on a neck strap and was surprised, but not embarrassed, to see Sam. Meanwhile, Bounty, that egg sucker, sat next to her, eyes blissfully closed, having his neck scratched.

"This is private property," Sam said, knowing that De-Wayne Sky would have hooted to hear him say so. "You're trespassing."

"Told you we should've carried a rifle," Brinkley said, coming into the barn behind Sam. Both men were dripping, and they faced the woman, Sam feared, as if they were a pair of hoboes and she the upright ranch owner.

"I knocked at the house," the woman said, looking past Sam at Phylly, a smile disfiguring her mouth. "No one answered."

"So," Brinkley said, "I take it you hauled your butt out to the barn to see if the owner was pitching hay or shooting rats."

"Not a stupid assumption." She nodded through the chapel-sized door. "After all, somebody left those trucks out front."

"What's your business?" Sam wanted to scare this self-assured person, for her stance—her entire attitude—implied that she had as much right to be here as Sam and the vet did, that she had the authority of a building inspector or maybe even a law officer. It was irritating, the authority she gave herself.

"I know you!" Brinkley suddenly boomed. "You're that stuck-up news cooze from Pueblo TV!"

The woman's lips set, and she scratched Bounty's head with harder and more rapid scratches—changes to which the dumb hound responded by leaning adoringly into her thigh. "My name is Karen Banks," she said. "'News cooze' is pretty neat, old man, but it isn't in my job description."

"No? Well, how about 'breaking and entering,' 'harassing and sassing,' et-goddamn-cetera? Are those in there, missy?"

"I've told you my name, old man. It isn't 'missy'—it's Banks, Karen Banks. Why don't you tell me yours?"

"It ain't 'old man,' Miss Banks—it's the Lone Ranger. This is my sidekick, Sammy Coldpony, alias Catchcougar. I call him Tonto, Spanish for 'stupid,' but you'd be almost as fucking stupid to call him that as I'd probably be to call you 'missy' again."

Brinkley's profane sarcasms, and possibly his size, were making this Banks person look past them into the rain for a likely escape route. But apparently she didn't like being buffaloed as Brinkley was trying to buffalo her, for she quickly lifted her chin and went hell-for-leather on the attack again.

"I uncover things," she said. "That's the biggest part of my job, Mr. Ranger. What I've uncovered here, trespassing or not, is what looks like some pretty sickening experimentation. What you've done to that creature"—she meant Phylly—"and what you're doing to these others"—she indicated the stalls behind her— "appears a helluva lot like cruelty to animals."

"The only cruelty I'm aware of around here," Brinkley said, "is your bosses' for turning you loose where you don't fucking belong."

"I'm on my own time, Mr. Roger—a private crusade."

"Well, if Catchcougar and I are the evil butchers you think

we are, Miss Banks, maybe I should start calling *you* Tonto for telling us so." Brinkley put a hand on Sam's shoulder. "The news cooze is here all by herself, Injun. What say we kill her and drop her body down a mine shaft? Who the fuck'd ever know?"

Things were getting out of hand. "Hey, Dr. Brinkley—"

"Someone *does* know I'm here," Karen Banks said hurriedly. "A friend at my station. And I know your names. Unless you're lying, they're Sammy, uh, Catchcougar and Dr. Brinkley."

"Right. *Doctor* Brinkley. But I'm a horse doctor, Miss Banks, not a Nazi vivisectionist, and I'm so all-fired tired of playing cowboys and Indians with you—a liar and a trespasser—that I'm leaving it to Tonto here and heading home. A good night's sleep. That's all I ask. Shit, four good hours."

He handed Telluride's reins to Sam, urged him to toss the woman out if she didn't leave on her own, and ran down some instructions for the care of the kar'tajans already under treatment.

"If something comes up, call. It'll take me thirty minutes to drive back up here, but right now, Catchcougar, it's either those suffering one-prongs or me—so I'm voting to save yours truly." He gave Karen Banks his you're-nothing-but-wet-weather-fungi scowl, tramped out to his truck, rattled its engine to asthmatic life, and drove away in the rain.

Sam was at a loss. Brinkley had deserted him. Or else the old vet—even after the cougar-roping incident below Abbot's Pate—had unqualified confidence in him. Sam wanted the Banks woman to beat it. He was soaked, the horses needed rubbing down, the kar'tajans wanted looking after, Phylly was skittish with a new person around, and he disliked Karen Banks a *bunch*, as much because of all these other things as because of her trespassing and her smugness.

In a way, Banks was merely tough and self-reliant, kind of like Libby. In another, though, she was pushy, opportunistic, and full of swagger, and Sam couldn't imagine liking her no matter which sex the Holy He-She had made her.

"Well?" she said.

"To hell with 'well,'" Sam said. "I want to hear 'goodbye.'"

"I have some questions that need answering."

"Yeah? I've got a toe that needs a fanny to boot." Of course, he made no move to carry out his threat. He let Phylly go, took the saddles off the horses, and watched disgustedly as Karen Banks aimed her camera at Phylly—an animal she had mentally dubbed, all doubts momentarily aside, a unicorn.

But that's what Phylly was. Sam didn't blame Karen Banks for being curious, but he resented her for assuming that her curiosity gave her a free pass to pry—as he resented the vet for dumping not only the sick kar'tajans and two tired horses into his lap but also this roving professional nuisance.

The woman's camera clicked, the print came whirring out (it was one of those expensive instant-picture cameras) and Sam got busy rubbing down Crip and Telluride, moving back and forth between them so that neither would chill out before he could finish rubbing them down. He tried to forget that Banks was trespassing and that he ought to run her off. Maybe, though—her questions unanswered and her photographs either under- or overdeveloped—she would wear down and leave. Sam hoped so. He no longer had the energy for an angry face-off.

"Can you explain this?"

Kneeling by Telluride, he looked up to find that the woman had stuck the print of Phylly right under his nose. It showed only a blurred fantail of light and some blue-ringed haloes that looked like water spots or acid stains. Against his will, Sam pinched the print by one corner and peered at it. Hints of the barn's interior appeared around the edges of the picture, but the foreground image was blotched, spun, flooded.

A flash exploded in Sam's face, and he knew that Karen Banks—without permission—had taken *his* photo. When the print whirred out, she tore it off and handed it to him, and he saw his startled features swim out of its chemical glaze like a drowned man rising from deep water. Sam flipped both prints aside and went back to gunnysacking Libby's horse.

"It's not the camera," Karen Banks said. "It's these animals. Before you and old Dr. Pantagruel got back, I took a shot of every 'unicorn' stabled up here. Not one developed. They all look like that print you just Frisbee-tossed into the hay."

"Get out of here, Miss Banks."

"I had reason to think something like that might happen, which was why I brought a camera that would let me find out on the spot instead of tomorrow back down in Pueblo. And so,

Mr. Catchcougar, that's one of the questions I have. Want to try to explain what's going on here?"

Sam stood up. "They don't picture-take."

"No kidding?" She dug into her pocket, fanned out six blotched prints. "Why don't they?"

Why, wondered Sam, don't we Mauche permit cameras in our Thirst Houses? Because they're an insult to something sacred.

But how did you explain that to a literal-minded Anglo looking for an answer to a physics question needing hard facts for data and leading from such facts to a bang-bang-bang mathematical proof. So he said nothing—even though he could have said that the kar'tajans didn't come from here; that they skewed the light entering the eyes of commonplace instruments; that even Over Here they carried within them a mystery that shone outward but that you couldn't herd into a camera lens.

"Why don't they picture-take?" Karen Banks insisted.

"You want one that does?"

"I want to understand what's going on. You're living in Disney World up here, Mr. Catchcougar."

"How about a deal, Miss Banks?"

"What deal?"

"I give you one that picture-takes, that pops out a photo you can show around, and you skedaddle back on down to Pueblo."

"Okay, but—"

"That's not all. You promise—you *swear*—not to play the news cooze with your photo for at least two weeks."

"You could slaughter these animals in that much time. Or ship them off to Canada or Mexico. You could—"

"Look, they're sick. There were maybe a hundred on the Tipsy Q last week, but these seven—Phylly and the ones in the stalls—are all the doc and I were able to round up since Friday." Sam grabbed her jacket sleeve, pulled her to a stall. "Look," he said, opening the gate and showing her a yearling that was holding its head up by sheer dint of will. "See. The doc put in that small-bore stomach tube. He did that for all six of 'em, and I'll be feeding all six through those throat holes for however long it takes. They won't be going anywhere for two weeks at least—they're too sick. So if you want a show-aroundable photo, better cut a deal."

The woman lifted her camera, took the yearlings' picture. The developed print, however, was another chaos of haloes.

"Okay," she said, shoving it exasperatedly into her pocket with the others. "It's a deal."

Maybe a half hour of light remained, but the rain—luckily, not a thunderstorm—had brought evening early. Sam drove Miss Banks up to Abbot's Saddle through the wet twilight in the pickup. From the highway below it, they could see buzzards outlined against the dome of the mountain, ragged wings in ever-circling silhouette.

It was Sam's grim pleasure repeatedly to gun and then ease off the gas pedal so that the pickup bounced Miss Banks and him silly on the ride up. Doing this, he frightened off all the buzzards, approached the pika colony, and angled close enough—at one point almost tilting over—for Miss Banks to take a flash picture out the window of the mutilated kar'tajan. Her print actually developed. Delight. Puzzlement.

Sam started to leave, but Miss Banks hopped out—ignoring the drizzle—to take several more photographs, some from three feet away and some from six or eight as she sighted down on her subject from the lowest of the rock tiers. She even took a couple of shots of the cougar that Phylly had impaled through the neck.

But her prizes were of the kar'tajan, prints that she handed to Sam under the pickup's wan dome light. What she seemed to like was that the animal's alicorn was visible in every one—sometimes just a corkscrewed section, sometimes the whole ebony spike.

Thought Sam: So now, if folks don't assume you doctored these pictures or rigged up this corpse out of a dead goat and a narwhal tusk, you'll have "proof" that unicorns really exist. But that's just what folks *would* assume, one or the other, and it amazed Sam that the woman was so damn pleased with herself.

"Why does this one picture-take? Because it's dead?"

"I guess," Sam said.

"But why? I don't get it."

Sam didn't get it either. He was no expert. He didn't know anybody, not even Papa Tuqú-payá or the good Dr. Brinkley, who was. Maybe someone who'd written a book about unicorns would know, but the only book about them he'd ever bothered to read had gotten a lot of stuff flat-out wrong. Sam had a maybe answer, but it was one he didn't plan to tell her. Namely, that you could violate the dead more easily than you could an animal that was still kicking—that was struggling, however weakly, to save its own life.

"You got more photos than we dealt for," Sam said. "It's your turn to pay up. By skedaddling."

"Are they real unicorns?" Banks had probably been holding this question back out of an up-tight professional pride. "Or did you people do something to some other kind of animal to make them look the way they do?"

"They're what they are," Sam said. "We haven't done anything to them except try to save them."

He drove Karen Banks back down the saddle, back down Highway 69, and back into the Tipsy Q's drive. After she had climbed into her yellow truck, he followed her all the way into Snowy Falls to make sure she was really leaving, then wheeled about and returned to the ranch to tube-feed his charges.

Later, as he was sitting on a hay bale in the loft overlooking the pickup (which he had pulled inside) and the stalls housing the sick kar'tajans (which he had already seen to), Sam realized that Paisley's Sun Dance ought to be wrapping up about now. Libby and Bo would be back tomorrow, and if things had gone well, Payz would come with them. This thought excited him, and as tired as he was, he was too hyper to stretch out for some shut-eye.

On the reservation, Payz was dancing. She was retreating from and then rushing God's Spine—trying to gain power for the people's sake. She was also trying to buy rest for her mother.

"Ssssssssssam." The hiss came from the rear tire of the truck below him—as air sighed through a sprung valve and the corrugated cargo bed began to settle to one side.

Damn. He'd have to change the stupid tire. Tomorrow, though. Not now. Now, all he wanted was to think about Payz and to get so far into such thoughts that they pulled sleep down on him as gently as snow falls or feathers swirl.

Then, in the opposite loft (in which the owners just before the Quarrelses had hung up two bearskins and stored both an antique jukebox and some sort of ornate fortune-telling machine), Sam saw Dolores Arriola's *ini'putc'*. D'lo appeared among the floating cobwebs over there just as she had appeared to Sam previously—with no head on her neck and no forgiveness in her heart. As on La Veta Pass, she was dressed in beads and fringed leather. However, she carried in one hand the alicorn that Bo had taken down to Sky to strap to the Tree of Life.

D'lo, thought Sam, I wish you no heartbreak. I'm sorry for all that I've got to be sorry for.

Once, he'd saved himself from her by throwing the alicorn of a long yearling at her ghost. Now, though, she had taken up the horn of another kar'tajan—a like weapon, a like wand—intending to kill him before he could taste the undeserved victory of Payz's return to him. D'lo's *ini'putc'* was too bitter to let him taste such a triumph. He would escape her this time only if he ran himself down in ways that were unstomachable, or if he fled the Tipsy Q and gave up all hope of ever reuniting with Paisley. Well, he would try to talk to D'lo, but he wouldn't—no, ma'am, *wouldn't*—get down on his knees and kiss her ghostly moccasins.

Four or five bulbs in cagelike metal hoods hung on nails on crib rails around the barn. By their light, Sam could look down into the stalls and study his charges. What he saw now was all six kar'tajans and both horses growing fidgety, for they had sensed the presence of the *ini'putc'*.

Crip, still nervous from that run-in with the puma, whickered, while the other animals either picked up their ears or struggled anxiously to their feet. Even old Bounty, whose nose had gone bad a few years ago and whose eyesight was unreliable, fell victim to their nerves. That hissing tire had awakened him, and now he was cowering under the wooden stairs to the other loft. Sam could see his dopey-looking eyes between two of the steps.

D'lo's ghost was straight across from Sam, about fifteen feet above the dog and maybe forty-five of empty air from the hay bale he was sitting on. She had pirouetted among the cobweb veils over there so that she was facing him (if she'd had a face to face him with), and she looked to Sam as if she were being beamed into those uneasy shadows by a movie projector: an image of grainy particles and shifting intensities of light and color. The hair on his neck and forearms stood up as if from a static charge, and fear began to gnaw him. Why in hell did she have to show up now? Would the damn woman never rest?

Apparently not. She walked or floated through the debris in the far loft to the head of the stairs. Bounty looked up, sensed something, ran tuck-tailed and whimpering to the truck below Sam, and squeezed under its off-center cargo bed.

Sam stood up. "D'lo, don't." As she came down the stairs and crossed the barn, surreal windows in her projected image repeatedly opened and closed. Had he fallen asleep in spite of himself? If he were dreaming, though, he'd done a damned good job of calling up the barn and the contagious anxiety of the animals.

In any event, D'lo's ghost ignored his plea. She climbed the steps to his loft and emerged through the hole in the planking to stand—to sway, actually—in the barn's darkest shadows, weighing his merits and passing sentence.

Except, Sam knew, she'd already done that. What she was doing now was relishing the fact of her ex-husband at her mercy and at a loss for some action that wouldn't cheapen his death if he couldn't keep her from killing him. She was dragging out the moment because he'd ignored both her and Payz for so many years and because he'd driven her to kill herself in a way that had mutilated not only her body but her spirit.

"D'lo, there's nothing I can do now. Cut it out."

First, today, that Banks woman. Now, his ex-wife's ghost. It was almost enough to make him hate women—but for his relationship with Libby and his unconditional love for Paisley. It just didn't pay to draw conclusions from worst-case scenarios. You had to keep your head on your shoulders.

Which was just what D'lo hadn't done. Brandishing the alicorn, she glided through the hay bales between them like a skier taking a slalom course in slow motion. Sam shook his head, denying what she wanted to do and watching her weirdly flickering body go in and out of this reality as she approached.

"Don't," he said again.

She was two feet away, close enough to hug, close enough to hit in the chest, but all Sam could think, now that the moment of his assassination had gotten here, was that he was taking it pretty well. He had even defeated the stupid male hormones that had made him go hard on D'lo's previous calls on him. He wasn't afraid. He wasn't shamefully horny. In fact, he wasn't anything except sad to go out this way and proud to be taking it so calmly.

D'lo lifted the alicorn like a dagger. She was gripping it so hard that she had squeezed blood—or, anyway, a thinner and blacker substitute—from the grooves in her palm. This stuff trickled down her forearm and dripped from her elbow, stinking like sulfur and La Plata County mud. The falling drops were hypnotizing.

"Dolores, I'm sorry."

She stabbed. The point of the alicorn plunged into his breast, bringing a terrible pricking pang and then an ache that spread out like the canopy of a shade tree.

"*Mother!*" a familiar voice cried. "*Mother!*"

Sam couldn't tell where these cries came from. If they were meant to stop D'lo from killing him, they failed, for D'lo struck him six or seven more times. Sam staggered, caught the edge of a hay bale behind his knees, and fell backward, his pain as big as the sky and his blood raying out like the crimson sprinklers of a Roman candle. Crip banged his stall, and one of the kar'tajans bleated in protest and terror. Who was going to take care of the poor bastards now?

"You are," D'lo said a short while later.

Sam sat up. His chest ached, but there was no wound above his heart, or anywhere else, and he wasn't bleeding. D'lo's *ini'putic'* had spoken to him, and she had spoken to him as most people usually do, through a mouth. With an elbow on the hay bales on either side of him, Sam struggled to his feet.

There was the *ini'putc'*, still going in and out of this reality like a remote network feed, opening and closing tinfoil windows on itself—but its body had a head, D'lo's as she had looked as Sam's young bride. Meanwhile, he kept obsessively examining himself for signs of her butchery. There weren't any.

"Okay," the ghost said. "Live."

More and more holes opened in her, this time without closing up again. Pretty soon, she had vanished. The alicorn with which she had tried to kill him lay abandoned on the planking.

To keep from falling out of the loft, Sam felt behind him for a hay bale and sat down. Amazingly, it was almost time to tube-feed the kar'tajans again.

# 32

"*The bastard. He better.*"

On their post-midnight trip home, these words kept popping into Libby's head, periodically putting a heedless smile on her lips as she drove the evergreen-lined roller-coaster highway home, gripping the wheel as if trying to splinter it. Bo was dying, but Bo had an ally in Paisley, just as Libby did, and surely, by now, Sam and the vet had done *something* to save a few of the infected kar'tajans (in addition to Phylly) on her ranch.

It was after 2:00 A.M. when they cruised past the Twin Peaks and came barreling down on the veterinary clinic on Huerfano's western outskirts. Libby slowed, not planning to stop, but simply to see if Brinkley were there, for he often slept in a room off the main examination areas of his cinder-block office. To her surprise, she saw yellow-orange light spilling from the blinds on a long window facing the Twin Peaks and the vet's truck and horse trailer parked between the railroad-tie planters.

"A five-minute stop, Paisley. That okay with you?"

"Sure."

"We'll hit Dr. Nesheim's next. Bo won't like that, but maybe, at the med center, they can prolong his life."

"No!" Bo said from the back seat. "No, no, no, no, *no*!"

Libby, parking in Dr. Brinkley's lot, was surprised to hear Bo speak. So far on their trip, he had either ranted incoherently or lain comatose in the sacred linen. She and Paisley looked into the back and saw Bo returning their stares from a sun-burned face with eyes as big and shiny as a newborn calf's.

"They can make it easier for you there," Libby said. "They can give you painkillers."

"They can keep me from experiencing my own death. And they can give me a place to do it"—he twisted the word—"alone."

"We'd stay with you, Bo."

"*Don't do that to me!*" Bo's face, in the sheen thrown into the car by the security lights, looked ghoulish, almost demonic. Also, he was burrito-wrapped in a sheet patterned like a dance diagram for a hit from the 1960s, "Barefootin'." She smiled. It was hard to imagine the Walking Man (Jesus, as Paisley had already told her) boogying to that ditty, a piece of throw-away Americana that Libby hadn't thought of in years.

"Bo, hush." She turned to Paisley. "Watch him, okay?"

Libby got out and jogged up to the clinic. Its front door was unlocked. When she pushed on through, however, a cowbell hanging from the inside handle clattered like a stack of soup cans toppling over. Startled, she clutched her heart.

"Dr. Brinkley," she called. "Hey, Dr. Brinkley?"

She followed the light seeping from under a nearby door—which stood an inch or two ajar—and peeked inside to find the old man perched on a stool at a Formica counter with a sink in it. He was sitting beside a rack of glass slides and a microscope that looked as old as an Anton van Leeuwenhoek original.

"What gives?" Libby said.

The vet did not reply, and she feared that he had died sitting over the microscope. He remained upright, though, because he had been too unbendingly focused on his work to fall over. This scare was even bigger than that provoked by the cowbell, and Libby heard herself gasp like a soap-opera heroine.

At that, Brinkley looked up. The whites of his eyes were as red as a bloodhound's; the bags under them were big enough to put sandwiches in. His gaze seemed askew and inhuman, and the wattles under his chin gave him the look of a drugged monitor lizard or a brain-damaged bull turkey.

"My God, are you okay, Dr. Brinkley?"

He was slow to come out of whatever trance he'd drifted

into, but Libby was eventually able to wrest from him an account of the events of the past four days. He had left her ranch only a few hours ago, intending to try to catch up on his sleep—but the call of kar'tajan-related lab work had sidetracked him and he had never managed to get to bed. He was pretty goddamn bogged out, Brinkley confessed, but an unshakable curiosity about the identity of the disease vector in the kar'tajans' mysterious sickness had made him forget about trying to sleep.

He had spent the past six hours studying the microscope slides that, during the untreated phase of Phylly's illness, he had made from her mucous membranes, various body sores, and other pertinent tissues. He had kept these slides frozen while trying to devise a treatment method for Phylly, but tonight pure research rather than out-the-barn-door medicine had called him and he had answered that call. Libby quickly learned that "out-the-barn-door medicine" was Brinkley's term for the kind that a vet resorted to when it was too late to prevent an epizootic—an epidemic among animals—by taking commonsensical measures in advance.

"What have you found out?"

"This fucking anemia-arteritis combination is a disease that an animal can recover from—Over Here at least—if given some TLC and kept away from the vector that injects the virus. In fact, it can probably develop a lifelong immunity if given enough time between exposures to the virus—say, seven or eight months. But your crazy unicorns, ma'am, they go back and get themselves fucking re-exposed even after they've gotten well, which they mostly haven't, and such behavior's likely to knock off the whole lot of 'em."

"Dr. Brinkley—" Libby regretted her audible impatience.

"Okay, you know that, but today Sam and I found out that one of the doors to Over There has been shut by a rockslide—the one near Abbot's Pate. Now we need to close the door in Naismith's Mine to keep the silly ninnies from reinfecting themselves forever, or till they all die—whichever comes first."

Brinkley's pouchy eyes glanced down at his hands.

"Okay, you know that too. What I've found out is that the vector's a fly the size of a protozoan, like the period at the end of a sentence. It lays its eggs near the nose, mouth, eyes, bunghole, or reproductive organs of the kar'tajan. Then its developing larvae grow up eating the soft tissues where their lovin' mamas have attached them. Call them muckflies, if you need a name. My Latin's lousy, and I'm not acquainted with a species quite like it Over Here." He nodded at his slides. "I've found the fucking boogers in both the adult and larval stages, and they're none too pretty."

He turned the microscope around for Libby, and she peered down, past her own lashes, at a tiny monster with hairy legs, bubblelike compound eyes, and transparent jaws similar to a crab's pincers. She raised her head and shoved the microscope back toward Brinkley, who adjusted the viewing tube with fingers that were perhaps better suited to squeezing pennies flat.

"Ugh."

"There she is, Miss Mucka Mosca, your ideal. But that filthy little wench is only responsible for surface sores and a few minor digestive problems. And she and her consorts can't survive here. Although their larvae eat kar'tajan flesh, the adults don't, and whatever they eat Over There isn't available Over Here—so they die not long after scumbling forth as grown-ups.

"It's the virus that Miss Mucka Mosca lugs around that's the killer, a virus that probably winters Over There in a host—maybe a vulture, or a greedy little desert rodent, or the fruit of a plant that the adult flies go dizzy over. If that's the way it is, which seems likely, I don't know how the fuck we'll ever figure out what the sonuvabitchin' virus's July-to-December host is or how anybody Over Here can do anything to solve the problem."

Libby thought, I need to get back to Paisley and Bo. And what good is knowing the identity of the vector if you don't know how to isolate or control the virus that causes the disease?

"We need to slam down that doorway in Naismith's Mine. We need to dynamite the sucker shut. It's the only way we'll save the ones Sam's looking after. Phylly, too. She's virus-free right now, and she can't be reinfected Over Here because there aren't any living adults to lay their eggs on her. But if she goes back through for the winter—our winter—those otherworldly muckflies will hit her again. Another bout of their lousy anemia-arteritis just might do for her, too."

"Look, Dr. Brinkley, you need to get some sleep."

The old man peered around. "Where the hell's Bo?"

"Outside in the car. Dying."

Brinkley stood up. "Let me have a look at him."

"It'll wait until tomorrow, Dr. Brinkley. Paisley's with us, and she's got poor Beaumont God-wrapped."

The vet may not have understood this remark, but he subsided, and Libby hurried back outside. Bo looked to be dozing again, and as they drove on into Huerfano and then up along the ridge behind the hospital to Dr. Nesheim's split-level house, Libby told Paisley all that Brinkley had just told her.

"Will you blow up the mine? To shut that second spirit door?"

"That mine's an accident waiting to happen, Paisley. We should have done it years ago."

"Wait another day."

Libby glanced out of the corner of her eye at Sam's daughter, seeing the man in the young woman and the young woman in the man. Meanwhile, as Bo's car climbed the asphalt road above the hospital, the lights of the shabby old mining community twinkled off to their left like grounded stars.

Nesheim heard a distant pounding. His first thought was that he was listening to a scene from the Charles Laughton version of *The Hunchback of Notre Dame*, when the mob puts a battering ram to the great wooden doors of the cathedral—but he had watched that late movie a night or two ago, to cool out from a frustrating day at the medical center, and he soon realized that there was someone at *his* door. He threw on his robe, groped his way through the dark house, and opened the front door.

"Dr. Nesheim," Libby Quarrels said, "Bo's dying."

He followed her down his inlaid-stone walk to the driveway and Bo's dusty automobile. He looked through the car's window to see his outpatient cocooned in a sheet with ocher, or blood-colored, footprints patterned across it, and a dark-skinned young woman in the front seat. He couldn't imagine what the hell they were doing, or where the hell they'd been or why the hell Bo looked as if he were undergoing some sort of crazy insectoidal metamorphosis.

"What do you want me to do?" he asked Libby.

"We all know he's dying. Should I take him"—she nodded at the hospital downslope—"there? Or carry him home?"

Bo's face was upside down to the doctor. But his eyes opened, rolled back in an attempt to focus, and blinked. "Snowy Falls," he pleaded. "Nobody wants to buy it in a place called Huerfano. Not even Alfie Tuck wanted that."

Nesheim opened the car door and placed a hand on Bo's brow. Bo felt feverish. His lips, ear tips, and nose had a muted ruddiness hinting at . . . sunburn. Did these folks have no sense? Did they think a person with a depressed immune system and visible cancer lesions could play in the sun with impunity? Where had they been? Picnicking in the Great Sand Dunes National Monument? Inner-tubing on the Cucharas River? If so, they all deserved a spanking. Hell, they all deserved to be shot—even if, in Bo's case, such a measure would soon be unnecessary.

"Don't put me in the hospital."

Nesheim recinched his robe. "You think the folks down there are chomping at the bit to get their rubber gloves on you? Come on, Beaumont—think again."

"Then I should take him home," Libby said.

"Yeah. Now. The sooner the better. I'd hate to die in this ugly burg, too. But I think I'd hate even worse dying in the back seat of a foreign car swaddled in Sasquatch footprints."

"Jesus's," the dark young woman up front said.

"Then he was a bigger man than I would've suspected," Nesheim said. "At any rate, get moving, Libby. Now."

"What should we do when we get home?"

"Wash him up. Put him to bed. Don't fret the details, though, because I'm going to drive up there behind you."

Nesheim watched Libby run around to the driver's side, give him a grim thumb's-up, hop in, and drive off. He dressed as quickly as he could, backed his Porsche out of the boxy garage slung under his cantilevered breakfast deck, and followed Libby Quarrels, his dying outpatient, and that young Indian woman—Sam Coldpony's daughter?—up the starlit highway to Snowy Falls.

* * *

At the Tipsy Q, Paisley felt—for the first time since they had left the reservation—uprooted and uncertain. She had traveled to various communities in western and southwestern Colorado with her debate team; she had even visited cities like Denver, Phoenix, and Santa Fe. But her father, who had come to see her only once in all the years since his and Mama D'lo's divorce, and who even then had tried to sneak away without talking to her, had invited her to come see him on this ranch for an extended visit, and the prospect of living somewhere other than La Plata County for a month or more had suddenly begun to frighten her.

It was all made worse by the fact that a man dying of AIDS—but kept from dying *right now* by the magic of the sacred linen that she had extorted from Papa Tuqú-payá—would almost certainly journey on to the spirit would on the first full day of her visit. What an omen. Maybe the Holy He-She, setting aside the apparent meaning of Paisley's Sun Dance visions, regarded this reunion with her father as a betrayal of their people. Maybe . . .

A dog stood in front of their headlamps, barking fiercely; it was also waggling its butt around. Its ferocious barking and the moist night air derailed Paisley's train of thought.

"There are lights on in the barn," Libby said. "Sam's probably in there. Why don't you go get him?"

Me? Why me? Paisley glanced at the barn, looked at the Anglo woman again, squeezed her blue-jeaned knees together, and shook her head. Not a "No," but a bemused "What's going on?"

"Go on," Libby said. "You came up here to see him. So you'll see him. Besides, Dr. Nesheim's not here yet, and we're going to need some help getting Bo inside."

Paisley got out and walked like a zombie toward the barn. The dog ignored her to wrap itself around Libby, repeatedly banging her on the legs and running in front of her as she tried to get to the house to turn on the porch light. Then Paisley saw her father come out of the barn and stop dead in his tracks. Seeing her, he had no better idea what to do than she did, and his uncertainty, a kind of guilty shyness, gave Paisley time to remember that the Ute gods have empowered her. She—Sam Coldpony's daughter—had made up her mind to do this, and her visions in the Thirst House had empowered her to follow through on her resolve.

"Papa," she said, hardly a sparrow's peep.

He looked at her as if she were an *ini'putc'*, a thing of smoke or shadow. Nearby aspens dripped from an earlier rain.

"Papa," she said more loudly. She crossed to the barn, put her hands on his shoulders, and, being almost as tall as he was, kissed him on the forehead. Guiltily, shyly, he let his arms encircle her and his fingers knot in the small of her back. His face remained as blank as a stone, not smiling, not frowning—a poker face, Papa Tuqú-payá would have called it, one full of neither apprehension nor glee—and yet Paisley decoded her father through this blankness and understood that he was both dumbstruck and moved.

"That Anglo man," she said, nodding at the car. "He's . . ."

Sam's brows knitted, and he released his daughter, only to take her hand again and to lead her at a brisk pace across the drive to the car. Here, he saw the god sheet, the dying Beaumont Gavin, and also the woman, his boss, who had confessed to Paisley on the first leg of their trip from Mama D'lo's vandalized house that she loved him. Paisley saw Libby smile at her father. She heard her father, unsmiling, say, "Let's get the white eyes to bed, ladies," and then she helped the two of them do just that.

"Get everybody here," Bo kept saying. "Get everybody here. I can't do this alone."

Libby, Sam, and Paisley rolled him out of his burrito wrap, the fabulous threadbare god sheet that Paisley had blackmailed Sky into loaning her, and Libby, trying to refold it, held it up so that she could examine the ocher footprints that the Walking Man had somehow burned into the molecular structure of the relic's fabric.

Just as Nesheim had said, they were *big* footprints, but comely, and Libby had to marvel at the phenomenon that had permitted their transfer to an old cotton sheet. It was a kind of wonky New World Shroud of Turin, and Libby was freshly boggled by it.

Once she had the sheet folded, Paisley took it, and the two of them visited the utility room so that Libby could show her new houseguest how to use the washing machine. The girl nixed the use of bleach, but agreed that half a cup of detergent in hot water probably wouldn't deface the artifact.

Although Paisley said that it would be okay with her if Libby added some other items—socks, underwear, jeans—to make up a full load, Libby refused. If the dye in any of these other garments ran and discolored the scared Muache relic, she would have felt like dog puke. She would have considered herself no better than a tomb robber or a monument defacer.

"Get everybody here," Bo was saying. "Get everybody here." On the bed in the converted study, he lay stripped to his skivvies and feebly thrashing. Sam was sponging him down with soap and a warm washcloth—under the direction, and with the occasional assistance, of Dr. Nesheim, who had arrived while Libby was showing Paisley how to operate her antique Maytag.

"There's something in his hand," Sam said. "He won't let go."

"Something?" Bo mocked his friend. "*Something?*"

Paisley knelt beside Bo, whispered to him. He unclenched his fingers and, to Libby's surprise, revealed a unicorn figurine—one of several she had shoplifted from Bali Hi Imports in Atlanta, but the only one that had made it back to Colorado.

It was the pewter toy she had retrieved from that gas-station rest room—the one that, stuck in Raton Pass between New Mexico and Colorado, Bo had pointed to and derisively called "fantasy," even while ranting that the foil-wrapped tickler was "reality" because it symbolized sex, and sex, of course, was "reality heightened, all your stakes raised, even your winnings on sufferance, your every loss potentially fatal."

What else had Bo said? Libby remembered: "Let no one hand you a two-bit unicorn when reality's so damned expensive that only your life will pay for it!"

Now, though, he was clutching that pewter unicorn—fantasy, as he had once decried it—for all he was worth, having seen that the mythological creatures it so sadly tried to represent existed in truth, in a way that redeemed them from both banality and wish-fulfillment daydreams.

But the figurine was digging a tiny horse-shaped wound into his palm, and Paisley, whispering again, relieved him of it. Then she stepped aside so that the two men would have room to work.

Eventually, Sam and the doctor got the half-delirious Bo into a clean pair of satin peejays, and Nesheim, over Bo's angry protests, administered a sedative injection.

Libby brought a television tray into the room and placed on it the triptych of photographs that Bo had brought back to the ranch from Atlanta—his dead father, Mama Josey, and little brother Ned. Maybe a glimpse of their photographed faces would soothe him, maybe it would make up for their physical absence from the room in which he was about to die. Paisley set the pewter kar'tajan on the tray with the photographs, and Bo, clearly growing woozier and woozier, widened and narrowed his eyes at the arrangement.

"Not just their goddamn pictures," he said. "Get the *people* here, m'lady. Get the people."

"Okay," Libby said. "I'll try." She meant it, too. There was no way short of resurrecting the dead that she could get Nathaniel Gavin to her house, but she would ring up Ned, she would telephone Bo's bitter and unforgiving mother, she would even try to run down Gary on the Prentice Ranch outside of Dumas, Texas—to inform that sweet-talking, two-timing asshole that the first cousin he had sent her off to save was now in the Grim Reaper's clutches and the only way to see him again this side of a problematic afterlife was to drop everything and get his calloused fanny one last time all the way up here to her—yes, *her*—ranch.

She'd do that for Bo because she loved the scrawny fag. There was a helluva lot about him to love, a helluva lot to celebrate. She'd make long-distance calls on his behalf until she had run out of bank funds, until the Russians lobbed a multiple-warhead nuclear device on the Tipsy Q, until the most tenderhearted archangel in God's heaven told her she'd gone overboard and was making the kind of show-offy display that gives love a bad name. That was how much she loved her rodeo-addled ex-husband's scrawny AIDS-stricken lesion-disfigured twinky first cousin, and she didn't give a flying fuck who knew it, either.

Suddenly, Libby felt Sam's arm around her shoulder. With his other hand, he was dabbing her eyes with a handkerchief that he had probably used to blow his nose in, twist the tops off dirty cans of axle grease, and wipe down dusty saddles. Well, so what? All that mattered was that he was beside her, trying, none too successfully, to dry her eyes, and letting the warmth of his body and the warmth of his concern do what they could to make the hurt go away. It was a lot, surprisingly—it was really a lot.

Nesheim had a pallet in Bo's room. Bo, he said, would probably get through the night okay, and if people began showing up tomorrow to see him, well, they'd have even odds of actually getting to talk to him before he "passed on."

Paisley, who was exhausted, took Libby's bed. Sam insisted on staying in the barn with the kar'tajans, and Libby, semirecovered from the emotions that had overwhelmed her at Bo's bedside, settled into the cushion-sprung sofa in her front room and made a series of long-distance calls.

It was no fun waking up people at four in the morning, and even less fun when you had to tell them that somebody was dying and that that unfortunate somebody wanted them to come to his bedside, hold his hand, talk to him, and experience with him the unoriginal agony of his goodbye. Ned, whom she called first, surprised her not by agreeing to come—Libby'd had little doubt on that score—but by announcing that he had already received permission from his boss to make a trip down from Denver tomorrow, anyway. He also said he was sorry for his part in creating a situation in which such a terrible burden could devolve to her, and he asked if there were anything he could do to ease it.

"Call your mother," Libby jumped to say. "Tell her Bo's almost gone. Tell her he wants her here."

Ned agreed to try, but said that he was in bad odor with Mama Josey himself and that it would probably take armed guards to get her to make such a trip. She had written Bo off long before Papa Nate's death, and she was in the process—if she hadn't already succeeded—of disinheriting him, Brother Ned, even from her memory, for his role in the development and promotion of a silicon condom called Kartajans.

"Just try," Libby said. "That's all you can do."

She telephoned Pamela Fay Quarrels, Gary's mother, in Colorado Springs, gave her the depressing scoop, learned that Pamela Fay had been ill herself and so wouldn't be able to come, and got from her, maybe as a sop for squeezing out her regrets, the telephone number of Gary's bunkhouse on the Prentice Ranch.

Wonderful, Libby thought. Just what I want to do. Wake up an entire barracks of cowhands to talk to the chief Ding Dong Daddy of Dumas, Texas, my ever-cheatin' ex.

As it happened, she got just one cowhand (a Hispanic, going by his accent), who told her—cordially—that Gary hadn't been around for two or three days and that he really didn't know who she could call to track him down.

After that, Libby placed telephone calls to Carrie Plourde, Jim and Tanis Watling, and another past associate at CCG whose number the Watlings gave her. Bo's former bosses expressed what sounded to Libby like genuine concern, although they both believed that it would be impossible for them to get away soon enough to arrive in Snowy Falls before Bo died, and the other man, obviously still half asleep, kept asking, sweetly, doggedly, where to send flowers or a charitable donation.

It was Carrie Plourde's response that croggled Libby. She had once let Bo live in her home. She had, in fact, been the immediate cause of his breach with his parents, for her concern for him had prompted her to telephone them with the unwelcome word that he was an AIDS victim. This morning, though, this Plourde person replied to Libby's news as if she didn't believe it, as if she couldn't quite remember who Libby was, as if the matter were in any event none of her affair and its recounting over a long-distance telephone line a tasteless intrusion on her privacy.

You bitch, Libby thought. You stuck-up, heartless bitch.

Aloud, she apologized for bringing such bleak news so early in the morning. She repeated that Bo had wanted her to know because Carrie's help at a difficult time in his life had *saved* his life—for a while, anyway—and he had never spoken of her to Libby or to anyone else without saying so.

Once off the telephone, her shirt wringing wet and a headache drumming at her temples, Libby cursed the woman long and hard. She stopped doing that to curse Bo's parents, and stopped doing that to curse his disease, and stopped doing that to rock back and forth on the edge of her beat-up sofa, softly crying. Life was a lead-in to death, and who could say if you were a lucky schmuck or a poor fool if your lead-in was longer than somebody else's?

Then she realized that there were some local people who should know what was happening to Bo, and she called Arvill Rudd's place to give him and his wife the sad news and to ask Rudd to pass word along to Brooklyn Terry and some of Rudd's other hands. She called Gina Thrower at the boardinghouse—Gina had already been up and at it for an hour, anyway—and left messages on the answering machines of the Methodist church in Snowy Falls and of Father Oskar Zinzalow at the Catholic church in Huerfano.

After that, she could think of no one else to call and sat back on the sofa listening to Dr. Nesheim's easy breathing, her sedated ex-cousin-in-law's occasional moans, and total silence from Paisley in her own bedroom. The little house seemed a world unto itself, a harbor on the shore of heaven. . . .

Paisley dreamed. Even after the visionary overload that she'd experienced a few house ago in the Thirst House, she dreamed. The Walking Man came to her, and again he came to her clad in the hide and head of a kar'tajan.

Mama D'lo also appeared—not, this time, as a headless specter but instead as the ghost of a perfectly made young woman closer to Paisley's age than to her father Sam's.

Paisley was also visited by the *ini'putc'* of Alvin Powers and that of the young Anglo dying in the adjacent room.

Even in her dream, however, she understood that Bo Gavin hadn't yet crossed all the way into the spirit realm. His presence among the other ghosts was as an initiate. When they talked to her, they talked around the Anglo's would-be *ini'putc'*. Yet they spoke *about* him, as if his fate mattered to them and as if what they said might eventually bestow true spiritual standing on him.

The Walking Man pointed toward the white mountains rising like white shadows from the white hardpan. He pointed, Paisley assumed, to inform Mama D'lo of something she had not known before.

Alvin Powers, Papa Sky's predecessor as Sun Dance chief, stood behind Mama D'lo pressing down on her head—a younger version of the head that she had shotgunned to Kingdom Come in March—as if to "cement in" the knowledge, and the *powa'a,* that the Walking Man was mysteriously passing on to her.

As for Paisley, she realized that she was watching these events not as an onlooker there among the *ini'putc'* but, instead, from a hole in the sky high above them. Still, all that they did was easy to see, and all that they told one another in their powwow was easy to eavesdrop on.

Like the Holy He-She, Paisley watched and listened for as long as this powwow lasted. When it was over, the Walking Man walked away to one horizon, Mama D'lo to another, and Alvin Powers to yet another—but the young Anglo's would-be ghost remained at the heart of their everywhere-at-once whiteness, looking after the three who had departed and fading fading fading from view. . . .

Libby tried to sleep on her sofa. It would not let her sleep on it. It bucked and rocked and doubled over and mounded beneath her without ever moving, and she realized that she would probably not sleep decently again until Bo died.

That was a good reason for hoping that he bought it soon, but, of course, she would happily contend with insomnia the rest of her days if God granted Bo a cure that returned him to physical health and likewise nudged him into the kind of creative renaissance that would make his life valuable to him and others again.

"Insomnia forever," Libby said to the empty room. "Give me Bo alive and I'll give you insomnia forever."

And then, knowing that she wasn't going to sleep, she let her thoughts drift to Sam, or was carried by her love for Sam to such thoughts, and got up and trudged across the tread-rutted mud of her front yard to the barn.

Phylly greeted her first, trotting from under one of the lofts and nibbling at her breast pocket to see if she had brought her a treat. Rum balls, Libby suspected, since the old vet had spoiled her that way, although she was sure that Phyl would accept a sugar cube or a piece of hard candy like butterscotch or horehound.

"Where's Sam?" she asked the kar'tajan, pushing the creature's muzzle aside. "Where's that damned Ute, eh?"

Libby walked deeper into the barn. Her GM pickup was listing to one side, and Bounty was nowhere about. She found

Sam kneeling in a stall using a dose syringe to glop a mixture of dehydrated alfalfa meal and Foal-Lac milk replacer into the esophagostomy tube of the youngest of the six kar'tajans in the barn.

Sam was holding the enfeebled creature's head up with one hand, supporting it under the jaw. With the other, he squeezed the bulb on the nutrient syringe. As he fed the long yearling, he crooned a tuneless song so that the kar'tajan, whose eye flashed blue when it saw Libby, would refrain from thrashing or trying to stand. Then Sam became aware of Libby too, and he finished pumping potassium-laden gloop into his patient, laid the syringe aside, and stood to greet her in a place where, surrounded by animals, they both felt that they had a measure of privacy.

"Hello, Sam Coldpony."

"Hello, Unicorn Libby Quarrels."

"I missed you."

"You took a damned long time getting out here."

"I had stuff to do. Important stuff. I'm finished now."

"No, you're not. There's still important stuff to do."

"I know. The kar'tajans. Was this all you could find? Only six? Out of seventy, eighty, maybe even a hundred?"

"I wasn't talking kar'tajans, hon."

Libby traced the line of Sam's jaw with her finger. There was stubble there. Ute men had beards—or, at least, their beginnings.

"I told you I missed you," she said. "Did you? Me, I mean?"

"I missed you. When I wasn't busy keeping Brinkley awake and Phylly from shish-kebabbing the local wildlife."

"Damned straight, you missed me. All the time. Even when you were keeping Brinkley awake and Phylly et cetera."

"Okay."

"What the hell do you mean, okay?"

"I mean okay. Okay means okay, Miss Libby."

"Stop that 'Miss Libby' shit. Coldpony, I'm in love with you. I want you to make a honest woman of me."

"Will the wages be any better?"

"Better than the wages of sin, you son of a bitch. Ten times better. Five, anyway. Try me and see."

"Okay."

"You've got to say something more than okay, Coldpony. Okay is not exactly the friggin' password to my heart."

"Okay, okay. I love you too."

"You bastard," Libby said mildly. "You better."

# 33

Bo woke up at 8:00 A.M. It annoyed him that he had missed the sunrise. This was going to be his last day. Although he had more energy than he had any right to expect, he had it only to take care of the concluding, and conclusive, business of his life—all of which he would jettison before nightfall and watch tumble away in a backwash of decaying memory.

"I want a bath," he told Dr. Nesheim. "You guys did the best you could sponging me down. Now, though, a bath."

Libby ran the water. Sam and the doctor carried him naked to the tub and eased him in. Lying there, his knees like pale islands and his sex floating as languidly as a sea anemone, Bo marveled again that the damned thing had betrayed him. It hadn't meant to, though, and in a different world it wouldn't have. To get to some other world, then, why not just slide down and drown?

"No pajamas when I'm finished," he said, erasing that option. "I want my Hawaiian shirt."

Hearing him say so pleased Libby. He had ticked her off at the Sun Dance wearing the touristy-looking thing, but who wanted to be anything but a tourist in death's territories? In any case, she gathered up the shirt, along with some of Bo's other dirty clothes, and put them all in her washing machine.

Paisley helped by carrying the damp god sheet out the back door and pinning it with colorful plastic pins to the clothesline. A breeze had come up, and the sheet whipped back and forth so that the Walking Man's footprints seemed to be doing a spastic boogaloo in the mountain-ringed dance hall of Remuda Creek Meadow.

Later, when Libby opened the curtains in Bo's room (where he lay in a terry-cloth robe waiting for his khaki trousers and his poinsettia shirt to come out of the dryer), Bo could look out the window and see Jesus dancing. It was not many men who got to see that, and he wished that Keith Jory could have seen it before *his* death. Of course, Bo had not been there at the end and had no notion of what Keith had or hadn't experienced before going down forever.

But seeing the Master dance, seeing the dawn-colored footprints of the Walking Man jitterbug the mountain air . . . well, could any leavetaking be better?

People began to arrive before noon. Libby hadn't thought about feeding everyone, but Gina Thrower and her girls took care of that by bringing fried chicken, cold cuts, potato salad, cole slaw, and a dozen loaves of bread from her boardinghouse. Arvill Rudd, who, Libby later learned, had paid for this impromptu feed, had three of his cowhands—under Brooklyn Terry's command—set up folding tables from the Methodist church to receive the food.

In spite of the unpredictable wind, nothing blew away; because of it, bothersome insects were few. Everyone but Bo was able to eat outside. Bo wanted nothing to eat. He lay in his room—in his chosen deathday outfit—receiving look-in visits from Snowy Falls residents and patiently awaiting the coming of his kin, including Ned and, God willing, his mother.

Ned Gavin, crusing up in his Continental, was taken aback by the crowd at the Tipsy Q. There were cars and pickups parked along Highway 69, in the aspen stand just below the highway, and in muddy pockets next to the barn and the house. The manager of a used-car dealership, Ned mused, would have enjoyed making offers for some of these clunkers; however, he did see Dr. Nesheim's Porsche, somebody else's Cadillac, and two or three tony imports among the automotive flotsam clogging the drive.

What the hell was going on? It looked as if the folks of Snowy Falls had turned Bo's dying day into a public carnival.

Ned parked on a precarious slant at the drive's northern end, then picked his way through the aspens toward the tables near the front porch. A lanky, mauve-lipped cowhand ambled toward him with a paper plate and a jelly jar full of iced tea. He welcomed Ned, introduced himself as Brooklyn Terry, and tried to hand over both the chicken and the tea. Ned said he wasn't hungry. Terry nodded, said there would still be plenty of food later, and told him to go on in to see Miss Libby's cousin.

"Cousin-in-law," Ned said. "*Ex*-cousin-in-law."

"Whatever," Brooklyn Terry said. "Glad to have you, Mr.—?"

Ned strode on by. He went inside angry with Elizabeth. Bo was dying. That was central. Everything else was gingerbread. These people didn't belong. Their presence robbed Bo's death of dignity and Ned of the chance to talk with his brother without distraction or interruption. For the last time in either of their lives.

So why had Elizabeth allowed a miniature Pioneer Days or Fourth of July celebration to spring up around the cruel imminence of Bo's death? Because castrating bulls and shooting magpies wasn't enough to keep these people busy the whole damn summer, that was why. It appalled Ned that boredom and bad manners could lead people to such grotesque excess.

It got worse. Inside, Sam Coldpony handed Ned an unpackaged and unrolled Kartajan and asked him to blow it up and tie it off so that Paisley could link it to several others. She would then hang the entire bunch from a light fixture or a door lintel. Already, Elizabeth's cramped house was a hotbed of these freaky bouquets. They hung from her large-screen TV like oversized organic vacuum tubes, and whenever someone opened the front door or walked briskly through a room, the "balloons" would lift or bob or flap, meanwhile emitting faint rubbery squeaks.

"There's a viricidal lubricant on Kartajans," Ned said. "I'm not about to blow one up."

"The lubricant's tasteless," Sam said. "It sure as hell won't make you sick. Bo want us to do this."

What Bo really wants, Ned told himself, is to laugh me to scorn with this outrageous display. To mock me—the person who got him his ad assignment—in front of all his new friends here in Remuda County. It's all part of a public rebuke. Bo is tweaking me for not taking him up to my place in Denver when—damn it!— there was no way for me to do that. It's not the viricidal lubricant on Zubrecht's condoms that's tasteless. It's what Bo is doing to me right now. It's what Elizabeth, Coldpony, and all the lowlifes in their jeans and shitty boots have conspired to help him do. . . .

Elizabeth appeared from the bedroom. She came to him, hugged him, put her arm through his. "Ned, we're glad you're here. Come on. Bo's been waiting for you."

Ned looks bad, Bo thought. He's getting around under his own power, but he looks red-eyed and pasty-faced and slack-jawed and crapped-out. Understandable. I haven't been so hot myself lately, and Libby woke Ned up at four this morning to tell him.

The next thing that Bo noticed was that Mama Josey wasn't with Ned. Bo said nothing until after Ned had kissed him dutifully on the forehead and taken up a nearby chair, but then he couldn't help mentioning aloud that Ned had failed to bring her.

"And suppose I had," Ned said, his baby-walrus neck bright pink against his lavender shirt collar. "Would Coldpony have given her a rubber to inflate?"

"That's just so people won't cry over me. I—"

"No worries there, Beaumont. After what I've seen, no worries in *my* case, anyhow."

Bo tried to explain. "It wasn't *just* for that. It's also more or less in memory of somebody I knew down home in Huerfano."

"Beaumont," Ned said, ignoring this. "You may have wanted Mama to come, but you didn't really expect her to. In your heart, you knew she wouldn't. Otherwise, brother mine, you'd've never asked Elizabeth and all her friends to hang silicon bladders around this place as if you were decorating the men's locker room at some sort of sleazy invitational sexual olympics."

Bo was startled to have this pointed out to him and even more startled to find that it was an accurate analysis of his submerged mindset. Until this moment, he hadn't realized what having Libby and the others decorate her house with Kartajans meant. But Ned had immediately understood.

Well, he should probably be ashamed of himself. That was

what all the Gavins seemed to want from him, a forthright acknowledgment of his sins and a little private wallowing in their shame. But the thought of his mother entering a house furnished with prophylactic globes tickled him. He shut his eyes, imagining the scene.

"Maybe Mama wouldn't recognize them, Neddy."

He kept his eyes closed, resisting the tug of a smile, until he heard Ned laughing—laughing in spite of himself. Ned's laughter was so amiable that Bo gave in to his own pent-up smile.

"She probably wouldn't," Ned said. "She probably wouldn't."

"She knows what they are and what they do," Bo said, "but it's possible she's never actually seen one."

Ned agreed, and they laughed together—Ned undoubtedly sharing Bo's vision of Mama Josey carrying on some hoity-toity chitchat under a bouquet of condom balloons and never grasping the absurdity of her obliviousness. There was a kind of carrion comfort in this vision, a kind of justice, but both the "comfort" and the "justice" quickly evaporated, and Bo understood that the woman whose womb had nourished and then evicted him had evicted him forever and that he would never see her again.

Libby asked, "What did Josephine say, Ned?"

Ned explained that to Mama Josey Bo was already dead. Why go sixty miles to sit beside his corpse? Right now, she was praying for Bo's soul. As for Ned, he was in an immoral line of work and should be doing everything in his power to get out. Soon.

There it is, Bo thought, my mother's goodbye. The last words that she'd ever said to him—caustic, revulsion-filled words—were "You're evil, Beaumont. So evil you can't even pretend any more you're not." Uttering them, she had condemned him to hell.

Just to entice her to Snowy Falls (even if only to lay a fresh curse on his head), Bo was ready to drag himself out of bed and to stagger from room to room taking down all the Kartajans bouquets. But Mama Josey no longer cared. There was *no* gesture he could make that would redeem him in her eyes.

"Maybe if *you* called her," Ned told Libby.

Libby left Bo's bedside. She returned moments later

carrying the telephone from the front room. She plugged it into a jack near the rolltop, placed the telephone on Bo's coverlet, and dialed the Gavin home in Pueblo. Bo watched her as if she were undertaking an iffy experiment in animal husbandry, like waking a colony of sleepy bees by poking their hive with a stick.

"Mrs. Gavin," Libby said after some waltzing-around-the-rose-bush preliminaries, "I'm going to put you son on." ("*I won't talk to him!*" Bo could hear his mother reply. "*I've said everything to him I intend to say.*") "But you have to hear him out, Mrs. Gavin. You're not an unprincipled person. You'd never slam a receiver down. It isn't in you to show your hindquarters, Mrs. Gavin, even if someone less gracious than you is doing just that." ("*How do you know what is or isn't in me? How do you—*") "It isn't. It just isn't. That's why I know you'll listen to what Beaumont has to say when I put him on. Okay? Okay. Here he is."

"Mama?"

Silence. Not an empty receiver, but silence.

"Mama, listen. I love you. Sweet Christ, woman, you've never known how much."

She's not replying, she's not acknowledging me—but she hasn't hung up. Libby's expertly manipulated her into listening to me. At this point, that's even more than I could've hoped for.

"Mama, just a couple of things. I also hate you. Along with this unshakable love, there's a load of raw hate."

There. That ought to be all the excuse my chain-smoking mama needs to slam down on me.

But no—she's still aboard.

"Listen, Mama, this hate is ferocious. I've imagined stripping you naked on a city street. I've imagined tattooing a smarmy Adolf Hitler mustache on your upper lip. I've even envisioned taking you on a TV talk show, putting my arm around you, and doing a stand-up routine about the vile ways you used to bully Dad, or condescend to Ned and me, or trot out your brain-damaged prejudices. It would've been hilarious."

Bo caught his breath, squeezed the handset. "And it would've been unfair—cruelly unfair."

Still with me? Yeah, apparently. My mother—humanity's answer to the smoke-belching steel mills of Pueblo.

"The only goddamn reason I hate you so much is because I love you so much I can't help but hate you for not loving me back the way I want you to. See? That's why I'm heaping all this upchuck and sugar on your head. Can't you damn-all see?"

"Bo—" Ned said.

Bo put his hand over the mouthpiece. "Ned, shut up." He took his hand away. "Mama, this is doing me in. This is really pushing me." From the corner of one eye, he saw Jesus's bloody footprints tap-dancing on the breeze. "So listen closely. Listen closely, Mommy dear, and you shall hear of the nitwit love of Beaumont the Queer." Not too bad for an expiring fag, consumed with that which he was nourished by.

"Beaumont, you can't talk to Mama like—"

"Neddy, stay out of this." Bo uncovered the mouthpiece again. "Mama, maybe you'll go to your grave convinced of my willful evil, sure that I'm down in Mr. Nick's Subterranean Bordello, buggering and being buggered by Beelzebub and the Boys. Maybe—God help me, God help us all—maybe that's where I'll be. If so, what I'm about to tell you probably won't seem to be anything but a smelly parting poot from the black sheep of the Gavin clan."

Or ewe-ram, Bo thought. (You ram, I ram, we all ram for Notre Dame, Beloved Lady of Our Bleeding Lamb.)

"Listen, Mama, it's okay. If it ever starts bothering you—consigning me to hell, I mean—just remember I loved you and kept on loving you, and that it's okay, it's honestly okay. You have no call to blame yourself for how I turned out, nor can I fault you for seeming to excommunicate me from your affections. I know more about betrayal than you'll ever know. It's that knowledge that'll send me to hell, not the other. If I can forgive myself, which I'm doing, or trying to do, well then, by God, I can forgive you too, can't I? You, the woman who pushed me out of darkness and who gave me the unspeakably precious gift of light?"

"*Beaumont*," his mother said.

"It's not you who's making me hand it back. It's not you. And I love you for the pain you bore to bear it to me."

A distant thump, plastic nudging plastic, and Bo knew that Mama Josey had hung up. That was that. He let the receiver drop to his lap. Libby, standing by his bed, picked it up and cradled it. No one said anything. Bo turned to his side and through the film on his eyes—like petroleum jelly on a camera lens—watched Papa Sky's disembodied, footloose Jesus dance.

A little later, Libby sent Ned out to his Lincoln to fetch his tenor sax and stop for something to eat if he felt like it. To Ned, the clear implication was that, considering his girth, he must surely feel like it, but maybe he was reacting like an out-and-out paranoid. He had been behaving that way since first driving up and finding the Tipsy Q overrun with cowboys and Indians.

Outside, the summer sunlight made him narrow his eyes. There were even more people on the premises, many of them cowboys hanging around the barn and the horse trap.

In the aspen stand ahead of him, some teenage boys were chasing one another in mad circles through the trees. Although they were taking almost supernatural pains not to laugh or shout—like mimes in an arty foreign film—they would sometimes lob a water balloon, halt dead to watch it burst among the branches or go *splat!* on one of their fellow hooligans' backs, then run back to a spigot on the side of Libby's house to rearm themselves. It took no imagination to figure out what they were using for balloons.

Ned got his saxophone and opted to go back to the house by way of the barn.

On his walk by, a Chicano cowboy waylaid him. "Hey, you should see what old Coldpony's got in there, man. I've never seen nothing like it in my life. Martinez and del Rio wasn't lying, and Gissing wasn't being square with us." The cowboy gestured excitedly. "Go see, man. It's fantastic. I mean, *really* fantastic."

"What is it?" Ned said. He had heard the names Martinez, del Rio, and Gissing before. Recently.

"Unicorns. Honest-to-gonorrhea unicorns, man. Go see."

"Cut the crap. My brother's dying. If you like games, there's a water-balloon war right over there you can enlist in."

The olive-skinned cowhand put a hand to his chest. "Insult me *after* you've seen them, okay? See if you still want to." Not much older than the kids fragging one another with Kartajan bombs, he wasn't yet Ned's age, either. He spat in an oily puddle, turned on his heel, and started walking back to the crowded barn.

"All right," Ned said, both remorseful and annoyed. He hadn't meant to insult the guy, and now he recalled the names Martinez, del Rio, and Gissing had appeared in a Remuda County newspaper that Zubrecht had made him read. Indeed, Zubrecht had sent him down here to Remuda County not solely to see about Bo but to check out the silly-ass rumors that real unicorns were roaming the Sangre de Cristos. "All right, I'll look. But if this is a practical joke, Pancho, I'll . . ." Ned stopped. The guy wasn't listening, and, in any case, what could he do to him that the Chicano and his pals couldn't revisit on him a hundredfold?

The central runway of the barn was packed, and Ned, in jacket and tie, felt like an idiot walking among all the lean, denim-clad cowhands. Worse, he was carrying a saxophone and trying to keep his cordovan wingtips free of both mud and horse shit, a completely hopeless task.

Sam Coldpony stood on a hay bale in the back of a red pickup— it had a flat tire, Ned noticed—signaling for silence. Amazingly, given the dozens of people in the barn, he was getting it. Ned was reminded of a holiday communion service. Except for the smells of hay and animal flesh.

". . . really don't want you in here," Coldpony was telling the crowd in as soft a hearable voice as he could manage. "We're not trying to keep a secret any more," he said. "We're just trying to make sure these sick kar'tajans get well. I don't blame you for being curious about them, but getting them well comes first. So I have to ask you two things. First, not to talk this up any more than you can help. Covarrubias's story in the *Warrior* last Friday made me cringe. Stuff like that doesn't help us to do what we need to do to save these animals."

Coldpony lowered his hands.

"So if you agree to keep this as quiet as you can for the next month, please let me know by raising your hands. Come on, now. Put 'em up."

So far as Ned could tell, everybody in the barn's center aisle raised his or her hand. Ned shifted his tenor sax so that he could raise his own. It was like a union meeting for mutes. The only noises on the Tipsy Q were the snorts of horses in their stalls and the foliage-crashing of the boys throwing water balloons.

"Okay, thanks. The second thing I've got to ask is for all of you to stay out of the barn. I know you want to see what we have here. I don't blame you. So I'm going to ask you to go out front, then between the barn and Miss Libby's house to the horse trap. My daughter Paisley is here visiting. In the horse trap, she's going to lead one of our kar'tajans around by a rope so that you can see it. No one can touch the kar'tajan but Paisley, though. No one can lead it around except her. The kar'tajans name is Phylly, and if you want to see Phylly, you should go out now and get you a good spot on the fence rail."

Suddenly, Ned was facing forty or more people who wanted to get outside. The Chicano who had advised him to come into the barn took his elbow, turned him around, and said, "This'll be better, man. You'll see a unicorn that's up and walking and not just one that's lying in a stall. Come on, man."

Bo—who'd just told Mama Josey things that Ned couldn't imagine telling her even if she were dead and buried—was dying, and here he was, hobbling through the mud and marshy grass to get a peek at a unicorn. He and everybody else were like marks on the midway of a two-bit traveling carnival. Meanwhile, his wingtips were caked, and his handsome but pushy Chicano friend was trying to help him get a foothold on a paddock rail.

What were these people going to do when Bo actually died? They were holding his wake in advance, and even Bo himself had okayed the party, it was backasswards. And wrong wrong wrong.

Then Paisley, Coldpony's daughter, entered the horse trap from the other side, leading a creature that Ned had never believed in, even in its incarnation as a trademark for Zubrecht Products, Inc. An admiring, disbelieving murmur went around the paddock, and Ned realized that he had contributed to it. The unicorn—the kar'tajan mare—stepped daintily behind the Coldpony girl, tossing its head and incidentally flashing the spike on its brow.

"Fantastic," said the cowboy next to Ned. "Didn't I tell you, man? I mean, *really* fantastic."

Ned thought, This is what Zubrecht wanted me to find.

This is what he wanted me to come down to Remuda County for. Not my dying brother, but . . . this. It *was* fantastic.

Coldpony's daughter, walking the unicorn, halted a few times to answer questions about the animal, but repeatedly had to admit that only Miss Libby and her father knew the whole story. Eventually, people stopped asking questions to drink in the undeniable reality of the unicorn. Everyone was smitten with the creature, including the bewildered and already grieving Ned.

Dr. Nesheim sat on the sofa in the front rom watching people come and go. He had mixed feelings about letting Bo die away from the hospital. There, he would've had far more control over events, overseeing them as a respected and deferred-to oncologist—but he had to confess that given a choice between Alfie's lonely death in an ICU and a twenty-four-hour going-away party in Libby's home, he, too, would have opted for the latter.

That, in fact, was why he was here. He had made up his mind to stay till the end, and he had telephoned the medical center's chief of staff to inform him of this decision. In the meantime, he was giving painkillers, offering reassurance without dispensing false hope, and staying out of the way to keep from becoming the godlike linchpin in a scene whose rightful hero was Bo.

Death is a crappy story ending, Nesheim thought. It's either too pat or too unexpected, and just as every person born has an umbilicus, every person ever born owes the world a death.

Alfie Tuck had had condom balloons by pathetic decree, and now Bo had them too—likewise by decree. Only Bo and Father Zinzalow had visited Alfie, but so far today Nesheim had watched forty or fifty people look in on and murmur both a greeting and a farewell to Bo.

It was discouraging, however, that most of these visitors were friends of Libby's rather than of Bo's. With the exception of the priest, the Methodist minister from Snowy Falls, and Bo's younger brother, these visitors had come less to show their support of the AIDS patient than to strengthen Libby in her role as the dying man's benefactor.

Well, that was okay too. At least they weren't turning their backs on Libby because she had given shelter to a "sick queer." At least they weren't pretending that he had already died. At least they seemed aware of Bo's human need for some simple acknowledgment of the fact that he, too, had lived and struggled.

Nesheim, ensconced on the sofa with a copy of *Western Horseman*, was vaguely heartened by the number of "at least" he was able to list. The circumstances of Alfie's death had left him with deeper reservoirs of cynicism than of unqualified regard for his kind, and it was good to witness behavior that brought the reservoir levels a little more into balance again.

Libby appeared in the hall. "Dr. Nesheim," she said, "I wish you'd come in here again. It's . . ."

It's what we've been waiting for, the doctor thought, and he was surprised—surprised and obliquely exhilarated—to feel a knot form in his gut. After all this time, he was supposed to be immune to attacks of angst over a bad outcome and of any resulting grief, but he was still experiencing them. He hadn't lost the ability to feel. He wasn't practicing medicine from force of habit. He was so relieved to discover these things about himself that he entered Bo's room heavy not only with concern but with gratitude.

Ned was standing in his stocking feet beside the bed. (He had returned from the paddock a short while ago, and Libby had made him take off his muddy shoes.) He had his saxophone at the ready, but, even in his lavender shirt and his blue rep tie, he looked a flabby mess, the sort of patient you would put on a diet with only a faint hope of his sticking to it.

Libby, meanwhile, had gone out to the paddock to fetch Sam and Sam's daughter back to the house. Once she had returned with them, and once everyone else including the two clergymen had been shooed from the room, Nesheim took up a spot in the corner. He would come out to give whatever comfort and assistance he could, but this was a family matter, and Nesheim didn't want to step on the toes of the people who had known Bo since childhood or who had been with him on virtually a day-to-day basis since his return to Colorado.

"Neddy," Bo said, and his voice now was a whisper and a croak, for he was having trouble holding himself in this reality, "you've got to go back by Mama's from here. Promise me."

"I promise."

"She's all alone. Papa Nate's dead, I'm going, and she's even said she doesn't want to . . . to see you any more, either."

"That's the truth," Ned said. "That's the rub, too, Beaumont. That's the rub."

"Don't let her get away with that. Impose yourself on her and then look after her."

"Beaumont—"

"Look, Little Brother, I'm giving you the word. She hates your job. It's a stupid hate, but she's too silly-proud to change, and she won't live that damn much longer, anyway."

"She'll outlive me, Beaumont."

"Like hell. Listen. Quit your job. Find something in Pueblo that won't offend her silly-ass Victorian sensibilities."

"Quit my job?"

"Right. Quit it. Then find a job in Pueblo—not move in with her, now. Just keep an eye on her till . . . till she goes."

"In the year two thousand A.D., when I'm a cool forty."

"It won't be that long. Seven months, tops—next February. So promise me, damn it."

"Bo, I'll never find another position like—"

"Look, you don't lip back at a dying older brother."

Ned unhooked the strap that supported his saxophone, laid it on the TV tray holding Bo's photographs and the pewter unicorn, knelt at his brother's bedside, and stroked Bo's wrist.

"Bo, it's shitty to use your dying to make me lie to you."

"Then don't do it!" Bo said, lifting his head. "Don't turn the promises you make me into lies!"

"The only promise I've made you is that I'll go see Mama."

"Promise me you'll quit Zubrecht and find work in Pueblo. Come on, you big goddamn baby."

Ned put his forehead on the edge of the bed, closed his eyes, and clenched his fists. "Bo, I'm afraid I'm . . ."

"I saw that you might be on your first visit here, Neddy."

"Just quitting Zubrecht won't solve the problem with Mama. It can't, Bo. I don't know who the hell I am."

"You're Theodore Gavin. You're an unhappy woman's son. Refuse to be disinherited. Everything else can come later."

Ned Gavin began to cry.

Bo said, "You know the money I made from Zubrecht for

my ad? Libby won't take any of it. So all but five grand's for you. That five thousand's for Mama, the rest's for you to start fresh with—severance pay, sort of. You've just got to promise me you'll quit Zubrecht's and go to Pueblo."

Ned turned his head from side to side on the robin's-egg blue linen. His shoulders hunched, rolled back, hunched again.

"Blast it, Neddy! Promise your dying damn older brother!"

"Okay, okay," Ned said at last, his face still pressed against the blue sheet. "I promise."

"You're my witness," Bo said, spying Dr. Nesheim in a corner of the little room. "You heard him, right?"

"Right, I'm your witness. I heard him."

There were four people at his bedside when Bo died: Libby, Ned, Sam, and Dr. Nesheim.

Paisley would have been there, but when she could see that Bo was going, she slipped out and crossed to the barn, where five of Arvill Rudd's hands were standing beyond its door talking about the "unicorns" and narrowly obeying her father's request to stay out of the barn itself. Of course, Paisley was exempt. Without saying a word to the cowboys, she entered the barn and ran into an enormous old man carrying a dose syringe.

In Bo's bedroom, Ned was playing his tenor sax. Bo had made two requests, "Kitchen Man" by Bessie Smith and "Goodbye" by the Benny Goodman orchestra, and although Ned usually played well only when backing up a recording, he remembered both these selections well enough to do them creditably. Then—when Dr. Nesheim made it as official as anyone needed it made that Bo had really died—Ned played "Amazing Grace," and that was the end of the music, the end of the afternoon, the end of a great many things.

In the barn, Paisley said, "He's dead."

She was squatting in a stall next to the big veterinarian as he examined a kar'tajan mare. They had already traded introductions, and the young woman's deftness with Phylly, who had taken to her at once, and with all the recuperating animals, had convinced the old man that she was "creature-wise."

Now, she put a hand on his shoulder and advised him to go

pay his respects to Bo Gavin. She also said that although Bo was dead. Brinkley should sit beside him and tell him the "muckfly" business that he had told Miss Libby last night. It was very important, Sam Coldpony's daughter said, that Bo have that information.

"The muckfly business?" Brinkley said.

"Yes, sir. Please tell him."

Brinkley ambled gimpily to the house. He took off his hat in the front room, nodded to everyone standing aimlessly in the little bedroom-study, and asked if it was okay if he paid the dead man his last respects.

Libby gave him a chair, and Brinkley turned it so that its back was at a cattywampus angle near the head of the bed, eased himself astraddle it, and leaned out sideways to whisper directly into the dead man's ear. The brilliant Hawaiian shirt in which Bo had just bought it was one that the vet greatly admired.

As the young Ute woman had suggested, Brinkley told Bo all that he had discovered and/or surmised about the disease afflicting the unicorns. He then told Libby that the animals in the barn seemed to be progressing nicely, added that he was sorry about Bo, grasped Ned by the upper arm, crammed his hat back on, and gimped outside to shoot the breeze with Rudd's cowhands and to watch the evening sunlight sparkle off Abbot's Pate.

"Bo wanted to be cremated," Libby told Ned. "Sam and I plan to drive him down to Pueblo to take care of things. Why don't you go on to Josephine's? We'll keep you posted, okay?"

Ned reluctantly agreed.

Libby pressed the toy kar'tajan into his hand. "For you, Ned. It hasn't exactly been a good-luck charm up to now, but Bo would have wanted you to have it, I think, and I've got a hunch that it's going to be. From here on out."

# 34

It wasn't like release. It wasn't like freedom. It was like dreaming that you weighed *tons*. Unless you got help, you'd sink through the bed, the floor, the surface of the earth—all the way to the molten furnace at the heart of the planet.

Bo hated the way death felt. He had believed that death would release him from the degradation of his AIDS—but now that he was dead, a down-bearing pain lay full length upon him, and he couldn't get out from under it. Would anything free him from the terrible heavy-limbedness imprisoning him in his own corpse?

Yes. A silent woman in buckskins, beaded leggings, moccasins, and a pair of long, silver-shot braids.

Bo knew at once that this was Sam's ex-wife and Paisley's mama, the suicide victim who had blown her head away with a shotgun. But when she entered his room tonight, not long after Ned had left for Pueblo, she had a head. She was a haggard, round-cheeked *ini'putc'* with transparent eyes, and her coming was so sudden and solemn that at first Bo was alarmed.

"Come on," the woman said impatiently. "Get up."

Bo couldn't turn his head. He couldn't even shift the irises in his death-stalled eyeballs. Although he could tell that no one living remained near his bed, he wondered if one of Gina Thrower's girls or Arvill Rudd's cowboys had sneaked into a corner to catch a glimpse of his dead body. Bo didn't really know if he was alone, and he was afraid to speak to the *ini'putc'*.

"There's no one here, white eyes. Come on, move your tail."

"I can't move." He tried. "I can't." He noticed that he had

spoken like a ventriloquist, without moving his lips. However, he *had* moved spectral lips that overlay his fleshy ones like sculpted eddies of air.

Whereupon Dolores Arriola walked through the foot of his bed—through its iron bedstand, its two stacked mattresses, and all of its various linens, coverlets, and ruffs. Then, seemingly trapped by the mattresses into which she had waded, she held out her hands so that Bo could take her fingers.

But because he couldn't raise his hands to her, Dolores reached down and clasped the immaterial hands inside the gloves of his dead flesh.

By these, the revenant pulled Bo out of himself, overcoming his death fatigue and the oppressive tonnage of his dead-weight self. She walked backward out of the bed, leading Bo clear of it with her. This feat permitted Bo's disembodied self to look back at the cold shell that had once housed his personality.

A major shiver seeing himself dead: a *major* shiver.

Especially spooky was the fact that he had arisen from his dead self wearing a ghostly set of the clothes still on his corpse—an indigo Hawaiian shirt with crimson poinsettias, and familiar khaki slacks. Both dead and resurrected, his feet were bare. Also, his resurrected body still carried upon it the ghostly prints of his cancer lesions.

Although now free of his dead self, Bo felt heavy. He was like a layer of plasma with the mass of a collapsing star, and the death fatigue on his shoulders got worse. He sank to his knees between the bed and the rolltop, and the dead Ute woman had to grasp him by the collar and wrest him to his naked feet again.

"You'll be better outside. Come on."

*Come on*. Her favorite command. Already Bo was sick of it. But he followed Dolores to the door by trailing her as if burdened with chains and padlocks. Then he turned to tell his disease-pummeled body goodbye, shocked by how thin and exhausted-looking it was. He felt a vast, unbecoming pity for himself.

"Christ," Dolores said. "Just like Sam, back when Authentic Ute Crafts was going under. Come on."

She led him through Libby's little house. There were still

two people in the living room—Arvill Rudd's wife, Bernadine, and Gina Thrower. They sat together on the sofa formulating a plan to help Libby get over her "loss" (Mrs. Thrower's compassionate word), but the two ghosts were invisible to the women, and Bo realized that he was eavesdropping on them from another dimension.

Then the weight of his death fatigue bore him down in front of the steamer trunk, very near the unseeing women, and Dolores had to return for him again. She lifted him to his feet and supported him until she had manhandled him outside into the starry dark.

Bo could hear an owl hooting from a cross strut of the creaking windmill. There were lights on in the barn. However, Dolores told him that he had no business going among the kar'tajans tonight. He must ready himself to climb Ptarmigan Mountain.

Bad news, thought Bo. He was so heavy, even in death, that he couldn't imagine getting halfway to Naismith's Cabin, much less to Ptarmigan's forested peak. He begged Dolores to let him lie down in a tire-rutted puddle near the house. He would wallow in it. He would pray for its cold scummy water to lend him buoyancy. Perhaps this buoyancy would enable him to climb the mountain.

"Dumb," Dolores said. "Dumb." She helped Bo around the horse trap, where both the darkness and the marshy grass were thicker, and where Bounty rose from the nest he'd made by circling himself a hundred times before lying down. The hound was aware of *someone's* presence but doggily ignorant of just whose.

Bo realized that, like the women inside, Bounty was unable to see Dolores and him, but that, unlike these women, he was picking up the fading death heat coming off their resurrection bodies. In fact, Bounty was nervous and hyperalert.

Dolores said, "He hid out here all day. Too many people."

"I thought maybe I'd outlive the bastard," Bo said.

Bounty backed away from what he couldn't see or hear. Then he tucked tail, hollered, and scooted off toward the house, helplessly spraying pee.

Bo collapsed. A ghost in the grass, he thought. I'll lie here until the cold fiery weight of my spirit burns me through the earth to hell. Maybe Mama Josey was right. . . .

"Get up." Dolores nodded at the skirts of Ptarmigan Mountain.

"I can't do it. I weigh too much."

"So we'll ride. The higher we go the less you'll weigh."

She pulled Bo to his feet and dragged him along the fence to a place under the frost of stars where the soil was strangely mounded and gravel in the hillock's crust had prevented any kind of plant—grass, marsh marigolds, snow buttercups—from growing. Here, still holding Bo's overweight ghost upright, Dolores began to chant in a tongue wholly alien to him. She chanted, paused, chanted, stopped, and changed yet again, her voice an animalish growl.

Suddenly, the gravel on the hillock began to dance, and then a jagged seam split the mound's crust and metallic rocks went flying like shrapnel. Some of this shrapnel pierced the glorified bodies of the two *ini'putc'* but did so, Bo noticed, without inflicting either injury or pain on their disembodied selves, as if they were . . . ghosts. Which, of course, they were.

Could a ghost be frightened? Bo knew only that in spite of the protection from physical harm that disembodiment seemed to bestow, he *was* afraid. In fact, Dolores scared him almost as much as did the frantic scrabbling from within the hillock.

More dirt flew out of the black mound. Then Bo saw a pair of hooves on a pair of dirt-caked forelegs clawing upward from the pit that Sam had dug to bury the two-headed calf—the "abomination," as Libby had called it. As Bo and Dolores watched, the deformed beast pulled its entire self from the earth, scratching and grunting its way to the surface as if summoned by a call ten times more powerful than the call to birth.

There stood the calf—its rear end as high as its head, its four eyes like four slugs, its coat pied with clumps of clinging soil. It was perplexed by both the starlight and the breathtaking liquor of mountain air, and each of its two heads was bawling, one protesting its entombment in the grave that Sam had dug for it and one bleating longingly at the shrouded mountains.

Bo could still remember the morning on which Libby had midwifed the grotesque beast. He could still remember his unreasoning anger when she'd said, "Abominations can't live—the world rejects them. Hermaphrodites can't live—nature weeds them out." Taking this as a personal attack, he had called Libby names and flicked her on the nose with his fingertip—until Coldpony had spiked his self-pitying boorishness by knocking him down.

Dear God, that had to've been in another lifetime, didn't it? Well, yes. And it had been, literally.

"Delores, what are you doing?"

"Get on. Ride. The calf will take you up the mountain."

Yet again, Bo fell. He sat on his butt with his knees up in front of him and his head hanging like an overripe melon. He was afraid of the calf. Because the animal appeared not to be a ghost like Dolores and him but instead a reanimated zombie creature, he was also afraid that it *wouldn't* be able to carry him.

After all, thought Bo, I weigh tons. . . .

"It can carry you," Dolores said. "Carrying you was one of the things Miss Libby's 'abomination' was born for."

Dolores blew the eagle-bone whistle hanging from her neck, and Phylly came trotting from the barn, a pale flame against the black outbuildings and the upright silhouettes of the fence stakes. Bo watched her float; she was a fiery myth interfacing magically with the reality that had demanded, and then extracted, his death. The two-headed calf stumbled to one side to get out of her way.

Dolores spoke softly to Phylly, then pulled herself astride the kar'tajan and rode over to Bo so she could again order him to mount the calf and follow her.

Bo stood. He still weighed tons. He always would, he feared. Nevertheless, the blind calf hobbled over to him on its abbreviated forelegs and accepted the freight of his newborn ghost. Bo clasped the deformed creature around the throat, laid his forehead on the V formed by its necks, and stretched out on its infant's body like an overcoat nearly too big for its wearer.

Dolores spoke to Phylly. Phylly trotted off toward the trail winding up the mountain. The calf galloped spastically after. If Dolores was Don Quixote on Rocinante, then Bo was Sancho

Panza on a burro. Their ascent through slapping fir boughs and up rock tiers from which their mounts' hooves struck sparks was a long nightmare of explosive jolts.

However, Bo did feel himself growing lighter the higher they climbed, and the sight of Phylly's incandescent butt and uplifted, flaming tail—encouraging signals to both him and the blind calf—helped him endure the jouncing. They passed Naismith's Cabin, and an overlook from which most of Remuda Creek Meadow gleamed under quivering starlight, and a rotting mine cart, and a family of mule deer that abruptly fled. Bo clutched the calf tighter, and soon they were on an apron of granite fronting the timber-propped mouth to Naismith's Mine.

Dolores dismounted. She led Phylly into the mine tunnel. Then she turned, looked back, and told Bo to come with them. He got off the calf—which hobbled away, fell, clambered up, and went crashing down the Remuda Creek Meadow side of the mountain. Bo watched it disappear into the night, all the while resenting the Ute woman for making him use and then abandon it.

"Come on, Gavin. Come on."

Phylly lit their way inward. Bo warily stalked Dolores and the glowing kar'tajan. Claustrophobia began to work in him. What if he hadn't chosen to be cremated? What if Ned, Libby, and Sam had decided to put him in a casket and bury him as Sam had buried that calf? He would have spent an eternity underground, confined and isolated. It would have been even worse than trailing these rusted tracks under the rotten support timbers of Naismith's Mine, feeling its ceiling drop closer as they advanced.

It was hard to maneuver. Although a petite animal, Phylly took up a lot of the forward portion of the shaft. The narrowing walls and the descending ceiling shoved the kar'tajan and the two ghosts close together, and the fact that neither Bo nor Dolores could walk through her—as Dolores had waded into the bed—led Bo to realize that Phylly had some of the same ghostly substance now constituting his and Dolores's resurrection bodies. In short, the kar'tajan was unearthly kin to them, even though she had transferred her primary allegiance from Over There to Over Here.

They came to a dead end. Dolores enticed Phylly to the

faceted inner edge of this cul-de-sac, and the kar'tajan lowered the tip of her horn to the glittering wall. A vertical crack appeared in the rock face, the rock fractured, and the tunnel walls near Bo turned into mirrors of frictionless tin.

Beyond the wall that Phylly's alicorn had touched, carved from the creation stuff of another reality, stretched a huge, uninviting desert. It was sandstone red, hazy with blowing dust, and knobbled across its daunting breadth by a myriad of pale boulders that from the vantage of Naismith's Mine looked whimsically eroded.

"Go," Dolores said. "Go down."

"What about you? What about Phylly?"

"I have another doorway. The kar'tajan has other duties."

Bo hesitated. He didn't like what he saw. He was afraid. On the other hand, standing on this sudden overlook, he realized that the oppressive weight that he had acquired in Libby's house—well, his recent ride had lifted that burden from him. He was now as close to utter weightlessness as one could become in death's territories.

"Go down," Dolores repeated. "Now."

And the dead Beaumont Gavin descended from Naismith's Mine into the full mystery of the other world.

# 35

Bo was cremated in Pueblo. Libby and Sam brought his remains back to the Tipsy Q. A day later, the pastor of the Snowy Falls Methodist Church held a private memorial at Libby's house.

After this service, Ned showed a tape of Bo's Kartajans ad on the large-screen TV and announced that he had just submitted his resignation at ZP Inc. He left the ranch with a small ceramic urn containing his brother's ashes. He would keep them, he told Libby, until Mama Josey either asked for them or died. If their mother died without asking for them, Ned would bring them back and throw them into the wind from Ptarmigan Mountain.

Paisley remained on the Tipsy Q. She had come to Snowy Falls to see her father again. Now, however, DeWayne Sky would expect her to return to Ignacio, go down to Hotevilla, Arizona, and begin training as a *po'rat* under a Hopi shaman of the Sun Clan.

In fact, LannaSue had telephoned Paisley from Ignacio the day of Bo's cremation to ask when she planned to return. Paisley had answered that she would stay until the sick kar'tajans were well, maybe another three weeks or so. A person could not hope to become a *po'rat* who turned her back on wounded creatures from the spirit realm, she argued. A person could not become a *po'rat* who refused to stand beside her father when he got married.

"Send the god sheet back," LannaSue said. "DeWayne's worried about it—so worried he wants you to send it Federal Express."

Paisley laughed. "It's cleaner than it's been in years, Mama Sky. I'll bring it when I come."

"Do what you have to, but come soon, kar'tajan gal. DeWayne misses his stupid sheet, but I miss you."

A week passed. Paisley, Sam, and Libby took turns staying up at night with the kar'tajans, all of which appeared to be rapidly recovering. Even Dr. Brinkley, who visited the ranch nearly every day, was encouraged. In fact, he began to fret over the fact that Sam still hadn't dynamited Naismith's mine—to "close forever that fucking doorway to reinfection and death."

Sam was willing, but Paisley kept finding reasons to hold off. For one, the six recuperating kar'tajans were confined to stalls and couldn't possibly cross back over. Second, Phylly, whom they had given a free run of the barn and horse trap, seemed to have no wish to follow the kar'tajans that had ignorantly returned to the spirit realm. And, finally, it was possible—dimly possible—that animals that had already gone back over might still return and thus save themselves.

"A piss-poor risk," Brinkley said. "Piss poor."

"We'll be careful," Paisley said. "And if a few kar'tajans sneak back over to us, that'd be great."

Brinkley harrumphed—the first person in her life Paisley had ever heard really do that—and popped a rum ball.

During this week, Paisley moved from Libby's house, where Sam and Libby were sharing a bedroom, to Naismith's Cabin. She didn't spend every night in the cabin—nursing the kar'tajans kept her in the barn one night out of three—but she was in it often enough to want some entertainment there. So Sam fastened Libby's prehistoric Bendix behind Crip's saddle as if Crip were a pack mule and goaded the poor horse up the mountain.

At the cabin, Sam hooked the set to his portable generator and guyed a small exterior antenna to the roof. He put the set in the sleeping loft, to get it as high above the surrounding trees as he could, positioning it at an angle offering the best reception.

On the evening after the memorial service, the telephone rang. It was Gary. He told Libby he was calling from Huerfano; he was visiting his attorney, Julio Covarrubias, and wondered if he could come up to the ranch and see her.

"No," Libby said. "I don't want to see you."

"Lib, I just want to thank you for what you've done—what you did, I mean—for Beaumont. It was above and beyond, baby."

"I tried to get you here. Too late now, Gary. Forget it."

"How about a neutral site, then. I won't stick my nose in, and you won't have to set foot in Julio's office."

"What does Covarrubias have to do with this? Nothing, so far as I can see. Back off."

"Suppose I said, 'unicorns,' Lib? Wouldn't me saying 'unicorns' make you think twice about telling me to back off?"

Sam was sitting beside Libby with his ear to the receiver. He put his hand over its mouthpiece and told Libby to agree to meet Gary; they might find out something useful, particularly since it sounded as if Quarrels and his attorney had some sort of devious scheme up their sleeves. Libby protested, but Sam said they'd do better heading off trouble early than allowing it to overtake them while their minds were busy elsewhere.

So Libby agreed to a meeting at the Prairie Schooner Café, and she and Sam drove down to Huerfano an hour after the phone call to see what Gary was up to. They found him and Covarrubias—a short, neat man typified by his bow tie and checkered vest—at a secluded booth inside the stucco covered wagon. (Outside, the place's neon sign winked on and off, lacquering and then dulling the grotesque wooden statue of an Indian.)

"You weren't on the Prentice place when I called," Libby said, sliding in beside Covarrubias. Sam squeezed in next to Gary, who looked at him as if he were a low-life strikebreaker.

"I was visiting someone in the Springs," Gary said.

"Another buckle bunny? Your mother didn't even know you were there. I called her about Bo, too." Libby looked at Covarrubias, whose hands resembled nicotine-stained porcelain. "What are you doing here, Mr. Covarrubias?"

"We have a business proposition."

Gary placed a copy of the *Huerfano Warrior* with the attorney's unicorn piece in it on the tabletop. "Soon as I got back to Texas, found this in my mailbox. Called Julio to ask what was going on. Found out poor old Bo had died, then came straight on back to check out this unbelievable unicorn stuff."

"It's true," Covarrubias said.

"I don't doubt Gary's word," Libby said. "At least when he's not trying to produce an alibi for catting around."

"I meant," Covarrubias said, grimacing, "that the 'unbelievable unicorn stuff' is all true. I've had confirmation that you have unicornlike animals on the Tipsy Q right now. Would you care to confirm it yourself, Mrs. *Quarrels?*" Gary's lawyer laid sarcastic stress on the last name. "True or not true?"

"It's Mrs. *Coldpony,*" Sam said. He was a little ahead of the gun, but it would be unequivocally true very soon, and the look of raw surprise on Gary's face delighted Libby.

"You married this goddamn Indian?"

Libby ignored Gary's question to answer Covarrubias's. "It's true," she said. "So what?"

"Then you're the owner of a potential gold mine, Mrs. . . . uh, Mrs. Coldpony," Covarrubias said, "and we want to help you realize its potential by purchasing shares and finding the most attractive methods of developing the property."

"Why the hell would you marry Sam?" Gary asked. "He's a stupid Ute. He's broke all the time. He's . . . he's *old.*"

"Because I love him," Libby said. "Mr. Covarrubias, I already have a gold mine—Naismith's Mine. What sort of development, and what kind of money, are you talking?"

"Half a million dollars up front, Elizabeth," Covarrubias said, obviously hoping that her formal given name would be an acceptable stand-in for her new surname. "After which you'll be a profit sharer along with Gary, me, and your neighbor Raymond Hilliard, who intends to purchase some shares too."

"Shares in what?" Libby asked.

"Coldpony, you bastard, why would she marry you?"

"I swept her off her feet," Sam said.

"Shares in a venture," the lawyer said pointedly, "that we want to call Unicorn Mountain, U.S.A. We'll build a lodge on the Tipsy Q, we'll hire an expert trainer for the unicorns, we'll offer both kids and adults rides, we'll license photographs and merchandise, and we'll all become very wealthy."

"Hilliard's already wealthy," Libby said. "Why would he want to mess with a pair of losers like you and Gary?"

Covarrubias's hackles rose. "Gary has money, inherited money, and I've done very well for myself as an entrepreneur. That new ski lodge near Cuchara, I have shares in that, and I've represented Hilliard's interests here in Colorado for many, many years."

"Then why mess with Quarrels here at all?" Sam said, grabbing Gary's wrist as if they were old buddies.

Julio Covarrubias was silent. Gary yanked his arm angrily out from under Sam's hand.

"Because," said Libby, "if we turn you and Hilliard down, you guys plan to press Gary's old suit against me and see if you can't win the Tipsy Q back for him, in which case your fee for doing so will be a sizable interest in the property thus won back. In the meantime, you've coopted Gary as a minor partner—insurance in the event that I refuse to be reasonable."

"'Unicorn Mountain, U.S.A.,'" Sam said. "'Unicorn Mountain, U.S.A.' It has a ring, don't it?"

"Well," Libby said, "the answer is 'No.'"

"You haven't thought about it," Covarrubias said. "You haven't considered all the ramifications of refusing our offer."

"Actually, Mr. Covarrubias, the answer isn't 'No.' It's 'Stuff it.' Come on, Sam."

As Sam slid out of the booth, Gary moved as if to grab him by the jacket sleeve. A hard look from Sam made him stop, though. Libby found that seeing her ex stymied in this way, by a man whom he had always regarded as a wage slave and the product of inferior genetics, gave her a small thrill. It was good-versus-evil in one of its mundane contemporary guises. Good had just triumphed.

Covarrubias said, "Listen, Elizabeth, these so-called unicorns of yours—"

"Kar'tajans," Libby said. But seeing the bewilderment on his face—why had she suddenly brought up this new brand of condoms?—she waved off the correction. "Forget it."

"These 'unicorns' of yours," Covarrubias began again. "There's going to be some heated debate about whether they're game animals, an endangered species, or livestock. If the state decides they're game animals or an endangered species, you'll lose them. I could help you keep them, Elizabeth. I could mount arguments that—"

"We'll cross that bridge when we come to it," Libby said. "For now, though, ownership is nine tenths of the law, and who the hell wants to hire on the one tenth that you represent?"

"Libby," Gary said plaintively. "Libby, wait a minute."

But she and Sam walked outside to the parking lot, got into her pickup, and headed home. Libby had the strongest feeling she'd ever had that she was through with Gary Quarrels forever, no matter how often in the future their paths might cross. That was a damned good feeling. Damned good.

Libby and Sam were married in the front room of Gina Thrower's boardinghouse. Paisley was the maid of honor, and Arvill Rudd, looking paunchy but pleased in his seldom-used Sunday suit, was the best man. Preston Brinkley gave the bride away.

There was no real honeymoon, for the kar'tajans in Libby's barn still required looking after, and it was becoming clear to everyone that word of their presence would soon explode in newspapers and on television screens all over the country. Sam knew that Karen Banks from that Pueblo station would soon be free of her promise to keep her mouth shut for two weeks, and he had little doubt that within days her photograph of the dead kar'tajan under Abbot's Pate would appear on an evening news broadcast.

To complicate matters, Ray Hilliard had begun buzzing the Tipsy Q in his light aircraft again, and so much unaccustomed traffic was going up and down Highway 69 between Snowy Falls and the ranch that Libby had almost asked the county sheriff to send a patrolman.

"I hate the way things are going," she told Sam on the night of their stay-at-home honeymoon. (Preston Brinkley had volunteered to kar'tajan-sit, and Paisley was up in Naismith's Cabin.)

"'Things'? Everything?"

"Not us. What I mean is, what's going to happen?"

"Damned if I know," Sam said. "Whatever happens, though, there won't ever be any rip-off Unicorn Mountain here."

"No. No, there won't."

"I've been the Authentic Utes Craft route once already. It was a disaster, m'lady. A disaster."

"'M'lady.'" Libby echoed Sam. "You said m'lady.'"

"That's who you are," Sam said, rolling her into his arms. "It took your asshole ex's first cousin to show us, though, didn't it?"

Libby laid her face against her husband's chest, and he stroked her hair as if playing a fragile harp.

On the reservation, Paisley had seldom watched TV, but up here on the Tipsy Q—at least while away from Libby, her father, and the kar'tajans—time weighed heavy, and Paisley watched. She watched all kinds of sorry commercial fare—sitcoms, docudramas, prime-time soaps—while on the bizarre stations that Little Ben began to bring in around midnight, she gazed goggle-eyed at some of the weirdest programming in the history of the medium.

"Tonight's is a very special episode of Mutual of Omaha's *Wild Kingdom*," Marlin Perkins said on the evening after Sam and Libby's wedding. Paisley lay with her nose ten inches from the set as the kindly looking Perkins opened the program from an expensive leather wingback. Behind him was a fireplace with an oaken mantel.

"Beaumont Gavin, a recent arrival to our wild kingdom, has told medical authorities in Hyderabad, including my old friend Prakash Chakravarty, that the terrible die-off that has been affecting the kar'tajan population of India, Africa, and northern Canada, is the direct consequence of a virus transmitted to these noble animals by a microscopic fly known as . . ."

"*Microtrichia*," an off-camera voice said.

"This is an important discovery," said Perkins, nodding, "but one we would have made long ago if our medical researchers were more responsibly funded. 'An immortal species is often a species that lacks compassion.' We prove the harsh truth of that epigram in our refusal to preserve the good gifts of Nature."

The camera dollied back to reveal two more big leather chairs, one on either side of Perkins. The people in these chairs were Bo Gavin—Paisley recognized him even through the electronic snow—and Perkins's old friend Prakash Chakravarty. A discussion began. Its gist was that the virus infecting the kar'tajans was the result of *Microtrichia*'s egg-laying and the parasitic feeding habits of its larvae. But the deadly virus's primary host was . . .

"Well, it is you and I," Chakravarty said. "All of us who have immigrated. The virus has no power to manifest clinically in us, considering who and what we are. Nevertheless, we are carriers. Indeed, one could even proclaim that humanity is an entire species of Typhoid Marys. This microscopic fly feeds on us without our knowledge, ingesting the virus, and then goes and lays its eggs and hatches its larvae on the kar'tajans. The kar'tajans acquire the virus, this viremia breaks out as an incurable disease, and the kar'tajans die: one, two, three."

"Why has this happened to our kar'tajans only over the past half decade, Prakash?"

"I don't know, Marlin. Perhaps some of us are arriving here in infected resurrection bodies, bringing our spiritual viremia with us. But I only guess."

"What can we do to save our remaining kar'tajans?"

"Usually, Marlin, one has three choices. Kill the virus. Kill the host. Kill the vector. So far, we've been unable to eradicate the virus. Because *we* are the hosts, we do not have the option of destroying ourselves, even were we altruistic enough to *wish* to do so, which we aren't."

"So we must zero in on *Microtrichia*, the vector."

"Yes. We must find a microscopic insect that is parasitic on the eggs of *Microtrichia* but harmless to macroscopic life forms, and release them so that they may eat the invisible flies that are killing—indirectly—our lovely kar'tajans."

Paisley continued to watch. Bo had very little to do, however, and only once did Chakravarty make a point of acknowledging that Bo was responsible for these breakthrough discoveries. Bo explained that he was a messenger, not a discoverer. Paisley was glad when there came a commercial break followed by a narrated film clip of a vast herd of kar'tajans migrating across the Great Indian Desert at night. The animals were taking in the moisture from the monsoon winds through their pores and foraging on sand plants and seeds no bigger than muckflies. Someone in a helicopter had taken this film, which reminded her of newsreels of Hawaiian lava flows shot at night, but paler, an inland river of pearl-white flame fingering forward, closing up behind itself, and utterly enchanting the eye. It was too bad that Bo had looked so sad. It wasn't fair for the dead, whether Anglo or Indian, to be unhappy.

If it hadn't been their honeymoon evening, Paisley would have hurried down Ptarmigan Mountain to tell Sam and Libby what had just happened. More than anything, she wanted to shout, "I've seen Bo on television! I've seen our dead friend on TV!"

Karen Banks showed her photograph of the dead kar'tajan on her evening news broadcast, during a ten-minute segment devoted to the revelation that she, her cameraman, and several residents of Remuda County had seen flesh-and-fire unicorns not far from Snowy Falls during that little town's Pioneer Days festivities. Further, she had found a small family of the sick fantasy beasts on a ranch near the town, and an Indian named Samson Catchcougar had convinced her—against both her better judgment and all her basic reportorial instincts—to hold off announcing the fact until he and his boss lady had gotten these unicorns completely well.

About ten minutes after Ms. Bank's segment had aired, Brooklyn Terry and some of Rudd's other cowhands set up roadblocks north and south of the Tipsy Q—with full connivance of Neville Fuller, Snowy Falls' chief of police. Then they screened every vehicle approaching Libby's ranch. Fortunately, it would soon be too dark for helicopter or light-aircraft overflights, but Libby and Sam both knew they would resume tomorrow.

Preston Brinkley, who had seen the "news cooze" do her stuff on his set down at the Remuda County Veterinary Clinic, telephoned to urge Sam to go ahead and dynamite Naismith's mine. The kar'tajans were well enough to let outside now, and the last thing anybody who cared about these fucking miraculous critters wanted was for them to disappear into an unhealthy Elsewhere. The human parasites who descended on the Tipsy Q from Pueblo, Denver, Los Angeles, and New York would be easier to deal with than the muckflies the kar'tajans picked up Over There. Lots easier.

Neither Sam nor Libby was sure about that, but Sam decided to uncrate the dynamite he had bought and to collapse the mine. Libby left this task to him and Arvill Rudd, and she and Paisley waited together in the sleeping loft of Naismith's Cabin. They waited for the echo of the blast, the tremulous buckling of the hillside, and Sam and Arvill's successful return. Waiting in the loft, Paisley turned on the old Bendix, rotated its ratchety dial, and fiddled obsessively with both the vertical- and the horizontal-hold knobs, trying to bring in a picture.

"I saw Bo on this thing. I really did."

"You've told us, Payz. Bo used to pull in some pretty far-out crap on Little Ben himself, but I'm afraid—"

"I saw him. I did. Here, let me prove it."

"That's all right. I'm too damned keyed up to watch TV."

But Paisley persisted, and eventually, even though it was still nearly four hours till midnight, she managed to bring in a station recognizable to her as a transdimensional affiliate. A music show, an early evening ballroom program devoted to nostalgic tunes from the 1930s, the 1940s, and the early 1950s. Keep your eye on this, Paisley wanted to say, but Libby's attention was obviously more on Sam and Arvill Rudd working to collapse Naismith's Mine than it was on the television set.

Finally, though, Paisley seized Libby's sleeve and

wrenched her down to the floor in front of Little Ben. "Look," she said. "It's the Benny Goodman orchestra." It was. They were playing in a vast ballroom decorated with bamboo stalks, palm trees, crimson orchids, and pale lilies. Astonishingly, some of the dancing couples were men, and some were women.

Right now the orchestra was doing "Sometimes I'm happy," and as the camera panned the exotic-looking hall, Paisley touched a finger to the screen and tried to locate Bo. He had to be there, she told herself. He has to. Otherwise, why would Little Ben have dredged up this oddball program at this oddball hour?

Sitting in a chair next to the bandstand was a woman, and when "Sometimes I'm Happy" was over, Goodman came forward and introduced her. She stood and moved to the microphone to deliver the vocal on "You Turned the Tables on Me." The camera continued to pan the hall, but still without disclosing anyone whom Paisley recognized.

"Paisley, I can't watch this. I'm trying to—"

"*There!*" she cried. "Right there." Her fingernail tapped the blond head of a slender man in the embrace of another young man who was both darker and heavier. But the camera wheeled past, and "You Turned the Tables on Me" ended.

Whereupon Benny Goodman, holding his clarinet, thanked everyone for watching and turned back to his orchestra to close the program with his melancholy sign-off "Goodbye."

Now Libby was watching too. About a minute into the Goodman sign-off selection, Paisley located Bo again, excitedly tapped his head, and was pleased when he and his partner revolved toward the camera so that Libby could see the warm, quiet smile on Bo's face as he swayed in the arms of the other contented young man.

Naismith's Cabin quaked, the set went out, the lights went out, the muted echo of the blast in the mine tunnel rolled down to them like thunder, and then all was silent.

Ouray reappeared the morning after the dynamiting of Naismith's Mine. But he had shed the humongous antler rack that he had worn on his last visit to the ranch, and at first Sam did not recognize the great elk as "his" elk. With help from both his wife and his daughter, he was busy escorting the six recovered kar'tajans out into the sunny horse trap from the barn. As soon as he realized that the elk was Ouray, however, he walked across the dewy grass, vaulted the split-rail fence, and approached the animal. A wistful ache clutched his heart.

Ouray, Sam knew, was no less magical than the fantasy critters that Brinkley, Libby, Paisley, and he had worked so hard to save, and he felt even more awe in the wapiti's presence than he did in the unicorns'. What this meant he couldn't quite imagine, or find the words to say, but it seemed to him that Ouray was rebuking him somehow.

Phylly, seeing Ouray, trotted to the fence and thrust her head over. She released a bleating whinny that made the elk's purselike ears prick up and quiver. Libby and Paisley laughed, and even Sam had to admit that it was good to be out in the summer sunshine with the kar'tajans, letting them eat grass and nibble at the hay in a covered rack instead of pumping moist gruel into their guts with a dose syringe.

It was even better to be tickling Ouray's long muzzle again and feeling the morning breeze kick in off Remuda Creek Meadow through the dancing water poplars. In the horse trap, seven kar'tajans and two lovely women. In the meadow beyond it, a wapiti of unswerving loyalty. All hell would soon be breaking loose up here—reporters, scientists, entrepreneurs, human scavengers of every kind—but, for now if not forever, the Tipsy Q was the god home of Inu'sakats.

How have I come to be so blessed? Sam wondered. Even if it all ends tomorrow, I'll die happy. Holy He-She, my thanks.

Paisley walked to the railing. With Libby's camera, she had been photographing the kar'tajans, certain that now that the spirit door in Naismith's Mine had been closed, their images would finally appear on developed film. "Daddy," she said, "it's time for me to go back to Ignacio."

"When? Right now?" Sam continued to rub Ouray's nose.

"Today," Paisley said. "This evening, I think."

"I'll drive her," Libby said, bringing a yearling kar'tajan to the fence with her. "I hate to leave at night, though, Payz. How about first thing in the morning?"

Ouray made a perfect circle of his mouth and bugled.

Phylly cringed back; so did the yearling and all the other kar'tajans in their places around the paddock. But none bolted.

"You won't need to be driven, will you, girl?"

"I'll ride Ouray and leave as soon as there's a moon."

Of course, Sam thought. The journey will take a few days, but no other way home is worthy of your going.

Libby didn't know what was happening here, but she was happy enough to let father and daughter settle the matter between them. But once it was settled, Libby turned and clasped Paisley in an emotional embrace.

"Godspeed," she said, certain that lately she had seen too many departures. "Godspeed."

That evening, Paisley kissed her father and Libby goodbye and set off through the Sangre de Cristos riding elkback.

She carried her clothes and some food in a saddle roll, but she lived primarily off what she could find in the mountains, including a scurrying ptarmigan that she killed with a dead-on rock throw and a bellicose porcupine that she beat to death with a stick, skinned out, and roasted over a tiny fire. She was also able to gather a good supply of piñon nuts and berries, to catch trout, and, with no trouble at all, to keep the old service canteen that Sam had given her full of stream water so cold it made her teeth ache.

Ouray stayed near whenever Paisley had to hunt for food or make camp, but in only six days they passed into the San Juans, entered the high meadow called Montezuma Park, and descended into Archuleta County. Even though it was mid-July, the nights at these altitudes were chilly, and often Paisley would wrap herself in the Muache Ute god sheet to stay warm. On several nights, she slept in it. Also, she almost always pulled it tight around her shoulders while riding Ouray in the post-dawn or the pre-midnight hours. It was no longer as spotless as it had ever been, Paisley admitted, but it had never had better use, ever, and Papa Sky ought to be glad.

Down from the mountains, it was harder to avoid being seen, but Ouray had an instinct for finding forested strips, dry arroyos, and tricky passages through rock canyons or even cultivated fields, and this instinct kept anyone—Paisley worried about law officers, game wardens, and jealous landowners—from discovering them.

On the tenth day of her trip, shortly before noon, Paisley rode Ouray up to the isolated enclave of housing where she and Mama D'lo had lived for so many years. She spoke softly to the elk, stopping him beneath a tree about sixty yards from her house.

Sitting on a cracked concrete slab behind the house—a slab her grandpapa had poured as the foundation for a never-acquired storage building—were Larry Cuthair, Timothy Willow, Tim's younger brother Jack, and old Herbert Barnes, a.k.a. Whirling Goat. They were sitting on that slab as if engaged in a ceremonial powwow, but Paisley soon realized that they were playing poker and had chosen this spot because it was conveniently hidden from the Cuthair and Willow houses across the road.

Whirling Goat playing poker? Except at Sun Dance—the one time each year that he pulled himself together—he never had any money. It was amazing that either Larry or Tim would cut him in. However, he had reformed well ahead of Sun Dance this year, because Papa Sky had made him gatekeeper, and maybe he planned to give up booze for good.

The wind was blowing toward Ouray and Paisley. The words from the men's jabber drifted toward her as clearly as autumn leaves on a stream.

Barnes was winning, and winning big. He wanted Larry, Timothy, and fourteen-year-old Jack to ante up and continue the game. Larry and Timothy were protesting that he had wiped them out. Would he take IOUs? Barnes, using the authority acquired from his role as gatekeeper, asked them to turn their pockets out. Disappointed with the results, the old fart asked to see the contents of their wallets, and this time the young men showed him something greatly more exciting.

"Ante up with those," he said. "Ante up with those."

They did. The game went on. While the four players yakked at one another and skirmished over their bets, Payz nudged Ouray and rode him right up to the slab. Jack, the youngest poker player, was the first to detect the elk's presence. He stood up abruptly, startling the other three players.

Paisley stared down at the pot that Barnes had just taken. It consisted of two Kennedy half dollars, three Liberty Bell quarters, five or six dimes, and a clutch of foil-wrapped

Kartajans, glinting blue in the evening sunlight, winking like the mythological coinage of another realm.

Barnes was the only one of the four poker players who didn't look totally astonished to see her there on the back of her daddy's semidomesticated elk. He grinned up at her as if she were the loveliest apparition in the universe.

"Welcome back, Paisley."

"It's Alma," she corrected him. "From here on out, Mr. Barnes, it's Alma Coldpony."

Somewhere in the San Juans, Mama D'lo passed through a spirit door into a territory of blissful hunting and happy dreams.

## About the Author

*Michael Bishop* lives in Pine Mountain, Georgia. He is the author of many fantasy and science fiction stories, including three collections to date, and is twice winner of the Nebula Award for best short fiction. Of his SF novels, several have been nominated for major awards and *No Enemy But Time* (1981) was the winner of the Nebula for best novel. His most recent novels are *Ancient of Days* and *The Secret Ascension*, and the Spectra Edition title *Unicorn Mountain*.

# Spectra Special Editions

Bantam Spectra Special Editions spotlight some of Spectra's finest authors in their top form. Authors found on this list all have received high critical praise and many have won some of science fiction and fantasy's highest honors. Don't miss them!

☐ **Out on Blue Six** (27763-4 • $4.50/$5.50 in Canada) by Ian McDonald. On the run in a society where the state determines one's position in life, Metheny Ard takes charge of her fate, turning from model citizen to active rebel.

☐ **The Nexus** (27345-2 • $4.50/$5.50 in Canada) by Mike McQuay. The tale of an autistic girl who can literally work miracles and the reporter who brings her story to the world.

☐ **Phases of Gravity** (27764-2 • $4.50/$5.50 in Canada) by Dan Simmons: An ex-astronaut goes on a personal odyssey to centers of power all over the earth in search of an elusive—but powerful—fate he senses awaiting him.

☐ **Strange Toys** (26872-4 • $4.50/$5.50 in Canada) by Patricia Geary. Winner of the Philip K. Dick Award. A young woman tries to come to grips with the supernatural powers that pervade her life.

Buy Spectra Special Editions wherever Bantam Spectra books are sold, or use this page for ordering:

- - - - - - - - - - - - - - - - - - - - - - - - - - - - - -